PELL PROVANCE

ERROL MARTINS

TATE PUBLISHING & *Enterprises*

"Pell Provance" by Errol Martins
Copyright © 2005 by Errol Martins. All rights reserved.

Published in the United States of America
by Tate Publishing, LLC
127 East Trade Center Terrace
Mustang, OK 73064
(888) 361-9473

Cover Illustration by Aron Nemeth
Photograph on back by Richard Materna

Book design copyright © 2005 by Tate Publishing, LLC. All rights reserved.

No part of this publication may be reproduced, stored in a retrieval system or transmitted in any way by any means, electronic, mechanical, photocopy, recording or otherwise without the prior permission of the author except as provided by USA copyright law.

This novel is a work of fiction. Names, descriptions, entities and incidents included in the story are products of the author's imagination. Any resemblance to actual persons, events and entities is entirely coincidental.

ISBN: 1-5988627-7-4
060728

ACKNOWLEDGMENTS

To Barbara Materna my editor and typist, I give my eternal gratitude for her superb work on Pell Provance. Her dauntless perserverance helped make this work possible and I consider her a true noble.

Thanks to Robert Radcliffe director of operations for his work, foresight and belief in Pell Provance when the work was still in it's infancy. His continued steadfastness and friendship helped make this all possible.

FOREWORD

Errol Joseph Martins was born in Providence, Rhode Island. Growing up in Rhode Island and New Jersey, he went to live with his father and grandmother until his father died in 1954. He later went to live with his mother, whom he did not know very well and his step-father, with whom he was very close to until the age of eleven. He then set out on his own to see the world. Martins grew up in foster homes and orphanages in Rhode Island.

Errol spent part of his life in an all girl's boarding school on Rhode Island, where he learned to respect the rights of women, a theme depicted in Pell Provance. One can see in the work that women are on the same level, if not higher than men. They are captains on freightliners and terraspans, which are air ships that travel along magnetic fields, and they also serve as Kungerods, which are equivalent to wizards.

There were times in Errol's life that were fun and exciting. However, he experienced a lot of dangerous times as well. At the age of fourteen, he lived on the streets and subways of New York City. Martins is an experienced and well-rounded person and knows the world in which we live which brings him to the foundation of who he is as a person today.

Although he studied theology and philosophy, Martins devoted his life to art, writing and the study of Roman and Jewish history. During the 1970's, Martins invented what was called "napkin art," a series of Roman and Jewish history depicted on paper napkins which were displayed in New York City and New Jersey galleries and critiqued personally by the Metropolitan Museum of Art in 1979.

Like Pell Provance, Martins is enigmatic in his own right and mischievous, but at the same time, honorable, loyal, fun, a great conversationalist, delightfully witty, cool and faithful towards his friends and his God. Martins currently resides in Montclair, New Jersey.

Let me introduce you to Pell Provance, an enigmatic, hypnotically charming figure. Ageless, desired by most women, feared and envied by most men. Dark and dangerous-looking with an ability to focus and magnify evil to the point of chaos, but unaware of his ability.

He travels from world to world, unaware of his mission, causing anomalies which none can explain, until he arrives on the present world of Agrimore, a world of unspoken wonders and Kungerods; a world without dust where the inhabitants have more substance and beauty than ours; a world of a constant partial eclipse where the sun is five times the size of ours and a large planet is continually in its orbit; a place of two moons which are blue because of the eclipsed sun.

On this planet, the wonderful continents as Athelone, Patamodia, Ilgestana, Can-Chimera, Pathenune and Vernace are each guided and protected by a Kungerod with his powerful tundril or staff.

Pell Provance is an individual who delights in his friends Darvin Scutter and Cremona Pinkerly, enjoying perlees, as well as parties and females, he also has the ability to inflame every female who makes contact with him.

His loyalty is legendary, but his power is fearful. He and his friends visit many enchanting cities such as Faxburn, Applendice, and Lethurnae. The means of transportation are terraspans, trains, freightliners and philbees, which are little cars.

This adventure will whisk you away into the pages of this book where you'll get to know, love and miss the characters.

Then there is the resplendent Grista, Pell's betrothed, whom he meets anew on each world he visits, always falling in love with her as she follows him from world to world.

Pell Provance is a classical, unique and masterful story unlike anything you've read. Agrimore is a world you'll hope exists. This book will become your Vade Mecum (go with me) book and you will become homesick for Agrimore when you leave it at the end of this epic.

Barbara Materna

Chapter 1

THE EYES OF EXTELLA

The morning rain ceded to the crown of the day, drippings of the fading rain change their key, as the prince of the day ascended. Cool breezes gently tugged at the tall green sentinels surrounding the tiny French Tudor in which Pell resided. The sunlight danced playfully on the fluted panes of Pell's bedroom, slowly feeling its way onto the redwood floor, discovering in each corner the treasures of darkness. It stopped at the bottom of the closet door of luxurious redwood, where a quarter moon was carefully cut toward the top. Inside were the secrets of fine haberdashery. The serenity was interrupted by the clarion sound of the faithful old wooden clock that sat on the mantle. Far to the left of the mantle stirred a form under a haphazard sculpture of satin sheets, another stir unveiling the form of Pell Provance. Bleary-eyed, sitting on the edge of his four-poster bed, he mused upon the dream he could not remember, fleeting shadows and the eyes of Extella. Stumbling out of bed, he felt his way towards the window, looking out through the colored glass, which painted a surreal picture of the garden.

    Moving away from the window and towards the archway that led to the bathroom, he began to draw his bath with essential oils and salts that befit a man of stature. He was of the mind that only peasants took showers, following the lead of the ancients. Emerging from the bathroom and making his way to the closet, he began the ritual of selecting his attire from his kingly collection of garments, beginning with an exquisitely tailored shirt, white with a slight embroidered motif of lions circling the cuff. The pants he selected were as black as the shadows in the "sea of tranquility," with a crease as sharp as Saladins Simatar, completed with a dark, shale-colored tie. His jacket was double-breasted of a rich and plush material, deep-indigo blue in color. Finally, he donned his ankle-high black boots.

As he opened the heavy, dark-green front door, he peered outside and caught a glimpse of the harbor cafe and train station. Closing the door behind him with a muffled thud, he meandered towards his favorite cabanered bistro. As he approached the cafe, his steps lost their cadence. He began fumbling with his hands in an attempt to direct them, as if his members were going AWOL. Struggling to gain a semblance of stability, he mustered the little fragmented coolness he had when he had left his home. He pondered the plight of his subordinates, "What is happening to me?" Aha, the answer came as sharp as the crack of an Enfield, "Extella!" He nervously sat in a position that seemed comfortable, wondering if he had been obvious in his clumsiness. No one could or had ever made him feel as unsettled as Extella Canterlane had. Seeking to capture secretly a glimpse of the siren, the majesty of her movements eluded him, but she could sense his presence and deliberately avoided his glance.

Chapter 2

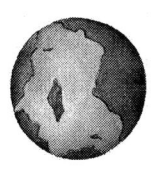

THE CARAPELLA

In the distance he could hear the screeching wheels of the Carapella as it began to curve its way into the station. With relief he rose to greet his steaming rescuer. He took great pleasure in riding this little local train, the wood paneling around the quilted seats, the green metal outlining the wood, the lights that would flash in sequence, denoting the route. Finding his way to his favorite corner seat and peering out of the window, he remembered his experience at the cafe and his ineptitude and defeat. As the Carapella began to pick up speed and the familiar sound of click-clack became evident, Pell noticed that there was a slight change in the tempo of the wheels on the tracks. It was no longer click-clack, but clack-clack-clack. Returning to the passing collage of running colors of the moving landscape, he anxiously anticipated meeting his two friends, Cremona Pinkerly and Darvin Scutter.

Cremona at first would remind you of spoiled royalty. Her emphasized manners and critiquing of speech was rather petulant, but under this facade lay an extremely loyal and courageous soul. With a smile on his face, he remembered his first encounter with Cremona at a Vistor concert. He recollected how during the concert he was edging his way through the throng and someone-stepped into him, forcing him backwards into Cremona, her beverage pressing against her maroon velvet skirt. The next few seconds were rounds of well-directed flames and magma. In an instant a menacing figure of a man was approaching, tall, lean as hickory, a well-chiseled face with dirty-blond hair like rows of wheat, with an edge of a Toledo blade. Pell thought to himself, fighting him would be akin to fighting a piece of hard wood with an ax blade attached. He stood poised for a few moments, then Pell unleashed a tiny smirk from the right side of his mouth. It was enough to disarm his two antagonists. Darvin's face softened with an even larger smirk and Cremona looked up from between the two titans, not exactly sure of what had just occurred. Then someone jostled Darvin from behind and this uncorked a bellowing round of laughter from the three of them. Thus began the foundation of a deep and rich friendship until time everlasting.

The Carapella began its approach of the Faxburn Station. With his attention now focused on his destination. Faxburn was a city of Tartanian architecture, very impressive, with tubular and oval shapes capped by colored spires. As the Carapella edged its way into the station he noticed the sunlight was not shining through the angular overhead panes as it was wont to do. With a final release of steam, the doors of the car folded open. As he proceeded to exit the train, he wondered where the overhead panes had gone.

Faxburn was a moderately large city, full of window shoppers and cataband transports. Noticing the time, he began to pick up the pace until he reached a side street, with tenements and a few stores sprinkled here and there. Turning left onto Alton Place, he approached the red stone three-story building in which Darvin and Cremona were waiting for him.

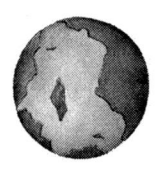

Chapter 3

REUNION

As he entered the swinging doors all heads began to turn as his leather-soled boots made sharp contact with the wooden and stone floor. He looked over to the left corner of the room and noticed Cremona giving him her silly, mischievous smile and Darvin looking out of the window with his perpetually wrinkled brow. Pell gave Cremona a silly look, took off his coat and sat himself next to Cremona across from Darvin. She turned to Darvin and said, "Did you notice how his majesty has to make a grand and noisy entrance every place he goes?"

Darvin, directing his attention to Pell, said, "Did you notice the second spire jutting from the building across the street?"

Pell moved to position behind Darvin's seat and craned his neck, looking up to what Darvin was looking at. "What in the...?!" exclaimed Pell.

Cremona just sat looking up at these two, wondering to herself, What is it now? It's always something weird when Pell comes around. But actually that's what she enjoyed about him.

"Cremona, look at this!" the two men exclaimed in unison.

"Oh, all right," Cremona replied. She lazily removed herself from her seat and there before her eyes, was a most bizarre spectacle of a building about two blocks away. It was forty stories tall, with a blue spire jutting into the heavens, with a second spire alongside of it, occupying half the space, as the first on a slight slant, with no foundation supporting a third of it. "What are we looking at?" asked Cremona.

Darvin abruptly sat down, took a sip of his warm wine and puffed on a puigo, filling the space in front of him with aromatic smoke. "Well, what do you think?" asked Darvin.

"Who cares," responded Cremona. "Some architectural error."

Pell slowly made his way back to his seat without saying a word. Then he looked around and motioned to the server that he was ready. The serving girl arrived and Pell looked up into her green-blue eyes. "Hot wine with herbs and a sweet and sour crescent roll." Pell watched as the shapely server moved gracefully away, with soft, tiny steps that didn't make a sound on the wooden floor.

"Well," remarked Cremona, "do you find her alluring? Does she ravish your heart? Do you wish to be her swain?" she continued with feigned emotions of a dreamy-eyed girl.

"Cremy!" retorted Pell. "If you want my undivided attention, all you have to do is pull up your skirt slightly and show me some leg."

Flutter, flutter, and flutter, Cremy motioned with her eye lashes in a mocking way.

Darvin, turning towards both of them, said, "What are you two going on about? Don't either of you have something to say about that spire?"

"Ah, yes, the spire. Well, Pell, you usually have the answers to all the mysteries of life in the universe. Say something," asked Cremy mockingly.

"What's to say? Someone made an architectural error," answered Pell. "Architectural error my hole!" Darvin shot back.

The discussion was interrupted with the clatter of cups and dishes, as the curvy waitress arrived with Pell's order. Pell looked up into her eyes and smiled. She responded by accentuating her curvy body.

"Oh! You cad!" A flurry of small fists landed playfully on Pell's left arm, and Cremy looked at him mischievously as if she was set for another volley.

Darvin sighed. "Pell, you're twenty-six. Creme's twenty-one. I feel like I'm sitting with a couple of crawlies."

"Look, Darvin, I don't know what the hell is with the spire and we're not going to figure it out, so can we speak about our trip?"

"Yeah, I rented the philbee," replied Darvin.

"What do you say? Shall we?" inquired Pell. They all rose to pay their bill. Pell walked over to the waitress and whispered something in her ear. She responded with a smile and a tug on his arm. Cremy and Darvin waited, as Pell made his way towards the door. Outside, the sun was shining brightly on the blustery, busy street.

Chapter 4

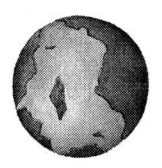

DO YOU HAVE A PHILBEE?

The three began walking down Alton Place towards the philbee station, passing tiny curio shops, booksellers and repairers. Cremy looked rather stunning, with the wind blowing back her rich auburn hair, revealing her exquisitely sculptured face and large dark-brown eyes, her little nose with a slight Roman curve and full red lips, the bright sunlight adorning a lovely crème-colored complexion. Her gait was graceful, admitting a refined background. She wore a dark-green dress of a velvety material that rested just above her knees with dark-brown leather boots. She was a sight to behold. She so enjoyed the times the three of them came together. Pell and Darvin were the two most important men in her life. Darvin, she thought to herself, ruggedly handsome, extremely loyal, all the qualities of a knight of yore. Then there's Pell, also handsome, courtly in his manners, refined but mischievous, every so often a strange and even dangerous look to him. She felt proud being with two dynamic men.

As they made their way to the rental depot, Cremy slipped her arms between both of their elbows and held on tightly to the two fast-paced men. "Well, here we are," said Darvin. "What color would you like?"

"Who cares," yawned Pell.

The agent, a man in his forties with a wide smile and a perfectly trimmed mustache, wore a gray suit with a bright red collar and lapel. "Well, hello, and how may I help you?" asked the agent.

"We need a four-seater for two days," responded Darvin.

"Any particular color?" asked the agent, stroking his mustache and looking over at the odd trio, Pell and Cremy dressed for the royal court and Darvin with his olive-green turtleneck and black leather jacket accentuating his strong, chiseled features. The agent motioned them to enter a large yellow door to his left, through a hallway that led to a large garage. He pointed and said, "Number sixty-two." There at number sixty-two was an orange and yellow philbee. They climbed in, Pell and Cremy in the back and Darvin at the controls. Darvin sat in the single front seat in the center of the vehicle. The philbee was so easy to operate that a child of five could negotiate it. One bar about twelve inches in length with two upright handles on either side swiveled freely for turning. There was also a red lever on the front panel that read "Forward, Backward and Rest." An actuating switch on the left side started the electric, steam-powered engine. From the outside, it looked like a mini steamroller with a dome atop. It had front and back cylindrical tires.

The machine hummed as it made its way smoothly and quietly out of the garage and onto the narrow side street, heading towards a busy intersection. Turning left, they headed towards the outskirts of Faxburn, passing some parks strewn with red pines, with a golden-colored lake in the center and a grayish-blue pillared monument in the distance. It was a breathtaking sight with a gray-blue and amber sky in the background. The scenery continued to roll by as Pell, sitting on the right, closed his eyes and began to dream, images of Cremy and Darvin passing through his mind, as well as Chantry, Faxburn and Extella. Her image was very vivid.

Chapter 5

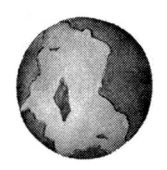

ANOMALIES

The philbee came to a sudden halt, shaking Pell out of his nap. The roadway in front was filled with philbees and people. "Now what?" muttered Darvin, unlocking the canopy and preparing to exit the transport, followed by Cremy and a bleary-eyed Pell. They began snaking their way through the fifty or sixty onlookers. Some officials arrived at about the same time. Making their way to the front of the throng, they ascertained what the commotion was about.

There, strewn before them, was a bizarre construct of trees and hills, with a piece of roadway set on an almost impossible angle, with two houses, a few philbees and a small Honey Creations plant. More officials began arriving, attempting to seal off the area to keep the crowd back.

Pell walked up to one of the officials, a rather burly man in his late twenties. "Hey, hold on there!" shouted the official, holding out his right arm in a straight stiff position. Pell continued to walk up to the outstretched arm, until his nose almost touched the upright palm. Peering between the fingers, Pell noticed that the face of the official had a quizzical look. "Here now. Didn't you hear me?"

"Well, I must see that sight that you sealed off." Pell directed his words between the thick fingers of the official. The man immediately withdrew his arm, feeling uncomfortable that some one was speaking through his fingers. "Look, if you let us pass to see that sight, everyone will think that we belong there and no one will be the wiser for it."

"And why should I do that?" replied the official.

"Well, everyone will think you're on top of the matter and are handling it. We will act like civilian officials by mulling about, walking to and fro and pointing at things."

"I guess that might work," answered the official.

"By the way, my name is Pell and these are my friends, Cremona and Darvin." "The name is Gully," the official said, his massive, hairy hand extended. Darvin took to the big man immediately, while Cremy and Pell walked over to the site.

When they arrived, they were astonished at the angle on which roadway sat in relation to the landscape surrounding it. There was seventy or eighty feet of road sitting on an inexplicable angle. Part of the underside of the roadway was exposed, revealing clumps of cement and steel rods, while part was sitting flush with the surface. Cremy and Pell ascended a small hill onto the flush surface of the roadway. They walked down the eerily quiet, misplaced road with some apprehension.

"I recognize this place," Cremy said, turning to Pell. "This is Halberry Place." Darvin and Gully had just arrived. Darvin, turning to Pell, said, "I told you something was awry. Everything just seems weird, like something is off somewhere."

"People have been saying things like that throughout the ages!" Pell shot back.

Cremy looked intently at Pell. "What's going on? You know more than you're telling."

"Why are you just dismissing this? Bloody Hell! You know something about this, Pell?!" shouted Darvin.

"Ladies and gentlemen," Gully interjected. "Do any of you know what's going on?"

"Ask him," Darvin said, pointing to Pell. "If there's anything amiss, you can be sure that Pell is in the middle of it."

Pell shrugged and walked away.

"See, he does know something," Darvin went on.

Cremy grabbed Pell by the arm and turned him around. She stood there staring at him with those luscious big brown eyes searching for a response, anticipating and cutting all avenues of escape. "Pell, talk to me. You're not going to avoid or distract us with some funny little quips," she charged.

"Cremy, I'm not really sure," he replied, turning away from her. "But you know something? Yeah, there's been a few things."

"Well, what are they, mate?" Darvin asked. Gully just stood there, not knowing what to say or what they were going on about.

Pell turned, looked at the buildings, then faced the Trio. "It started when I woke up this morning. Everything felt different. First off, look at the motif on the cuffs of my shirt."

"What?" asked Cremy, shaking her head quizzically.

"Why, they're facing the wrong way. The lions should be facing the hand, not the arm," explained Pell. "Not only that," he went on, "the chimes of the mantle clock were different. Oh, at first I just dismissed it as my overactive imagination. But there were other things that didn't make sense, such as the cadence of the Carapella, or the missing triangular overhead glass of the Faxburn station, then of course the things that the three of us witnessed."

"What overhead glass?" inquired Cremy.

Gully finally issued his observations on the matter. "Look, we've had reports of other anomalies occurring in Chantry and Faxburn. But they seem to be limited to these two locations."

"But," Darvin added, confronting Pell, looking intently into his eyes, "they seem to be focused around you, mate."

Cremy stopped in between the two and looked straight at Darvin and shouted, "We still don't know anything. So don't draw conclusions. Got that?!"

Darvin backed off, completely cowed by Cremy's ferocity. "Well, what do we do now?" Darvin asked, changing the subject.

"Well, I could go for a nice pint of perlee right about now," said Gully, grinning.

This evoked an ear-to-ear smile from Darvin, who immediately threw his right arm around Gully's shoulder and said, "When's your shift over, mate?"

"In about two minutes."

"It's settled, then. Let's all jump into the philbee and find a cob," offered Pell.

"Now there lay the answers to all questions, at the bottom of the perlee," groaned Cremy.

Pell and Darvin looked at each other, then down at Cremy, put both their arms around her waist and whisked her away towards the philbee, with Gully following behind.

• • • • • • •

All four climbed into the little transport, with Cremy in the middle and Pell and Gully on either side. Darvin at the controls turned and asked, "The Olivevat?"

"Good choice, mate," answered Gully with glee.

"By the way, it's on me," offered Darvin.

The philbee slowly and quietly edged its way past the onlookers to the roadway and hummed away, past the parked philbees, with Gully occasionally waiving at some of the dutiful officials. They made their way up a steep incline and circled the Tanesh fountain, where they turned off of the highway and entered the little town of Wetchpot.

After Darvin parked the philbee, all four made their way down a narrow, winding alley of cobblestones and a stone wall strewn with ivy. Halfway down the alley was The Olivevat. A wooden sign hanging over the front door read, "The Olivevat. Our cupboard of dreams is always available to both the bold and the foolish." The Olivevat was well known throughout the entire Athelonian continent, especially for the cupboard of dreams.

The Olivevat was full this late afternoon with Hogomeans, Tendrats, officials and fenfitters. As the four entered, they witnessed a scene reminiscent to a festive medieval pub. The place was full of puigo and swagg smoke. The walls were adorned with wooden barrels of exotic brews, banners hung from the rafters, crystal glass decanters were set in stone, containing the more elegant cordials, and amber lamps sat on all of the supporting beams and posts.

• • • • • • •

Far to the left corner were the boisterous Hogomeans, a poor man's version of varsity jocks, throwing balls of paper at each other and occasionally glancing over at the Tendrats in the opposite corner. The Tendrats on the other hand, paid little attention to the Hogomeans, enjoying their Pashoow bubblers, rather than noticing the Hogos. Whereas the Hogos were noisy, the Tendrats were quiet and cerebral, looking more like Goths, with long leather coats opened, but belted at the waist, and dark blue ties knotted off-center on their bare necks, settling on the collar of their bright white shirts. The Hogos were quite different, however, with their loud orange and black horizontally stripped shirts and black pants with a thin orange stripe down the side, broken towards the hip, with an emblem of an animal that resembled a boar. Brown and white shoes finished the outfit. They would occasionally stamp their feet on the floor in unison in response to some witty comment one thought he might have had. Every city on the continent had a compliment of these two groups.

Then there were the fenfitter girls occupying the center tables and part of the bar, feral and slightly surly, flirting with all the males, rather attractive in a primitive, uninhibited manner. Their garb was the same, a black sleeveless top made of satin-like material and dark green denims with tan sandals. Their faces and arms were darkened from the sun, dirt and sweat. One of them looked over at Gully, shouted something at him, then threw her dark tan arms around his thick neck and kissed him hard on the face. "Gully, you are a big, thick, hairy, adorable Terraquin!" she bellowed.

"Cherwyln, you sultry moon bat," he whispered. He looked into her dark green eyes, formatted by a dark, tight, tan face crowned with short hair as black as hot tar.

"By the gods," exclaimed Darvin. "Would you look at that woman?!"

"Cherwyln, I would like you to meet Cremona, Darvin and Pell," said Gully introducing them. "It's with great pleasure that I give you Cherwyln, longtime lover, friend, lover and now friend again," said Gully, smirking. She then invited them to join her, motioning towards one of the center tables, where two of her friends were waiting.

Making their way through the onrushing serving girls towards their table, Pell and Darvin noticed one of the Hogomeans staring at them and gesturing in their direction. "That one's going to be trouble," said Darvin, turning his head towards Pell, while looking at the antagonist, a young man, slightly corpulent, with sandy-colored, uncombed hair, wearing the Hogomean colors. "Just ignore them, mate," whispered Darvin.

"If that's possible," answered Pell.

They all took their places at the center table with the two other Fen girls. "I'd like you to meet Gully and his friends Cremona, Darvin and Pell," said Cherwyln introducing them.

"Well hi, I'm Grista," said the girl to the left of Pell, fixing her eyes on his. "You can call me Gris." Pell moved uncomfortably in his seat, trying to divert the female's attention. This made her all the more aggressive, now posturing her entire frame in front of him, as if preparing for a sumptuous meal. She was licking her lips, as if she were about to consume him. She was a big-framed girl, with thick, firmed, tanned arms and a well-developed upper body, with a rather lovely face, and a strangely delicate, long neck. Her face was beautifully oval shaped, with a little pixie-like nose smudged with dirt and sweat. Her mouth was rich and full, with a smile that rivaled the rising sun, accentuated by large shapely dimples on either side. Her eyes were large, blue and full of mischief, capped by sharp golden eyebrows. Her hair, short, golden and curly, crowned her beautiful tan forehead.

Pell excused himself and made his way to the bar to peruse all of the different blends of liquors set in stone at the front of the bar. Just then, Darvin noticed one of the burly Hogomeans following behind him. As Pell arrived at the bar, the Hogomean bumped into him sharply with his shoulder. Before he had time to respond, Darvin was there behind the Hogo and in one fluid motion, thrust the Hogo behind the head into the stone face of the bar. The Hogo fell to the floor like a crumpled piece of paper. Four other Hogos approached, with Darvin and Pell poised like sharp pieces of flint about to run through all that approached. The Hogos stopped. Glancing down at their fallen comrade, they began to be filled with apprehension at the demeanor of the two men they faced. Sentinels on the walls of a tower and themselves strewn at the bottom, they began to back up, searching behind them for their seats with their hands. Pell extended his hand to the wounded Hogo, helped him to his feet and ordered a round of perlees for the Hogomean table.

All watched in silence as the two made their way back to the table, all the women admiringly glancing at them. "Something like this always happens when these two get together," Cremy went on. "Two heroes back from the wars, the hope and desire of every female on the planet."

Darvin smiled sheepishly at her and Pell kissed her brow. "Only in the service of my lady," Darvin uttered.

"Yes, and if I had a castle, you'd both be in the dungeon for the safety of the world," she sneered.

"Fascinating," said the quiet fenfitter, sitting across the round table from Darvin.

"I'm called Misteena, and I have never seen the likes of you. Are you intending to keep them both to yourself?" she asked Cremy. Cremy blushed and turned away, ignoring her question. Misteena was rather intriguing, with dark red long hair hanging loosely over her right eye, shading her tan complexion, large dark red eyebrows outlining slightly slanted large hazel eyes, an aquiline nose buttressed by two full, colored lips, teeth set as a crown of pearls, a rather strong neck and a well-defined thorax.

Grista looked over at Misteena and said in a voice feigning a lovesick teenager, "What do you have in mind Misty?"

"Yum," she sighed, licking her lips.

Pell and Darvin looked at one another, with Cherwyln smirking at the other end of the table. The scene was interrupted by a serving girl announcing the new brews, aged perlees and delicate liquors. "This round is on the table to your right," she announced, pointing to the group of four Tendrats, who lifted their goblets in a toasting fashion. They all responded with a courteous nod.

"Five perlees and one boswith, thank you," ordered Darvin, who then rose up and walked over to the Tendrats table and invited them to join them.

The four Tendrats lifted their rectangular table and carried it across room to where Darvin and his party were seated, then began introducing themselves. "I'm Thackry and these are my companions: Fontana, Sawra and Quill." The two male Tendrats were tall and lean, garbed in black and brown leather. The two females were clad in dark green sleeveless tops, with soft leather vests and pants girded with gold belts. "So what brings you lot to this place?" asked Thackry.

"We needed some perlee," offered Gully.

"Your moves were quite impressive," said Quill, addressing Darvin.

"Just did what had to be done, nothing that impressive," droned Darvin. "By the way, I'm Darvin and this is Cremona, Grista, Misteena, Cherwyln, Gully and Pell."

"Listen," said Thackry. "We were going to walk around the town after we finished our brews. What are you bunch up to?"

"This town? There's nothing here. It's so tiny," Cremy volunteered.

"Yes, but there's a Nails End shop here," Quill offered. Quill was an interesting gnome-like character in his twenties with bushy brown hair, bright small blue eyes, a small nose, a little smirk of a smile and an almost perfectly round face.

"Those shops are everywhere!" asserted Pell. "Filled with useless goblets, shiny stones, common candles and stupid writings that pretend to be profound."

"Yeah, but not this one, mate," interjected Quill. "This one has a Kungerod."

"A Kungerod!" shouted Darvin in disbelief.

"Well, that's just mythical stories you tell little scrubs," said Pell.

"Let's just go there," yawned Sawra. Sawra was a Tendrat, a slight girl with black hair, ordinary features, but with enormous lips. Fontana was quiet and withdrawn, with long brown hair covering most of her face. What little could be seen of her was quite dazzling. Thackry was sort of their leader. He was in his twenties, very tall, with short blonde hair combed straight back, a dark green sleeveless shirt revealing well-developed arms and upper torso, girded with a thick gold belt and reddish-tan leather slacks.

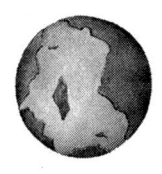

Chapter 6

THE KUNGEROD OF ATHELONE

Pell and his party, along with the Tendrats, stood and bid farewell to the three fenfitter girls. At that moment Grista stood up. "I'm going, too!" she said assertively, looking straight at Pell.

"We're staying," said Gully and the two fenfitter girls seated at the table."

Cremy, annoyed at Grista, shouted at Darvin and Pell. "Well, say something!"

Pell looked at Cremy resigningly. "Oh well, let's move." Cremy pouted and stamped her heals behind them with Grista smiling at her. The eight of them made their way up a slight hill towards Mitlex.

The town of Mitlex was tiny indeed, comprised of ten narrow streets, with a bridge leading to a fountain in the middle of the town, all the shops circling the fountain. Right next to a puigo shop was a hanging sign that read, "Nails End." In the window were the usual goblets, fake parchments, stones and assorted old candles. "Fotfit, fuzzel," said Darvin with mock enthusiasm.

The shop was quiet, dingy and dimly lit. They all walked in together, creating a cacophony of creaks on the wooden floor along the quiet isles. In the shadows appeared a figure walking hastily to the front of the shop. It was the Kungerod, a severe spectre of a man with a firm and menacing appearance. His hair was black, with white streaks combed upward into a bun at the top, firm, up-slanted brows with eyes that exhibited no fear, a long scaline nose, with firm lips and a protruding jaw, which gave his face a fierce, determined countenance. He was wearing some sort of green velvet jump suit with a high stiff collar, which wrapped around both ears and slightly opened at the throat, completed with knee-high white knickers and low-cut soft brown boots. "Who are you people?!" he demanded, glaring at the group, which now felt ill at ease, including Darvin. Pell cracked a little smirk, thinking to charm and disarm the Kungerod.

"Don't you try that nonsense with me," he said, confronting Pell and looking straight into his eyes without flinching. "You, a messenger of death to an entire world, with a careless devil may care attitude, going about drinking perlees and charming females, while destroying their world."

The group turned and stared at Pell. "What does he mean?" demanded Cremy.

"He knows," the Kungerod went on, looking intently at Pell and in a quiet and threatening voice. "Tell them, tell them what you know. You've seen your shadow. Look down all of you. Look at his shadow. See how it's doubled there on the floor." In the orange lights of the shop, was a shadow of Pell with another shadow emerging from the first. "I'll say no more of this matter," sighed the Kungerod.

"Wait," pleaded Pell. "Where shall I inquire about this? To whom do I speak to regarding this?"

The Kungerod softened its countenance. He looked carefully into his eyes and said, "You must go to Bretyun and inquire. Someone there will further instruct you. Now you must leave," he said, opening the door and showing them out.

They all stood looking at Pell without uttering a word, with Grista clutching tightly on his arm. "Hey, let's go back and get Gully," she said, breaking the tension. So they made their way back to The Olivevat to retrieve Gully.

On their way back they were rather quiet, with Grista firmly gripping Pell's arm in support. Upon arriving at The Olivevat, they noticed that Gully was engrossed in conversation with a rather tall, tanned man. His graying hair was neatly cropped in a crew cut. "Well, Gully," demanded the man, "are you going to give up your career and everything you've worked for, to go on some aimless journey with these newfound friends of yours?"

"Speaking of newfound friends, here they are," said Gully, rising from his seat. "I'd like you to meet my friends, Cremona, Darvin, Pell and this is Grista, whom we've just met. And of course, you know Cherwyln and Misteena."

"Pamater's the name," the man said with a scowl.

"He's my boss," Gully volunteered.

"Yeah, I'm trying to convince him not to throw away his career as an official on some whim, with some people he just met!" injected Pamater.

Gully turned and faced the man eye to eye. "Look, mate, I don't exactly know where I'm going, or what I'll be doing. I only know that these people have become my friends and wherever they're going, that's where I'll be. Got that, mate?"

The man shook his head and turned, looking back at the group. "I hope you know what you're doing, giving up everything to go with this lot." With that he stormed out the door.

Chapter 7

PELL AND THE KUNGEROD

"Well, what happened?" asked Gully, seating himself and ordering a round of perlee and waving at the tendrats who took their leave.

"Yes, tell us. Did you see the Kungerod?" asked Misteena.

Everyone stared at Pell, awaiting an answer. "Yes, we met the Kungerod," sighed Pell.

"Well?" Gully's eyes searched Pell's for an answer. There was a still silence for a few moments, which seemed to never end.

"Would you tell us what happened?" demanded Cherwyln, leaning on her thick soiled arms, as if she were about to lunge across the table. She stared at Pell and Darvin menacingly, while she awaited an answer to her query. "Unless I get an answer, soon I'll leap over on both of you," she threatened.

Pell rose up, saying, "I must return."

"Return? Return to where, mate?" asked Darvin.

"To the Kungerod," he replied.

"Are you out of your bloody mind? That's one dangerous fellow!" exclaimed Darvin.

Grista gripped his arm firmly and looked up at him. "I'm going, too."

At that, he bent over and whispered in her ear, pulling back her hair and gently nibbling her ear lobe. "Not this time, love," he whispered, while unprying her grip. "I must go alone," he said, addressing everyone. "I'll be right back." Then he turned and left.

Grista had a look of apprehension on her face, fearing to lose him, even though she had just met him. Pell walked up to the circle, stopped at the fountain and thought to himself, What's with Grista? She's not going to be easy to shake. With that he made his way to the "Nail's End."

Opening the squeaky door, he peeked in slowly as not to stir up the creaking wood floor. "What! Grown tired of the perlees and all of the doting females?" spoke a voice behind him. Pell turned slowly and faced the severe spectre of the Kungerod.

"You knew I'd return," he said in a slow, deliberate voice, this time staring unflinchingly into the eyes of the Kungerod.

The Kungerod turned and commanded, "Follow me." He moved sprightly down the aisle and unlatched a thick wooden door with hinges and hasps, which led to a circular staircase. They both descended deeper and deeper, until they came to a wonderfully well-ordered and charming room.

"Have a seat," ordered the Kungerod, fetching a flask of a light gray liquid. He filled two goblets, handed one to Pell and reclined, staring curiously at him. Sipping the cordial slowly, he looked up at Pell and did something astonishing. He cracked a tiny smile, and then said, "You're quite a character, aren't you Mr. Provance? As long as I have been in this world, no one, no not one person has ever stared at me unflinchingly. In fact, if I hadn't turned, I probably would have flinched... Yes, you are something. Do you know you are the first person that has ever been in this room?"

"I'm honored, sir," Pell replied respectfully.

"Honored my tundril," said the Kungerod, smirking. "Walking about with that damned double shadow, matter being transported before your eyes, finds out he's the unwitting lord of destruction and what's he do? He drinks another perlee and not to overlook the reassuring nibble on some female's ear lobe," he said with mock concord.

"Anyone else would be beside himself with guilt and fear, but not Mr. Provance. Oh no! Not you! Lavishly dressed, head in the clouds, champion of all females and loyal to the core. Amazing." With that he sighed and stared silently into his goblet. "I'll tell you all you need to know," he said calmly. Then he walked over to the other side of the room, as if he were looking for something on the shelf and muttered to himself, "Why? Why do I feel so ill at ease in the presence of this Pell? Who is he and why this feeling of dread?"

Composing himself, the Kungerod sat across from Pell, refreshed his drink and began, "I've arranged passage for you and your group, as many as you wish to bring. By the way, I know you're thinking of leaving Grista behind. Well, don't. She's a formidable ally and a terrible enemy. She'll sink the damned freightliner if you leave her. That one's the most ferocious female on this plane of existence and for some reason that escapes me, she's completely devoted to you."

"Now, you will go to the city of Firwith, along the coast there will be a freightliner called "Lamberant" docked at the Skidamore Yards. Your quarters will be statesman class and the liner is bound for Patamodia."

"Patamodia," remarked Pell.

"Oh, don't act so damn surprised!" shouted the Kungerod. "Mr. Pell Provance, who believes that new worlds are his portion in life and it is their pleasure to be visited and included in the life experiences of Mr. Pell Provance." The Kungerod sat back in his seat and sighed, "And he actually believes it."

He continued, looking at him rather sternly, as a father to a misbehaving son. "When you arrive, you will seek out a place called the 'Maiden's Beard.' I'm sure you'll have no trouble finding it. It's filled with riff raff, soiled sultry females and sailors from the five continents. You see, it's the only place that's not off limits to them, your sort of appetizing fare. Someone will meet you there who is called Faengle. He will guide you to the interior of the Patamodia, to one Crofty Bellar and you will follow her instructions precisely. Now, if you will take your leave of me. I have to make some preparations for you."

• • • • • • •

After escorting Pell out of the shop, the Kungerod hastened back down to his dwelling. He quickly slid the center table in the room which they were sitting to the side, unlocked a latch in the center of the wooden floor, lifted a small square panel and set it to the side. He then carefully removed the intricate stone work where the panel was, carefully placing them in order piece by piece beside the panel, slowly revealing a circle of five dark blue ceramic-like balls, which were half set in the stone base. The Kungerod turned the balls by hand, revolving them until a gold-engraved emblem was in view and upright. In the center was a round hole for the setting of his tundril—a long staff, five-sided, rounded at the bottom, made of rich amber wood with an oval-shaped piece of dark red glass in the center and an intricate carving of a flower at the top. He lifted the decorative staff into the air, muttering to himself, "Eight hundred cycles, eight hundred cycles and Mr. Pell Provance has to show up and now, the whole world's upside down. Damn you! Pell Provance!" With great force he jammed the tundril in the center of the stone platform, creating a blast of electric blue light, as the stone platform began to rise out of the floor. He moved his hand away from the tundril, as the platform continued to rise, until it reached the height of his waist and stopped. "Blast, Mr. Pell Provance," he continued to mutter. "You would have to come here to my shop. Couldn't go somewhere else, could you? Now an entire chain of events will begin to take place which will most likely reshape everything."

Pell entered The Olivevat with a somewhat puzzled look on his face.

"Well," demanded Darvin, "what happened? Did you go back to the shop?" Everyone waited with silent expectation.

"Yes, we sat together and had a cordial and talked at length."

Cremy's mouth dropped. Gully looked over at Darvin. Grista looked up and smiled. Darvin stood speechless, searching his eyes as if waiting for the punch line to a joke. Pell quietly sat down at the table. Grista gently slid her arm into his with an occasional reassuring grip.

"You're not joking, are you?" asked Darvin. "You had a drink with a bloody Kungerod and lived to speak of it?"

"What did he say, Pell?" Gully quietly asked.

"We must leave here," he answered. "I don't mean The Olivevat or the city, but the entire continent." Everyone stared at each other astonishingly, except Grista, who smiled to herself, as if nothing that had to do with Pell surprised her because wherever he was going, he was not going anywhere without her.

"I know I did the right thing in hooking up with you lot," said Gully.

"Well that settles it. Where to now?" asked Darvin.

"To Firwith," answered Pell.

"Along the coast?" asked Grista, her beautiful face brightening with a huge smile.

"Who said your going?" shot Cremy, her eyes filled with fury.

"The Kungerod," answered Pell, fixing his gaze on Cremona, allaying her volley.

With that she gave off a slight "Hmph," then grabbed Darvin's hand.

"What about us?" asked Cherwyln and Misteena, in unison.

Gully turned to them and gently stroked their shoulders. Pell then stood up, with Grista still holding onto his arm, followed by Darvin, Cremy and Gully. Cherwyln stroked Gully's forearm. "Your not going to forget about me, are you?" she pleaded.

"Now, what sort of nonsense is that? Of course not," he said and kissed her forehead. They all turned, saluted the two women and left.

Chapter 8

TROPICAL CAN-CAN

As they approached the parked philbee, Cremy noticed that there was only seating for four, to which Grista explained that her home was just a short distance and she would sit on Pell's lap. They crammed into the philbee, Cremy on the left, Gully in the center with Pell on the right, Grista straddling his lap and Darvin at the controls. The philbee hummed and purred as it made its way down the scenic causeway past the place of the last event where they had met Gully and towards Faxburn.

"Pell, are you stopping over at my place?" inquired Darvin.

Cremy leaned forward and looked at Pell. "No! He's coming home with me!" she answered for him. "You've got a large wardrobe there and the guestroom is always ready for you," she added.

"Oh, I don't know," replied Grista mischievously. "I thought he'd be coming home with me."

Darvin looked at them through the rear view and smiled. Gully also found himself completely amused at the back seat shenanigans. Cremy stared viciously at Grista, her eyes throwing darts of flame.

"Grista, stop!" pleaded Pell. "Of course I'm going with you, Crem," he assured her and closed his eyes, trying to assimilate the day's events.

As the little philbee made its way down towards Faxburn, Pell's thoughts were distracted by the shapely form sitting on his lap, her freckled back and arms still slightly soiled from the Fens, her aroma rather primitive, bespeaking henna, mead, honey and fauna, her fragrant hair occasionally tickling his nose. He began struggling to keep the stature of his manhood under control, his temperature rising and his heart beating rapidly. Grista sensed it and began rhythmically nuzzling and moving her sensually exquisite body. "Stop that!" he demandingly whispered.

She stopped, turned and looked at him, her lovely face revealing a schoolgirl smile. Darvin looking back at them through the rear view. "What's going on in that corner, you two?" he asked, feigning severity. Gully was asleep. And Cremy was glaring at both of them.

The city of Faxburn was becoming visible, as they descended down a long hill, past the shimmering forests and monuments. "Would you drop me off at the bottom of the hill?" asked Grista.

"Right, we'll pick you up the same time and place tomorrow," offered Darvin.

The philbee came to a slow stop at the intersection. Grista lifted herself off of Pell, turned to him, held his head with both hands fingering his hair, and kissed his forehead. "Tomorrow, my prince," she whispered. Gully nodded and smiled politely, while Cremy looked out the window without saying a word.

Darvin looked at Cremy disappointedly and turned to Grista. "Same time, same place, love," he directed. With that she looked at Pell, turned and walked up the street towards a row of small well-kept buildings. Pell didn't take his eyes off of her, until she entered one of the buildings and was out of view. "Where to, Gully?" asked Darvin.

"To the Faxburn praetodal," he answered. "I've got to officially resign my post and clear out my status charts."

"Pick you up there tomorrow?" Darvin inquired.

"Sure, same time," Gully answered and said his farewells.

Chapter 9

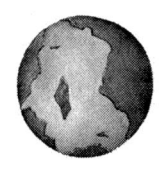

CREMONA'S DILEMMA

Darvin turned off the philbee and unlocked his seat so that it swiveled around to face Cremona. "What is it, lovey?" he asked, addressing Cremona.

Pell turned to look at her. "What is troubling you sweetie?" he gently asked.

Cremy just stared out of the window, not answering a word. Darvin noticed that her lovely face was wet. He stroked her hair and gently turned her face towards his. Her face was flushed and wet. Her eyes were closed and teary and her little nose exhibited an occasional little bubble from running.

Pell immediately moved next to her and held her in his arms. "What's all this?" he whispered, wiping her face and eyes. She began sobbing uncontrollably.

Darvin wiped her nose. "Come on, lovey, speak to us. What's all this?" he probed.

She took a rapid succession of short breaths and looked at them. "I'm terrified of losing you," she said, turning to Pell and trying to catch her breath. "You see, all of these cycles," she continued, "I've felt like a queen, having the two most handsome and gracious men fussing over me, protecting me, admiring me, waiting on me hand and foot. It made me feel so special. We were always together. We did everything together, shared everything. Oh, I know that the maddening Pell would always play with and enjoy other women, but they never joined us. It would always be the three of us," she said, composing herself.

Darvin and Pell looked at each other. Pell held Cremy tightly and spoke gently into her ear. "We both adore you. We will always have you and you must believe that. A series of events has changed things and I don't know where they're taking us, but you can be sure of this: we both cherish and love you. That will never change. You're Cremona Pinkerly, first lady of the realm, and we are in your service."

Darvin smiled and brushed her hair back then kissed her runny nose.

"Stop that!" she ordered. "I look terrible. My nose is all yucky."

"That nose is the fairest of all noses," he asserted.

"Yes," said Pell, "the most desirable in the realm." Then they both began playfully kissing her nose, with her laughing uncontrollably.

• • • • • • • •

The blue light from the Kungerod's staff reached into the heavens, piercing the clouds, as the Kungerod peered up into the thin shaft of his ceiling, watching the shaft turn to a darker indigo blue, as the stone in the center of the tundril began to pulsate. "This is knowledge to be shared," he muttered to himself. "Now all of them that have been idle all of this time are to take part in the events of Mr. Pell Provance."

Just then a figure appeared in the room. "Departing, sir?" the figure asked.

"Yes, Migely," answered the Kungerod.

"Destination, sir?"

"Pathenune," he answered.

"Sir?" Migely stood hesitant, his face full of questions.

"Yes, Migely, Pathenune," said the Kungerod, looking at him reassuringly. "It was visited last by a reaper, a spectre, a harbinger of destruction."

"Sir," said Migely alarmingly.

"Oh! He's not what you think, my old friend," he said in a calm tone. "No raggedly black drapes or faceless Phantom or anything like that. No, Migely, if only he were. No, this is a maddening person, exquisitely dressed with poise and manners, a suffocating charm, dashing good looks, setting the hearts of females ablaze with his wit and demeanor and drinking all the perlees he can bottom out. That's not all my faithful friend; this being does not have a clue, not an inference of who or what he is. Sitting there in that very seat," he motioned, pointing to a recliner, "he looked at me without flinching, with a roguish smile on his face. I actually poured him a cordial!" he shouted.

"Sir," answered Migely in a state of semi-shock.

"I actually rather liked the rascal," he said, looking puzzled.

"I'll ready the philbee sir," replied Migely as he left the room, leaving the Kungerod in deep thought, staring at the shaft of light.

• • • • • • •

Darvin was now bringing the philbee to a stop in front of Cremona's home. Turning back in his seat to face Cremy, he asked, "How's it, my lady?"

"Some lady," she replied. "I really laid it all out, didn't I?" she said, exiting the philbee.

Pell walked around to the other side to talk to Darvin, while Cremy waited in front of her home. Darvin looked up at Pell. "Well, he whispered. What do you think?" he asked.

"We'll take care of our love, don't sweat it, mate," Pell assured him.

With that he nodded to Darvin and walked over to Cremy, put his arm around her and walked over to her door. She unlocked the door, looked up at Pell and invited him in. They entered the round, towered house and Pell made his way to the guest room. Upon entering, his thoughts meandered through the events of the last two days. He reclined back into the easy chair and closed his eyes, thinking about the Kungerod, then the lovely Grista and Cremy. How he groaned inside to see her weeping.

There was a quiet tap at his door. "Pell, are you decent?" said the soft voice of Cremona.

"Yes, lovey, come in," he answered.

She entered, still slightly wet from her bath. Her beautiful auburn hair was almost black from moisture. Her tiny bare feet made their way to the bed, her satin robe still wet in spots. She sat on the bed and emitted a long sigh, her large lovely eyes staring intently at him."You must think of me a fool," she stated.

He rose from the chair and sat next to her, staring up at the ceiling, then said, "Cremy, you are a queen amongst women. How could I ever think such of the one I adore?"

"But, I'm jealous for both you and Darvin," she admitted. "I don't want to let go of either of you. I know everyone says it's impossible, but I think I love you both. Oh my," she sighed, "I think I'd marry both of you."

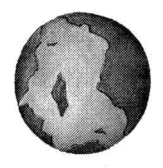

Chapter 10

BECKONING BEACON

Darvin parked the philbee next to his home on the outskirts of Faxburn. His little home was out of a fairy tale, very rustic looking, with part of the hill covering the roof. He unlatched the large wooden door decorated with designs of black iron and rivets. Inside, was like seventeenth-century America. There was only one room, but it was very large, spacious and extremely well kept. The room was about the size of five average rooms, with a black, wooden, rectangular table in the center, set about with fine leather-covered chairs with high backs. Two tiny bay windows appeared on the left, with a pillowed window seat and the ceiling was of carefully cut, black wooden rafters. There was a fireplace in the center wall, with a stone cooking area protruding from it. A thick mantle of rich, dark red wood crowned the fireplace, adorning what at first glance, looked like rows of shields, but were delicately cut forms of mica outlined in gold. On top of the mantle were gleaming bronze plates set on either side against the stone wall, centered by an exquisite brass compass of some sort. These were margined on either side by two translucent stone candle stands.

Darvin took off his thin leather jacket and hung it on a hook against the wall. He then took his turtleneck off, revealing a well-defined, wiry torso, reminiscent of hard white stone. "Bloody, bloody, bloody," he muttered to himself as he was undoing his belt and pants. "Where in the phantoms lair do these people come from?" he said, referring to Pell and the Kungerod. He then moved to the right side of the room, unhinged a latch on the floor and with a tug, lifted the handle. A portion of the floor folded back, revealing a small bed that settled sturdily on the floor.

• • • • • • •

Migely opened part of the canopy and the door to the philbee until the Kungerod was seated, latched the canopy, and then closed the door. Migely sat in the single seat in the front and waited until the Kungerod looked up. "Caerilon, sir?" asked Migely.

"Well, it's closer than Phaelton. Caerilon it is, my friend," said the Kungerod, as he was positioning himself in the back. "Why don't they ever build a larger philbee?" he muttered to himself.

The philbee purred down the causeway towards the outskirts of Faxburn on route to the terraport. They passed the area in which the event had taken place, where the trio had met Gully. The Kungerod craned his neck to catch a glimpse, his vision obscured by onlookers and officials. "Blast you, Pell Provance!" he yelled. "You're probably thinking of your next conquest or a pint of perlee. Blasted rascal," he went on until he was interrupted by Migely.

"Can't something be done about him, sir?" Migely inquired.

"Not a thing, my friend," he answered. "The whole world is at the mercy of Mr. Provance. We dare not take any action. We'll know more after we convene at Pathenune."

• • • • • • •

Far off on the continent of Patamodia, a figure was stirring in a darkened room. Awakened by a clamor outside of his estate, the figure arose to investigate the source of the disturbance. Walking towards the window, he looked down to see many townsfolk gathered in front of the gates of the estate conversing with one another and pointing up into the night sky. The Kungerod looked up and was astonished. Peering up through the glass, he saw a sharp shaft of indigo-blue light piercing the night sky.

In a frenzy, he rushed towards the other side of the room, stumbling over articles on the floor. "Oh, dear! Dear me! Oh my!" he exclaimed to himself. He found the master switch and the room became flooded with light, revealing books, parchments and unidentifiable devices strewn over the exquisitely carpeted floor. "How can this be?" he asked himself. "What could have caused the Athelonian to light that beacon?"

The Kungerod of Patamodia was a very striking man, tall, well built, in his early forties, black hair almost parted in the middle, reminiscent of men in the forties era. He had flashing blue eyes accentuated by a deep tan face due to the climate of Patamodia. He had a sharp nose, two sharp dimples, a strong chin and a moustache that slanted upward on each side towards the nostrils. He threw on a pair of trousers and ran barefoot to the balcony, pressed a lever that opened the front gates and motioned to one of the natives to come forward.

The crowd outside of the gates looked stunned, as the one chosen carefully made his way up the stone path until he reached a point under the balcony. He looked up and bowed his head. "Vinestu," he said in his native tongue.

"Yes, yes. Enough of that," said the Kungerod, answering him in his own language. The Kungerod threw down a piece of mica, rich and dark red, with an official crest on it worth about a hundred of US dollars. The man picked it up with wonder and looked up. "That is yours, my friend. I would like you to go to Selverna as soon as possible, in fact, immediately, and use the langline, ask for number forty-one seventy-six. When the person answers, you will say to prepare the conference room. You must go immediately," he said in an alarming voice. The native backed up and bowed, turned and ran off towards Selverna.

Crofty Bellar had seen the shaft of light and the commotion it caused in Selverna. She knew it had something to do with the Kungerods. Just then the light on the langline began blinking red. The color indicated the seriousness of the message. She lunged forward and pressed the white button. The native on the other end spoke quietly and nervously. But she understood the message.

Crofty Bellar was the administrative secretary to the Kungerods. She had been prepared for this position since the age of five. She was now in her late thirties and knew exactly what had to be done. She was a rather big blond, slightly corpulent, with a rather attractive face and a large dynamic smile. She had received an allowance from the Kungerods of one thousand royal micas – the equivalent to two million dollars Earth currency – per cycle since the age of twenty-two in preparation of this event. One person was selected every one hundred and forty cycles and she was it. She gathered the clothing she needed, parchments, maps and a device that looked a mini tundril.

Chapter 11

AN OFFICIAL RETIREMENT

Meanwhile, back at Cremona's, Pell was holding her against his chest and realized she had fallen asleep. He lifted her in his arms, opened the door and headed to her bedroom. Her robe and hair were still wet from her bath. He opened the door to her bedroom and carefully laid her on the bed. Her bedroom was truly fit for a queen, full of deep red velvets, pinks and whites. He quietly closed the door and ran into Janimere, an older woman, who had nursed Cremy since she was born. Pell quietly told her that she and her clothing were wet. The woman smiled and entered the room, closing the door behind her. Pell then retired to his own room.

• • • • • • •

Gully entered the Praetodal and greeted the man at the desk. As he past some open doors, he could hear greetings as he made his way downstairs past the chart room. He stuck his head into a file room to see a young, brown pony-tailed woman standing on a chair, attempting to reach a box of files on top of a metal cabinet. He snuck up behind her and lifted her onto his shoulders. At that she let out a shriek and said, "I'm going to pound you when I get down, you lout." She held onto his head to balance herself, as she pulled the box off of the cabinet.

Gully stooped over while the woman climbed off of his shoulders. Gully grabbed her around the waist and pulled her close to him. "Thayty," he said, "you looked very appealing up on that chair."

"Hmm," she answered. "Not enough to keep you from throwing away your career. Am I?"

"That's a different matter, love," he answered.

"Is that what you call it?" she shot back. "Everything you worked for, everyone had high hopes for you, your family, friends, me," she said firmly. He looked at her, hardening his visage.

"I've made my decision, I won't discuss it any more."

"Fine," she said and stormed out.

Gully continued down the hall, until he reached the locker room and proceeded to his locker, squeezing past some of the officials that were changing and preparing for the next shift. A young man approached him, still in his undergarments and blocked his path. The young man stood there and stared back at him. "Flossy," he said. "It's been a sum, hasn't it?"

"It's been a sum!" the man shot back. "Is that all you can say?! Gully it's me, Flossy! We went through the academy together! We hung together, had many perlees together. What were you going to do, sneak off?!"

"Listen, I was going to stop off at your place because I didn't want to talk here," answered Gully.

"Gully, what in blazes are you doing?! You're throwing everything away! What's gotten into you?!"

Gully edged past the man, walked over to his locker unlocked and began emptying everything into a brown case he had in the locker. "I've got to leave. I'm going to Patamodia."

"Patamodia?!" asked the shocked man. He grabbed Gully by the arm and turned him to look at him. "Gully, what in Mythellas tight pants are you talking about? There are only two people in the whole continent of Athelone that can go there and not without a very, very rare invite."

"It's all arranged," Gully asserted.

"Arranged?" asked the man facetiously. "Arranged by whom? You?"

"No, not by me," answered Gully with newfound courage.

"Then by whom?" inquired the man meekly.

"By the Kungerod of Athelone," answered Gully authoritatively.

The man's expression changed as he sat down on the bench. "Well, I hope you know what you're getting into, Gully," he said quietly.

Gully placed both hands on his shoulders and said, looking at him intently, "That's just it, mate. I don't know. That's what's so exhilarating. I don't know." Then he turned and left.

Chapter 12

THE TERRASPAN

Migely had already given instructions to the terraport concerning the Kungerod. Upon their arrival, everything was ready and awaiting them. The maintenance crew was just finishing warming up and restocking the terraspan. The private jump platform was elevated with the private terraspan awaiting. Migely stopped the philbee right next to the elevator access. Both he and the Kungerod disembarked and climbed on the elevator access. The smaller platform slowly rose to meet the larger one, which cradled the terraspan. Both figures entered the strange-looking machine. Migely opened the inner hatch and the Kungerod followed behind. Migley made his way to the forward section, the thick carpeting cushioning his steps.

The Kungerod took the nearest stairway down, which led to four cabins. He entered the first cabin on his right. The cabin was exquisitely furnished with a writing table, a sofa and an easy chair. A small doorway led to an alcove with a variety of refreshments. The walls were lit from within and were made of rich red and tan woods, with an inch separating the inner and outer walls. The Kungerod leaned back on the sofa and closed his eyes, the soft whine of the engines lulling him to sleep. Migely was steady at the controls of the terraspan. The control room had a large captain's chair in the center, light gray in color, with strips of decorative redwood veneer at the base. The rest of the control room was dark Pompeian green and cream-colored, with blue-green glass on the windshield and observation windows outlined with wood. The control panel was rather simple, one dark green lever to raise the machine and a gray one to lower. A blue ignition toggle switch, a large, brightly lit altimeter and a field density meter.

The Kungerod was awakened as the vehicle lunged to and fro, searching for a magnetic corridor to ride. Once the vehicle found the corridor, the electric field in the abdomen of the craft began to quietly hum and the Kungerod again shut his eyes.

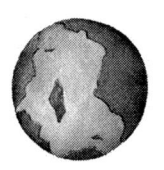

Chapter 13

ON TO FIRWITH

Pell awakened to a rap at the guestroom door. It was Janimere asking what he would like for breakfast. He rose from bed and made his way to the bathroom and drew himself a bath. He then entered the walk-in closet to peruse his haberdashery. He selected an exquisite light tan suit, a midnight blue shirt, soft brown shoes that resembled Bassweegans and a thin gray tie with a small crest of a woven gold lion on his hind legs covered by a shield. He then filled a suitcase for whatever he needed for the trip.

He walked down the winding staircase to the breakfast room. It was a delightful room full of sunlight, with the overhead panes open and breezes gently blowing in. The table was set for two. Dark blue glass plates adorned the table with the dark amber goblets containing some sort of fruit salad. Janimere was busy around the stone oven baking poscen rolls and sautéing some sort of meat that looked like goose pate with malen chips that resembled thin slivers of carrots, but when golden brown tasted like bacon and mushrooms. He greeted the large, robust woman with a loud, "Good morning Janimere!"

The woman turned and smiled and said, "Sit yourself down, Mr. Pell. Miss. Cremona will be down shortly."

Cremy slowly made her way down the staircase, partially dragging her feet. She was still tired and bleary eyed from the events of the previous day. Her attire was enchanting. Her auburn hair was slightly hanging down the sides of her face, with the rest pulled back in a loose ponytail, crowned with a very thin tiara of fine gold. Her blouse was something to behold. It was sort of a pinkish-gold, as if it was spun of gold and pink yarn and she wore a fine thin necklace. The sleeves were very short cut, almost to the shoulders, and it hung over a short, forest green skirt. Her soft, tan, leather boots complimented her shapely legs. She sat down and plopped her head down on her arms and without looking up said, "Good morning, Janimere. Good morning, Pell. Forgive me, but I feel sooo tired."

"You'll feel better once you've eaten sweetie," Janimere answered. Pell just stared at her. Even though she looked tired, he had never seen her more beautiful.

• • • • • • •

The sunlight danced through the window of Darvin's elegant hut. The trees outside caused it to play on his face. He turned away, covering himself. Blast, he thought to himself. I've got to get up. Why does the bed feel so comfortable when you've got to rise? He rolled himself out of the bed and staggered towards the alcove and the stone bath.

• • • • • • •

Gully was already up and wide awake. He was anxious to leave not knowing what adventures awaited him. He sat down to write his mother a note: "Lovey, I'm going on a journey. Not sure how long I'll be away, but will keep you posted. Your son forever, Gully." He quietly made his way upstairs and to her bedroom, tiptoed beside her bed, gently kissed her forehead and left the note beside her.

• • • • • • •

Grista opened her eyes and stared at the bright sunlight glistening off the panes in her bedroom. She ran her fingers through her short, blond, curly hair and then stretched out her arms as if reaching for the ceiling. There was a rap at the door and a voice. "Mmmm," said the voice on the other side of the door, "the caone smells sooo good."

Grista sat up and smiled. "Twilly, come in!" she shouted enthusiastically. The door opened and in walked a tall girl with short dark hair and a cup of hot caone in her hand. A caone was a coffee-like a beverage that tasted something like hot cocoa with rum. Twilly sat on the bed and handed her the cup.

Twilly and Grista were roommates; in fact, they were inseparable, having grown up together since infancy. Both girls were orphans, which was very rare in the world of Agrimore. They were cherished by the entire community of Faxburn. The entire city was one large family to them. In the world of Agrimore, orphans were given special attention, not only by the authorities, but also by the entire city. The orphanage was a private home purchased by the city and every family in the city stayed at least one week with the orphans. The community formed such close ties with the orphans that it was like having an entire city of parents, brothers and sisters. It was difficult for the orphans to purchase anything, for everything was given to them. Twilly and Grista also had four families that were their benefactors, which saw to all of their needs. The authorities also furnished them with an allowance for housing and education. There were very few who were loved and cared for, more than orphans in this world. The love that Twilly and Grista had for one another was deeper than sisterhood, but never diverted from that.

Twilly looked at Grista and combed back her hair with her fingers, playing with her tight little curls. "You came in last night and went right to bed," she said with concern, looking over her face.

"I know," answered Grista. "I was so tired."

"You must have had some day. What happened?" asked Twilly.

"I've met someone," she said, smiling and looking down at her feet. There was a pause and Twilly continued to question her.

"Someone?"

"Yes, someone marvelous, someone so different from anyone in all existence!" she said with enthusiasm.

"Whoa, slow down girl," admonished Twilly. "We're not talking about a Kungerod, here. He's just a man."

"Just a man?" asked Grista, looking away. "No, not just a man. Even the Kungerod of Athelone was no match for him. Truthfully, I don't know what he is, all I know is when you look into the deep dark marvelous eyes of his, you see wondrous and terrifying sights." Grista then looked up at Twilly, held her face gently between her hands and said, "Sweetie, I'm going away and I don't know when I'll be back."

Twilly stood up and walked to the other side of the bedroom. She turned away and looked out of the window, her throat beginning to close and her heart groaning with pain. "You cannot do this," she said without turning around, her voice shivering. "We've never been separated. We were infants together." She continued,

a flood of tears streaming down her lovely face.

Grista ran to her and held her close. "I know," she whispered, holding back sobs. "I know. We'll work something out. How could I ever think of going anywhere without you? Can you forgive me?"

"Yes, of course," sobbed Twilly. "How could I not?"

"Come, lovey. You'll have to pack. We have to meet up with them shortly."

• • • • • • •

Darvin closed the door behind him and walked over to the parked philbee. He turned the ignition and headed down the avenue towards Cremona's. Pell and Cremy were waiting in front. Darvin pulled the philbee next to them and greeted them, noticing how chic Cremy looked in her iridescent pink and gold blouse glistening in the sun. He was transfixed by her beauty. She entered the philbee, admiring Darvin's strong good looks. Pell sat in the corner, amused by the attention they were giving one another.

They headed back down the avenue to pick up Gully in front of the Praetodal. The big man strapped his travelon to the back of the philbee with the other travelons and looked in the compartment with a wide grin on his face. His face lit up the entire compartment. He sat between Cremy and Pell, looking so self-content with a big smile on his face. "My, my, don't you look majestic, Cremy." The curly red-haired man's face was beaming. "What say you, lads? Isn't Cremy breathtaking this morning? Darvin?"

Darvin looked through the rear view. "Yes, quite," he said with a little embarrassment.

"And what about you my dark, quiet, mysterious friend?" he asked turning to Pell.

Pell leaned forward and looked at Cremy. "I've never seen you so ravishing Cremy. We're all completely enthralled."

Cremy's face turned slightly red and flashed a little smile. She raised her head in a queenly fashion and said, "Oh, sirs, how does a lady react to the praises of three handsome gentlemen?"

The philbee continued down the main avenue of Faxburn until it reached the corner of Grista's handsome apartment building. In front of the building stood Grista and another young woman. Darvin turned the philbee and parked it in front of the carpeted entranceway of the building. Darvin and Pell exited the philbee and walked over to the two young women. Grista's eyes were fixed on Pell.

"Have everything you need Grista?" asked Darvin.

"Yes, thanks. Oh, by the way, we've got one more traveler. I'd like you to meet my dearest friend, Twilly." Twilly was a tall, young, beautiful brunette with hair so black that it shown blue in the sunlight. Both girls were dressed in khaki shorts, with soft brown leather shoes.

"Grista! It's just the five of us!" asserted Pell in a firm voice.

"No! It's the six of us. I don't go anywhere without Twilly," she returned, hardening her stance, "and if she doesn't go then no one goes!" The girl was determined and Pell and Darvin knew that they would not be able to dissuade her.

Pell looked at Darvin. "What do you think?" he asked.

"What do I think? Is that what you asked me?" Darvin became more agitated as he continued, "Look at the girl. She's more ferocious than a bloody Gantho and you're asking me what I think. Listen, mate, that girl is determined to bring her girlfriend and there's nothing you or I, or anyone else in existence, can do to stop her. What do I think," he concluded sardonically.

Gully got out of the philbee and looked up into the heavens. "Oh, the adventures and misadventures of being associated with Pell Provance. I knew when I hooked up with you lot that I was going to experience situations just like this."

"Look," he continued, "we don't have to go far, just to the Faxburn station. The girls can sit on our laps until then." Pell knew all he could do was acquiesce, so they all piled into the philbee, Twilly on Gully's lap and Grista on Pell's, with Cremy laughing to herself at the concept of Pell being bullied around by Grista. She actually began to like Grista and found her to be fascinating.

"We're approaching the station, so I'll drop all of you off and return the philbee to the garage, then I'll meet up with you on the Taponella," said Darvin. They all piled out of the philbee and Darvin rode off towards the garage. The group, all carrying their travelons made their way to the Firwith window to acquire a destination schedule.

A voice greeted Grista from behind. It was Mrs. Gridfige, one of the women that had spent time with her at the orphanage. "Hi sweetie," she said affectionately, "and where are you off to?"

"To Firwith," Grista answered.

"Oh, and there's Twilly," Mrs. Gridfige noticed, "with a group of people. So both of you are going to Firwith with your friends? Do you have enough mica?" she asked, whispering.

"More than enough," Grista answered, thanking her.

"Oh, well, I guess it's time to board the Taponella. You there!" shouted Mrs. Gidfrige, addressing Pell and Gully. "Make sure you take care of these two and they get everything they need, you understand?"

"Of course, we do," replied Pell.

They made their way through the station towards the Taponella platform. As they made their way, Pell glanced up at the ceiling looking for the triangular-shaped glass, which was not there, only marble slabs.

As they ascended the stairs to the platform, they were met by a silver-haired man with a neatly trimmed moustache. "Mr. Provance?" he inquired. "Mr. Pell Provance?"

"Yes," Pell answered.

"Would you follow me please?" the man directed.

• • • • • • •

Meanwhile, the Kungerod of Patamodia raised the platform in his basement similar to the Athelonian Kungerods after he had set the orbs. He then jammed his tundril in the center, and the room became filled with streaming magenta light, as the gem set into the center of the tundril began to glow and then sent a stream of magenta light knifing through the heavens.

Far away, on the continent of Ilgestana, a tall shadow of a feminine figure had just completed the ritual of jamming her tundril into the slot. The room swirled with purple and violet, revealing a tall, beautiful woman with a severe countenance. The purple and violet climbed rapidly into the heavens, the heavens being set ablaze with purple, violet-magenta and blue light. Off in the far distance, two more beacons were slicing their way into the heavens, a pearl white beacon from the continent of Vernace and an emerald green beacon from Can-Chimera. Each Kungerod made their way to their own terraports.

• • • • • • •

On board the Taponella, the three girls were scurrying to get to the window seats ahead of the men. Pell looked at them and said with a smile, "Silly girls. We have the entire car to ourselves." Gully laughed and shook his head.

The door between the cars opened and the silver-haired man entered. "My name is Muswick and I'll be seeing to all of your needs." The car was elegant, with rich woods and brass piping and wonderfully comfortable window seats of a soft leather. There were six sleeping berths and a dining table. Gully's face brightened, as a steward entered with six perlees. "I'll return to take your order," he said, as he was leaving.

The girls were engrossed in conversation, giggling and throwing silly glances at the men sitting across from them. Grista asked Cremy if she had ever seen Darvin or Pell in a bathing suit. With that she broke out in uncontrollable laughter, pointing at the two men. "Sinister looking. Darvin!" she screamed and laughed. "And his majesty over there in bathing suits. Oh, what a sight that's going to be." All three girls continued to laugh hysterically. Pell and Darvin just looked at each other and sighed. Gully was fighting to maintain a straight face, but caved in and just burst with uncontrolled laughter, before they knew it Pell and Darvin were holding their sides in pain from laughing so much. The entire car was filled with a cacophony of laughing men and screaming girls.

The gaiety was interrupted by the entrance of the steward, looking smart in a white suit with maroon piping. "Shall we start with hot todo pan rolls while I take your order?"

Everyone shouted, "Yes," in unison.

The steward continued, "We have mutrish with delicately prepared tandelon silk strips topped with gretheline sauce. Or you may choose the plaporis carib covered with seasoned fig nuts. For dessert, we have moon struck cadenate or merokosian canae."

Everyone ordered mutrish, which was a sort of a meaty olive soup. Everyone, except Gully ordered tandelon silk strips with gretheline sauce. Gully loved plaporis carib with seasoned fig nuts. They all ordered the merokosian canae, which was an exquisite dessert served in a large silver and glass goblet consisting of a piece of the softest, most delicate cake, covered with a hot sauce akin to chocolate and rum and topped with quante berries, which were large, white and juicy.

As the brunch was being served, the Taponella began leaving the station of Faxburn.

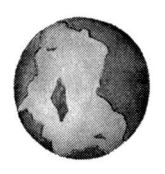

Chapter 14

PATHENUNE

Crofty Bellar's terraspan was beginning to descend on Pathenune's terraport. Peering out of the viewing glass of the terraspan, she marveled at the order and the breathtaking beauty of the isle of Pathenune. She remembered her childhood memories, as the Kungerods prepared her for this purpose. The grounds were well kept and attended, red pines and violet spruce adorned the horizon. On the south side of the main building, was a clear violet lake. The conference center itself was a shimmering ice blue building, with a half-moon-shaped glass dome in the center, filled with symbols and legends.

The terraspan gently touched down on the elevator. Crofty Bellar opened the hatch and inhaled the fresh cool aromatic air of Pathenune. Stepping off of the passenger elevator, she made her way down the stately marble roadway that led to the conference building, flanked by red furs set ablaze by the ever eclipsed evening sun. There at the entrance of the grand building, was a small army of staffers waiting for her, from fen fitters, to chefs, to houseboys, serving girls, electrical workers and finally stewards. They stood in a semi-circle waiting for Crofty to address them. She stood in the midst of the semi-circle and began her address.

"Hello everyone, it's so nice to see all of you again. And a special greetings to all the new appointees. Well, as you know, we're preparing for a most momentous event. In just twenty-four annots all five Kungerods will be gathered here for a conference. This is a unique and singular honor for all of you. As you know, most of them are very particular and somewhat demanding. But I'm sure you'll all perform your duties with exemplary alacrity. By the way, the grounds look superb. I salute you fen fitters and I'm sure the conference center and adjoining buildings are in pristine condition. So I look forward to an efficient, attentive and fascinating two weeks for us all. I myself will be coming and going during their stay, but I'm sure every one of you will be up to the task. Remember, that the Kungerods picked each and every one of you and prepared you for this time. So I'll leave everything in your very capable hands. Thank you for your time and attention."

After she had dismissed the entire staff, many came over to invite her to their homes and to meet their families. The staff of Pathenune lived their entire lives on the island. They wanted for nothing. There was a town called Gledifiel with schools, shops, even a train service from one end of the island to the other and philbees. A freightliner docked once a cycle to supply all of their needs.

• • • • • • •

Aboard the Taponella, the group had dozed off with the dreariness of full stomachs, the men on one side and the girls on the other. They awakened as the Taponella came to a stop at the Lethurnae station. They would have some time to walk and stretch as the engines were being switched.

As they stepped off the open platform, the man with the silver hair and moustache appeared. He gathered them together and told them to stay together as a group and he would inform them as to when the train will be leaving.

The air was fresh and gusty, with a hint of ocean aroma. Cremona put her arms around the waist of Twilly and Grista and said, "Girls, let's do some shopping since we have to stick together as a group. We can force the men to follow us to some female finery shops and watch them squirm as we try on some alluring female temperature risers." They all screamed with laughter as they made their way down a cobblestone path towards Lethurnae, with the three frustrated men following behind them.

As they turned the bend to the entrance of the town, they were fascinated at the number of shops, inns and pubs for such a small town. It was a busy little town with outdoor cookeries, cabanas, philbees traveling to and fro and crowded sidewalks. What was particularly noticeable was the sound of streamers and flags adorning all of the buildings furrowling in the gusty wind. They made their way slowly through the throng, trying to stick close together.

Darvin ran up to the girls. "Hey! We're not going to some female finery shops while you lot spend your time trying on different outfits."

"Yes, you are Darvin Scutter" Cremy asserted. "You heard what that silver-haired man said. We have to stay together, so you all will have to watch us change our lingerie." With that the girls all giggled.

They found an expensive finery shop next to an outdoor cafe. The shop was full of female dainties and lingerie made of rich pherleon, a silk-like material that grew deep in the soil.

"Isn't this fun?!" exclaimed Grista. "Plus, we can torture the men." Twilly giggled.

Cremy looked over at the three forlorn men and said, "Oh Grista! How could you be so cruel to our manly champions? You're right. It is fun!"

The three men looked at each other and shook their heads. Pell turned to walk out of the shop. "I don't know about you lot, but I'm going to wait outside," and left.

Pell, standing outside of the shop, began to catch the eye of not a few of the females. One tall red-haired maiden winked at him and smiled. The only trouble was, was that her escort, a tall muscular man, noticed this and began aggressively making his way towards Pell. Pell, steadying himself, began positioning himself for combat. In an instant and out of nowhere Grista lunged at the man, thrusting her fist into his abdomen, as if to disembowel him. The man was taken aback in shock and pain with a clear understanding that to strike a woman would bring ruination to his reputation and career. So, he covered himself and pleaded for her to stop. Darvin and Gully lifted her off of the defeated man.

As they pulled her away, she shouted, "How dare you! How dare you try to put your hands on someone like him! He's not just some hunker that works at the corner store! This is Pell Provance, you maeldon egg worm!"

The man hid his face with embarrassment and took the hand of the red-haired girl and rushed to get away from the ferocious female. A large crowd had gathered to view the spectacle. The men's faces were pale with shock and the women looked at Grista with great admiration.

One stately, platinum-haired woman came over to her and said, "My my, lovely lass, that was the most amazing thing I have ever witnessed. Let me have the pleasure of you and your company joining me for a cordial." The serving girls and boys rushed to the table to bring extra chairs and to sneak a peak at the lovely and feral Grista. "Well, sit down my dears and order anything your heart desires." They all ordered saermet cocktails, which were native to the region. "By the way, my name is Pernis Huelet."

Pell stood and introduced the group and himself.

She turned to Grista and said, "Grista, yes, the name is appropriate. I have never seen such a display of courage in my life and with such fervor. So where do all of you come from? If I may."

"We are from Faxburn, on our way to Firwith," Twilly offered.

"Yes, we're going to spend a few days at the shore," Gully added.

"What about you? Tell us about yourself," Pell inquired.

"Well not much to tell. I'm a very rich and very bored widow looking for some adventure or excitement. I would dare to say that everyone here is a little bored. That's why Grista's spectacle received so much attention. Listen, my loves, how would you like to come to my home tonight?"

"I'm not sure," answered Pell. "We were on board the Taponella and we have to be back after they've switched engines."

"Well that's no problem, no problem at all. I'll have my terraspan deliver you to Firwith in the morning. You'll arrive there way before the Taponella. You see, my niece is having a party and we'll have Pac-Nostre performing."

"Pac-Nostre!" exclaimed Twilly. "Why, that's just the greatest female band on the planet!"

"Listen, mate," said Darvin to Pell quietly. "If we go it's just going to muck things up."

"Look, Darvin," answered Pell. "We'll stay the night and leave first thing in the morning. We'll even wait for the Taponella at the Firwith station."

The girls all supported Pell's advice with assuring words directed at Darvin. "Come on, Darvin. It'll be fun!" shouted Cremy.

"Yes, come on you eternal beacon of practicality. Let's have a night of it," added Grista.

"Please, Darvin. Oh, please, please," pleaded Twilly.

"Come on mate. You and I will look after this lot," assured Gully.

Darvin relented. "All right, all right. Enough of your whining, but remember this: I'm personally going to throw all of you out of your beds in the morning."

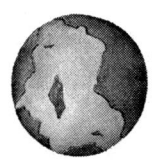

Chapter 15

DRUE LICHENS

On the isle of Pathenune, Crofty Bellar was going about her business, making sure all the quarters of the Kungerod's were prepared and stocked. She then made her way to the conference center to place daily bulletins, briefs on the disposition of each continent, census data, transportation advances, calamities, torts, crimes if any and decorbans or deaths.

She could smell the aroma of hot caone being brewed coming from the kitchen. She followed the smell through the circular corridor to the enormous kitchen. The place was alive with activity, as chefs and assistants were preparing for the Kungerods' arrival. The Kungerods came there from time to time for leisure and to visit the inhabitants of Pathenune. But this was a gathering of all of the Kungerods and the entire island knew how serious this was. This was a conference.

Crofty approached the large brass caone maker to pour herself a cup and immediately one of the assistants rushed over to serve her. She could tell that he was from Patamodia. He was tall and extremely attractive, with an orange hue to his skin, hair blacker than the dark caverns of Ilgestana and piercing violet eyes. He bowed to her slightly. "We have a refreshing repast waiting for you in the Floriana room, Miss Bellar. Please let us see to your refreshments and comfort."

She smiled and followed the young man. The Floriana room was breathtaking, with four white marble pillars in the center. And six dining tables were placed between the pillars, surrounded by a mini forest of a sample of all the fauna of Agrimore. There were walking paths leading to a waterfall and two fountains; it was like a dark sacred grotto. Above, were three large panes of arched glass separated by a white marble roof. The glass extended along the width of the roof and was colored blue-amber and smoked, with the brilliant eclipsed sunlight pouring through.

The steward presented himself at attention upon reaching the table and then seated her. He served her an ice-cold frothy fruit parfait served in an ice blue goblet, paired with tecadorman egg droplets covered with bellamura mushrooms, pecans, pendleta onions and finally hot-brewed caone, topped with whipped mocha. After eating, she strolled out to the patio to rest before the arrival of the Kungerods.

• • • • • • •

Pell and his group had just arrived at the stately mansion of Pernis Huelet. It was a sprawling estate, built in a classical style, with buttresses, arches, fountains and a cupola on top. Philbees were strewn everywhere. "Well, this is going to be some soiree," noted Gully.

Grista, Cremy and Twilly went up to the front door ahead of the men. Pernis Huelet was just exiting her philbee with the help of a young attendant. "My, my, my!" she exclaimed. "Those girls are very rambunctious, aren't they?" she asked. Then she laughed and said, "You boys certainly have your hands full, don't you?"

Pell, Darvin and Gully strolled into the large narthex, which led to a grand ballroom, filled with four to five hundred teenagers. In the middle of ballroom was a mountain of perlees with a waterfall of swemorize, a bubbly champagne-like beverage, with so many bubbles that it was as if steam was rising at the bottom of the huge mountain of bottled perlees.

Gully was completely enrapt by the scene. "Now, this is a party. Yes, yes, a thousand times yes," he said gleefully.

"Easy now, mate," warned Darvin. "Remember, we've got to leave first thing in the morning."

Pell separated himself from Darvin and Gully and made his way through the throng, to the other side of the huge room, to the right of the stage where Pac-Nostre was about to perform. He walked over to one of the ice trays and pulled out a perlee. He looked over the throng. There were Hogomeans, Tendrats, aristocrats, idle rich, or so he supposed and some not so rich or idle. He noticed Grista, Twilly and Cremy in the center of the room, surrounded by eighteen or twenty dazzled young men completely enthralled by the three beauties. They were enjoying every bit of attention they were receiving, playfully teasing the poor pie-eyed young men. Grista was tantalizing them with her feral, curvy body movements; Cremy was beguiling them with her beautiful big eyes and regal disposition; and the tall, sultry Twilly had them entranced with her childlike innocence. Pell laughed to himself and shook his head, thinking, "Those poor sops don't stand a chance against those three. They'll retire to their beds tonight with a pain of enflamed passions and unfulfilled desires," and he continued to laugh to himself.

Just then he felt a hand on his shoulder and turned to behold a most intriguingly stunning creature behind him. "I wanted to meet the man that a woman would put on such a public display for," the young woman said.

He was at a loss of words at the apparition of this dazzling young woman partially obscured by the lights and the shadows. She was in her early teens with silver hair, which seemed to shimmer in the lights, a dark tan complexion and fascinating blue-green eyes. Her features were almost pixie like, with her hair in bangs and the sides swept back and braided down her back. Her eyebrows were also silver. Her nose was small, delicate and lovely. Her lips were small, but full. She had a long neck adorned by a platinum chocker. The light silver dress she was wearing accentuated her curvy body. Her legs were strong and well defined and silver shoes gilded her delicate feet. He found himself completely bedazzled by her.

"Now that I've seen you, I understand. By the way I'm Drue, Drue Lichens and you are?" she asked.

"I'm Pell, Pell Provance."

"Fascinating name for a fascinating person," she noted.

"Oh, I'm not that fascinating."

"Yeah, right," she answered. "My aunt considers you one of the most intriguing people she's ever met as does every female in this entire place and so do I. I would love to give you a tour of the mansion," she offered. She stared into his eyes, as if she was trying to hypnotize him.

Pell looked away at the stage as the female group Poc-Nostre was about to perform. The entire hall grew silent, as the five provocative-looking females raised their instruments. The lead singer stepped forward to the front of the stage and announced, "The first selection is Velvet Curtains."

Pell knew it would be very easy to find the three girls. All he would have to look for was a group of twenty to thirty forlorn males. Sure enough, there they were in the middle of a group of men, frolicking, dancing and just carrying on. Drue walked up beside him, looking at the band and over at Pell, scanning all of his features with admiration. Pell caught her stare and began to feel ill at ease.

Pac-Nostre was now well into their routine and the young woman had moved closer to Pell, stroking his arm and trying to catch his eyes, when all of a sudden the music went chaotic, into a screaming cacophony of sound and chords that were impalatable to the ear. The musicians stopped and stared at one another in shock and disbelief. The entire audience looked up at the stage, some staring and lowering their drinks. The lead singer stepped forward to apologize. She began to speak in broken sentences, as if she had lost the ability to form words. All the performers were at a loss as to what had happened. The young woman standing next to Pell noticed his perlee bottle unattended and walked over and dropped two small rectangular blue tablets into the bottle.

Pell took a sip of his perlee and began to feel sleepy. His eyes were getting heavy and he began to stumble, looking for a place to rest. Drue grabbed his hand. "Pell you look so very tired," she said. "Maybe you should come with me to lie down a bit." She led him away to the other side of the great house and unlocked a heavy door, which lead to a small circular staircase. She helped him up the stairs to a room with a bed and bath. She helped him onto the bed and began removing his clothing, admiring the contours of his physique. "Ah, my great prince," she whispered, "It's no wonder the girl fought for you."

His head was spinning, as he struggled to open his eyes to see Drue leaning over him. He could see her lips moving, but couldn't hear what she was saying. She straddled his waist and whispered in his ear. "Now you belong to me. No other woman will ever have you. In a few weeks, we'll be husband and wife." With that, she left the room and locked the door behind her.

• • • • • • •

The Kungerod of Athelone's terraspan began its descent onto the landing platform and the slight thud of its landing awakened the Kungerod. He began to stretch out and as he peered out of the small observation window, he could see the beautiful isle of Pathenune and some of the staff rushing to meet his arrival. Migely undid the hatchway and waited while the Kungerod exited the hatch and made his way to the boarding stairs. Migely came up behind him. "You look troubled sir," he noted.

"Migley, my good friend. We may be facing the greatest crisis in the history of this world all because of Pell Provance."

"Pell Provance?" Migely asked.

"Yes, Mr. Provance has no idea the danger he poses."

After that, they quietly made their way to the conference center, with a team of staffers following after them. The large doors laid open for them, with two staffers on each end. One came forward. "Will you be using the atrium sir?"

"Yes, I think I will," answered the Kungerod cheerfully. The man who led him to the atrium was from Ilgestana. Ilgestanians were quite tall and pale with delicate features, almost feminine in appearance. They passed the Floriana room and walked through a narrow hall to a room filled with marvelous light. The roof was an open rectangle with round corners. The walls were light-green marble with decorative brass fluting, sealed at the top with the most beautiful orange wood. There were eight tables and chairs. The table top shimmered, as if made from pure crystal. The edges of each table and chairs were made from a precious pearl-like material. The tables were separated by four great vernatian pines. The pine needles were violet, in contrast to the golden brown trunks. The floor was very decorative, made of marble, glass and ceramics depicting the history of each continent.

The Kungerod sat himself at one of the tables and contemplated how well kept everything was. Everything was in perfect order. A staffer came over. "Will you have a refreshment or cordial?" he asked.

"Yes, I will thank you. By the way, do you have a fresh hot caone?"

"Oh, yes sir. I'll bring you one immediately."

"Thank you," responded the Kungerod. He sat back and contemplated the meeting and looked forward to seeing the other Kungerods.

• • • • • • •

Meanwhile, back at the soiree, Darvin and Gully began looking for Pell. "Where's he gotten off to now?" asked Darvin.

"Well, you know Pell. He's probably up to some intrigue, or chasing some females," answered Gully, totally unaware of Pell's plight.

"What about those girls? They're getting rather wild out there," said Gully.

Darvin snickered to himself and noticed the three surrounded by a throng of pie-eyed men. The heavens pity those poor sots, he thought to himself.

Drue, in the meantime, had located her aunt in the sitting room on the second floor. She sat next to her. "Auntie, remember when you promised me to give me anything my heart desires?"

"Of course sweetie. You've been with me most of your life. Have I ever denied you anything?"

"No," she answered, "but this request may seem a little unusual."

"What is it, my sweet?" asked the woman, looking into her eyes tenderly.

"Well, you know that group which you met at Lethurnae?"

"Oh! You mean the ones I invited to your party? The ones with that exotically beautiful and feral female?"

"Yes," she answered.

"Well, what is it dear one?"

"Remember that tall raven-haired man that seemed to be their leader?"

"Oh! You mean Mr. Pell Provance. Yes, he is rather dashing, isn't he? But a little old for you, don't you think?"

"He is the one I want," she said sternly.

"Well, how does he feel about that?"

"Auntie, there's no one else in this entire world that I desire except Pell Provance."

"Well, my sweet, there's not much we can do about that, can we?" she asked rhetorically.

"I've already taken steps to obtain him!"

"He's not a piece of property that you can obtain. He's a being and a rather fearsome at that!" exclaimed Purnis.

"Well he's not so fearsome now."

"What have you done?!" she asked, her voice trembling.

Drue stood unmoved by her aunt's emotional outburst. "I drugged him and locked him in on the third floor and I'm holding you to your promise."

"Oh, my poor Drue. My poor child, what have you done to us?" Her aunt put her head in her lap and began weeping and moaned. "What have you gotten us into? No, I must take steps to protect you and extricate ourselves from this situation."

"I'll be all right, auntie. Eventually, he'll come to accept his situation and even enjoy it. Am I not beautiful? Could we not offer him more than anyone else in this world?"

"Oh, you poor little fool," she said, her throat sore from weeping. "Don't you understand anything? These people are not like us. They don't care for trinkets or riches. They're most unusual, that's why I invited them. That Pell Provance is unlike anyone I've ever seen. He has a strange look to him, almost dangerous, and have you forgotten that female, Grista, I told you of? She was ready to slay a man six times her size for threatening him. She had the poor creature whimpering. What will she do when she finds out that you've drugged and locked away the love of her life?" At that she rose and wiped her eyes. "Well, what's done is done. We'll have to decide what to do next."

• • • • • • •

Crofty Bellar was back at her home in Patamodia. She was resting after her trip to Pathenune and awaiting the arrival of the group. When the langline blinked, she walked over to the instrument and answered, "Crofty Bellar."

The voice on the other end of the line was rather frantic. "Miss Bellar, this is Muswick. I was to guide the group to Firwith. Well, we changed the engine at Lethurnae and then went off to town for two hours until the Taponella was ready. Well, they didn't show up and the train is about to leave without them. I cannot hold it up any longer. What should we do?"

"Blast it!" she muttered. "I've heard about this wild group, especially Pell Provance. Parties, perlees and females are his daily fare."

"Well, what should we do?" asked the man frantically.

"Look, don't worry about it. Just take the train to Firwith. I don't think all five of the Kungerods could keep that group in check. I'll contact the Kungerod of Athelone and see what must be done." She hung up the instrument and settled down on her easy chair. "Blast it, the Kungerods are going to be furious," she muttered to herself. "Oh well, I'll just have to blink the Kungerod of Athelone and let him know that the pack of Veracodas may not be showing up for the conference." She pressed the buttons for Pathenune and asked for the Athelonian Kungerod. She related everything that Muswick told her to the Kungerod. There was a long pause at the other end. Then there was an unintelligible interruption and the instrument seemed to vibrate.

"By all the moons of Detrius! Blast that bunch of insipid, perlee drinking, prancing horde of Aextori! That's Provance's fault!. He probably led them off on some gala where he could chase females and sate himself on perlees!." The Kungerod went on and on, "Blast! Blast! Blast!" After a while he calmed himself down and said, "I'll inform the other Kungerods when they arrive. There's nothing to be done at this time. This world is going to shake when they find out that they're going to be at the leisure of Mr. Provance and his party." With that, the instrument went dead.

• • • • • • •

Pell stretched himself on the bed and grabbed his head. Everything was spinning. He struggled to his feet and stumbled back onto the bed. "Bloody hell," he murmured to himself. The room was very dark and he attempted to rise up again and held onto the bed post for balance. He had no idea what had happened to him. He began feeling his way across the dark room and bumped his shin on a piece of furniture. "Oh, did that smart!" he whispered to himself. He found the wall and fingered his way across the mantle of a fire place. Feeling the wall for a light or a door, he found a door knob and turned it, opening the door, which led to an empty closet. Another door knob was turned and there was a small amount of light. He was in the bathroom. The light was coming from a small barred window. He looked out to see the shimmering moons of Agrimore. Below in the distance, he could see trees and a lake. He realized that he had to be in the rear end of the huge estate. "How did I get here?" he asked himself. "I remember being at the party with Drue, but can't remember another thing. Did I pass out and was brought here? I only had a half of perlee." His eyes began adjusting to the darkness and the light through the bathroom window helped. He walked carefully to the far wall and found a large, heavy door. He turned the knob to discover that it was locked. He now realized that he had been locked in. But who? Why? He thought. Drue. Her image came to him like a flaming arrow.

He thought of the journey, the train waiting their arrival and his friends Darvin, Cremy, Gully, Twilly and Grista, especially Grista. Would he ever see them again? Would he ever see Grista again? He began missing her, thinking of all of her antics and mischief. Thinking of her curly blond hair, her great beauty, he began to panic, but caught himself. I'm Pell Provance, he thought to himself. I don't panic.

He shouted a controlled shout at the door. "Hello, is there any one there? Drue, are you out there?" No answer, so he made his way back to the bed to think of what he should do next.

Darvin became concerned when he and Gully couldn't locate Pell. "Where in the blazes is he?" he asked Gully. "If he went off with some female... Damn, Pell, where in the trifords are you?"

"Should we tell the girls?" Gully asked. "I'm afraid to tell Grista. No one knows what she might do. She'll take this estate apart stone by stone, until she finds him."

"Your right," Darvin affirmed. "Leave them be. We'll try to find him on our own! Let's ask Purnis, maybe she's seen him about."

They left the ballroom in search of Purnis Huelet. Darvin walked over to one of the servers rushing into the ballroom with a tray of canopes and asked about Pell. The server hadn't seen him, but directed him to a room up the large staircase. They entered the large room, which resembled a smoking room. There were books, games and wooden boxes of assorted puigos. "Pardon us Purnis, but we can't seem to locate our friend, Pell Provance. Have you seen him?" asked Gully.

"Why no," she answered. "Isn't he at the party?"

"Well, he was, but he has a tendency of wandering off," stated Darvin.

"Oh my, this won't do. We must find him. Don't you people have an appointment in the morning to meet up with the Taponella?" she asked concernedly.

"Yes, we do and we don't have that much time," answered Gully.

"Well, not to worry. I'll have my staffers do a thorough search of the grounds and the entire estate. We'll find him," she assured them.

She immediately left the room and called the staffers together and directed them to thoroughly search the entire estate and grounds, until he has been found. She then left to find her niece. Purnis found her in the ballroom dancing with a young man. The music had somehow corrected itself and the female band was blazing. She interrupted the couple, grabbed Drue by the arm and led her away to a small sitting room adjacent to the ball room. After she had locked the door, she sat down next to her. "Drue!" her tone was sharp. "Do you see what is happening? His two male friends are searching for him. I have all the staffers looking for him. It's a good thing for you that no one knows about the hidden staircase and bedroom on the other side of the house, or we'd really be in trouble. Well, what do you have to say?"

"Auntie, everything is under control. A rumor is already being spread that he went off with another female in a philbee. All they will have is the description of the female and the philbee, which are rather obscure. Plus, there's no way he can get out of that bedroom."

"Do you intend to keep him there forever?" she asked. "You must be mad child!"

"Auntie, I'm going to handle this myself. It's my design, not yours. I'm keeping you out of this," she assured her.

"But, child, I'm already involved. You've told me everything you've done," she said anxiously.

"If, by any chance anything goes wrong, I will deny that you had any knowledge of this. But nothing will go wrong. Eventually, Pell will accept me and we will become man and wife," she said with a reassuring smile.

"Oh, my poor, deluded child. Things don't work that way. This person has friends, powerful friends. Have you forgotten about Grista?"

"No, I have not," she asserted. "He belongs to me. If I can't have him, then no one will! He'll stay locked up for good!"

"Oh, Drue." With that, the older woman put her head in her hands. "This is one time, if anything happens, I will not be able to protect you."

• • • • • • • •

The Kungerod of Athelone had finished his small repast and made his way to the outdoor gardens. It was quite a lovely and serene place that was a favorite of the Kungerods. It resembled an Italian Grotto or a Chesterfield maze, with many walking paths that led to earthen sitting rooms. He made his way to one of the cozy sitting rooms to contemplate what to do when the other Kungerods arrived and there was no Pell Provance. He was very concerned about the female Kungerod from Ilgestana. She was known for her short temper. He had to assure all of them that no action should be considered against Pell Provance, or they could all be held accountable.

• • • • • • •

In the meantime, Darvin and Gully had no success in locating Pell. One of the servants espied them from afar and made his way through the throng to them. He confronted Gully and Darvin and said, "Sirs, one of the other staffers related to me that she had seen Mr. Provance leaving in a philbee with a female."

"Bloody hell!" exploded Darvin. "We've so much to do ahead of us and he reverts back to his old tricks. Bloody bloody hell!"

"Well, what now?" asked Gully.

Darvin, turning to the servant, asked, "Would you be able to describe the female?"

"Well, he only caught a glimpse of them leaving, but she was tall with red hair. He said they entered a white philbee," answered the servant.

Purnis walked over to them and said, "I heard he's left with someone. Not to worry. I have people trying to track them down as we speak."

Grista, Twilly and Cremy noticed the commotion and saw Purnis and her staff speaking to Darvin and Gully. They immediately left the crowd of enthralled young men and made their way to where Darvin and Gully stood. "What's going on?" Cremy asked them. They looked at each other, hesitant to speak, fearing Grista's reaction.

Grista looked intently at them. "Well, we're waiting," she said impatiently.

"Pell is missing," Darvin answered.

"Missing, what do you mean missing?" asked Cremy with concern.

"It seems that he went off with someone a while ago."

"Who?" asked Grista, trying to control her emotions.

"He went off with a female in a white philbee. We're trying to track him down and we don't have much time," answered Gully.

Grista grew very somber. Walking away from the group, she raised her head to the ceiling, with her face tensed up. The vein in her neck became exposed. She let out a sound, an "URGHUR!" that startled everyone.

Darvin looked over at Gully. "Even the gods are shaking."

She came over to where they were standing and whispered to herself, "Pell Provance, you are going to know what terror really means when I get a hold of you."

Twilly said to Cremy, "I've never seen her this way, but I would not want to be Pell when she finds him."

Grista composed herself, her face still red from rage, glanced at Darvin and Gully and turned to the staffer. "Do you have any more information than what you just gave us?"

"No, miss. That's all we know right now."

Purnis walked over to her. "Calm yourself, child," she said, holding her wrists in a reassuring manner. "We are going to find him. Right now, I have an official investigating the matter. He'll find the town they went to. My langline should blink at any time."

"Look, we've got to be at that station in Firwith ahead of the train. Maybe some of us should leave now and a few stay behind, in case they track him down," suggested Gully.

"I'll stay," offered Grista. "The rest of you leave and catch the terraspan. You don't want to be here when I find him."

Darvin looked at the group and rolled his eyes. "I think Pell has had one too many of his silly detours. Let's go people." With that, they all left, leaving a seething Grista by herself.

• • • • • • •

Morning was approaching as Pell opened his eyes. He had a pounding headache and the room was still dark, except for a little light coming from the small window in the bathroom. He stumbled out of bed and made his way towards the light. Finding his way in the bathroom, he began opening all of the cupboards and drawers to find something that he could use to open the large door of the room. He found an assortment of soaps, toiletries, razors and to his amazement, a couple of candles. The sunlight lit up the bathroom enough to see himself in the mirror. His hair was disheveled and his clothes were wrinkled. He thought the proper thing to do was to draw a bath for himself. It would calm him and help him to think of what to do next.

Drue was in the main kitchen, having the chef prepare a sumptuous breakfast for herself. "Well, miss," said the chef, "that party certainly gave you an appetite."

"It sure did," she answered. "I'm famished." He then filled her tray with brown malen chips, poscen rolls, assorted fruits, berries and a hot foamy caone. She took the tray to the back staircase and up to the room where Pell was locked in. She put the tray down and listened at the door. She could hear the water running in the tub. She quietly unlocked the door and entered carefully and quietly, realizing he was in the bathtub. She laid the tray at the foot of the bed and left, locking the door after her. She smiled to herself and thought, Yes, take your bath my love. Prepare yourself for me.

Pell emerged from the bath feeling refreshed, wrapped the towel around his waist and lit one of the candles with his puigo lighter. He walked into the bedroom and peered around at the wall and mantle. The room was stark and bare, no windows or pictures, just the bed and a large dresser. He then caught sight of the tray at the foot of the bed. "Blast it!" he shouted, "That little vixen was here. Blast it!" He calmed himself and sat down on the bed to partake of the morning repast. He hesitated, then thought, She wouldn't drug me again. After all, she has me locked up in this damn room. So he partook.

Everything was extremely tasty, especially the hot caone. He then heard a voice outside of the door. "Are you enjoying the present I left you my prince?"

"Who is it? Who's there?"

"Why it is I, Drue, the niece of Purnis. Have you forgotten me so quickly, oh fickle one?"

"I knew it!" he shouted. "You're the one that was following me at the banquet hall. You're the vixen that locked me in here, aren't you?!" he demanded.

"That's right, lover and now you're mine. You might as well forget about your friends and that wild girl Grista, for you'll never see them again," she said confidently.

"Oh, you don't know my friends, especially Grista, do you?!" he shouted through the door. "They'll take this place apart to find me! And when Grista gets a hold of—"

"They won't find you," she interrupted. "They think you've gone off with some red-haired female in a philbee. Right now staffers and officials are trying to track her down, including Grista."

The room was quiet, then Pell asked her calmly, "Why, Drue? Why have you done this?"

"I saw you," she whispered. "I've never seen anyone like you. Other men are so ordinary compared to you. Those kingly features, those dark eyes, that beautiful form. No, Pell Provance, you belong to me now. Eventually you'll accept your fate and we'll marry, but you'll stay there until you do. This is my secret bedroom. No one knows of it, except me. No one's ever going to find you up here. Don't you find me beautiful?" she asked.

"But you're a child and you don't even know me. Perhaps, as you get to know me you'll not find me as desirable as you thought."

"Oh no!" she asserted. "There's no one like you in all the world. You're like a king. Even your friends are loyal. They would gladly lay down their lives for you and Grista, look at her devotion! Why, she'd take on entire armies for you. No use trying to convince me of your flaws," she said, "but I have to go now. I'll be back later with a change of clothes and refreshments. We'll have to devise some way of providing you with these things without you trying to escape." And she left.

• • • • • • •

Meanwhile, Darvin, Gully, Cremy and Twilly were heading towards the terraport in Purnis's philbee. Darvin shook his head in frustration. "What in Gantho's kidneys was he thinking?" he muttered.

Twilly and Gully were quiet. Cremy spoke up, "I don't believe it."

"What are you saying?" asked Darvin.

"Something doesn't smell right," she said.

"But he's done this before!" exclaimed Darvin.

"Sure, for a brief time, but not this, not like for an entire night, especially when we were on such an important journey." Offered Cremy.

"But he's done so many crazy things in the past according to the rest of you," interjected Twilly.

"That's true," admitted Darvin.

"Well, let's just get to where we're going and wait for word from Purnis," said Gully.

"Yes, let's leave it in her hands," Cremy said resignedly. "After all, the woman has everyone looking for him and she doesn't even know us."

"I know," answered Darvin. "She's even enlisted the aid of officials and private professionals."

Purnis walked over to them, as they were about to board the terraspan. "I know you are all concerned about your friend, but don't trouble yourselves. Everything is being done to locate him," she assured them. They all thanked her and boarded the terraspan that would take them to Firwith.

Chapter 16

CHAMPIONSHIP WRESTLING

Crofty Bellar was back in her home waiting for word from the Kungerods, or the silver-haired guide, hoping there would be word of the group's arrival. She wondered about the group she had yet to meet and why there was such a fuss being made over them. Just then, the langline lit up. It was the Kungerod of Athelone. "Crofty?" he calmly asked. "Any word of Mr. Provance and his group?"

"Not yet, sir," she answered. "I'm still waiting to hear from Muswick, their guide. I should never have left poor Muswick alone with that bunch. Even all the Kungerods combined wouldn't be able to keep them in check." With that, the line went dead.

• • • • • • •

Pell was awake lying on the bed in the darkened room. He began musing about his life and what he had done, his adventures, romances, parties. He began to miss his home in Chantry and especially his friends. *But, I'm Pell Provance. How could I fall victim to this lovely little wench?* he thought. It did not trouble him at all that most of his life was spent traveling, buying exquisite clothing, partying and carousing. It all seemed normal to him and he enjoyed it immensely. Nor, did he question the fact that enormous amounts of mica were deposited in the local exchange for him and that he had no recollection of his childhood. That did not trouble him in the least.

He had always had powerful feelings that Agrimore was not his place of birth, but he was completely comfortable with this and the inhabitants of this lovely world. He marveled at their sundry systems of politics, economy and manufacturing. It ran so smoothly in concord with everything in creation. He thought of those little philbees that people used all of the time, how safe and practical they were. There had never been a philbee mishap since their invention. But every so often, he would have fleeting visions of a nightmarish place, where there were no gentle philbees, but roaring pieces of designed metal, with cruel and annoying sounds, swiftly moving from point A to point B. The silence of the room seemed to calm him and he began to focus his thoughts. In a strange way, he enjoyed the solitude. It gave him time to think and to reflect. He thought of the superb economy of this world, how a city like Faxburn could produce all of the trains of the entire world and how every person in Faxburn would take part in their construction. Besides having other professions, every citizen would receive a residual from every train that was used in Agrimore. Amazing, he thought to himself. The same with Selverna and the terraspans and Muesly with their philbees. Also Firwith with their great freightliners. Such an ingenious idea. The whole idea of orphans and how they were loved by entire cities, how possessive each citizen was, as if they were their own. Also, the way no one traveled between continents, except for trade. Everyone is at home in their sundry stations.

His concentration was broken by a sound outside of the door. "Pell?" a quiet female voice asked.

He did not answer, but quietly waited thinking, If she opens the door, I could make my escape. Then he heard footsteps moving away from the door. He jumped out of bed and called, "Drue?"

"Pell?" Drue asked. "I didn't hear anything, so I thought you were sleeping and would have returned later."

"Yes, I was resting," he said. There was a pause.

"Listen, Pell, we've got to come up with a way for me to get in and out of your room, without you trying to escape," she said urgently.

"I know," he said with clarity.

"When you were bathing, I was able to bring you breakfast. So I want you to keep the tub full of water and disturb it with your hand when I come back. It will give me enough time to slip a tray into your room and lock the door."

"Do we have to go through all of this Drue?" he asked, losing his patience.

"It's the only plan I could come up with for now."

"Listen, Drue, this is not going to work. You can't keep me here forever," he said quietly, trying to contain his frustration.

"Of course I can. No one knows you're here. My aunt's going away. Also, the staff is leaving and there's no way out of this room," she said confidently.

"What about school?" he asked.

"Oh, that's easy. I'll just postpone it for a while."

"You know," he said, "if you unlock the door and let me go, I'll never implicate you. You know I'm telling the truth, don't you?"

"Yes, I actually believe you," she said, "but, I can't let you go. I'll never see you again." She turned to leave and said, "I'll be back shortly with a change of clothing and your soiled clothing, I shall send to another town to clean and press." And she left. Pell sat on the bed and ran his hands through his hair with frustration.

• • • • • • •

Meanwhile, on board the terraspan the group was very quiet. Cremona was looking out of the window, as the terraspan ascended high into the clouds, thinking of all the wonderful times she had had with Pell and how incomplete they felt without him. "Where is he?" she asked herself. "How could he do this to us?"

Darvin, who was sitting across from Cremy asked, "Are you all right love?"

"No I'm not!" she shot back. "How could he do this to us on such a journey?!" Her voice was shaking.

"Well, he is Pell Provance," added Twilly. "Intriguing, rambunctious and completely unpredictable."

• • • • • • •

Meanwhile, Grista and the officials were closing in on the location of the person Pell had supposedly gone off with. They tracked the philbee's registration to a little hamlet called Pollandace and found the home of the female who had rented the philbee. It was a small, quaint little house, gray, with turquoise shutters and many window plants. The two officials, along with Grista, walked up the stairs to the front door. One official rapped gently on the front door, with no answer. Grista immediately pushed him aside and banged with a closed fist, almost cracking the door. A voice from inside said gently, "One moment, please." The door was unlatched and a blurry-eyed, red-haired girl appeared. "May I help you?" she asked cautiously.

"Sorry to bother you miss, but we're trying to locate one Pell Provance. You were seen leaving with him last night, during the party at the Huelet estate." Grista was losing patience, but bit her lip.

"I left with no one last night," she offered. "I was tired and left the party early. I don't know of this Pell Provance you're seeking."

"May we look inside miss?" the official asked courteously.

At that, Grista pushed her way past the girl and entered the house. She looked everywhere, but no sign of Pell and no smell of his fragrance that she would always detect. The officials apologized to her and took their leave. Grista became troubled in her spirit and began to be concerned at not finding him. She did not suspect that he was being held at the estate, for she had never met Drue, only her aunt, whom she suspected nothing of.

"Well miss, where to now?" one of the officials asked Grista.

"Back to the estate," she answered exhaustively.

"Miss, you haven't slept all night. Don't you think it would be best to sleep for a while before you continue your search?" asked one of the officials gently.

"Yes, we might as well return. No use searching aimlessly," she agreed.

They arrived back at the estate where Purnis was preparing to leave for Lethernae. She came over to Grista and asked, "Didn't find your sweetheart?"

"No," she answered, "it was a dead end."

"Well love, you can select any room in the estate to rest, or I'll have a terraspan at your disposal and you can sleep on board, whichever you desire."

"Thank you, Purnis. I think I'll take the terraspan and meet up with the group."

• • • • • • •

So Pell was now alone. He was lying on the bed, trying to devise a plan of escape. He was becoming increasingly restless and impatient. All of a sudden, there was a sharp rap at the door. It was Drue. "Are you awake, my love?" she asked mischievously, toying with him.

"Stop calling me that!" he said sharply.

"But you are my love. You belong to me and no one else."

"You stupid little churlish wench. I will never be your lover, never, do you understand?!" he shouted.

There was silence for a few moments, then she began to giggle. "You should calm yourself, my sweet. After all, you are Pell Provance, whom nothing can unravel, the coolest person in the world," she said teasingly.

"You won't be so smug when Grista gets a hold of you," he said.

"Oh, I failed to mention, Grista and the entire group left for Firwith. Also, my aunt and all of the staffers are gone. We are all alone."

He was silent for a moment. "All of them?" he asked. "They all left?"

"Yes, my love. Now I have you all to myself. You'll soon understand to accept your circumstances and to appreciate the fact that here is a beautiful young woman that will go to such extremes and even peril to have you. Why, you should be flattered." Then she left.

• • • • • • •

The terraspans of the other Kungerods began circling and landing on the isle of Pathenune, with all of the staffers running to and fro preparing for their arrival. The Kungerod of Athelone entered the conference room of the main building preparing to greet his fellow Kungerods. The Kungerod of Patamodia was the first to enter the conference room. He was exquisitely dressed in a dark gray, double-breasted suit, white shirt, dark blue tie and tan leather boots. The Kungerod of Athelone greeted the handsome figure of the man, with much affection and a rare smile.

"Well, my dear friend, what's all the commotion? And where is the character called Pell Provance?" asked the Patamodian Kungerod.

"Well, that's the problem," answered the Athelonian. "We can't locate him."

"Tell me about him," asked the Patamodian.

"Well, he's a unique character to say the least, completely oblivious to what he's causing in this world. He's extremely handsome, enough to swoon every female in existence, with a totally careless attitude of partying, drinking perlees and chasing females. He's the most dangerous person this world has ever encountered."

"Tell me more," asked the Patamodian.

"He came into my shop. I looked him straight into the eye and he did not flinch. In fact, I flinched!"

"What?!" asked the Patamodian, his interest growing with every word.

"Yes," the Athelonian continued, "and besides that, he has a double shadow."

The Patamodian was aghast. "What's to be done?"

"That's why we're meeting here," the Athelonian replied, "precisely to find out what we should do and who or what this being is."

Just then, the Kungerod of Ilgestana entered the room. She was tall, beautiful and very severe looking. Her long black hair was pushed back into a ponytail, revealing a strong, chiseled face, accentuated cheek bones, a small, perfect nose, eyebrows that slanted upward and rich, full lips. She was wearing a brown leather jacket, with a forest green blouse and skirt and tan boots. She looked over at the other two Kungerods, her expression unchanged, walked over to the two and smiled broadly. They embraced each other, then she asked if the others had arrived yet.

"We're still waiting for the last two to arrive," said the Patamodian.

"What do we know of this Pell Provance?" she asked.

"I know him better than anyone here," answered the Athelonian. "I'll fill you in when the others arrive."

• • • • • • •

Back at the estate, Pell was lying on the bed, thinking of all the things that had happened in the past few months. He thought of the strange changes he had noticed when he left his home, his stumbling upon seeing Extella, the new friends he had met – Gully, Twilly and the feral and beautiful Grista. Strange how he was beginning to long for her. Now he was the prisoner of a mad sixteen-year-old vixen.

All of a sudden, there was a knock on the door and the voice of Drue. "Pell, I've brought you something. You know what you have to do. Turn on the tap in the tub and splash the water with your hand, or I won't unlock the door."

He did as she asked and walked to the bathroom. When she heard the water running, then the splashing, she unlocked the door and slipped the tray in, then quickly closed it and locked it. He picked up the tray of assorted fruits and hot caone, which he drank greedily. After a few moments, he began to feel sleepy and his head began spinning. He laid back on the bed. "Blast, damn little wench did it to me again," he muttered, and closed his eyes, not knowing what to expect. He struggled to stay awake, but his head was reeling.

After a few moments there was a voice at the door. It was Drue. "Pell my love, are you awake?" He could hear her, but his head was spinning so much that he could not answer. She unlocked the door and came into the room, carrying a candle. She looked at him lying on the bed adoringly. She slowly undid her beautiful silver hair, letting it hang on her tan shoulders, all the time not taking an eye off of him. She undid her skirt, revealing beautifully-shaped, well-developed tan legs and shapely thighs. Lastly, she sat on the bed and took off her tan boots, again never taking an eye off of him. She leaned over him and straddled him, running her tongue over both his eyes and whispering in his ear. "I knew from the first time I saw you, that you were going to be mine, my love. I'll fill your life with pleasures unheard of, unspeakable pleasures from dark and forbidden places. I'll make you dizzy with inexpressible ecstasy and quicken you with far off desires."

She began wildly kissing him and growling like a wanton beast, ripping open his shirt, kissing and biting his chest. He struggled to open his eyes, trying to dislodge her. He managed to pull her off of him, but this only made her more passionate. She jumped on top of him again, trying to hold his arms with her knees and kissing him wildly. He lifted his entire body up into a sitting position and threw her off. The struggle was wearing him down. The drugs were taking affect, with the entire room spinning. He struggled to get to his feet, tripping and falling in the attempt. She immediately jumped on him and straddled him, this time reversing it, attempting to bind his hands behind him. He pulled his hands free and lifted himself up, as if he were doing pushups with the girl on his back. He managed to get to his feet, the girl toppling to the floor laughing hysterically, as Pell stumbled around the room. She continued to laugh and said, "This is the most fun I've had in my entire life." With that, she left and locked the door behind her. Pell could hear her laughing, as she made her way down the hall. Pell was determined to get out of there the next time she came by.

Chapter 17

THE GATHERING OF THE GREATEST

At Pathenune, the Kungerod of Can-Chimera had just landed and entered the conference room. He was a strange and imposing figure. He was tall, with long black hair and a gold head band adorned his forehead. He had dark, foreboding eyes, thick eyebrows, a long scaline nose, high cheek bones and a mouth that was set with small, but attractive muscles around his lips. In Earth terms, he would have been taken for Asian and Spanish, but he was neither. He was the Kungerod of Can-Chimera. He was wearing a long flowing jacket of pearl white, which shimmered in the light, with a high collar similar to what was worn by Indian Royalty, white flowing pants and high, black, shiny boots that covered his knees. He walked over to where the other Kungerods were gathered. Without changing his expression, he nodded to the male Kungerods, turned to the severe-looking female, kissed her on the cheek and smiled. "Young beauty never fades," he said to the tall menacingly beautiful Kungerod. Then, turning to the others, he asked, "What's all the fuss about?"

"We're awaiting the Kungerod of Vernace. Everything will be revealed as soon as he arrives," said the Athelonian.

• • • • • • •

Meanwhile, Grista's terraspan arrived at Firwith and a philbee took her to the train station. There she found the group quietly sitting around, with the silver-haired guide standing near by. Grista walked up to Darvin, who looked up and asked, "Any word?"

"Nothing," she answered. She sat down placed her head in her hands and stared at the train station floor. Twilly then came over to her and embraced her.

Combing her hair with her hands and looking up steadfastly, she said, "Grista, sweetie, we'll find him. I promise you, no matter what it takes, we'll find him."

• • • • • • •

Back at Pathenune, the Kungerod of Vernace finally arrived. He was different from the other Kungerods, in that he was a short and rather stocky rotund man with disheveled clothing. He was in his late fifties or sixties with a round head, white curly hair, thick white eyebrows with little blue eyes, a large round nose with a little white curly beard. He was wearing a little dark green jacket, which he could not button because of his little pot belly and a thick black belt held up his little green pants, and he wore enormous, funny-looking boots on his little feet. He was quite comical looking for a Kungerod. The other Kungerods turned to look at him, as he entered the room. Then they all smiled and cheerfully greeted him. In spite of all of his eccentricities, they were all very fond of him. The Kungerod of Athelone was the first to walk over to him. He put his arm around his shoulders and told him how good it was to see him again. In fact, his presence seemed to lift everyone's spirits. The female Kungerod smiled warmly and kissed his curly white head. The others followed to express their appreciation for his presence. The little Kungerod chuckled at the attention he was receiving from his fellow Kungerods. "Well, what's all this about?" he asked. The Athelonian suggested they move into the conference room, adjacent to the Pollidecreum.

The Pollidecreum housed a massive glass globe, with a smaller globe within. They all sat at places specified for each Kungerod. The conference room was a large room, with no windows. In the middle, was a large rectangular table with five seats, one for each Kungerod. The room was neat and bare, except for two large urns set in inclaves on either side of the room. The large table was made of a tan and green marble material with thick, round, dark, wooden legs. The room was illuminated from within the walls.

"Well, tell us more about this Pell Provance," asked the Patamodian Kungerod.

The Kungerod of Athelone rose to his feet and leaned over. He placed his clenched fists firmly on the table and looked at each face intently.

"Some time ago, a group of interesting individuals entered my little shop. I was surprised to see them, for all I have there are useless items, you know, silly maps of places that do not exist, useless crystals and old candles. I confronted these people in my shop, but there was one that stood out, a tall, roguishly handsome character of impeccable taste. This creature had two shadows." All were silent when he stated that and began staring at each other. "Yes, my friends," he continued, "two clearly-defined shadows."

The female Kungerod put her hand to her mouth and exclaimed, "He's been to both worlds!"

"Yes, and there's more," the Athelonian continued. "He returned and I faced him..."

There was silence in the room. "Yes, yes, go on man," asked the Vernacian greedily.

"Well, I stared him right into his eyes, but he did not even flinch or blink. In fact, I began to flinch and started to become terrified."

The sound of "Ohhh" resonated through the conference room.

"Yes, my dear friends. He is the destroyer of worlds, the undoer of matter, the most dangerous creature in existence. But not in the way you imagine. No not at all. He has a captivating charm. In fact, I invited him to my chamber and found him delightful to speak with. You see, he is totally oblivious to who he is and what he's doing. The only things on his mind are females, perlees, parties and buying exquisite clothes. This person is not innately evil, but his presence is the downfall of both worlds." He went on, "You noticed the anomalies occurring around the world?"

"Oh, you mean the ones we're trying to restrain?" asked the Patamodian.

"Exactly. He is the cause. Both Agrimore and Algenmere are at risk."

The female Kungerod of Ilgestana rose to her feet. "Well, what do we do? Just let this creature roam about freely destroying both worlds?"

"Be careful what you are about..." interjected the Kungerod of Can-Chimera, who had been silent all the while. "We must not be hasty in any decision, for we've never come across such a creature before."

"I concur," said the Athelonian. "Let us retire today and tomorrow we will enter the Pollidecreum. That will give us the information we need, should we see fit to take any action." They all agreed and adjourned.

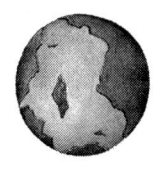

Chapter 18

ESCAPE

Back at the Firwith Station, the group was still waiting, not knowing what to do. Their silver-haired guide walked over to them. "Children. There's no sense moping in this station until we hear word. Look, why don't you all go to the town and refresh yourselves? I will stay here and keep watch for your companion." He walked over to Grista and crouched down to look at her, her eyes red from weeping. He said to her gently, "Especially you, miss. You'll need to be at your best when Sir Pell returns." He stroked her hair and wiped her eyes with his handkerchief and reassured her. "Listen, Miss Grista, this is Pell Provance. In all my years, I've never seen the likes of him. I know he'll return to you." She looked up at the handsome gentleman and found new strength. She held his hand, thanked him and went off with the others.

• • • • • • •

Back at the estate, Pell was just awakening. He had lost track of time and did not know how long he had been there, but he was ready to make his move. The chances of her drugging his next meal were very good, seeing that she had derived so much pleasure at their last encounter. He would accept the meal and feign being drugged, when she returned to harvest another erotic episode. He would then grab her and make his escape. Sure enough, there was a rap at the door.

"Pell, lover, are you awake? Pell, come on, sweetie, wake up. I've prepared something delicious for you. Pell!"

He answered, as if he had just been awakened. "Yes, is that you, Drue?"

"Who else, my prince?" she answered. "You know the routine, go to the bathroom and run the water." He complied with her request. Sure enough, there was a lavishly set tray of Athelonian delights. He lifted the tray to the bed. The hot caone was very aromatic and tempting, but he would have none of it. It would take some time for her to return, so he waited.

A short time later, he could hear movement outside the door. Then a key entered the latch. He waited patiently, knowing one wrong move and he would lose his chance, maybe forever. The door opened slightly. The key was still in her hand, as she began entering the room. Her silver hair shimmered from the light in the hall behind her. She was naked. He was taken aback at how breathtakingly beautiful she was. He reaffirmed his resolve and grabbed the young girl by the wrist and flung her onto the bed. She was taken completely by surprise. He leaned over her and kissed her ferociously, until he had wrested the key from her hand. He turned towards the door, when the girl jumped on his back, wrapping her strong legs around his waist. She was incredibly strong. They both fell backwards onto the bed. They kissed each other greedily, Drue's upper body heaving with passion. "Let me take off my clothes," he whispered to her.

"Yes! Yes my love. I knew eventually you would want me," she moaned. He rose up from the bed and began undoing his shirt. The girl was on the bed waiting for him, blinded with ecstasy.

In a moment he was outside of the room, locking the door behind him. Drue ran towards the door pounding and screaming, "Pell no! You can't leave me, Pell please!" she pleaded. "I love you beyond what anyone could. There's nothing I wouldn't do for you. Pell, you inflame me more than I thought was possible. And I know that you desire me, Pell. Please!"

Pell quietly listened to the girl. She began sobbing next to the door. Her sobbing moved his heart. "Drue," he said quietly. "Drue, you just cannot have me. I don't know if anyone can. Yes, you are very beautiful and very desirable, but this is not the way."

"Then what's the way? Tell me and I'll do it," she whimpered.

"I don't know, lovey. I don't really know who I am."

"Pell," she pleaded, "let me go with you, just to be next to you. Please, Pell."

"Listen Drue, I've got to leave now, but I'll make sure your aunt knows where you are."

"Pell!" she screamed. "Please don't leave me!"

"Sssh, quiet yourself. I'll go downstairs and prepare enough food for you, until your aunt arrives and I'll not implicate you, or your aunt in this mess. But I must go."

"Please, Pell. Please don't leave me," she sobbed.

"Stop that!" he demanded. "You are young and beautiful. Most men would sacrifice anything to be with you."

"I don't want most men!" she shouted angrily. "I want you, Pell Provance, the most intriguing man in the world. There's no one like you, Pell. You're a king amongst men. When I saw you in the banquet hall, every cell became inflamed, every hormone activated within me. My heart almost leaped out of my breast."

"Well, love, I'm very flattered, but I must take my leave of you now. I've much to do. I've a big tray to prepare for you. Then I've got to contact your aunt, then I must find my friends." He turned to leave.

The girl shouted, "Do you think you're just going to walk away from me?! I will find you wherever you go. I'll hunt you down, Pell Provance and the next time you'll not escape. Do you hear me?!"

Pell made his way down the secret staircase to a large hallway. The estate was vast. How could he ever find the kitchen? Finally, he smelled an aroma of caone and followed the aroma to a vast kitchen. He quickly put together a large tray of assorted fruits, dates the size of melons, punis rolls, meats, ferigots, which are long, yellow, crunchy vegetables and three huge olives. He carried the heavy tray in one hand, balancing a large hot caone in the other. He finally arrived at the door of the bedroom. "Drue?" he asked. "Drue, come on now, answer me. I've got a huge tray of goodies for you." He heard movement at the foot of the door. He crouched down to speak through the keyhole. "Come on, baby, answer me."

"I hate you, Pell. How could you do this to me?" she asked indignantly.

"Bloody hell!" he shouted. "You're the one who locked me in that bloody room! At least in a day or two you'll be out of there, whereas you were going to keep me in there for who knows how long. Plus, I've taken the liberty to prepare for a huge tray for you and I'm not reporting you as you deserve, but I'm going to look for your aunt so you don't get into trouble."

"Well that's why I love you so much, Pell. No one else would do that," she answered, having gained her composure."

"Now, Drue, you know the routine. Go to the bathroom and run the water."

"Why? Don't you trust me?" she asked.

"Of course not! Now do it!" She complied and as soon as he heard the water running, he unlocked the door and slipped the tray inside and locked the door after him.

He had left her enough to last three or four days. By that time he would have located her aunt. He made his way through the vast estate to the second floor bedrooms, looking for the clothes he was wearing. Finally, in a bedroom closet he found that everything was cleaned and pressed.

He changed and left the estate. It was getting dark, as he began his trek to the nearest town. The two moons of Agrimore were beginning to rise, with an indescribable blue moon light, which made everything shimmer. Walking on Agrimore was easy and enjoyable because the gravity was slightly lighter than on Earth. This was a uniquely beautiful world, with sumptuous plant life and colors beyond description. He walked past fields and glens and thought of the events that had transpired. Drue, he could never imagine that someone so young and beautiful could be so cunning, possessive and dangerous. Yet he felt such compassion for her. He believed that she truly loved him. He hoped that she was all right in the bedroom. It was frightening to be locked in a bedroom, in such a vast and empty estate.

He decided to turn back to the estate until daybreak. He was worried that the night might be too hard for her to bear alone. He grabbed some blankets from one of the bedrooms and made his way back up the secret staircase. He reached the bedroom. "Drue?" he asked quietly.

"Pell! Pell. Is it you?" she asked earnestly.

"Yes, it's me," he answered.

"I knew you couldn't leave me here! I knew it!"

"No. I was just worried about you alone in this big house. I'll sleep here outside your door until morning."

"Yes, I was terrified being all alone. At least with you I was always close by."

"I know," he answered. "That's why I returned."

"Then you do care for me, don't you?"

"Of course," he returned. "What do you think I am? But not in the way that you desire, my sweet."

"But, Pell, don't you know that I could give you love and pleasures beyond your imagination? I'm to inherit all that my aunt has and already have vast resources. There is nothing you would want for."

"I have enough," he answered. "In fact more than enough. Plus, I've some things to settle in my own life."

"Let me help you Pell," she pleaded. "Let me become part of your life."

"No, no, lovey. We have different paths to follow. My path may be very dangerous."

"I don't care!" she shot back. "As long as I share them with you."

"We've been through this already, Drue. It can't be. It's impossible." The girl was quiet and became weary from the day's events. She closed her eyes and slept. Pell also decided to sleep.

• • • • • • •

The glory of Agrimorian sun began to rise, crowning everything it touched with a golden parade of light. The inhabitants of Pathenune arose in celebration of the daylight. Every plant and tree invited its warmth. The Kungerods were awake and about to breakfast together in the atrium. Grista and Twilly were sharing a bed together at an inn at Firwith. Cremona had her own room. Gully and Darvin shared a room. They all gathered together at the dinning hall, preparing for breakfast. All felt refreshed.

Pell opened his eyes. He slept well in spite of being on the floor. He whispered, "Drue, are you awake?" There was no answer. He decided to let her sleep and go downstairs to make some hot caone for both of them. He also prepared an extra small tray of fresh fruits for her. "Drue?' he asked gently. "Are you up?"

"Hmm Pell, is that you?"

"Of course, who else? I have hot caone and another small tray of fruit for you."

"Well, can you at least have your breakfast with me?" she asked.

"Yes, but then I must leave to find your aunt. In fact, last night I forgot to ask you where she was."

"She's back at Lethurnae. She has a home along the coast," she answered.

"Well, Drue, I'll never forget this experience, flattering and slightly terrifying."

"Pell, I would never do anything to harm you. You know that don't you?" she asked.

"Of course, but I cherish my freedom. Bye bye, sweetie pie, must be going now. Not to worry. I will contact your aunt." With that he left the estate.

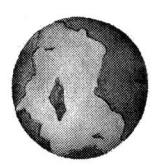

Chapter 19

THE POLLIDECREUM

The Kungerods had just finished their morning repast. The Kungerod of Athelone arose from the table. "Well, shall we proceed to the Pollidecreum?" They all rose together and followed him into a huge room with two globes. Each Kungerod stood at their assigned position. They stood in front of the huge glass globe, waiting for the cue from the Athelonian. In unison with the Athelonian leading, they all raised their tundrils and thrust them together into the slots in front of their slits. An explosive impact was made by the five tundrils. The globes came to life like golden blood scurrying through the glass as patterns and legends were fully illuminated. Things unperceivable to the average mind were revealed as both globes were now fully illuminated, with rich golden light reflecting off of the faces of the Kungerods. The globes began to hum and turn.

"Well," asked the female Kungerod, "what are you waiting for? Are you going to ask it anything?" she asked, directing her irritation at the Athelonian.

"Patience, my dear. Patience," he answered. "We must clearly delineate all of our inquiries, not just fling questions around as in a game of fluguote." Fluguote was a game where balls were thrown at multiple moving targets.

"Well, what is our first question?" asked the Can-Chimeran.

"Who or what is Pell Provance?" answered the Patamodian.

"Well, then," said the Athelonian, "that will be our first inquiry. Ready?" asked the Athelonian. They all gently nodded and grabbed their tundrils, which were still fixed in their slots. In unison, they all turned the tundrils to the right. They were immediately engulfed with golden light, which illuminated their entire bodies. Strange symbols appeared on the outer globe and fixed themselves, still illuminated. The Kungerods relaxed their grip on the tundrils, removing their hands and began moving about, circling and scanning the outer globe.

"Oh my! Oh my!" exclaimed the little Kungerod of Vernace.

"Yes, you see it, don't you?" said the Athelonian.

"Yes, I see it," said the Can-Chimeran. "He is the destroyer, the destroyer not only of worlds, but of entire systems, dimensions and planes of existence. Yes, this is our darkest hour."

"Well, what are you waiting for? Let us take action against this rogue!" shouted the female Kungerod.

The Athelonian approached her slowly and deliberately, looking at her intently as he spoke, "We do not know what we are dealing with here! Do not! I say again," turning to all of his comrades. "Do not take any action, until we have more information. This person, Pell Provance, does not even know who he is or what he is and he has never taken any provocative action against a single creature. Why, he even has compassion on the smallest and most insignificant creature. All he cares about are females, parties, perlees and his friends. Also, we have yet to ascertain who this Grista is for I would fear for all of us if we should ever try to harm this person. Now, let's get back to work," offered the Athelonian.

• • • • • • •

Meanwhile, Pell made his way to the estates garage, for Drue had told him of an extra philbee that was rented monthly. He found the philbee and made his way towards Lethurnae. He drove past lovely glens and little hamlets. Finally, Lethurnae was in sight. He could have spoken to her on the langline, but, he needed to speak to her face to face concerning Drue. Also, he needed transportation to Firwith. He longed for Grista and his friends.

• • • • • • •

The group had finished their morning repast and were considering what to do next. The silver-haired man saw them all mulling about the lobby of the inn, so he walked over to them and spoke to the group, "Listen, children. This is a wonderful resort town with wonderful beaches, bistros and shops. Why don't you all go out and enjoy yourselves. I will keep watch here and at the station for any word from Pell. You can shop, buy yourselves some exotic bathing suits, or just enjoy yourselves. Everything has been taken care of by the Kungerod of Athelone, so why not enjoy yourselves? After all, these last days have been hard on all of you." They accepted the man's advice and went off to the center of Firwith.

• • • • • • • •

Pell entered the city of Lethurnae, passing the cabanas, shops, bistros and all the buildings with numerous colored banners blowing in the wind. He made his way through the town to a little bridge on the outskirts of the town, as Drue had directed him. Finally, past a cheerful dale, he saw a charming cottage facing the sea. It was surrounded by the large red borteus pines and beautiful flaxinate trees. The cottage was covered with leaves and vines that resembled encanthus. He parked the philbee and walked on the stone path, leading to the front door. He rapped on the door twice, then three times, without any answer, so he walked around the back of the cottage to find the stately woman tending a small garden. He made a soft sound so not to startle her. She looked up and rose to her feet when she noticed it was Pell. She looked around for Drue and asked, "Is my niece-?"

He interrupted her and told her not to worry, everything was fine. She invited him into the cottage and brewed hot caone for both of them. She sat across from him and looked at him intently. "What happened Pell?" He related the entire story, deleting only the indiscretions and liberties, which Drue had taken with him. "Then she's all right?" she asked concernedly.

"Yes, ma'am, she's fine."

"So you actually took the time to come all the way over here to settle my mind and to make sure Drue is tended to after all that is happened to you? Well, Mr. Provance, I've never seen the likes of you in my whole life. I can see why you are so cherished by your friends and loved by Grista. Even my niece, though she acted wrongly, saw how unique you are from others. Well, I guess I'll have to face the official music now. Oh well, it's only right.

"Now, Purnis, there'll be no music to face or reprisals. I'll just have to explain to the group that I was unavoidably detained. That's all I'll divulge. They'll believe me because I have never lied." Purnis looked at him lovingly, rose and walked over to where he was sitting. She leaned over and kissed him on the forehead.

"Oh, you dear, dear boy. So strong and yet so gentle. You know, in some way I would have wished for you and my niece to come together. I would have been so honored to have some someone like you as part of our family, but I realize that this is not to be."

"Drue is a very spirited young woman and quite beautiful I must add, but you must keep her under tighter controls," he offered.

"Yes, you're absolutely right, of course. Thank you for being so kind to an older woman. If there is anything, anything at all that I could do for you and your friends, please, just ask."

"Well, Purnis, just one thing."

"Yes, what is it? Anything. I have homes and estates, shops, bistros, so ask what you will."

"No, no. You're overwhelming me. I just need transportation to Firwith and my friends."

"Is that all? Could I not do more for you?"

"No, Purnis, that's all I need for now."

"Of course," she said. "I'll have a terraspan at your disposal immediately. In fact, I'll leave the terraspan at Firwith. The best terraspan I have, equipped with everything. Just consider it as your own for as long as you wish. It will always be at your disposal." He bowed to the woman and turned to leave. "Pell," she asked, "Will we ever see you again?"

"Perhaps," he said, opening the cottage door. He then bowed his head in thought. "Perhaps you and your niece are in some strange way important to me, so perhaps we will see each other again." With that, he left and headed to the terraport.

• • • • • • •

Grista and the group entered one of the shops of Firwith. For some reason their spirits were lifted, as if they anticipated some good news. They were looking at the bathing suits. The girls looked over at Gully and Darvin, Darvin with his thin, lean frame and Gully with his thick, massive frame covered with red hair. The girls looked at each other and let out a burst of laughter, thinking of these two in bathing suits. Then the laughter became contagious, as the men joined in. It was the first time they had laughed in a while. It felt good. Grista found a red suit lined with very thin gold borders. "Oh my!" exclaimed Cremy. "The entire city of Firwith will come to shop if you put that on!" Grista gave her a whimsical smile and went to the dressing room to change. Cremy found a dark gray suit lined with thin spun silver. Twilly found a blue-green suit of a material that resembled rich silk.

Grista emerged from the dressing room, with every eye on her. There was an "Oooh," that was repeated from the entire staff. The staff of the shop circled her in admiration, looking at each other with wonderment. Grista began to turn red from the attention she was receiving. She stood there in the red and gold bathing suit looking like a dream that only gods could have. Potentates would have given up their realms at the first glimpse of her. Breathtaking was a word that one would have despised concerning her beauty. The word had yet to be formed by tongues unborn. She glowed with beauty. Her body, tan and defined, seemed to shimmer in the suit.

Gully found himself staring to the point of embarrassment and Darvin had to leave the shop to compose himself. Cremy emerged from the dressing room wearing the gray suit with spun with silver, her queenly auburn hair adorning her porcelain shoulders and back. The only things lacking were courtiers and ladies in waiting.

"Exquisite," whispered the staff. Gully immediately went out to join Darvin in moments that were personal to men. Then Twilly emerged from the dressing room, her short black hair looking more boyish in the blue-green suit. She was like a maiden that ruled all the forests of the world, unspeakably lovely, almost elfish.

Poor Darvin and Gully were to accompany these three, that all the kings past and present could only hope to possess. Finally, the men entered the dressing room to put on their conventional, ordinary suits. Darvin emerged wearing a blue swimsuit revealing a thin, white, lean and well-defined frame, but oh, those skinny white legs. Gully had on an orange slightly baggy suit. He had a massive upper body covered with red hair and thick legs also covered with red hair. The three girls screamed with hysterical laughter, pointing at the two distinctively different men. The female staff joined in. The men stood there looking at each other, the center of everyone's amusement.

"Bloody hell," Darvin said to Gully, "you're the hairiest thing I've ever seen!"

"Well, what do you call those things?" said Gully, pointing to Darvin's skinny white legs. "I'm amazed those things supported you all of these cycles." Both men burst out in laughter at one another. It was exactly what they needed after the events of the past few days.

As the group left the shop and made their way towards the beach, every eye was on them. Philbees came to a halt and people rose from their cabanas to get a better look at them. Even married couples found themselves staring. As they entered the beach area, people moved and made a path for them, each hoping that they would place their blankets in their areas. The females were in wonder of their beauty and the males were afraid to say a word. That beach had never been so adorned.

• • • • • • •

Meanwhile, Pell had reached the terraport. The staff rushed over to accommodate him. The terraspan was the most luxurious he had ever seen, with carpeted gangways, tinted windows and it was beautifully furnished. The galley was filled to the brim with every refreshment Agrimore had to offer and the staff was extremely courteous. He made his way downstairs to an exquisite apartment-like compartment. He settled down on a thick-green leather couch looking forward to the trip to Firwith.

• • • • • • •

Grista and her friends found a spot next to where children were building sand cities. She crawled over to where three boys were working on their construct. The sand of Agrimore was denser and more substantial than that on Earth. When the water mixed with the sand, it became like a mixture of silly putty and light cement. Therefore, the sand castles were much more detailed. Grista was amazed at the creation of the boys. "How wonderful!" she exclaimed loudly. The boys were startled by Grista and rose up from the sand. They stared with wonder at the beauty of Grista. The Agrimorian sun highly favored her, as the liquidy residue produced by the sun dripped off her wondrous body. The children stood there tongue tied and embarrassed. She crawled closer to the boys, looked at them and down to their creation. "How amazing! What is it?"

The boys felt more at ease and began to explain the structure. One dark haired, freckled-faced boy offered, "It's an assembly plant where they make the trains of Faxburn."

"May I sit here and watch?" she asked.

"Sure," they all said gleefully. An adorable little girl strolled over with a yellow pale and shovel in her hand. She walked over to Grista, who was occupied watching the boys work the sand. The little girl came up behind her and touched her shoulder.

Grista turned around and looked at the little beauty. She smiled broadly. "Well, hello," said Grista's, her voice filled with sweetness. "So, what would you like?" she asked the little one.

"My mommy and daddy said you were so beautiful, so I wanted to see you up close."

"What a compliment from someone so lovely. I'm Grista, and you are?"

"I'm Glessy."

"Well, Glessy, I'm so happy to meet someone so pretty who also finds me pretty."

The little girl extended her arms with the pale and shovel in each hand and twisted her body from left to right. "But everyone thinks you're the prettiest and so do I." Grista kissed the little girl one the forehead. When she turned around, all the children of the beach had crowded around to catch a glimpse of her.

Cremy looked over at Twilly. "Amazing," she noted.

"It's been that way ever since she was little," said Twilly. "She's adored by everyone. She's easily the most beautiful female in the whole world," she said with wonder, as she watched Grista frolicking with all of the children.

• • • • • • •

Meanwhile, the Kungerods were busy in the Pollidecreum. Led by the Athelonian, they grabbed their tundrils, which were set in their slots and turned them in unison. Once again, their bodies were illuminated with golden light. The outer globe came alive with golden light rushing through the veins of glass. Emblems appeared and legends, words upon words, which were undecipherable to the average eye. They released their grips and turned to each other silent and thoughtful. The Athelonian spoke, "Well, my friends, this sheds new light on things, does it not?"

"But his age!" shouted the Patamodian.

"We're speaking of aons upon aons. Can this be?" asked the Ilgestanian.

"He's beyond the ages and does not realize it," offered the Athelonian.

"Let's find out more about him before he was the destroyer," asked the Vernacian.

"Yes, we must know more about his origins," agreed the Athelonian. They anxiously grabbed their tundrils and turned them. Once again, light filled their bodies and the globe came alive with legends and symbols. Then it concluded abruptly with a large purplish-golden symbol and seven large indecipherable letters beneath. The Kungerods stopped and stared at the letters, working hard to decipher them. "Activate the orthosphere," commanded the Athelonian.

• • • • • • •

Pell awakened as the terraspan made its descent. He was anxious to see his friends, wondering if they were still at Firwith. There was a knock at the door of his compartment. He opened it and an attractive female attendant informed him that they were landing at Firwith. She looked very smart in her uniform. She was tall, with very dark hair and flashing blue eyes. Her complexion was ruddy and robust, as if she had been out in cool autumn weather. Her uniform tugged lightly at every curve. It was dark green with a thin silver border, a two piece suit. Underneath, she wore a white silk blouse with ruffles at the throat area. Her dark green skirt was short, about six inches above the knees, revealing well-developed legs and completed with dark brown knee-high boots. Her scent was fresh, like a child that had been playing outdoors. Pell thought it strange that she had informed him before the machine had landed. Usually it was after the terraspan had landed. "Did I wake you?" she asked, her smile revealing a perfectly beautiful mouth, outlined by luscious red lips.

"Uh, yes, but no matter since we'll be landing soon," he answered. The girl walked into the compartment towards the galley.

"Oh, Pell! You did not make use of all the wonderful cordials that Purnis had us stock for you." Pell watched the girl walk around the galley reaching for an exquisitely adorned bottle. "Oh!" she exclaimed. "Cadinea." She held the light blue bottle with the embossed metal label up to the light. "Do you realize that only a few people in this world had ever had the pleasure of partaking in this?" she asked.

"Listen, we only have a few minutes before we land."

"How about having a drink with me?" she asked boldly.

Pell was amused at the female's forwardness. He smiled and nodded, noting that taking such liberties made her intriguingly alluring. She sat down and poured the rare cordial in two ice goblets. She lifted her goblet in a toasting fashion. He in turn did the same. "What do we toast to?" he asked, still amused by the girl, noting her boldness that rather lifted his spirits.

"Well, why don't we toast you," she said, "and the successful completion of your journey." They lifted the goblets to their lips, never taking their eyes off of one another.

"What is your name?" he asked.

"Oh, forgive me, I'm Denara." she answered.

"Denara, aren't you a little concerned? The captain may be looking for you," he asked.

"Oh, I'm the captain. Does my presence here disturb you?" she asked.

"Oh, not at all. You're so vibrant and you smell so fresh that you rather invigorate me," he said.

"I'm so glad," said the captain. "Well, I must prepare for us to disembark." She turned and looked into his eyes, "I know you're looking for you friends, but if you don't find them, come back here and I'll take care of you until we locate them." She smiled girlishly and left.

He felt the terraspan settle down on the elevator and walked over to the hatchway. The hatchway slowly opened, revealing the bright Agrimorian sun. He descended the small stairway with the crew standing at attention – three men on each side, with Denara standing at the bottom of the gangplank. She walked over to him and said, "Remember, Pell, we are at your disposal for as long as you need us." She smiled and touched his arm reassuringly. He smiled at her and began to make his way to the passenger elevator, then turned and walked back to Denara.

"Listen, after I find my friends, we'll have to make our way back to the port to pick up a freightliner. So I don't know if I'll need the terraspan again."

"When you find the freightliner, pick up the langline and inform me. We will land on it so that we will be able to continue to transport you," she answered. "Oh, by the way, Purnis ordered a philbee that will be parked outside of the terraport. The driver will spot you. Remember, if you need me tonight, I'll be here," she said smiling.

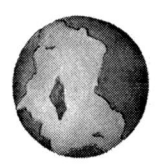

Chapter 20

GRISTA!

Purnis entered her estate and made her way to the secret staircase. She walked up to the bedroom door and unlocked it. She found Drue under the covers, her eyes still red from crying herself to sleep. She shook her. The girl cried out, "Pell, is it you?"

"No, my sweet. It's me," she answered. "Here's some clean clothes. Get dressed so we can leave for the cottage." She sat down in the room while the girl bathed herself, speaking to her while she was in the bath. "Are you feeling better love?" she asked.

"How can I?" she answered. "I've lost the love of my life. What's the use of anything?"

"Stop that!" Purnis answered crossly. "You had no right doing what you did. I've never heard of such a thing. How dare you put us at risk that way. It was only the graciousness and kindness of Pell that kept us from official trouble. I've been a little too lax with you my dear, but that's going to change."

"Don't you see, auntie? Only Pell Provance would be so gracious. Who else would have reacted in such a way after having been in prison for a time?" the girl asked.

"Yes, he is gracious, more than any one I've ever known!" she shot back. "You had no right to do what you did. That poor boy," she continued, "has to explain his disappearance without implicating us. I don't know how he will do it," said Purnis.

Drue dried herself and began to dress. "Auntie, do you think Pell will ever return to me? Do you think he will ever forgive what I did?"

"I think he's already forgiven you, but as to returning, I don't think so, sweetie," she answered. With that, they both quietly left the estate for Lethurnae.

• • • • • • •

Pell exited the terraport to find a bright-colored philbee parked nearby. The driver exited the philbee, greeted Pell and opened the door for him. "Where to, sir?" he asked.

"Firwith station please," he answered. It was a short ride to the station. Pell thanked the driver and made his way into the station.

He noticed the tall, handsome, gray-haired man sitting in the waiting area. As he saw Pell advancing towards him, he rose and smiled broadly. "Mr. Provance!" he exclaimed. "I'm so happy to see you're well, sir," he said.

"Good to see you," Pell returned.

"Grista and the others are at the beach. They were very worried about you."

"Take me to them," he said anxiously.

"Of course, sir."

They made their way past the shops and to the beach. There, near the shore, he saw Cremy and Twilly, with Darvin and Gully sitting next to them. He laughed to himself when he saw Darvin and Gully in bathing trunks. The beach was crowded, as they snaked their way to the group. There, far to the left, was Grista playing with a bunch of children.

The children enjoyed her frolicking with them, playing with her curly blond hair and covering her legs with sand. She turned slowly, as if sensing his presence and saw him. She stood up, the sand falling off her legs in clumps. She stood there looking at him as if she were dreaming. He had never seen anything as beautiful in all of his life, like a bronze statue of forbidden beauty. She stood there staring at him. They walked over slowly towards each other hesitantly and longingly. The entire beach was transfixed by them, including his friends. They ran towards each other and embraced. She clutched him closely. Beach sand and liquid sun covered his immaculately-tailored clothing, but it did not matter to him. They kissed each other, as if they were trying to emboss the image of their lips on one another. There was no time, no beach, no people, except them. Not a word was spoken by them, or anyone. Everything became silent as all watched them.

Pell gestured to Grista that everyone was watching, but to no avail. Her arms were like a vice around his neck and she would not let go, as if she would lose him if she relinquished her grip.

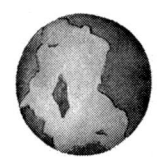

Chapter 21

THE GREAT AQUIDALE

Cremy came over and asked, "Could I have him for a while?" Grista turned and smiled at her. Then, looking into her lover's eyes, unlocked her arms and moved back, as Cremy jumped up to hug him ferociously. Twilly stood behind her waiting for her hugs and kisses. Then there were the two men waiting, feeling ridiculous in trunks.

• • • • • • •

The five Kungerods moved over to one of the alcoves to remove the urn. They slid it out of the way, revealing a pattern on the stone floor of floral designs with five circles and slots for their tundrils. They all removed their tundrils from around the globe and set them into the circled slots on the floor. They all turned the tundrils in unison. With that, the stone slab rose silently, revealing a glass cylinder with emblems and legends at the base. The platform rose up to about waist high. The Kungerod of Athelone removed his tundril from the stone slab and placed it into a slot at the base and turned it. The glass cylinder came to life with bright magenta light turning a bright pink. The swirling stopped, the legends and symbols disappeared, leaving just the bright pink light. The Athelonian turned his tundril and a symbol sprang up, another turn retracted the symbol. He continued this process until the correct symbols appeared that matched the ones in the globe. After all the symbols he needed had been retracted, he selected a symbol to decipher the seven letters. After deciphering the letters, they stood there silently looking at each other, astonished, flabbergasted, their eyes blank as if they were stripped of all their Kungerodian power.

They all turned quietly and slowly made their way towards the conference room. They sat down, staring at the surface of the large table. The Can-Chimeran tried to speak hesitantly, his voice shaking with fear. "He, he's one of the rulers, one of the twelve great kings."

The female from Ilgestana put her head down into her hands. "I proposed to take action against him. What have I done?"

The Kungerod from Athelone spoke and said to her, "My dear. Get a hold of yourself. None of us knew who we were dealing with; anyone of us could have suggested taking action against him."

"Yes, but I'm the one who suggested it. No one else, but me."

"Yes, but you were acting as a true Kungerod, seeking to protect your world," he said, reassuring her.

• • • • • • •

Pell, Grista and his friends left the beach area and returned to the station to decide what to do next. Muswick, their guide, suggested that they spend the night at the inn and leave for the port area in the morning, where they would find the Lamberante, the freightliner, which would carry them to Patamodia. Grista, Twilly and Cremy shared one room together, while Pell, Darvin, and Gully shared another. Their guide had a private room.

Pell entered the room, with Darvin and Gully following behind. No one said a word about Pell's whereabouts for the previous four days; they knew that he would speak about it when he was ready.

Grista began to change while Cremy was bathing. "Aren't you curious?" asked Twilly, removing her undergarments.

"Curious about what?" asked Grista, sitting on the edge of the bed.

"About Pell and where he's been for the last four days and nights," Twilly returned.

"Of course I am. I'm itching to know, but I'm not going to assume anything, nor will I ask him. When he's ready, he'll speak to me and the rest of us about it."

The men were quiet as they began dressing for dinner. Muswick had all of their luggage transferred to the inn a few days before. Gully looked handsome in a maroon turtleneck, dark brown pants, shoes similar to penny loafers and a green windbreaker. Darvin looked handsomely provocative in an electric blue shirt, thin black tie, black pants and ankle boots, topped off with a black leather jacket. Pell laid a chocolate-brown jacket and pants on the bed. The material was like rich, soft cashmere. He put on a bright white, exquisitely tailored shirt sewn with gold threat that was barely visible. Everything was tightened up with a thin gold tie and light brown, plain-toe ankle boots.

The girls were frolicking in the bedroom. They were laughing and jumping around on the beds, talking about the spectacle of Gully and Darvin in their bathing trunks and the mysterious appearance of Pell. The three men stood outside their door listening to all the mayhem and cavorting goings on in the bedroom. Gully looking at Pell and Darvin, grinned widely and said, "Forget it, boys. They're not going to be ready for a while." Pell enjoyed the familiar sounds coming from the bedroom.

They all looked at one another and made their way down to the lobby. Pell walked over to the desk clerk and asked for some hot caone for him and his friends. The female clerk complied with a smile and a wink. Gully noticed and said grinning, "It's good to see everything back to normal."

Darvin frowned slightly and said, "Yep! He's back to his old tricks."

The men sat down, waiting for their hot-brewed caone. Pell looked over at them. "Well, I guess I owe you some sort of explanation." They didn't say a word, just stared at him. "Well, all I can tell you is this: in the last four days I was prevented from joining you. The experience was not all together unpleasant, mostly annoying, but I cannot give you details of the experience. But know this: if I could have, I would have joined you."

Gully, with a light smirk, said, "I bet it had something to do with a woman," looking over at Darvin.

Darvin shrugged and said, looking straight at Pell, "If you say that you were prevented from joining us I believe you, because I know you never lie, but could you not use a langline?"

Pell shook his head. "No, I was not able to."

"Well," said Darvin, "you're obviously protecting someone, so we will drop the matter forever."

Gully concurred and thought to himself, What an amazing group of people I hooked up with. He felt quite honored to be amongst them.

They could hear the girls talking and laughing loudly on the way down to the lobby. They were all gorgeously attired in rather formal dress. Twilly was wearing a dark, rich, blue, form-fitting, satin-like dress with a jeweled, dark velvet-chocker, which accentuated her lovely long neck. Her feet were shod with lovely soft open-toe shoes. Cremy was elegant in a plush maroon, corduroy-type suit with a white, pearl-colored satin blouse and an exquisitely crafted necklace of unidentifiable jewels. She also had a bracelet of crafted gold on her wrist, covering her cuff. She was shod with soft red pumps. Grista appeared as a queen from Greek or Roman mythology. She was wearing a long dress of a silvery white color, made of a material like the richest silk of India hanging just below her shoulders. Another garment of the same material wrapped around her left forearm and wrist. It was tightened just above her left breast by a blindingly beautiful brooch of fiery ice blue jewels. Her neck was adorned with a white satin chocker with an emblem of gold hanging from it. She was shod with pearl-white, shimmering sandals. The three women looked like a dream that someone was yet to awaken from.

Gully began to look at Twilly in a different way. He began to notice her beauty and especially her boyish haircut. The female clerk arrived with the hot caone, which the men shared with the girls.

Muswick had informed the Kungerods of Pell's arrival. They were all relieved and informed Crofty Bellar in Patamodia. The group finished their caone and prepared to leave the inn. Grista grabbed Pell's arm and nuzzled her head against his shoulder. She whispered in his ear, "Hi, gorgeous. Are you married?"

"Yes," he said playfully, smiling at her.

"Well, I guess you'll just have to leave your wife," she whispered and nibbled lightly on his earlobe.

His entire body tingled. He said to her quietly, "Grista, behave yourself." She smiled at him playfully.

Cremy grabbed Darvin's arm. "My, my, aren't we handsome this evening!" Darvin blushed slightly and stuttered as he tried to compliment her. She noticed that he was embarrassed and clutched his arm tightly and drew him close to herself.

Gully walked over to Twilly and said, "Well, well, aren't you an image of loveliness. May I have the pleasure?" and extended his forearm, which she immediately grabbed, looking up at him and giving him a tom-boyish smile.

As the three couples made their way out of the lobby to the front doors, the doorman rushed over to open the doors for them, tipping his hat and smiling at them as they left the inn. Cabanas and throngs of people were strewn over the main avenue of Firwith. Shops, eateries and elegant restaurants were all busy with nocturnal patrons. As the three couples passed the cabanas, shops, restaurants, etc., they drew attention. Every eye was on the handsome sextet. Some pointed and some rose up from their seats to get a better view of them. As they passed the restaurants, the maitre d's would bow and welcome them, hoping the three couples would grace their establishments.

They found a wonderful restaurant called Folineese. The maitre d' rushed to welcome them and opened up an alcove facing the sea, which was usually reserved for dignitaries. After seating them, he insisted on serving them a complimentary cordial. The owner came over to introduce himself to them. He was a tall, dashing man about thirty with large handsome dimples. He was anxious to make sure everything was perfect. The maitre d' insisted on serving them himself and two staffers were assigned to assist him. The cordial they brought was the best the house had to offer. It was a rich, juicy, heady drink, like nothing they'd ever tasted before. The owner made sure the bottle remained in the ice tray beside the table and ordered their goblets to be continually filled as they desired.

The staff came out to the open portico, carting a huge table with them. The table came with its own cooking pit in the center. It was filled with flaming delights. On Agrimore, due to the lighter gravity and everything being more substantial, they could actually stylize and shape the flames. Swirling plums of silver and blue flame twisted itself upward like braided hair licking the darkening sky. Four big, powerful-looking chefs dressed in tuxedo-like garments, plied their trade with pleasure, smiling at the guests as they made the flames change color and shapes. They presented the exquisite fare before them and waited for their approval. Silk strips, palpeon sides, dorcimel wings filled the air around them with tempting aromas. They had never seen such a cuisine.

• • • • • • •

The Kungerods sat in the conference room deliberating. "Well," said the Kungerod of Athelone, "we should continue in the Pollidecreum to discover more concerning his majesty."

They entered the Pollidecreum quietly, all moving to their assigned places. Once again, they all turned their tundrils in unison until the outer globe came alive. The Kungerod of Athelone spoke, "My friends, we know his majesty has been to our two worlds, which is evident by the anomalies, which were occurring until we arrested them. Now we should discover the extent of his rule and power." They turned their tundrils, all were illuminated from the power of the Pollidecreum, symbols appeared and legends flashed, until the information was clearly displayed on the globe. They all left their seats and circled the globe, deciphering the legends and symbols.

The Kungerod of Can-Chimera stared up at the globe. "The extent of his rule is vast," he said with astonishment written on his face.

"Yes, yes," replied the Vernacian. "Our entire universe is one of his domains. He's not just a king, but he is our king."

"The king of our two worlds," continued the female Kungerod of Ilgestana, "and I planned to devise action against him," she said with sorrow.

The Athelonian took hold of her firmly with both hands and looked at her. "You must cease this self-deprecation. You did exactly what his majesty would have intended to protect his world and his people. We have much to do. Now cease!" he shouted at her firmly. Everyone was taken aback at the force of the Athelonian.

The female Kungerod composed herself and nodded. "Forgive me," she asked.

"There's nothing to forgive," said the Athelonian gently.

"What about the female, this Grista?" asked the handsome Patamodian. "She seems to play a part in his activities and seems to be part of his destiny."

"Yes, let's find out more about Grista, for there is not the likes of her in all of Agrimore," said the Athelonian.

They all returned to their places and activated the Pollidecreum again. Once again, the globe came to life differently this time. The color changed to a pinkish-gold with different symbols and legends than Pell's, but all connected to his own. "Oh my! Isn't this wonderful!" exclaimed the Vernacian. "Why, she's his queen," he stated with a smile. "Of course. She's been with him since the beginning of time, searching and protecting her beloved. Her love is vaster and deeper than the universe." They all smiled with delight.

"She's our queen," declared the Can-Chimeran with joy. They all smiled and marveled at this. Even the globe seemed to turn warmer at the revelation of Grista.

"Well, dear friends, let's adjourn for today and muse upon this," offered the Athelonian. "We'll discuss this during our repast." They all concurred and left the Pollidecreum.

The Athelonian picked up the langline and spoke to Crofty Bellar, informing her of all the details concerning Pell and Grista. She was flabbergasted at what she heard. The Kungerod continued, "Crofty, make sure that they are offered every dignity that their rank demands, every comfort and convenience, but do not reveal anything to them. We'll inform their majesties when they arrive." She fully concurred and complied.

∙ ∙ ∙ ∙ ∙ ∙ ∙

The three couples continued their sumptuous meals and the maitre d' came to announce the arrival of the specially prepared desserts. Everything was cleared from the table except for hot-brewed, delicious caone, which was perking freshly on a little stand next to the table. The maitre d' clapped his hands and through the doors that led to the portico, came a splendidly adorned table with a chef dressed in a semi tuxedo. On the table surrounded by flowers and leaves was a dessert that would need a poet to describe. On a glass pedestal, was cakey dessert called Paximunte. The base was surrounded by large white berries, circling first a layer of thick, blue, flowery-shaped crème. The next layer was a thin cake lid. On top of that was a bowl-shaped cake with large, thick, blue and red berries in the cup of the bowl. In the center of the bowl, suspended on blue and white crème was a large, thick, meaty fruit called aspicone, very rare, extremely delicious. More than one serving of this dessert could be harmful. The chef stood there with his small table, proud of his creation.

Once again, the maitre d' clapped his hands and another table emerged through the doors. This table was adorned with lovely ribbons and precious gems, surrounded by a white, edible goblet made of heated custard and pastry. In the center of the goblet was a creamy cake filled with light blue gretheline sauce. Under that, supporting the cake was a hot, boiling, potent wine. Lastly, was the peste-resistance. The owner came carting in the third table. The table was adorned with six goblets of pink, twisted, shaped flames that lit up the faces of all present, bordered by dark green vines, similar to encanthus. In the center, was an unusually-shaped goblet, wide at the bottom and tapered up the stem. Beneath the goblet was a blue flame that heated the fruit inside, which appeared to be liquid crystals. As the crystal boiled and melted, it created an eruption of dark blue liquid and white foam pouring over the stem. The face of the owner beamed and he said, "Let me present to you, Aquidale." Everyone at the table was impressed with the presentation. It was an unforgettable night.

It was growing late and everyone was tired after their sumptuous meal. They rose and Pell left the group to speak to the owner concerning the tab. The owner looked at him and smiled. "Was everything satisfactory?" he asked.

"Beyond our dreams," he answered. Pell removed crowned mica from his breast pocket.

"No, sir!" exclaimed the owner. "Everything is taken care of by the Kungerods, including a substantial gratuity." Pell thanked the owner and the staff bowed respectfully.

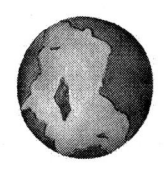

Chapter 22

THERMEDYTES AND EXTELLA

The couples made their way back to the inn. All had the dreariness of full stomachs. They walked quietly pass the shops that were beginning to close. The restaurants were pulling in their tables. The two moons of Agrimore were full, illuminating the avenue with blue light. Their footsteps echoed, as they walked along the quiet street. Pell broke the silence. He stopped and turned to Grista, Cremy and Twilly. "I know I owe you an explanation," he said, "but as I have told Darvin and Gully, I was prevented from joining you or using the langline."

"By whom?!" Grista shouted, staring intently at him.

"I will not go into more details. That's all I can say."

Cremy looked up at him. "Pell, were you harmed in any way?" she asked.

"No, I was not harmed at all."

"Why are you protecting the one that has done this?!" Grista shouted angrily.

"Grista," he replied and held her upper arms. "I'm fine. I will not divulge any more of the matter." She knew that no power in the world could make him divulge anything, so she turned away full of rage and walked back by herself.

Pell decided to let her cool off and told the other two couples that he would join them later. He walked in the quiet blue moonlight, with a gentle breeze blowing his tie and hair. He continued to walk pass the restaurants, which were now all dark. The town of Firwith was asleep. He walked down to the quiet harbor, looking over at the serene bay. In the distance, he could see a freightliner making its way to some unknown port. He stood at shore thinking about the events that had taken place, the Kungerod, Grista, his friends and Drue. He began thinking about his own life and the things which the Kungerod had told him. He was a stranger here in this beautiful world, a world that was threatened by his very presence. But why? he thought. Why would I threaten such a wondrous place? Who am I? What am I?

He became uneasy with his questions and continued walking along the shore. He walked passed a café that extended into the bay supported by a wharf. On the other side of the café, he could see the shoreline continue.

Just then, he thought he saw a figure on the far end of the shore. He picked up his pace to where the figure was. As he drew closer, he could see the figure of a woman facing the bay, the breezes blowing her long, black hair. He continued to walk towards the figure, straining to look at her face. He was now only a few feet away. He recognized her. It was it was Extella, the waitress at Chantry. She did not turn to look at him, but stared out at the bay. "It's good to see you again, my lord," she said, looking straight ahead.

"Extella?" he asked.

"Yes, my lord, it is I," she answered, still looking straight ahead.

"Why do you address me in that manner?" he asked, trying to look at her face.

The beautiful woman turned and looked at him. "Because that is who you are – my lord." She looked at the night sky and extended her hands. "All of this is your realm, as far as the eye can see and beyond," she explained.

"Who are you and how do you know this?" he asked.

"I am one waiting upon you, my lord." She turned away and looked out at the bay.

There was a momentary silence. Then she spoke, "I am a Thermedyte, my lord."

"What in the world is a Thermedyte?" he asked.

She turned to him and said, "Everything will be explained when you meet with the Kungerods, my lord." With that, she seemed to open a door that was not there and walked through, disappearing from his sight. He stood there, staring at the spot where the woman had been. Then he turned and began walking back to the inn, thinking upon all that he had heard.

• • • • • • •

Grista silently entered the bedroom, with Cremy and Twilly following behind. She threw herself upon the bed, stuffing her head into the pillow and screamed, "Oh, I could just kill him!" She turned over and stared at the ceiling with Cremy and Twilly looking at her. "What do you do with such a man?!" she screamed, not addressing anyone in particular. "When he does not want to talk about something, there is no power in existence that will change him or make him speak. Why? Why do I have to love such a man?" She continued her tirade while the girls undressed and tried to ignore her.

Pell had made his way back to the inn, up the stairs and to the bedroom. Gully and Darvin were already in bed, but had left the light on. Gully raised himself against the backboard, placed his hands behind his head and grinned. "Whew, are you in trouble. I would not want that girl mad at me," he said. "No, no, a thousand times no." His eyes followed Pell, as he undressed.

"You're enjoying this, aren't you, you red Pargemeste?" said Pell quietly. A Pargemeste was a big, red powdery moth found on the continent of Can-Chimera.

"Ho, yes, yes in deed," laughed Gully. Darvin was quiet just observing the two men.

"What about you? Aren't you going to join in?" asked Pell. Darvin shook his head, muttered something to himself and covered his head with the sheet. Pell shut the light and climbed into bed, still thinking of what Extella had told him and what she was. What in creation is a Thermedyte? he thought to himself.

All of a sudden, the bedroom door flew open, startling all of the men. It was Grista, dressed only in a slip, revealing her wondrous body. Her eyes were wide open with rage. Gully shrunk under the covers and Darvin turned, covering his head with the pillow and covers. She walked slowly towards Pell, until she stood beside the bed, looking down at him. He shrunk back on the bedboard, not knowing what to do next. He tried his little smile, which had always worked in confrontational situations. This enraged her even more. "Don't you dare, Pell Provance!" she shouted. "Don't you try that silly stuff on me!" She could see the covered heads moving under the covers, trying to see what was happening, without uncovering their heads. "How could you just give me some glib answer like that?!" she shouted, turning red. "Don't you know what I was going through these four days?! How worried I was and the fears that were rushing through me?!" she continued. "Don't you dare try to give me that little smile. Not on me! I'm the woman that loves you beyond time, beyond eternity, more than all existence. I deserve more than just a glib little answer!" She continued to shout. He was almost paralyzed by her ferocity and the other two men wanted no part of this. They could hear voices and movements outside of the door, as the other patrons were awakened by her tirade.

Pell thought to himself, I pity the poor creature that opens that door or tries to calm her. It would be easier to cap a volcano than try to quell Grista. He just stared at her silently. He dared not say a word, but noticed how alluring she was standing over him. All that passion encased in that exquisite body, he thought. He wanted her so much more now than ever before. His joints tingled and his heart raced. He was becoming dizzy looking at her.

She noticed that he was rather enjoying this. She stood speechless for a moment. She turned towards the door, raising her head screaming, "I'm going to kill him, he's enjoying this!" Then she screamed as she slammed the door.

The other patrons cowered, as they saw the girl emerge from his room. Gully was the first to slowly uncover his head and look at Pell, then burst out laughing. Darvin was laughing under the covers. Then Pell began laughing. Their laughter was so loud that the patrons gathered in the hall again.

The girls could hear the laughter coming from their bedroom. Grista, who was on her bed, turned on her back, facing the ceiling. "Laughing?" she said, not looking at any one, just staring at the ceiling. "Laughing?!" She began to seethe. She could hear the muffled laughter coming from Cremy and Twilly. "Cremy? Twilly, you too?!"

Cremy turned on her pillow, her face red with laughter almost to tears and Twilly had fallen out of bed kicking her legs in the air with uncontrollable laughter. "I've got to go to the bathroom!" she screamed.

"Me too," Cremy said, both girls still roaring with laughter. They both ran into the bathroom together. Cremy had to use the tub. She could not hold it long enough for Twilly to finish. They both emerged form the bathroom completely spent from all the jocularity.

"Well, what was so funny you two?" asked Grista.

"Oh, Grista, you are the wildest girl in the whole bloody world!" exclaimed Cremy. "The image of you busting into that room and confronting Mr. Pell Provance is legendary," she continued. "Mr. little charming smile, Mr. smooth talker, Mr. royalty, who always knows what to say, was speechless." She began laughing again and so did Twilly.

Grista began giggling at the scene and said, "You should have seen the other two under the covers, not knowing which way to turn, or what I was going to do next." She too began laughing. They all began roaring uncontrollably. Finally, everyone laughed themselves to sleep.

• • • • • • •

The Agrimorian sun arose on Pathenune. The Kungerods awakened and assembled for their morning repast. After finishing, they all assembled in the conference room. They sat for a moment staring at each other. "Well, my dear friends, what do we look into concerning his majesty Pell Provance?" asked the Athelonian.

"What about his last sojourn?" asked the Vernacian.

"Yes, we can gather more information concerning his sojourn with us," affirmed the Ilgestanian. So they made their way to the Pollidecreum.

• • • • • • •

Grista opened her eyes, the morning sun fingering its way into the room. She looked over at Cremy and Twilly, who were still asleep. She thought about Pell and her tirade the night before. She smiled, thinking of Darvin and Gully hiding underneath the covers. Cremy turned on her pillow and faced her, slowly opening her sleepy eyes. "Hey," she said, stretching her arms.

Grista leaned against the backboard, looked over at Cremy and said, "I really let lose on him last night, didn't I?"

"Uh, huh," responded Cremy, still cuddling her pillow.

Grista stretched her neck to look at Twilly. "Look at that little cutie pie over there still sleeping." Cremy turned on her pillow to look at the little lovely black-haired beauty, her head half covered with part of her thumb in her mouth.

Cremy turned lifted herself up slightly and looked again at the cute little head with the boyish haircut, half covered with the sheets, then turned to Grista and laughed. "She's got her thumb in her mouth," she said with amusement.

"I know, isn't she adorable?" said Grista lovingly, "She's been doing that since she was a baby."

"You really love her, don't you?" asked Cremy.

"Are you kidding?" responded Grista. "I adore her."

"I think Gully finds her adorable too," said Cremy.

"Mmm," she replied, "I'm rather glad about that. I really like Gully," continued Grista. "His smile is contagious and he's become very close to all of us in such a short time."

Cremy concurred with her. "Yes, he's warm and wonderful, a good counterpart for those two icons in the next room."

Grista laughed and shook her head. "Those two icons weren't so mighty last night," she said and continued to laugh.

"Oh, Grista, you are so naughty," smiled Cremy. They could hear little baby noises coming from the last bed, where Twilly was sleeping. Grista and Cremy walked over to her bed and sat on either side, looking down at her. Grista started tickling her nose. The girl made some unintelligible noises and wriggled her nose. Cremy started shaking the bed, Grista stuck her nose onto the nose of the sleeping girl. "Hey," she said in a low voice as if she were talking to a baby. "Bubble, bubble, boop, boop." She continued making silly noises, pressing her nose tightly against Twilly's.

Twilly opened her eyes. "You look like a big bug," she said, yawning. Then Grista and Cremy began tickling her. Twilly screamed and fell out of the bed. "No, no!! I've got to go to the bathroom!" They continued tickling her. "Stop it or I'll go right here!" They let her up and she ran to the bathroom. She yelled out from the bathroom. "I'll get even with both of you!"

Grista smiled at Cremy and asked, "What about you and Darvin?"

Cremy blushed. "He is handsome, isn't he?"

"He shaw is," Grista said with a drawl.

"You know what's strange?" asked Cremy. "I've always loved Darvin, but I thought I loved Pell also. I guess I still do. I used to fantasize about being married to both of them."

"Greedy little girl," said Grista playfully.

"I know, aren't I awful?" she said sheepishly.

Twilly emerged from the bathroom. "What are you two scheming?" she asked, jumping on her bed.

"Oh, we were thinking of how good you and Gully looked together," offered Cremy.

Twilly cradled herself with her arms and swooned. "Yes, he is rather hunky, isn't he?" Then she turned to Grista. "Grista, are you planning to do some bad things to our poor swains?"

"Naw," she said, "I think they are going to be on their best behavior after last night." The girls all laughed.

Pell opened his eyes and looked over at Darvin, who was propped against the backboard reading something. Pell stretched and yawned loudly. "Bloody hell, what a night," he said, continuing to yawn.

"They're up," said Darvin, as he gestured to the next room where the girls were, "and they're laughing like hell."

"Bloody females," muttered Pell. "What are they up to now?" Gully was still asleep. Darvin looked at him and threw a folded map he was looking at, which bounced off of Gully's head.

Gully turned over on his left side and muttered to himself.

"Wake up you damn furry Pargemest," Darvin shouted at Gully, smiling. He looked over at Pell. "There's no getting him up, mate," he said.

"That's all right. Grista will be here in a minuet to knock him out of bed!" shouted Pell.

Gully opened his eyes and propped himself up. "Grista's coming in here?" he asked. Pell and Darvin laughed to each other at Gully's reaction to Grista.

"Bloody hell," said Darvin to Pell, "you brought that wild thing with us."

"Yeah, it's all your fault," Gully shouted at Pell.

"Ah, but gentlemen, have you ever seen anything as beautiful as that wild thing in all of your lives?"

"Yes," said Darvin, "an Agrimorian typhoon." They all laughed loudly.

The girls could hear them laughing through the wall. Grista put her head to the wall to listen. "Shh, I'm trying to listen," she whispered. "I can't hear. It's too muffled, but I wonder what those three rascals are up to. I know! Let's do something bad to them."

Cremy giggled and said, "Grista, you're so terrible."

Twilly's eyes widened with enthusiasm. "What do you have in mind?" she asked.

"Hmm, let me think," she said mischievously.

"Stop it, you two," commanded Cremy. "Those poor guys have already been tormented enough."

Grista shook her head. "Uh, uh. No, no, no," her voice drifted with a far off look in her eyes. "One more bad plan to make them a little crazy." Twilly giggled, perched on her knees watching Grista.

The men noticed it had grown quiet in the next room. Darvin looked straight ahead and said, "They're planning something."

"Bloody females," muttered Pell. Gully was laughing in his pillow.

"Are you enjoying this, mate?" asked Darvin sharply.

Gully raised his curly red head, his freckled face smiling. "Yup! Best fun I've ever had in my life," he said gleefully. "It's you two the girls are really after," he continued. "Mr. Pell Provance and Mr. Darvin Scutter, two statues of sophistication. Quiet, deadly, handsome men. They can't resist going after you two and doing crazy mischievous things to you," he laughed.

"Bloody tar pits of Phaldegon," muttered Pell.

Darvin looked at him quizzically. "Where the hell is Phaldegon?" he asked.

"Forget it, mate," said Pell. "Just muttering to myself."

Chapter 23

A SERENADE OF SORROW

The Kungerods entered the Pollidecreum to their assigned positions. They all turned their tundrils in unison. The globe came to life with symbols, emblems and legends, like golden blood running through the globe, until an image of the earth appeared. "Ah," said the Athelonian. "This, my colleagues, was the last place his lordship sojourned." They all turned their tundrils to exact more information. The globe turned with more legends, emblems and symbols. The Athelonian grabbed his tundril and forcefully turned it to the left. The globe stopped its activity. The Kungerod of Athelone turned to face his colleagues. "My dear friends, the things we're about to witness may be unsettling even for us. The reason his lordship left that poor world is because he finished his task, so be prepared for what we are about to view."

After that, he walked over to his position and turned his tundril once again. The globe once again came to life. Symbols, legends and emblems formed images in the minds of the Kungerods. The activity continued for a while, when the Kungerod of Vernace shouted, "Stop! Please, stop the globe!" He was visibly shaken. He left his seat and walked out to the conference room and sat down. The other Kungerods left their positions to join him and comfort him. He looked up at them with a question mark on his disturbed face. "How? How can this be?" he pleaded.

The Athelonian sat next to him and put his arm around his shoulder. With his face close to the Vernacian's, he said gently, "My dear friend, I know how hard it is to look upon that most woeful place, but remember, we are Kungerods, the protectors of these two worlds, and this is our duty." The Vernacian, being strengthened, took courage and proceeded to the

Pollidecreum with the others in tow. They returned to their assigned places and continued viewing the globe.

The globe once again came alive – emblems, symbols and legends – until finally the Earth appeared. They continued turning their tundrils as more symbols appeared. Images formed in their minds, causing their countenances to change. Their faces tensed, filled with horror and sorrow. The Can-Chimeran spoke, "How could such creation exist?" he asked, his face red with anger and shame.

"It's outrageous!" shouted the female.

"Yes, pure sewage!" exclaimed the Patamodian.

The Athelonian calmed them, gesturing with his hands. "There is much more, but keep in mind that there was a time they had honor and nobility."

"They are a flimsy species, aren't they?" asked the Vernacian.

"Did you notice their means of transport?" asked the female. "Their philbees are a vision mobile madness. They're made of thin, sharp metal, which pierces and penetrates their bodies when they collide with another object. Yes, they race head long in these monstrous inventions."

"What about those large structures that look like castles or citadels? They crowd into these places with one accord at certain times. They comport themselves in ritualistic fashion, with two or three others either leading them, or yelling at them, or speaking to them of inane impossibilities or rhetorical bozwix," said the Patamodian.

The Athelonian laughed to himself. "Oh, you mean their religion or forms of worship?" the Athelonian offered.

"What is religion?" asked the Vernacian.

The Athelonian continued, "It's some sort of, theological system of logic and auditory mathematics to communicate the metaphysical concoctions of their minds." They all looked at each other and burst out with laughter. The Athelonian was not laughing. His face grew severe. They looked up at their colleague and noticed his countenance and abruptly stopped the levity.

The Athelonian walked around the globe to face them, his face stern and menacing. "Do you find this amusing?!" he shouted, pointing to the image of the Earth. They all lowered their faces in shame. The Athelonian pointed to the Earth. "That poor orb suffered great torment because of those serpent-spawned hatchlings. The royal seed was there," he added.

"Oh!" they all moaned thoughtfully. "How? How did they get there?" asked the Can-Chimeran. The Athelonian's face grew dark. "The bright ones grew dark, the high ones slipped low."

"Corodorbus!" they all shouted and rose from their seats in alarm.

"Aye, Corodorbus," concurred the Athelonian. "He sojourned on that poor world, spreading his filthy seeds everywhere." The female put her hand to her mouth in horror. The others looked at each other, their faces white and pale with fear. "Chaos, darkness and confusion emerged as their daily fare," continued the Athelonian.

• • • • • • •

The three couples left the inn and stepped into the Agrimorian sunshine. They were all refreshed and dressed casually, as they walked arm in arm looking for their guide. They espied Muswick sipping hot caone and puffing on a puigo at one of the cabanered tables of a café. They all joined him. He looked at all of them. "Well, children, are you ready for your voyage?" he asked.

"Looking forward to it," answered Pell.

"Well, after you've had some refreshment, we'll depart," said Muswick. Muswick looked over the group thoughtfully, wondering to himself why they were so important to the Kungerods. The girls changed their seats to sit together, as did the men.

Pell looked over at Darvin and Gully, while sipping his hot caone. "Well, mates, we're about to embark," said Pell. Darvin and Gully concurred. Gully was looking forward to the journey. He was gratified that he had joined Pell and his group, he had no regrets. Darvin too, was looking forward to the journey. Drinking his hot caone, he starred out at the bay, wondering about the adventures that awaited him. The girls were engrossed in conversation, occasionally glancing over at the men laughing and whispering.

Muswick stood up. "Well, shall we?" he asked. They all stood together, Grista with Pell, Cremy with Darvin and Twilly with Gully. "I've two philbees waiting for us," said Muswick.

They made their way down the main street to the two waiting philbees. The drivers were standing outside the vehicles and opened the doors and lifted the domes as the group appeared. They piled into the philbees and made their way to the port area. As they approached the port, past large warehouses and quarters for seafarers, they noticed the freightliner. It was nothing like the freightliners on Earth. There before them was a huge, white and green shape sitting in the bay. At first glance, it was like an upside down turtle shell with a bridge section and four massive cylinders protruding into the sky.

They exited the parked philbees and made their way towards the gangway. The gangway was covered with a green awning, with two men in immaculate uniforms at the foot of it. After saying their farewells to Muswick, they approached the two uniformed men. The two men were natives of Patamodia, the orange hue to their skin betraying them. The two came to attention, then called attendants to carry their luggage. They asked the group to follow them. They walked up the long gangway, higher and higher, until they reached the main deck. The deck was very wide, made of rich redwood. They followed the two briskly-walking men past cabins, a glass-enclosed café and finally to a wide staircases that led up to the officers' deck. The two men continued to lead the group onto the glass-enclosed officers' deck, past more cabins, with gold symbols embossed on them denoting rank, and finally to an archway, at which they turned left to the interior of the officers' deck. The officers' deck was quite unique in that the doors to each cabin were made of thick-frosted, beautifully-decorated glass.

The bulkheads were made of soft ivory like material as they were illuminated from within. The wood from this deck was a rich wood, ochre in color. They walked through this section, up another wide stairway to the promenade deck. The breeze was gently blowing and the sun was gleaming off of the huge cylindrical turbines. They continued up another section of the deck, until they reached another section of cabins. They proceeded indoors through a huge, frosted glass door. They entered a large lounge area that was beautifully carpeted. The carpet was a rich, dark-green, with brass-colored piping on the edges. The carpet was so thick it seemed to absorb sound. The walls were a white ivory color, with thick-veined tan marble molding around the lower and upper edges. The floor lamps were long metal stems, with fluted glass globes on top. The stems were made of a reddish metal. There were also tables, recliners and caone makers. Their two guides motioned for them to sit, bowed and left the lounge. Everyone was quiet, taking in the beauty of the lounge.

Cremy turned to the others. "I've never been aboard a freightliner before, but I never imagined these vessels would be so gorgeous," she said, looking around in admiration. A moment later, the hatch at the rear of the room opened and a very tall man emerged, followed by a woman. They were both garbed in immaculate white uniforms with touches of green and gold circling each sleeve. The tall man had a slightly thick green and gold stripe on the left side of his uniform from the shoulder to the bottom edge of his jacket. He walked over to the group and smiled broadly at them. They could tell he was from Ilgestana, from the long tear-shaped eyes, not unlike the ancient Egyptians' eye makeup. Their eyes were common to the Ilgestanians. His hair was thick, dark, like fine gold, as was his moustache and beard. His skin was tan and weathered, but not in the least unattractive.

"Welcome!" he said in vigorous booming voice. "I'm captain Daghre and this is my second in command, qarde Furia." The woman bowed respectfully. She was quite lovely, with rich brown hair hanging loosely over her white uniform. Her eyes at this time were greenish-gray. Ilgestanians eyes changed with lighting when standing in direct sunlight. Their eyes turned gold and purple and gleamed visibly. Her uniform caressed her opulent body. She was staring at Pell. When he caught sight of her, she turned away embarrassingly.

The captain sat across from them and spoke, "My vessel is completely at your disposal. Please feel free to enjoy her. Her name is Lamberante and she's a most accommodating vessel. Please take in all of her delights. The only area which is restricted, is the rear hold area. We are carrying partially-assembled terraspans in crystal polymer cases. But other than that, my ship is yours." He spoke affectionately of his vessel, as if it were alive. He wished everyone to enjoy his vessel the way he did.

The qarde, which was a mariners' rank on Agrimore, gestured for the group to follow her. She walked beside Pell, every so often trying to steal a glimpse of him. She led them to the guest section, which was on the same deck as the lounge. The bulkheads were white as ivory, with strips of green bordering the edges and the halls were lushly carpeted on this deck. They turned right, down another corridor to a series of cabins. There was an individual cabin for each of them.

The three girls spoke to Furia, requesting that they bunk together. Furia picked up the internal langline and asked for three crewmembers. At the arrival of the crew, they began moving furniture into one large cabin. The men were content with individual accommodations. She lead Darvin and Gully to their individual cabins, then walked quietly with Pell to the end of the corridor and unlocked a cabin door to a huge stateroom. She entered and pulled back the drapes, revealing a series of large, bridge-like windows exposing a wonderful view. "There is not a more exquisite cabin on the entire vessel," she said, not looking at Pell. Pell was slightly overcome with the beauty of the stateroom. The girl continued rushing about the stateroom. Then she proceeded to pull back a folding door, revealing a quaint mini galley with a butcher block-type eating table in the center. She opened the cupboards and the mini fridge to make sure they were properly stocked. He wondered to himself why she was giving him all this attention.

After all were there not attendants on board that would tend to these things, rather than the second in command?

The girl kept rushing about the cabin, dizzying him as he watched her rapid preparations. She walked over to the left side of the huge windows to a door, which she unlocked.

Pell walked over to the open door and peered in. There before his eyes, was a marvelous bedroom with twin beds. The rug was like maroon grass under his feet, rich and lush. The decorative edges of the rug were gold-colored. The portals were wide and rectangular, with round edges covered with deep maroon and gold drapes. The bulkheads were a rich crème color, with tubular lighting extending from the deck to the overhead in each corner. The lighting blossomed into intricately designed crystal at the top. The two beds were covered with maroon and gold covers, with an exquisite emblem of Patamodian royalty in the center. The backboard was of clear, light blue glass, thick, with a golden design set inside of the glass, as if suspended on nothing. There was also a handcrafted ivory dresser. There were two walk-in closets. The bathroom was past the portals on the right side of the room. It had a huge, marble-like stone tub, the spigots were made of precious metals, like a mixture of gold and platinum and some other metal that made them shimmer. It was stacked with every conceivable bath salt, precious oils, soaps and aromas. The girl kept rushing about when Pell finally grabbed her arm to stop her. "What is all this?" he asked quizzically, gesturing with his hands.

She looked up at him hesitantly, slightly unnerved by his piercing eyes. "Why, these are my orders, to give you the finest accommodations we could afford you."

"Who ordered this?" he asked, quietly yet intently.

"The Kungerods, sir," she answered. He gently released her arm and she continued where she left off.

As she was bolting about the room, he asked, raising his voice, "But why are you, the second in command, attending to me?"

"Orders sir," she replied, craning her neck as she was fluffing the pillows to look at him. "I'm to see to all of your needs until we dock at Patamodia." After that, she left the stateroom, catching a glimpse of him before she left.

He walked around the opulent accommodations to the walk-in closet, revealing that all of his clothing had been unpacked and carefully hung. He walked back to the lounge area of the stateroom and peered out the huge windows. He could hear the overhead turbines begin to whirr, as the vessel began to disembark. Everything was filled with a low, rather soothing vibration.

The three girls were unpacking and preparing their stateroom. Cremy was hanging her clothes. Twilly was straddling the bed with her knees, jumping slightly up and down. "Oooh!" she exclaimed. "These beds are cushiony."

Grista emerged from the bath, clad only in a short-white silk slip, shaking and combing her wet, curly hair. "Why didn't the men bunk together?" asked Twilly.

"Oh, they hate bunking together. They love privacy," answered Cremy.

"Boy, men are strange, aren't they?" asked Grista.

"Sure are," answered Twilly. "I love bunking together with you two. It's so much fun."

Darvin was unpacking and thinking of the journey, Pell and what the Kungerod had said about him. "Who or what is Pell Provance?" He left his cabin and made his way to Gully's stateroom and knocked on the door. Gully was finishing stuffing his clothes in draws of a dresser, when he heard the rapping on his cabin door. It was Darvin, looking rather dower. Gully invited him in. Darvin made his way to the portals, pulled back the drapes and stared out into the bay. Looking straight ahead, he asked, "Ever wonder about all of this, Gully? I mean, Pell being this harbinger of disaster, about all of the madness, adventures and such?"

Gully gently grabbed his shoulders and turned him. "What's going on with you?" he asked sharply. "I've never imagined that life could be so rich, until I met that marvelous person," he said reassuringly. "I, for one, am honored to be associated with him. Look at us, traveling to places where no one has ever been, personal guests of the Kungerods no less. Look how this association has drawn us all together. Why, you're all closer than my own family. Open your eyes, man!" Gully shouted. "You and Cremona have become much closer and I know how you feel about her. Me, I adore that girl Twilly, her boyish loveliness," he said smiling.

Darvin lowered his head in thought. "Please don't misunderstand me, Gully," he pleaded. "I love the man and am his friend to the end of time itself. Why, there's nothing I would not do for that big rascal. But once in a while I think of my life before I met Pell, what road I would have taken," he said quietly.

"Oh! Clear your damn axe-blade head of that stuff!" shouted Gully. "Look at yourself. You look like a damn weapon, mate. You were made for just such a situation as this. And if you think about it, you wouldn't have it any other way," he said, now whispering in his ear and smiling.

Darvin turned and smiled at Gully, nodded and said, "You're right, you bloody Parmegest. Let's go and see if his highness is finished unpacking."

Grista, Cremy and Twilly were still dressing. Twilly, was twisting into a pair of black pants that appeared to be thick, lush corduroy. She looked stunning as the lush black material bordered her shapely navel area. Grista looked at her. "Look at her. Isn't she a sight to behold?!" she exclaimed, caressing Twilly's waist.

"Oh, my!" said Cremy, kneeling on her bed. "Those pants make you look irresistible, Twilly," she said.

"Come on," said Grista. "Let's finish adorning the little forest nymph." Twilly loved the attention she received from Grista and now from Cremy. She tingled, as the two beautiful women were fussing over her. It made her feel more feminine and attractive. Grista went to the closet and found a white, sheer silk blouse, sewn with pure silver thread. They both helped her with it. Then Cremy went to the closet and took a pair of hand-crafted, knee-high black boots that were her favorite walking boots and put them on Twilly. The girls stood back to admire her. "Oh my!" said Grista, beaming. "Extravagant beauty. Wait till Gully beholds you!" Cremy went to her draw and pulled out an emerald and silver bracelet and put it around Twilly's wrist, covering the sleeve of the blouse. Grista fetched a fine silver choker and clasped it around the girl's lovely neck. "There," she said, stretching her arms around Twilly's neck and placing her forehead next to Twilly's. She looked into the girl's eyes. "You know, you are the most alluring creature in creation. You know that, don't you?" she asked.

The two men approached Pell's stateroom and knocked. "Enter!" shouted Pell. Darvin entered, followed by Gully.

Both men stood in the middle of the stateroom with their mouths open. "Bloody hell!" shouted Darvin, looking around the opulent stateroom.

"Only Pell Provance could rate a kingly stateroom," said Gully, as he made his way into the galley. "Would you look at this mini galley! It's stocked with everything, I mean everything!" he exclaimed.

Grista was getting dressed, Cremy and Twilly helping her. She donned a short leather skirt made from Patamodian leather plants. It was dark brown, soft and supple, covered with individual leather-shaped leaves. Cremy was buckling a thin gold belt around her waist. Twilly carried a soft white, short-sleeved blouse from the closet. Each sleeve had had a thin gold border, as also did the neckline. Then Cremy grabbed a matching leather vest. Twilly grabbed her own tan boots to put on Grista's feet. They stood back to look at her and looked at each other. "Keagles bingles!" exclaimed Cremy. "This ship is not going to survive you two."

"Well, let's get to work on you," said Twilly.

The girls were giggling, as they brought varieties of velvets, silks and leathers out of the closet. Cremy stood there being fussed over by the two girls, Grista brushing her beautiful auburn hair and Twilly laying out garments on the bed. "You know, you have hair of a queen," she said, carefully brushing and admiring each thick strand of hair in her hand.

"I could get used to all this attention," Cremy purred.

"Look at these slacks!" shouted Twilly, holding a pair of dark green, soft, plush velvet slacks in her arms. Cremy stood, as the two girls helped her snuggle and twist her shapely body into the slacks, her legs perfectly filling out the velvet. Grista shod her feet with gold leather sandals. "What about the top?" asked Twilly.

"Oh, I don't know if we should hide the top of rich Cremy beauty," laughed Grista.

"Stop it, you two!" shouted Cremy, laughing.

"Oooh! Look at this!" exclaimed Twilly. She was holding a blouse that was light tan. There were patterns of vines sewn around the short sleeves, with three pleats on each side of the breast area, accentuating the breasts, fastened with dark gold buttons. "She is a queen, isn't she?" asked Twilly, as they put the blouse on Cremy. Finally, they placed a garment over her left shoulder, wrapped it around and clipped it with a brooch at the forearm, not unlike the ancient Roman and Greek senators of Earth. It matched the slacks of dark green, plush velvet. They were ready. The three queens would rival the beauty of the Agrimorian sun.

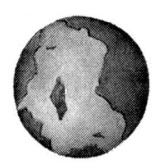

Chapter 24

THE TERROR OF THE THERMEDYTES

The Kungerods were busy in the Pollidecreum. Their eyes were fixed on the globe with fascination and amusement, focusing on the Earth, which was Pell's last stop. They mused upon the images that flashed into their minds. "Why!" exclaimed the Vernacian. "Those creatures were so enamored with themselves that they could barely function in their mundane tasks."

"Yes," concurred the female with a smile, "their energy was mostly spent upon gazing at themselves. It's almost comical that they even set up huge mirrors in their cities and hamlets, so they could admire themselves continually, even bumping into one another in the process of their self-adoration."

"Hmm, yes, the poor wretches," interjected the Athelonian. "Even their industries took full advantage of this, pumping out day and night self-enhancing elixirs and myriads of beauty concoctions. All it did was to rob them and make them uglier. Their self-absorption was decaying them at a rapid rate. Our lord Pell Provance was there viewing the absurd miscreants, walking amongst them quietly in his regal form, steadily destroying their entire civilization."

"But, how?" asked the Can-Chimeran.

The Athelonian continued, "You see, my dear colleagues, Pell Provance is the perfect weapon. Look at him. Charming, debonair, dangerously handsome and rapt in mystery. You see, he is the focal point of their final destruction. He magnified and intensified every decaying factor lying dormant within them, bringing it to its final apex." He continued, "And they had no idea, as he walked through their world completely undetected. Men were fearful of him and would avoid him and their women were feverishly trying to get his attention. Their authorities completely ignored him, as some obscure taddybit. Even if they had become aware, it would not have availed them, for he is well supported and equipped. But also, there is the beautiful Grista at his side, even now, intrepid, full of courage, blindingly beautiful, the envy of every female on that woeful orb. She is his queen!" he heralded in a booming voice.

"Oh!" exclaimed all of the others in wonder and awe.

"Yes," he went on, "and her highness is our queen." They stared at each other in astonished amazement. "She has followed him to numerous worlds, as on Earth the lion watching over her whelps, Grista watched over Pell," he added.

• • • • • • •

The three girls emerged from their stateroom wonderfully attired. The attendants male and female stood in their tracks, smiling with admiration at them. They continued down the corridor towards Pell's stateroom, holding each other around the waist, walking three abreast, swaying playfully, as they approached the stateroom. They stopped outside of the stateroom, looked at each other and grinned, without saying a word. Grista turned the knob quietly, until the door was slightly ajar. Then, as one, they kicked open the door. The three men were startled by the door flying open. Grista led the way. Without saying a word, she walked over to Pell looking mischievous and dangerous. She looked deeply into his eyes, searching, then grabbed his thick black hair and kissed him ferociously. Cremy approached Darvin, who began backing up as if stalked by a huntress. She cornered her prey, grabbed his shirt, pulled him towards her, gently and lovingly kissed him and embraced him. Gully was smiling, as Twilly made her way towards him like a cat, wriggling and swaying from side to side. She closed slowly, as Gully watched her every movement, smiling, but not sure what the boyish beauty was about to do. She moved closer to him with her pixie-like smile, swaying until she reached his massive chest. She pressed herself tightly against him, looking up at him, hands behind her back, swaying as if she would snake up the massive chest. She smiled broadly, as he held her close to himself, looked at her, admiring her, perusing every feature of the girl's lovely, delicate face, then slowly and gently kissed her.

Grista looked up at Pell and said, looking around the stateroom, her arms still clasped about his neck, "I see they're taking good care of my beloved, aren't they?"

Cremy released her grip on Darvin's shirt and exclaimed, "Would you look at this place!" She extended her arms and moved about the stateroom in wonderment. Twilly wasn't paying attention. She had her eyes closed, as Gully caressed her. Pell and Darvin were still flustered and dazed by the amorous sortie of the two women.

Grista sat on the divan, her legs slightly apart with her elbows on her knees supporting her head. "Well, this is what it means to be Pell Provance," she said.

Twilly turned her head, still in the arms of Gully, and smiled. "We should throw him out of here and take this room for ourselves," she said playfully.

"No," said Grista quietly, "this suits my lord," she said, looking up at Pell.

• • • • • • •

The Kungerods had recessed for refreshment and to discuss what they had viewed. They retired to the Delurian room, which was a quaint, glass-enclosed capolla. It had a stone floor with light tan wooden pillars, separating the fluted glass every ten feet. The canopy was wood and glass with vines strung overhead. The attendants rushed about them in preparation for their repast. After the Kungerods had ordered, the attendants came in with hot foamy caone and a golden pitcher of Agrimorian water. The Athelonian leaned back in his seat and scanned the faces of his colleagues. "Well," he demanded, "give me your thoughts."

The Vernacian leaned forward, sipping his hot caone, and said, "It's a dusty world, isn't it? Dust everywhere," he continued.

"Did you see them eat?" asked the Patamodian. "Very unattractive foods and noisy. What a noisy place," he added.

"Yes they're always chattering, mostly about subjects devoid of substance. They actually carry langlines on their person!" shot the Ilgestanian. "It's as if keeping their mouths in constant motion, they can bypass the use of their minds," she added.

"Not only that, they're so flimsy," offered the Vernacian. "They're bodies are susceptible to viruses, vermin and a host of other things."

"They're smelly," said a voice.

"They're what?" asked the Athelonian.

"They're smelly!" shouted the Patamodian.

"Yes," offered the Ilgestanian, "a stinky species full of foul odors."

"These jackonates slay the innocents!" boomed the Can-Chimeran. "Those poor helpless creatures that are much higher and cleaner than they are!" His anger rose. "They don themselves with the outer coverings of the poor creatures and keep them in captivity in their ugly homes and institutions, then they come and view them!" he shouted, slamming his fist on the wooden table.

"The miscreants slay their women," offered the Ilgestanian in disgust.

"Did you notice their ugly, primitive terraspans?" asked the Patamodian. "They pack themselves together into these objects and every so often fall from their skies and pierce and burn themselves."

"Ugh," groaned the Vernacian. "All of those creatures stuffed together in one of those flimsy and noisy things. They haven't even discovered the basic principals of wedding the natural forces with man-made inventions," the Vernacian concluded.

"Their freightliners sit flat in the water, impeded by waves and storms," offered the Patamodian. "Their entire world was up in arms against them with uncontrollable wind storms, quakes and volcanic activity," the Patamodian continued. "They cannot even control the basic element of fire. The smallest creatures pierce them through with ease."

"What are those things that they preoccupy themselves with, sort of like a show ball, but with a flat screen and numerous buttons?" asked the female.

The Athelonian looked at her from across the table and smiled. "I believe you're referring to the camp-no, computer I think," he said comically. "This device," he continued, "facilitates the non-use of their minds. It actually thinks for them," he laughed. The others looked at him, hanging onto every word. They were speechless. "Yes," he continued, "instead of developing their minds to reach their natural potential, they decided to short circuit it, so they could serve, facilitate and maintain these objects. Some crude form of limited and circular reasoning from one computer to console to the other."

"Quite absurd," interjected the Can-Chimeran.

• • • • • • •

Pell looked over at Darvin and chuckled, as he was holding the purring Cremona. Darvin in turn looked at Gully, who had a large Cheshire-cat smile on his freckled face. Darvin jerked his head towards Pell, motioning to look at Gully. Pell leaned his head forward, with Grista still holding him, and grinned. Pell broke the amorous atmosphere by asking, "Well, little chumlies, shall we adjourn to the promenade deck?" The girls would not budge, completely content with holding their men. Pell gently tugged at Grista's arms. She only tightened her grip at his feeble struggle.

Cremona held Darvin around the waist and looked up at him. "Going somewhere?" she asked. He tried to wriggle himself free, only to have Cremy hold him tighter around the waist, nuzzling her head against his chest. He looked at Pell helplessly. Pell squatted down, trying to get out of Grista's clasped arms, but she merely squatted down with him, smiling. Gully and Twilly were laughing at the antics of Grista.

Pell put on a severe face feigning anger. "Grista," he said, "let go!"

"Sure, baby," she whispered and gripped him tighter.

"Oh well," he said, surrendering. He then lifted her up by her legs and carried her, with her arms still tightly gripped around his neck. Darvin tried walking with Cremy, still holding him around the waist and her feet on top of his. The scene was comically absurd as he lumbered towards the door. Gully and Twilly were so overcome with laughter that they fell on the carpeted floor.

They were rescued with the entrance of an attendant announcing that they were about to embark and that dinner was being prepared in a private dinning room on the promenade. She struggled to keep a straight face at the hilarious display in the stateroom. Pell dropped Grista on the divan and asked the attendant if they could dine with the captain and the crew. The attendant said hesitantly, "But, sir, the private dining room is even now being prepared and is far better than the crews' accommodations."

"But we'd like to sup with the captain and crew for tonight," stated Pell. "Plus, it gives us a chance to know all of you," he added.

"Well," she said, "I suppose it's all right. We are to provide your every comfort. If you will follow me," she said, with a scintillating smile.

• • • • • • •

The Kungerods entered the Pollidecreum, having discussed at length what they had viewed. The globe came to life, as the Kungerods turned their tundrils. The Earth once again came to view. The Athelonian addressed his colleagues. "My dear friends, now we shall see the final work of our lord Pell, the intensifying of evil which lay in them, the protection and rescue of the royal house, the final conflagration and purging of that doleful orb."

They once again turned their tundrils, as images flashed through their minds. They all removed their tundrils and stared at one another. All remained silent, until the Athelonian spoke, "Well, my dear brethren, there you have it."

"The end of those creatures was unimaginably terrible," said the Vernacian.

"Yes," added the Ilgestanian, "it was so chaotic that it became a blur, as if we were viewing a collage of blood and heat, scored with a cacophony of screams and thunder."

"The evil had reached its apex and turned on themselves, feeding continually, feeding forever, feeding until there was nothing left to feed upon," offered the Athelonian. "They fed on each other for self-gratification. Their name became the feeders. A frenzy had taken hold of them. Most of their innocent creatures were slaughtered, the rest were taken from them. The royal house was gone and they were alone. Shortly after that, came the Thermedytes to purge the Earth and expel them. The Thermedytes are fearful creatures to look upon, composed of many unidentifiable elements. Their appearance is like lightening, fire, ice, diamonds and platinum. The conflagration was rapid. They would land in the middle of one of their cities, with all looking on in awe. In an instant, they were gone, no residue or debris, not a shadow of anything, just Earth unharmed, not even warm, just clean. After expelling these parasites, they brought the poor Earth back to the center of its galaxy and reformed it tenderly with great care, beautifying it, placing it with its sun in new families of systems." With that, the Athelonian concluded his discourse. They all rose and retired for the evening.

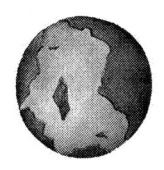

Chapter 25

THE KINGDOM OF GRISTA

The three couples followed the attendant past the promenade deck to the officers' deck and down a corridor that led to two large, smoked glass doors, with an insignia on each side. They entered a room that looked like the crew's lounge and through another door that led to a stairwell. Pell was impressed with the wonderful craftsmanship of the vessel. Even this obscure stairwell was made of rich red woods and ivory bulkheads. The hand rail was a clear, pearl-like material. The stairwell led them to another series of glass doors and finally to the crews' mess.

The mess was very large, with flags of every continent hanging from the bulkheads. The trio stood on the upper platform above a short staircase leading to the main floor. They noticed the captain with his qarde seated next to him. Everyone sat together despite their rank. The captain was seated at the head of an enormous table filled with crew members engrossed in conversation, while eating and drinking. The scene was lively and the aromas were whetting the group's palates. When they descended the stairs to the mess, one of the crew espied them and immediately rose to attention, followed by the entire table, including the captain.

Pell didn't wonder about these honors any longer, but just rather accepted them. Pell, to his surprise, noticed a familiar face at the left of the captain. It was Denara, the beautiful captain of the terraspan. She looked and smiled at Pell. Grista, who was holding Pell's arm, noticed this, looking first at the woman and then at Pell. Some of the crew members ran to set up extra places at the table close to the captain. They all sat down together, with the captain last to be seated. Pell was seated between Grista and Denara, the young woman trying to keep her composure by not looking at Pell.

The captain addressed Pell and his friends. "Mr. Provance!" he said in a booming, cheerful voice, his smile brightening the table. "We were just discussing you and your friends," he continued. "First, I want to thank all of you for honoring us with your presence and gracing my table." Pell nodded courteously. "Well, I've already received six calls on the langline from the Kungerods inquiring as to your comforts and accommodations. Before this I had never spoken to a Kungerod. I hope everything has been to your satisfaction?" he asked.

Pell smiled at the captain and said, "Quite, quite overwhelming. I've never seen such a stateroom in all of my life and your crew has been most hospitable, but this vessel," he said with wonder, "this vessel is the most beautiful craft I've ever seen. The comforts it affords are almost legendary. Why," he continued, "every part of her is meticulously crafted in warmth and beauty. Quite impressive," Pell concluded.

The captain's smile broadened. Pell had endeared himself to the captain by speaking of the thing closest to his heart, his ship. Denara was fighting to not look at Pell, but was feeling unsettled being so close to him with Grista present. Her breathing quickened, her temperature rose and her heart was beating rapidly. Finally, the girl rose to excuse herself, stating she had duties to attend to. Everyone stood until she left the mess, Grista studying her as she left. They continued their meal and hot-brewed caone, as the crew enjoyed their company. The females among the crew, changed places so they could speak to Grista, Cremy and Twilly. They were laughing about the antics they witnessed earlier and were fascinated with Grista's beauty. The men were inquiring about Pell's clothing and where they might purchase them. Gully was talking to them about his official service and Darvin about his pugilistic expertise. The crew was having a great time with them, with the captain enjoying the scene. Pell decided to excuse himself. He kissed Grista on the cheek and told her that he would meet her later, that he needed to be alone for a while. Grista understood and smiled adoringly at him.

Pell made his way back up to the officers' deck and up to the bridge deck. He ascended the ladders to a catwalk that led past the massive cylinders, which contained the turbines. He relished taking this out-of-the-way trek to the bridge area, climbing another set of ladders to the outside of the bridge cabin. He enjoyed the high-up view of the setting Agrimorian sun, the deep gold colors that were playing off of the massive ship and the gleaming humming cylinders. The multicolored clouds were forming over the horizon, with flashes of violet-blue and red-horizontal lightning from cloud to cloud. In Agrimore, small windstorms occurred over the sea and never over the land area. This world had no hostility against its inhabitants. He was quite taken by the beauty of this world and was determined to do no harm to it.

All of a sudden the bridge hatch opened and a female crew member invited him in. She was a perky little blond with bangs and she was very talkative. He entered the bridge behind the girl, who began talking about her duties and their position in the water. She was so bubbly and radiant Pell noticed. "Oh," she said apologetically, "how rude of me. I'm Hevla," she said, extending her hand. Pell smiled at the girl and introduced himself. "I know," she said excitedly. "The whole crew is talking about you and your friends," she said energetically. "Please let me show you my bridge duties," she said proudly. She began explaining certain functions of some of the instruments.

The wheel was attached to a domed white cylinder, which was bolted to the deck. The wheel sat horizontally, about three-quarters of the way up the cylinder, with two up right handles attached. She explained that four huge fins that protruded from the hull to the water all turned simultaneously with ease. She showed him the instruments that measured depth and wind velocity, screens that showed schools of teradorfils and other sea life, so they could avoid them. Pell thought to himself of how much he loved and admired the people of Agrimore, how they cared for every living thing.

He then began remembering bits and pieces of the Earth where he had been. The memories troubled him and he questioned why they were now surfacing. He shook off the troubling images and concentrated on the delightful creature explaining her vessel to him. He thanked her for all she shared with him and took his leave, as he opened the main hatch that led to a wide staircase. Hevla ran over, grabbed his arm, looked up at him and said, "Please come back anytime you wish, Mr. Provance. I'm sometimes here for hours and would love to have the company of you and your friends."

Pell smiled at her and thanked her. "Oh, by the way," he said, "the name is Pell, and we will visit your bridge again," he said assuringly and left. Pell made his way down the staircase, past the officers' deck and towards the promenade deck. As he passed the railing of the deck, looking out to the sea, he noticed a figure in the shadows walking towards him. It was Denara. She had changed out of her uniform and had donned a most alluring short skirt of brown and gold mesh, with a dark brown turtleneck and a gold necklace to be worn to formal affairs in uniform. She was shod in open-toe brown pumps that accentuated her beautiful legs. Her black hair was blowing slightly from the gentle sea breeze, with her eyes occasionally capturing the blue Agrimorian moonlight.

She walked over to him and looked over at the sea. Pell was perplexed by the girl's presence and said, "Denara, why are you here?"

"Orders from Purnis," she responded. "Don't you remember?" she asked, turning to him. "We are to be at your disposal for as long as you need us, so we stored the terraspan in the hold and boarded. I had to see you again Pell," she said softly, looking into his eyes. The girl slid her hand along the railing, moving closer to him. He backed up, nervously looking around for Grista.

"You cannot be here with me, Denara," he said to her anxiously.

"But, Pell, don't you find me attractive?" she asked, moving closer to him.

"I certainly find you attractive," he noted cautiously. "Denara!" he said sharply. "It's dangerous to be so close to me."

"Why?" she asked. "You would never harm a woman, would you?" she purred.

"No, but I would!" a voice shot out in the dark like the report of a rifle. Then Grista appeared out of the shadows. Pell backed up as Grista closed menacingly on the girl. Fear was rising in Denara, as she looked at Grista's face, fury and rage mounting in her. Grista turned to Pell and said, in a calm voice, "I'll handle this, my love. Please leave us."

"But, Grista," said Pell, trying to mediate for the girl.

"Leave, now!" she shouted. Pell knew that this was no time to argue with Grista, not while she was in this condition, so he left. Grista watched Pell leave then turned towards the girl. The girl was clutching the railing with her hands behind her, her knuckles white with fear. Grista slowly closed in on the girl, their faces only inches apart. She stopped and stared into the girl's eyes. There were a few moments of silence. The girl's heart was beating rapidly. Then Grista spoke slowly and quietly, still staring into her eyes. "This is the only time I'm going to say this. That man, Pell Provance, belongs to me, and I to him. No one in this world or any other world will come between us. The next time I will not speak and you will never come close to him again, or speak to him unprofessionally. Is that clear?" she asked, calmly, but menacingly. The girl nodded nervously. She turned and left slowly, not saying a word, knowing a sense of terror she had never before experienced.

Grista turned and left for Pell's stateroom. Pell waited for her arrival. He thought to himself that he would have never let anyone speak to him in that manner, but in Grista's case it was different, it was right. She opened the door to the stateroom quietly and stood there for a moment, looking at him, but not saying a word. The blue light of the Agrimorian moons seemed to search for her, donning her in its wonderful blue light, content to rest and caress her lovely features. She moved towards him slowly, Pell's eyes never leaving her, until she was inches from him. She looked at his features adoringly and searched his eyes silently, admiring the regal crown of his forehead. "Is my love cross with me?" she asked softly, touching his cheek with hers.

He moved her back from him gently, slowly exploring her beauty with his eyes. The moonlight played and hid in the shadowy contours of her face and body, frolicking in her splendid eyes playing hide and seek. Worlds have come and gone, dazzling empires containing the composite beauty of conquered realms, he thought, but this before me is an unexplored world. His eyes moved rapidly. He was falling headlong into a dark cavern of soft black velvet, past creation, into eternity, into Grista, like death and life itself. She, he thought, the envy of the stars. He then moved closer. Her internal aroma was a heady, dizzying aphrodisiac. He fell deeper into the world of Grista. Their lips met and he was lost, with no way out of the unexplored regions. He embraced this world. He went forth, the king he was, to establish his kingship in her realm. She welcomed him, opening the doors to her inner chambers and closing them behind him. They stood there in the moonlight, knit and sewn together as one. He had found his queen. With their lips, they embossed the seal of their kingdom.

Chapter 26

PREVARICATION, FURY AND PELL PROVANCE

The Kungerods rose with the Agrimorian sun and made their way to a small anteroom next to the kitchen. They enjoyed the little room because of the aroma of hot-brewed caone and baked aldapore, which was a Pathenune delight. The staff was scurrying about preparing for the day. The Athelonian leaned back comfortably in his chair and looked at his colleagues. "Well, my dear friends," he said, "have you all recovered sufficiently to discuss the past events?"

"Well," said the Vernacian, yawning, "we know the final chapter of the Earth before it was scraped clean by the Thermedytes."

The Patamodian rose up from his seat and offered, "Let us consult the inner globe to see what our lord is up to here, his past actions, encounters and finally what it was that drew him to us."

"Aye," concurred the Can-Chimeran.

After refreshing themselves with hot caone and aldapore, they walked slowly to the conference center. The Vernacian lagged behind and thought to himself out loud, "Their bathrooms are awful places."

The Athelonian stopped and turned, looking at the little Vernacian, who was muttering to himself. "What is it, my friend?" asked the Athelonian.

The Vernacian looked up at him. "Their baths, terrible, terrible!"

The Athelonian put his arm around him and gently spoke, "They were not always that way. Pell Provance magnified the latent evil that was in them. They had eras of nobility and promise," he continued. "What you saw was them at their worst. It was not always that way."

The female Kungerod turned and asked, "But why? Why at that time? If, when he arrived, some years prior to their demise, why, why did he come?" she asked, walking slowly on the stone path.

"It's rather complicated," answered the Athelonian. "You see," he continued, "they began in their last phase or century coming up with preposterous conclusions about their origins and mores. Mindless discussions, fruitless investigations, on and on with committees, conferences and conventions, some believing this, some that, until they began to lose all grip on rationality and reality, continuing in this mindless dance of religion and philosophy named after one of their ancients. Finally, some turned to the squeaking things that dwelt in darkness, things that hid in dusty corners that were not worthy of them. This caused the circle of their ignorance to broaden. The result," he added, "was a frenzy, fanatical, noisy banter of schisms, confusion, loud, stupid men and women leading more confused, deluded followers to the paths of profound ignorance and despair, like an ocean of dirty water and filthy foam lowering them to a condition below their insect life."

· · · · · · ·

Pell stood in his stateroom alone after Grista had left. He turned to look out of the bridge-like windows, with many emotions running through him. He began remembering more of his sojourn. The thoughts and images troubled him, how different this world was from where he had been. He turned to the two white, cushiony squares on the rug, which were about the size of foot rests. He dragged the cushion by the big bridge window and pressed down on one corner. The cushion unfolded and rose into a white, soft captain's chair. He walked to the galley, prepared a cordial, lit a puigo and sat back, looking out at the blue-gold sea.

Darvin knocked at the stateroom door. "Enter," said a voice through the door. Darvin entered the darkened room, slowly looking at the back of the captain's chair, with a plume of blue-green smoke rising. "Help yourself to a cordial and a puigo," said Pell, "and pull up a cushion," he said, as if he knew that it was Darvin. The cushion undid itself and Darvin sat back, lighting his puigo. Both men puffed without saying a word.

Darvin looked over at Pell and asked, "What's it all about?"

"What's what all about?" asked Pell, looking straight ahead.

"You know, all of it," continued Darvin.

Pell turned to Darvin, studying him. "What's going with you, mate?" he asked.

Darvin continued puffing his puigo, looking straight ahead. "I've always been the pilot of my life, in command, totally in control," said Darvin, still staring straight ahead and puffing the puigo, "but ever since I've met you, it's been one adventure after the other, like being stuck in a magnetic corridor rushing headlong with no port of call," he said. "I mean, look at what's happened," he continued, "anomalies, Kungerods, fierce and beautiful women, parties, disappearances, freightliners to unknown destinations, then there's you, mate. What in the bastions of creation are you?" Pell didn't say a word, but stared straight ahead and listened.

Darvin looked over at him and said, "Listen, mate, I'm your friend. I've never been closer to anyone in my life, except maybe Cremy." Pell smiled to himself, the puigo still in his mouth. Darvin continued looking at Pell. "Double shadows?" he asked quizzically. "How?" He sat back and sipped his cordial, staring out at the sea. "I suppose the Kungerods will sort it all out," he said resigningly.

Grista entered her stateroom slowly with a far-away look in her eyes. Twilly and Cremy studied her. "Grista?" asked Twilly. "Is anything wrong?" Grista laid back on her bed, her hands clasped behind her head, cushioning her. She looked straight ahead and smiled slightly. Twilly looked at her, waiting for a response.

Cremy turned and leaned on one arm, saying, "I don't think anything is wrong with her, Twilly. Why, look at her, all aglow."

Grista turned to the two girls. "What are you two going on about?"

"Come on, Grista, tell us," asked Twilly, anxiously propping herself up.

"I have him," she said, clasping her arms around her knees and looking up at the ceiling. She turned toward the others sitting on the side of the bed. "He's in here," she said, making a circular motion encompassing her breasts and solar plexes." The two girls looked puzzled. She tried to explain, "I'm not sure, but part of the essence of Pell Provance is inside of me, like some indescribable union. He's the only one that can fit in there."

"You mean the conjugal union?" asked Cremy.

"No," answered Grista, "that will happen in time. But this is ecstasy beyond that. It's like," she continued, searching for words, "like the physical is a shadow of that, something like a down payment, almost like an ocean exploring its own depths of pleasure."

"He can do that?" asked Cremy. Twilly was aghast. "But?" asked Cremy. "Do all men possess this ability?"

"I'm not sure," answered Grista, "But I don't think so. You see, he's not like other men. I'm not sure what he is, but I'm sure of this: He's never given this to anyone else. I'm the only one who is able to contain it. It's like he came home."

"What's it like? What does it feel like?" asked Cremy.

"No words have ever been formed, or will ever be formed to describe it. It's impossible to relate this," she concluded. Cremy and Twilly looked at each other astounded and slightly envious.

Darvin and Pell continued to enjoy their cordials and puigos, when Gully knocked. "Come in, mate," said Darvin lazily. Gully entered the darkened room filled with green and blue smoke and looked for a place to recline.

"In the walk-in closet," said Pell to Gully. Gully returned with a cushion in hand, pressed on the corner, until the cushion unfolded itself. He grabbed a perlee and puigo and sat down to join his companions. They all sat quietly, staring out at the sea, enjoying their puigos and cordials. Then Pell spoke, "The dark part of my journey is about to begin, my friends," he said. Both Gully and Darvin turned to look at him. "Yes," he said, still staring straight ahead, "something drew me to this lovely world, something dark and malevolent. This time I'm going to deal with it. I'm determined to protect this world," he said quietly.

"When are we to face this darkness?" asked Gully.

"Not we, me. You cannot join me in this. I'm the only one on this world that can face that," he said.

• • • • • • •

The Kungerods made their way to the conference center and then to the Pollidecreum. They entered the large, globed room and made their way to their positions. This time they fixed their tundrils into a slot to the left of the previous slot, which had activated the outer globe.

• • • • • • •

Darvin and Gully excused themselves, deciding to look for the girls. Pell sat there in the darkened stateroom contemplating the events that the future held in store for him. He was watching a school of terradorphils skimming the surface of the water at high speed. He felt the vessel's turbines slow down to give way to the creatures. He began again thinking of the Earth, as flashes of his last sojourn became more frequent. He knew that this meant he was about to conclude his time on Agrimore. He began to be troubled, not wanting to leave Agrimore, his friends and the incomparable

Grista. He was determined to find the evil that had drawn him to this world and to vanquish it himself.

He thought about that miserable place he had resided before he came to Agrimore. All of the activity, constant activity, useless activity, summit conferences, annual this and that, moratoriums, speechifications, dizzying debates, equal rights, human this and that. They were caught in such webs of deceit that it became more and more risky and dangerous to be truthful. The ignorance and futility was quite evident in their religions. He visited some of these institutions and was appalled. They were completely devoid of even the basic knowledge of themselves. Loud, boring dissertations and orations about nothing, temples of debasement and self-gratification. They became serviceable to slippery, shiny-faced men and women and to others with oversized hats that walked slowly, muttering unintelligible words, carnivals of futility. Their scientific propositions were convoluted, more and more inverted, collapsing in on themselves, redundant systems constantly being serviced and upgraded. He smiled to himself, thinking of their attempts of trying to reach the celestial bodies that were so close to them, completely ignorant of the coxidail, delvithren and numerous other fields that surrounded their world. Instead, they tried to force themselves into the void by shooting themselves into it, a time-consuming, slow and ponderous plod, sterile and futile. Their ancients, he recollected, had clearer presuppositions on all of these subjects. Given time, they would have achieved a more advanced and civilized society, but somewhere there was a shift, a paradigm that brought them to this most lamentable condition, completely pregnant with wrong presuppositions, so that eventually nothing worked, constantly feeding on wrong premises.

He continued to muse upon his time spent on Earth and what caused him to leave. All he could remember was, when he had intensified the evil on Earth to a certain crescendo, there was a flash and he was gone. He knew he still had time, for the evil had not yet manifested itself on Agrimore.

Denara had made her way to her stateroom, still shaken from the encounter with Grista. She thought to herself, Why? Why did she have to be on board? She walked over to the mirror, wiping her eyes and combing her hair. Who does she think she is? She doesn't own him, she thought. Why am I shaking and so upset? I've always acquitted myself well in personal conflict. Thoughts kept racing through her mind and anger was rising. Why am I so angry? she mused. I've never felt this way before. She! With one swipe of her hand, every item on the table before her – bottles and liquids – were sent bouncing on the thick blue carpeting.

Just then, there was a rap on the stateroom door. "Enter!" she shouted. A small-framed young woman opened the door slowly. She looked around, alarmed at the disarray of the room. Denara, still seething, asked, "What is it Fluice?"

The young terraspan crew member spoke hesitantly, "We were preparing the terraspan for departure." The girl looked around the stateroom and wearily at Denara, who was red with rage. This was not a normal experience for Agrimorians. "Commander?" she asked looking up at her.

The commander turned away, staring at herself in the mirror. "I'll be there soon. In the meantime, ask Brighel to come here," she commanded.

The girl left, looking perplexed. Brighel gently knocked on the door. "Enter!" Denara ordered. Brighel entered, looking puzzled at the condition of the room and the commander. Brighel was her second in command. He was a man with a rather large girth, broad shoulders, tree trunk muscular legs, a square jaw, brown hair and fierce set brown eyes. He was garbed in his dark green uniform, which strained to contain his massive frame. He looked at Denara compassionately, having hidden feelings for her. She could sense this and decided it was time to employ them to her advantage.

"Denara," he asked in a deep voice, "what is all of this?" He gestured to all of the items strewn on the carpet.

"That female attacked me!" she shouted.

"Wha, who?" he asked.

"The female that was with our illustrious guest, Pell Provance," she sobbed.

"You mean that beautiful wild woman sitting next to him in the mess hall?" he asked, his voice rising.

"Yes," she sobbed, "she thought I was after Mr. Provance and threatened me, grabbing me ferociously." Rage was rising in the heart of Brighel. He left the stateroom, slamming the door behind him.

Pell sat in the captain's chair, puffing on his puigo, staring out at the sea. All of a sudden, as if a claxon rang an alert in his head, he rose, put out the puigo and said to himself, "It has begun." He immediately left the stateroom to search for Grista. Grista was standing alone on the promenade, looking at the darkened sea with her hands on the railing.

• • • • • • •

The Kungerods watched, as the inner globe came to life. The events of Agrimore and Algenmere were being disclosed to their minds, golden legends, symbols and emblems, the characters slightly different from the large globe. They viewed Pell enjoying the life of a rascal, complete with perlees, haberdasheries, parties, concerts, his friends, cavorting with and swooning numerous females of both worlds. The Vernacian laughed. "He is quite the rogue, isn't he?"

The female Kungerod of Ilgestana said, "He is rather dashing, though."

The Athelonian interrupted, "Shall we keep our concentration on the subject at hand?" he scolded.

They all came to a leisurely attention. "Ah, look," said the Patmodian, "that's sort of different." They viewed Pell struggling to get his composure, uncoordinated, hesitant, fighting to look like his old self.

"Now, that's something to behold!" exclaimed the female.

"What in the world would cause him to lose it to such a degree?" asked the Can-Chimeran.

Then they all viewed the small bistro at the harbor of Chantry. Then they saw the cause of the stumbling of Pell. It was the mystifying Extella. "Wow, we must find out more of the creature that could so undo our lord Pell," offered the Patamodian.

"Aye," concurred the Vernacian. They began to concentrate on Extella. The globe searched and probed, legends, emblems rushed to life, focusing on the elusive Extella. There, before their eyes, stood an indescribable being, lightening, ice, flames, gleaming metals and elements, which could not be identified. They stood astonished, slowly removing their tundrils.

They gathered together and slowly left the Pollidecreum, passing the conference center onto the stone path, which led to their quarters. They stopped in the middle of the walkway. The Athelonian stood in the center of them and studied each face then asked, "You know what we were looking at, don't you?"

"Yes!" responded the Can-Chimeran. "A Thermedyte."

"Aye," added the Vernacian fearfully.

"The time is short!" shot the Patamodian.

"Yes," concurred the Athelonian, "a Thermedyte, the most fearful beings in existence and they are here amongst us. It means," he continued, "that our Lord Pell's work is nearing its conclusion." They were all aghast. "Also," he went on, "the evil has awakened."

• • • • • • •

Grista continued to look out at the sea, thinking of her beloved, thinking of ways to please him, when she heard a sound behind her. She turned to see Brighel closing dangerously, then rushing headlong like a linebacker. She was caught completely by surprise. Then out of the darkness, a figure appeared as fast as mercury, fiercer than a Thermedyte, full of fury like a gleaming blade burnished with flame. The figure was that of Pell. The contact he made with Brighel was like a comet hitting the surface of a moon. He sent Brighel reeling against the bulkhead, the man's body crashing with a sickening thud. Grista watched her king, like a lion with his black mane hanging over his eyes. With the speed of quicksilver, he deployed several well-directed blows to the man's sternum. Brighel crumpled in a heap. The assault by Pell was complete. Another blow would have resulted in irreparable damage or even death. Grista had never seen Pell engaged in violence. It was a fearful sight. The speed and power of her beloved was dizzying. No man on this world is his match, she thought. Yet she knew he did it for her. His great love and care only deepened her love and admiration for him.

The commotion had attracted a crowd of attendants and crew members, some assisting Brighel, who was not permanently harmed, but ever mindful of the battle with Pell. Darvin and Gully had arrived on the scene with Cremy and Twilly following. They watched as the throttled man was assisted by the crew. Grista was looking up at Pell, comforting her head against her champion's chest, like a child who had been rescued from an imaginary closet monster. Darvin and Gully walked up to the couple looking at Pell. He had a look that they had never before seen: fierce, implacable, a legendary king who had just fought a dragon. Cremy and Twilly stared with fascination, never having viewed Pell this way: feral, mighty, his beautiful mane hanging over his eyes, the way some children read about in stories of great heroes. They liked it, Pell's hair uncombed, his clothes slightly disheveled, a look of war on his handsome face.

Chapter 26

TEARS, THE DIET OF A BROKEN HEART

The attendants helped Brighel to his stateroom, with Denara following. Brighel laid back on the bed, still dazed. He looked up into the concerned face of Denara. "Denara," he whispered, "you provoked me into going after that woman, didn't you? You played me like flute. That woman was innocent. I could tell after battling with her lover. I could have lost my life!" he strained, still feeling pain. "He could have easily killed me, but you didn't care. All you care about is your own selfish desire for him. I've never battled with someone like that, lightening swift and as powerful as Togorus, the legendary beast of great strength."

Denara felt shame and fear that she had put Brighel at such risk. A tear fell from her cheek, as she kissed his forehead and whispered, "Forgive me, my sweet."

• • • • • • •

The Kungerods reached their quarters, each troubled about what they had viewed – the presence of evil on Agrimore and the appearance of a Thermedyte. They sat in the main vestibule area and just stared at each other, speechless. The Athelonian broke the silence, "I know what you're all feeling, that Pell Provance is somewhat responsible for all of this." He continued, "But remember this, our lord Pell would not be here unless this evil had not been spawned here. Imagine, would you, if he had not come? Our condition would be far more terrible, for we would be helpless against such."

"Aye," reiterated the Vernacian, "we would be completely alone."

"Not only that," added the Athelonian, "our lord is on his way to us and will face the evil for us." The Vernacian's face brightened with a look of far-off admiration.

· · · · · · ·

Pell made his way back to his stateroom, with Grista by his side. She enjoyed this new side of her beloved. It was warm and comfortable. He reached his stateroom and turned to dismiss Grista, but she would have none of it. She pushed him back playfully, smiling as a huntress about to capture her prey. His strength made him more desirable to her. His uncombed hair and disheveled clothing made her temperature rise. She was sweating droplets of liquid from her forehead, which found a path to her lips. She pushed him again, circling him like a cat after her prey. "I'm going to take you," she growled. Pell put both of his hands in front of his chest, pleading with her. She would have none of it and continued circling around him, smiling hungrily, whetting her appetite. She knelt down, crawling towards him, with him backing up until he was at the edge of the bed. She slithered towards him, twisting her neck erotically, looking up at him. Then she stopped at his feet.

"Grista!" he shouted. "Stop it!" She completely ignored him and grabbed his ankles and flipped him onto the bed, taking his feet out from under him. She lunged on top of her prey, straddling him and pinning his hands. He tried to speak, but she muffled his mouth with her lips. She wanted to devour him. Knowing her love was so strong, made her more feverish. She wanted to overcome him forever. He lifted her with care and laid her on her back. She marveled at how effortlessly he flipped her. Then he held her and kissed her powerfully. She was so overcome with pleasure that she thought she would expire. He then kissed her left ear and whispered, "Not now, my beloved. After our coronation."

"Coronation?" she asked, looking puzzled.

He rose up from atop of her, questioning himself. "Why did I say that?" He shook his head at a loss for an explanation. All of a sudden, there was a rap on the stateroom door. Grista quickly rose up from the bed and attempted to compose herself, irritated that her moment was interrupted. Pell walked through the lounge area, combing his massive mane, as he approached the door. He opened the door to the presence of the captain, qarde and two official-looking crew members.

The captain's face was grim and set. He tipped his hat courteously and said, "Sir, the events that took place on the promenade deck have come to my attention. Also, the attempted attack on the lady Grista. We thought it wise to speak to you first, as to the disposition of the one named Brighel."

Pell asked the captain and the attendants to enter and went to the bedroom to speak to Grista. He related to her what the captain had said and asked her what her pleasure was. Her eyes twinkled and she smiled warmly. "You," she swooned, "my delicious morsel, you are my pleasure."

"Grista," he said gently, "this is urgent. They are about to take official action against Brighel."

She turned back to him. "He was manipulated into taking that action," she offered. "It was Denara," she said sharply.

"Wait here, my sweet. I'll handle this."

She grabbed his shirt and drew him to her, then gently kissed him and said, "Show them mercy, my love. There's something more afoot here."

Pell understood what she was saying. "I'll see to it," he replied and kissed her forehead.

He asked the captain if he could speak to Brighel and Denara before they took official action. The captain looked at him intently and said, "Of course, sir. We are at your disposal," then turned in smart, coordinated fashion and left, with his subordinates following.

Pell made his way to the officers' deck, past the crew quarters to the guest crews' deck. He walked up to the white stateroom door and gently knocked. "Come in," said a female voice.

Pell slowly entered the stateroom. Denara was standing over Brighel attending his bruises. The sight of Pell terrified both of them. Brighel lifted himself against the backboard. Pell allayed their fears by gently calming them. He sat down and looked up at them, feeling pity for the two. He spoke softly, "Listen please, I'm not here to do you any harm," he assured them, "but tell me, why? What motivated you?"

Denara hung her head in shame. "It was I," she said repentantly. "Please, Pell," she pleaded, "don't blame this poor soul. I am the one that provoked him, knowing how he felt towards me," she continued. "I was jealous of Grista and incensed by her threat. My pride motivated Brighel, who I knew loved me and would do anything for me. When I told him that Grista attacked and harmed me, he lost control. Blame me, not Brighel," she pleaded, her eyes filling with tears as she gently stroked Brighel's brow.

Pell was moved with compassion for the couple and said, "The determination of your disposition is in my hands," swallowing hard as he looked at the fearful duo, his throat slightly swollen with compassion. "Nothing more will be said of this incident. The matter is closed. No official action will be taken against you and..." he added, "I will give strict orders to the captain not to inform Purnis. You will both continue in your duties to help me, until the completion of my journey." He then moved over to both of them, gently laid his hands on them and whispered, smiling slightly, "Love one another deeply. It will heal both of you."

Denara grabbed Brighel's head and held him tightly. She wept and said, "Thank you, sweet Pell."

Pell left the stateroom and saw the captain and his entourage approaching Brighel's stateroom. They stopped in the middle of the corridor. "Sir," said the captain, "what is your pleasure concerning Brighel?"

"The matter is closed," said Pell in a quiet, but firm voice.

"Sir?" queried the captain, puzzled.

He approached the captain and attendants, comporting himself as the king that he was, stared intently into the captain's eyes and ordered, "The matter is closed. There will be no official action taken. Also, you are not to inform Purnis Huelett of this matter. Is that clear?" The captain knew that this was the end of the matter and that he was commanded by someone of very high rank. The matter was closed.

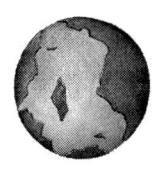

Chapter 27

THE MAIDEN'S BEARD

The three couples were enjoying a tour of the bridge given by the thrilled Hevla. She was so proud of the vessel and more than happy to show her off. The group so enjoyed the conversation of the perky blond, whom Twilly thought was adorable. They watched, as the skilled Hevla guided the massive freightliner to a Patamodian harbor. The group was amazed, as Hevla was able to maneuver the great craft with such ease, settling the great ship in the docking area. The crew was assembled at the awninged gangplank, with a thick, blue carpet that had been laid down for them. The crew was standing at attention on either side of the gangplank, all wonderfully attired in uniform. The captain and qarde were waiting at the bottom of the gangplank. They could see the terraspan rising slowly and quietly out of the hold. The captain saluted the group and told them how pleased he was to accommodate them. After saying their farewells, they noticed the terraspan landing and Denara and the crew disembarking.

Denara and Brighel walked over to the group, garbed in their smart uniforms. They saluted and said, "We are at your disposal, sir."

Pell walked over to the couple, smiled mischievously and asked softly, "Are you two..?"

"Uh huh," they said, smiling at each other.

Brighel grabbed Pell's hand tightly looking into his eyes. "I don't know what to say, sir," he said thankfully.

Pell whispered to him, "You make sure you take good care of her and love her to distraction. You got that?"

He smiled and said, "You bet, sir. You bet."

Denara moved over and kissed Pell on the cheek and said, "You darling man. You are really a king amongst men, but if you ever get tired of Grista…" With that they all laughed heartily.

Two philbees were prepared for them, as they made their way to the Maiden's Beard to meet Faengle, their guide on Patamodia. Darvin, Gully, Cremy and Twilly rode together in one philbee, while Pell and Grista rode alone in the other. Grista was playful as usual. "I'm driving," she said sternly, "because I'm taking you away."

"Oh yeah," he said, tickling her until she fell off the seat.

"No more! Please!" she screamed.

"Are you going to behave?" he demanded.

"Yes, yes. Just stop," she pleaded.

The other philbee pulled up beside them. The dome slightly opened. "Hey!" shouted Darvin. "What's going on in there, you two?"

Twilly began laughing. "Can't you two control yourselves?" Gully was red with laugher, as he saw Grista getting off the floor of the philbee and running out to look for a place to comfort herself in privacy.

"Pell!" shouted Cremy. "You're bad. That poor little girl." The laughter continued until Grista returned, her face slightly flustered.

She walked over to the other philbee and whispered to the girls, "Oh! I'm going to get him for this, believe me. This one I'm going to carefully plan out. Oh yes," she said to the giggling girls.

Gully laughed and thought to himself, Is this world going to survive those two?

• • • • • • •

The Kungerods came back to the Pollidecreum and took their positions. The Athelonian stepped forward to say, "Good news, my dear colleagues. Our lord Pell, I was informed, has arrived at Patamodia, they're now on their way to the meeting place of Faengle and then to Applendice to Crofty Bellar." They were all elated to hear the news and continued in their duties of exploring the inner globe.

"Now," said the Athelonian, "we will explore the evil that our lord Pell must face. So prepare yourselves." The Vernacian's face grew white and he backed away from his position. The Athelonian came over to his colleague and gently stroked his back. "My dear friend, do you need more time to prepare yourself?"

The Vernacian looked up at the strong Athelonian. "I have never looked at any darkness in all of my days," he said.

"I know," said the Athelonian, gently comforting his little colleague, "but this, my dear friend, is what we must do. This is why we are Kungerods. We protect and guide our lovely world."

"I know," said the Vernacian, "I know."

The Athelonian went on, "Think, my friends, think. We only have to view the images, but our lord Pell must face the darkness." He paused, then said loudly, "Alone." They all looked up sadly. "Shall we continue?" asked the Athelonian. They all concurred.

The inner globe came to life with images, legends, symbols and characters, like a golden network. Then the globe went dark. Everything ceased. Nothing, no activity. The Kungerods rose in stunned amazement. They looked to the Athelonian for guidance, "Wha, what happened?" they all began asking, their faces confounded.

The Athelonain motioned with his hands. "Calm yourselves, my brethren, calm yourselves. I know what has happened," he assured them. "You see, only our lord the king can access this subject. His imprint on the globe will bring it to life. He alone may access the knowledge of darkness." With that they retired.

• • • • • • •

Both philbees made their way past the harbor area to the guest settlements. Everything past this area was off limits to visitors. No one was allowed to venture inland on Patamodia except Patamodians and, of course, Pell and his party. In the world of Agrimore, there was no such thing as intercontinental tourism. Everyone was content with their own continent and there were no curiosity seekers nosing their way into the affairs of other nations as on Earth, where there were cohorts of noisy, nosy tourists pointing at this and that, depositing their waste in other lands, infuriating natives, exasperating officials and pillaging artifacts germain to the places they visited. These activities have resulted in thievery, wars, murders and rapine. Hordes and hordes of invaders stepping on everything, sneering at customs, loud buffoonates seeking how to take advantage of those that were not as astute in the art of larceny and flim flam. Their women were laden with lusts and forbidden passions. Fantasizing about the bizarre, the profane and the exotic mores of sheltered jungle dwellers. They were cargos of abominations to a primitive society, which in reality were more civilized. By the time they'd finished, the buffoonates and dirt hags had carried away the most precious artifacts of each culture they had visited. Another misery of Earth.

The continent of Patamodia was filled with gigantic fauna, exotic trees, vines as thick as pines, olive groves with olives as large as beach balls, large, translucent, white melons, multicolored grapes the size of baseballs, plants that produced leather stronger and more beautiful than animal coverings and rich-red pine forests. Breath-taking falls short in description, even the aromas in the air caused the most wondrous dreams.

On the outskirts of the harbor area, they espied the establishment called the Maiden's Beard. It was a large and busy tavern with a stone and wood floor. It looked like a cathedral transformed into a beer hall, complete with flying buttresses, rafters and ornate metal lamps hanging from the high ceiling. There was a wide walkway from the entrance to the main bar. The stone walkway had two high railings on each side made of wood. The bar was high, like a police bench. The place was teeming with patrons – Tendrats, Hogomeans and an array of characters you would find in a Dickens novel, crews from all over Agrimore, Athelonians, Can-Chimerans, Ilgestanians and Vernacians. All eyes were on the group as they walked in.

· · · · · · ·

They walked up to the high bar, as the bar tender buzzed them in, as part of the railing swung open. They made their way into the center of the great hall, with all eyes still fixed on them. There were female and male seafarers, officers, officials and a host of serving girls rushing about.

Then a very wiry man appeared. He had a thin, scaline face and nose, with comical bushy eyebrows. His hair was brown, bushy and uncombed. His garb was rather tattered, a blend of thick tweeds of green and maroon. His jacket had a large lapel with a fur outline. His pants were wrinkled and tight on the cuffs, with funny-looking strapped high boots that appeared two sizes larger than his feet. He approached the group and stared, looking at them up and down. "Pell Provance party?" he asked in a coarse, elfish tone. Pell nodded warily at the strange figure. "The names Faengle," the man offered. "I've a table reserved just for us." He led them through a myriad of characters, all staring at the out-of-place group. They settled themselves at a table by the back wall, with a candle lantern flickering and dispensing violet and orange lights that played off of their faces. They sat around the table, waiting for Faengle to cue the conversation.

Faengle looked over the round table at them smiling to himself and said, "My, my, my. I've been waiting for the group that has caused such a stir in Agrimore and here you are before my eyes. I mean, everything is astir because of you lot. Kungerods, specially reserved freightliners and Crofty Bellar anxious for your arrival. Official permission to travel anywhere you wish and everything at your disposal," he concluded. The entire establishment was quiet with fascination, whispering about the strangers that visited their noisy perlee center. Faengle raised his right hand and immediately three young serving girls rushed to the table, all giggling and looking at Pell.

Cremy rolled her eyes. "Oh, blast," she moaned. "Here we go again." Pell didn't react to the attention he received and ignored Cremy's comment.

Grista smiled at him and whispered in his ear, "My love is most desirable." She loved the attention he received because he was hers and no one else's. The girls came to Pell first to take his order and he directed them to take his order last. They all ordered perlees and broiled acalard leaves, filled with muttrish, which was a Patamodian delight. Faengle sipped his perlee with great pleasure, with foam settling on his thin nose. They were all amused by the comical figure of a man.

"Well, my sweethearts," he said, looking up from his perlee, "it is my and your pleasure for me to guide you to the town of Applendice to meet the ever incomparable Crofty Bellar. We will leave at your pleasure," he concluded.

There was a commotion two tables away. Serving plates and perlees went sprawling across the floor in the direction of the group's table. Pell turned and looked over his left shoulder to see what the matter was. He noticed two large figures facing off against each other. One of the men, a large Can-Chimeran, caught a glimpse of Pell. The man, a crewman from one of the docked freightliners, had black, full hair parted in the center and pony-tailed, deep-set dark eyes with thick black brows, a rather bulbous nose and thin lips with slight growth around the edges. He had the distinctive Can-Chimeran look, which was at first appearance similar to Asian and Spanish.

"What are you looking at, mate?" the big man said, directing his comment at Pell. Pell ignored the man. The man moved closer and stared at the back of Pell's head. "I said, what are you looking at?" Pell continued to ignore the man. Faengle began cowering in fear. Grista was set to lunge. Pell steadied her with his hand, still ignoring the man. "Ignore me, will you?!" the man shouted, enraged and began moving closer to Pell.

Gully rose from his seat, smiling at the imposing man. He walked slowly around the table, never taking his eyes off of the man. Gully was also an imposing figure. Darvin watched the scene, poised as a leopard preparing to strike. Grista was uneasy, shifting in her seat, with Pell's hand calming her. Gully made his way to position himself between Pell and the Can-Chimeran. "What's all the fuss about, mate?" he asked, trying to allay the man's anger.

"Get out of my way, mate!" shouted the man. "I want that one there," he said, pointing at Pell, "to turn around and face me!" Pell continued to ignore the man, infuriating him. Gully moved closer to the Can-Chimeran, with all eyes fixed on the two large men.

The Can-Chimeran threw a blow at Gully's face. Gully, surprisingly fast for a man of his size, ducked under the outstretched arm and took a step past the man, holding the outstretched wrist. He then directed a sharp and telling blow with his elbow into the big man's ribs. Still holding the arm, he swung the big man around and projected an open palm, smashing into the big man's mouth and nose. The man's knees buckled, as if they were filled with jello and he sat down on the floor in a heap. Pell turned to Gully, looked up at him and smiled. "Artfully done, my good friend," he said.

Two big attendants rushed over to the crumpled man and hastily escorted him out of the premises. Gully sat down, with Darvin smiling in approval and Twilly wrapping her arms around the large girth of his waist, her eyes looking adoringly up at him. Faengle, feeling secure in the presence of these titans, ordered another round for everyone. The place went back to normal, with noisy conversations and rushing serving girls. After finishing their perlees, they all rose together to leave. The serving girls rushed to ask Pell as to their service and sneak some flirtatious glances. Faengle walked proudly through the hall in the company of such honored guests. He wanted everyone to see that he was the guide of this group.

Chapter 28

PATAMODIA

They entered the philbees with Faengle riding with Pell and Grista, who was slightly disappointed, wanting to cajole and frolic with Pell. As they left the harbor area, they were astonished at the thick and beautiful fauna of Patamodia – plants that glowed at night lighting the roadway, fascinating and beautiful insect life that seemed to take a curious interest in travelers. No one swatted or killed these creatures as on Earth, for they were not at war with the inhabitants. In fact, they seemed to show some small affection for the occupants of Patamodia. The smells were wondrous, as they passed the Ocla forests of purple oak-like trees.

Patamodia was teeming with natural life, in complete cooperation with the natives. They even understood the constructed limits of highways and cities, never intruding past their borders, as if a treaty was signed between the natural and manufactured, each one respecting the other without tension. The more Pell saw of this world, the more he loved it. His face was set like flint that nothing, no matter how dark, was going to harm this world. He was anxious to get to Pathenune and deal with whatever darkness was threatening the twin worlds of Agrimore and Algenmere. Then there were his friends. Grista he knew would be safe, but Darvin, Gully, Cremy and Twilly would be at great risk. By no means would he lose his friends, even at the cost of his life.

The city of Applendice appeared on the horizon. First, there was a wonderful natural archway that welcomed travelers into the city. Two massive Torennite trees formed the arch, entwining their massive vines above the roadway, like two lovers embracing. These trees were grayish-green in color and about a hundred times the size of an oak with yellow, white and magenta shoots. These trees would occasionally dislodge one of their massive branches and grow a new one, sort of a peace offering for the inhabitants. One branch would take about eighteen tractor trailers to move.

Applendice was a stunning city, with many pastel-colored buildings because of the warm and moist climate of Patamodia. There were wonderful turquoise-colored, teapot-shaped structures, with subtle red lights inside. Others were ice blue, some orange and white, some lavender, all distinctively shaped, like toys one would find in a child's bedroom. The city was lush with Pacalanta trees. Pacalanta trees were similar to palms, except had leaves and branches spiraling up the trunk. The green and violet leaves of the Pacalanta trees emitted a rich, heady, intoxicating aroma at night, that seemed to encourage the erotic arts of love making.

The city was teeming with inhabitants – beautiful orange-hued men and women stronger and thicker than the inhabitants of Athelone because of the climate. Everything was festive, filled with color and life, with beautifully decorative awnings, banners and floating Retazuna plants. These Retazuna plants would float just above the rooftops. They looked like large, multicolored balloons with sparklers inside. Some were round, others ovoid. They would continuously visit Applendice. They were traveling pollinating seeds.

"I've never in my life imagined anything like this!" exclaimed Gully, looking around at the sights, completely overwhelmed. Twilly and Cremy were speechless, just staring out of the philbee at the slightly-clad inhabitants.

Grista looked at Pell and asked, "You know what this place produces, don't you?" Oh, Pell knew. Oh did he know, but tried to shake off her question. She began poking his ribs. "Come on," she said playfully, smiling erotically. "You know."

"Grista, stop," he whispered, acting annoyed. Then she put her mouth tightly next to his ear and began making Grista sounds of "Mmm, grr." Then she said, "This is the place for yum, yum, yum."

Faengle, who was operating the philbee, said, "The lady's correct, sir. This is the place of all that she said and much, much more. Look at them," he said, laughing pointing to some of the female inhabitants. "Why, they're designed for pleasure. Besides the exporting of exotic plant life, their main production is pleasure, which they do not export. A paradise of the senses," he said, pointing at the most alluring creature standing near a bakeshop. Her orange skin like a rich tan, with copious curves, woven gold hair, pomegranate-colored lips and silver-colored eyes filled with lightening as the colors of the city reflected off of them. But for all of their beauty, Grista was still the queen of all females in beauty and sensuality.

Grista began nuzzling her body against Pell's rhythmically, as a cat does when showing affection, making "Mmm" sounds and kissing her beloved's eyes.

"Grista, stop," whispered Pell. "Think of Faengle. It's not proper with him here," said Pell, assuming he was alone.

"It's quite all right, sir," said Faengle. Pell was astonished at the man's acute hearing. "I have my sweetie back at the Maiden's Beard," he said with a broad smile.

The inhabitants of the Earth would appear anemic and sickly next to Patamodians. Even their blood was vitally charged and fast. The blood had a silver substance mixed in, and if their skin was cut, the blood would find its way back into the cut, closing the wound behind itself.

• • • • • • •

They parked the philbees and decided to walk the rest of the way past the throngs of scantily-clad orange inhabitants who would nod at them courteously and stare at Pell and Grista. Though they were an attractive race, they'd never seen the likes of Pell and Grista. The group made their way up a narrow, winding street higher and higher, passing the most adorable homes and shops. Faengle was leading the way to Crofty Bellar's place. "I would not recommend you staying out too long at night," warned Faengle. "The atmosphere becomes more and more irresistibly erotic," he said, laughing. The handsome inhabitants would occasionally come to their doorsteps and greet the passing travelers.

A gorgeous little silver-haired girl ran up to them and said, "My mommy and daddy asked me to tell you if you're thirsty to come with me right there," pointing at a lovely little home that looked like a child's spin top. They decided to follow the child, who immediately took Grista's hand. She led them up the stairs of the top-shaped home where the child's parents were waiting. They smiled and escorted the group into their home.

"I'm Forste," said the handsome Patamodian, "and this is my glory, Corindel," he said, gesturing to his wife. The woman was silver haired with silver brows and lashes, a perfectly-shaped nose and extravagant magenta lips. She had a delicate choker of turquoise and fine gold adorning her neck and was wearing a matching sarong that caressed her marvelous body. She wore an engraved silver armlet on her upper left arm, with a piece of beautiful blue fabric hanging down past her legs. She was clad with silver sandals. This woman would have closed every beach on Earth with men trying to catch a glimpse of her.

Forste had the appearance of an ancient Egyptian prince, but was far more stunning as a man. He was tall with hair of spun silver. A thin gold head band enhanced the beauty of his brow. His brows and lashes were also thick silver. He had violet and orange eyes and a full, strong nose. His lips were pink and sensual, with handsome dimples bordering them. He had a strong, well-defined neck and shoulders. His powerful chest was bare, with a plated silver necklace hanging over it. Around his muscular waist was a plated silver belt holding a blue-green tunic. His feet were also shod with silver sandals. There was also a large silver wristband on his left arm. They both nodded courteously and welcomed the visitors into their home.

Cremy and Twilly were having trouble trying not to stare at the handsome figure of Forste, trying to occupy themselves by looking around the house. The couple invited them to sit, with Corindel staring at Pell and Forste focusing on Grista. Corindel reached over and put her fingers through Pell's massive black mane. "Beautiful!" she exclaimed with wonder, touching his exquisite face. She then looked over at her husband, who was completely enthralled by Grista.

"Marvelous," he said, looking up and down at Grista. "Oh, forgive us. You must be thirsty after your walk," said Forste, who joined his wife in the kitchen to prepare some frosty cordials for their guests.

"Well, I don't even know if we were actually here!" shot Cremy.

"Yes, it's rather unsettling," said Twilly.

"Didn't it bother you to have that woman fawning over Pell?" shouted Cremy to Grista.

"Sssh, keep your voice down," Grista warned. "They may overhear you."

"Well?" whispered Cremy. "Didn't it bother you?"

"No, of course not. In fact, it was kind of nice to see someone so beautiful admiring my love. Forste was admiring me," she added, "and it didn't disturb Pell, did it, my love?" she asked.

"No, my queen," he said. "Anyone who admires you, honors me."

"You two are so weird," said Cremy.

"Not at all," offered Gully. "I understood it perfectly."

"Mr. Pell and Miss Grista understand it perfectly," added Faengle, knowing the mores and customs of Patamodia. "They were both honoring and admiring them. There was nothing disorderly about what they did." He went on, "In fact, they were giving them one of the greatest honors that Patamodians can give."

Forste and Corindel emerged from the kitchen area carrying two trays of frosty, creamy, ice blue and orange cordials. They both inquired as to their destination. When they heard that they were on their way to Crofty Bellar's, they looked at each other with awe. "Why we've heard rumors of travelers coming to Patamodia, travelers of great rank. We are so honored," said Forste.

"Well, how could we resist the invite of that little beauty over there?" asked Grista, pointing at the quiet little girl sitting in the corner. The little one smiled warmly at Grista.

Forste went over and picked her up on his shoulder and spoke to her. "Hear what the beautiful lady said about you?" he asked. The little girl nodded, sticking her finger in her mouth. Grista asked to hold the child, which the father proudly gave her.

"Listen," offered Corindel, "it's going to be evening soon, so if you would like, after you have met with Crofty, we would be honored if all of you would spend the night with us. We could show you some of the sites of our beautiful city. By your leave, my love," she said, turning to her husband for approval.

Forste grew with excitement. "Oh, yes, yes! Please, we have more than enough room. I, myself," he went on, "was hesitant to ask, but I thank my lovely wife for her boldness. Please, I beg of you. You would make us so happy if you would return here." Pell agreed and the group took their leave until later.

Faengle was happy with the events and said, "You know that the greatest honor a Patamodian can show is to ask you to abide in his home for the night. To Patamodians it is very significant, for it means friendship for life and all they possess is yours," he smiled.

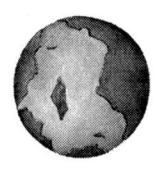

Chapter 29

A NIGHT TO REMEMBER

They continued up the winding, spiraling street until they came to a small estate with a wooden gate, at the end of the street. They unlatched the gate and walked up a stone path, surrounded by all sorts of flowers and a thick blue-green lawn with little stone seats hidden here and there, similar to a grotto. They approached a Chatham blue door with a small window and knocked. There was a voice inside which shouted, "Be right down!" They could hear footsteps running down the stairs and the door opened. Standing in the doorway was Crofty Bellar, a rather large blonde-haired woman, with a contagious smile. "Come in, darlings," she said with glee, looking over the group, then walking over to Pell looking intently at him. Turning to Faengle, she said, "Please, Faengle, help yourself to anything in the kitchen and pantry."

She invited the group into the parlor and sat herself across from Pell and Grista. "Well, well, well," she went on, "the enchanting Pell Provance and the beautiful lady Grista." Then, turning to the others, she said. "You must be Cremona and you Twilly." Then turning to the men she said, "Ah, the courageous Darvin and faithful Gully. Well, I'm so happy to finally meet all of you." Then she turned and shouted towards the kitchen, "Faengle, would you put on the caone?!"

Faengle stuck his head out of the kitchen. "Already done love," he said.

"Well, let me look at all of you. My, my," she went on enthusiastically, "The whole world abuzz with your exploits." She then lit a puigo and offered the box to the group. The men helped themselves, with the women declining. They puffed quietly for a few moments, waiting for the hot-brewed caone that Faengle was preparing. Faengle entered the room with the millstern, which brewed the caone and a tray of china. He then excused himself, retiring to the kitchen to avail himself of Crofty's delicacies, which he loved.

"Well, my sweeties, I must langline the Kungerods at Pathenune and then arrange transportation for you, but it's late and that can be done in the morning. In the meantime, I've a large house with plenty of bedrooms. So why don't we retire until the morning?" Pell related to Crofty about Forste and Corindel and about spending the evening with them. She was impressed and said, "I know them both. They're descendants of a great line of mighty ones of Patamodia, going back thousands of cycles. For them to open their home to you is no small honor. Please go, don't let me hinder you. You're in for an unforgettable evening."

They left Crofty's small manor and trekked back down the spiraling street to the home of Forste and Cordindel. The beautiful couple came out as they approached. There were two other couples with them. They wanted to show off their newfound friends. As they approached the house, their friends were stunned, the males by Grista and the females by Pell. The two males surrounded and stared at Grista adoringly, admiring every nuance of her face and body. The females slowly approached Pell, looking at each other with astonishment, studying every detail of his face and form, but not touching him. That was a liberty that only Corindel could take, the same with Grista and Forste. Pell and Grista seemed to understand this custom completely and were completely comfortable with it.

Corindel took Grista, Twilly and Cremona into the house to share her splendid wardrobe with them. Forste invited Pell, Darvin and Gully to his wardrobe. Corindel and her friends helped the girls disrobe. All were astonished with Grista's great beauty. They swabbed their bodies with orange Apicella leaves, which were used by all of the women of Patamodia. They gently applied the leaves, until every inch was covered. In a few moments, their skin began taking on a golden hue. Corindel and her friends smiled in approval. Corindel gently removed a translucent blue bulb from a plant nearby. She squeezed the bulb, surrendering the most fragrant light blue liquid. The other women did the same, but she alone would apply this to Grista. She approached Grista and slowly, bent down before her and applied the rare fragrance to every inch of her glorious body, beginning with her feet and legs. Corindel began humming a melody never heard by Grista or the others. The sound made her limp, more relaxed than she had ever been. It was a melody from one queen to another.

Corindel continued admiring every inch of Grista's superb body, adoringly applying the sultry liquid. Then, looking deeply into Grista's eyes, the beautiful Corindel kissed her forehead. Grista felt warm with emotion and sensations arising within her that she hithertofore had never experienced. She was almost overcome.

Then Corindel and her friends opened the wardrobe, revealing a collection of garments that would give a different name to global warming. These worn by Grista could set a world aflame. Corindel chose a garment that was the deepest brown Grista had ever seen. It had gold embroidery and trim. Corindel smiled, as she approached Grista and began carefully wrapping the glorious garment around her. She covered the upper part of her legs, wrapping twice then three times, then pinning at the hip with a silver broach that had a shimmering orange stone set in the center. Everyone in the room was stunned with Grista's beauty as she began to glisten. Corindel then took the matching part of the garment and began covering her breasts and upper arms, wrapping the garment slowly as she whispered, "I have never been the presence of such comprehensive loveliness and uniformity," her eyes glistening, as if filling with tears.

The others were silent, as they watched the two queens. Grista was growing in beauty and stature. The more her beauty was admired, the greater her beauty became. After Corindel had clipped earrings that matched the brooch, she pulled a chest out of a draw. Inside was a tiara of fine gold, set delicately with the most precious stones. She set this carefully upon her golden head, then bowed before her.

Forste and his friends were busy with Pell, Darvin and Gully. Forste looked at Pell's naked form and remarked, "Sinewy, mighty, wrought of tempered steel and the strength of a Targamar." Forste referred to a mythical beast that roamed the heavens laying waste to star systems. Forste helped him apply the Apicella leaves to his body, as his friends did with Darvin and Gully. Pell's skin glistened like Grista's. Every nuance of his magnificent physique became visible, with Forste admiring a mighty warrior, a king. Pell's eyes flashed and sparkled when he thought of his queen, the beauty of his manhood increasing as he grew in love for her. Forste carefully removed a bright red bulb from a plant. He spread the liquid on his hands, slapped them together, then briskly applied it to Pell's face, giving him the bulb so he could applied it to the rest of his body. The aroma was extremely masculine and captivating, enough to incite a rebellion in the body of every woman on Earth.

Then Forste took an indigo-blue tunic with a silver border and firmly wrapped it around Pell's waist, fastening it with a thin spun silver belt. Then he took a crimson garment long, like a robe, but tightened with a silver ring that sat on the wearers shoulder. He placed it over Pell's left shoulder, crossed it over his bare chest and clipped it to his right hip, with the rest hanging loosely down by his muscular legs.

Then Forste looked at him firmly, king to king, walked to his draw and pulled out a chest that contained a most beautiful gold headband, with a precious blue stone in the center. He placed it around Pell's handsome forehead, then bowed on one knee, showing him great honor. They were ready.

Corindel led the glistening Grista, full of splendor, by the hand, with all the other girls following after as a queen's entourage. She continued to lead her to the front steps, as if to present her to Applendice, both women full of wonder and majesty waiting for their consorts. Forste led Pell by the arm, with Darvin and Gully following. As they approached the waiting women, Grista's heart melted within her, as she beheld her beloved. She was speechless at his magnificent beauty and strength. Pell stood stunned captivated by the splendor of Grista. He thought to himself, Is this the light of creation? The deep caverns of Cronox could not withstand her glory. This, he thought, is my glory. Grista, the beautifying factor of my life. A tear descended down Pell's cheek, as he beheld his queen. She, being moved by the sight of this, approached him and drank the tear. Everyone was silent, as if they were in the presence of something sacred, holy, even the worlds must have stopped in their orbits at this moment. The universe stood still to behold the spectacle. Grista then broke the silence, smiling mischievously at Pell and gently gnawing on his well-defined shoulder. They began to laugh and continued down the stairs onto the winding spiraling street towards Applendice.

As the custom was, Forste took Grista, placing his arm around her exquisite waist and Corindel put her arm around Pell's waist, looking up adoringly at him. Cremy still didn't fully understand this, but kept silent nonetheless. Gully smiled, understanding it perfectly.

The six couples made their way past the onlookers towards Applendice, windows filling with onlookers beholding the wonder of this most enchanting entourage. The night was sultry and erotic. As they entered the festive city, the Pacalanta plants were beginning to open, emitting their erotic mixture. They walked past cafes and pondora clubs, which were filled with Patamodian dancers. The group walked into one of the Pandora clubs. The music was erotic and heady, quite intoxicating. The club was full of couples, lovers all, husbands and wives. When the six couples entered, the music immediately stopped. As everyone made way for the entourage, everyone nodded their head respectfully, paying homage to Forste and

Corindel. Corindel held Pell and presented him to all of the merrymakers, as did Fortse with Grista. They then did the same with the others. Everyone stood in amazement at Pell and Grista. Both were clothed in splendor and grace. Forste motioned them to continue the gaiety.

The music changed and began a slow, rhythmic, climbing, deep-toned, fast-fugue, rising in sound, climbing to a frenzying crescendo. Forste grabbed the glistening Grista, purple and blue lights shimmering off of her glorious form. Forste bent her backward until she was kneeling on one leg. The two began a dance that would be described as a ritualistic rhapsody, inflaming all that watched the couple. Forste grabbed Grista by the ankles and swung her high into the air, catching her on his broad shoulders. Grista sat on Forste's shoulders, swinging her head rhythmically with the music. She then slowly snaked her way down his chest, her legs wrapped around his mighty frame, until she reached the floor, snaking away, then bending her body in a perfectly-shaped, upside-down "U." She flipped herself to her feet. The onlookers stood there quiet, astonished and not sure what they had just witnessed. Grista stood there in composite beauty and majesty, with Forste bowing before her on one knee.

The lights then turned on Pell and Corindel. The music was different, slow and deep tones, much richer, with the sounds vibrating off of the frames of Pell and Corindel. The lovely silver-haired queen approached him, staring intently into his eyes, as the music gained momentum. She circled him, slowly drinking in his wondrous form. As the music rose, she grabbed his massive black mane, pulling him backward. He complied with her, settling down on one knee as the ravishing Corindel swung her body around him, stalking him menacingly, as if she were a lioness preparing to lunge, the music still rising to a flaming crescendo. It was a conflagration of complete ecstasy, maddening and dizzying, the onlookers aghast at the spectacle. Then Corindel climbed his shoulders from behind, while he was still on one knee, her exquisite legs wrapped tightly around his arms and chest. The music still rising, Pell stood up with the woman still locked around his form. Then she preformed a maneuver that could be described as Olympic. She leaned forward and threw herself down Pell's chest, her silver hair swinging in the orange and red lights, grabbing him around the waist and snaking under his legs, ending up behind him. Then she rhythmically walked around Pell, smiling sensually. Pell grabbed her hard, pulled her close to him, then lifted her around the waist higher into the air until her feet were in his palms. He turned around slowly, the woman now high in the air, as if presenting the queen for all to admire.

Grista and Forste were enthralled by this maneuver. Some of the female patrons had fainted. The music came to a slow finale and the lights dimmed, cueing him to lower Corindel. Corindel then bowed before him, with Forste and Grista smiling in approval. Crofty Bellar was right, thought Pell. It was an unforgettable evening.

Cremy looked at Darvin. She was astonished. "Did you see that spectacle?!" she exclaimed, trying to contain herself.

Darvin shook his head. "I don't understand this."

Gully, overhearing them, came over and put his arm around both of their shoulders and asked, "Something troubling you two?"

Cremy turned to Gully. "Don't tell me that didn't bother you," she said sharply.

Gully smiled. "Not at all. We officials we have records of the customs of all continents. This, though very rare, is the dance of Monarchs. No greater honor can be given, but," Gully went on, "you think this is improper? Wait till you see the conclusion of the evening," said Gully laughing. Cremy looked annoyed. Twilly was at a loss.

Darvin shook his head and smiled. "It's just Pell," he said to himself.

The proprietor came over to the two couples, bowed and thanked them. Forste took Grista around the waist and asked, "Thirsty, my beauty?"

"Mmm yes," she said, always glancing over at Pell and smiling. Pell, who took the beautiful Corindel around the waist said, "My lady must be thirsty."

Corindel's eyes flashed and smiled broadly. "Oh, yes, my beautiful prince," she said and kissed him playfully on the cheek. Pell seemed to understand this custom perfectly and so did Grista. They had no apprehensions at all at this display of affection. It was a family matter that few understood.

• • • • • • •

Crofty Bellar was on the langline with the Athelonian. She was excited as she spoke to the Kungerod, "They're all here and they're having the evening of their lives. Oh! They're just adorable, all of them." She continued. "They're little babies," she laughed. "All of them look up to Pell. They don't take a breath, it seems, without his approval," she said, giggling.

"I think it's marvelous," the Athelonian laughed. "But remember, Crofty," he continued, "he is our king."

"I know," she laughed. "That's why it's so wonderful. He's absolutely adorable, and Grista," she added, taking a breath. "You have never seen such an unimaginable beauty in the entire creation!" Her voice rose with excitement.

"Did you say Forste and Corindel?" asked the Kungerod.

"Yes," she answered, "the most prominent couple in Patamodia," she concluded.

The Athelonian excused himself and rushed to gather his colleagues. They all rushed to the Pollidecreum and activated the inner globe. Legends, symbols and emblems appeared, golden lines threading their way illuminating sections of the globe. The Kungerods all looked at each other and smiled. "Forste and Corindel," said the Athelonian with excitement. "Why," he said, stuttering. "Why, he's Pell's brother!" he shouted and began laughing. The Pollidecreum was filled with laughter. They were all delighted.

"Corindel?" asked the Can-Chimeran. "She's Grista's Sister?" he asked, smiling. "Her great beauty betrays her."

"But how, how did they get to Patamodia?" asked the Vernacian.

"I think I'm beginning to understand," offered the Athelonian. "Pell's with us!" he shouted with enthusiasm. "He's an Agrimorian. He came home!" The atmosphere of the Pollidecreum became more celebratory. They were all elated, hugging and smiling, happier than they'd ever been.

• • • • • • •

Pell and Corindel walked out of the club arm in arm, Corindel looking at him. "Was I satisfactory, my sweet?" she asked, smiling.

Pell looked down at the wondrous woman, smiling with that captivating smile, which was uniquely Pell's. "You are a bottomless treasure chest of hidden delights, enough to enrich the man you're with eternally," he said, stroking her beautiful cheek. Corindel was delighted and honored to be with Pell. She put her arm around his waist and held him close, as they walked down the wondrous streets of Applendice. Grista and Forste emerged from the club, Grista filled with excitement from the dance. Forste looked at the exquisite beauty, admiring her as one would admire a newly discovered treasure which one dug for with much labor. There were new facets of Grista, new revelations of her beauty. He was pleased that she was with Pell. Anything less would not be worthy of her, he thought.

"Were you pleased with me, my lord?" asked Grista.

Forste turned to her, held her face with both hands and kissed her adoringly on the forehead. "A world of bards would not be sufficient to describe thy beauty, beloved," he said, smiling proudly. She grabbed Forste around his waist and walked, swinging her opulent body from side to side, forcing him to do the same.

Corindel, holding Pell's waist tightly, looked up at him. "Shall we proceed to the Island of Delights?" she asked, her eyes flashing wondrously, reflecting all the lights of Applendice.

Pell smiled, looking straight ahead. "Lead the way, my queen."

Corindel was pleased that Pell was with Grista. Only Grista could be a counterpart to this vision of splendor, she thought.

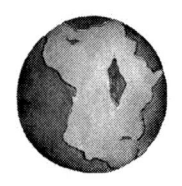

Chapter 30

THE ISLE OF DELIGHTS

They approached the harbor where a small, translucent, pearl-white boat was waiting. The two orange-gold rowers helped the couple aboard. After seating them, they slowly began rowing and singing an enchanting tune that only lovers could understand. Their voices were inexpressible, one high alto, the other basso. Corindel and Pell held each other tightly, as they slowly approached the Isle of Delights. Pell was astonished at the way the two moons of Agrimore shown solemnly on Corindel, delighting to play in her eyes and her silvery hair. Pell thought to himself that only Grista was her equal in beauty and majesty. Corindel seemed to sense Pell's thoughts and her beauty seemed to increase.

Forste and Grista approached the harbor, watching as the small boat carrying Corindel and Pell was well on its way. Grista felt so honored that her love was with Corindel. She, she thought, is the only one worthy to accompany my beloved. The vision of the two sailing in the Agrimorian moonlight gave her a sense of excitement and pleasure she had never known.

"Shall we join them?" asked Forste.

"Oh, yes, yes, please," she answered with enthusiasm.

Forste smiled. "As my queen wishes," he said softly, looking into her eyes. "I would gather even the stars for thy pleasure." The couple made their way to the dock where two orange-gold attendants bowed in honor of them. The two attendants helped the couple into the boat, which shimmered like an indigo-blue gem. They rowed slowly and sang an indescribable ode to the two glories. Grista was being transformed, her beauty intensifying and the moonlight of Agrimore also remembered her. The two blue companions were anxious to shine their light and discover her great beauty. Forste was almost overwhelmed by the spectacle, beauty redefined, laws changed to accommodate the wonder. Silently he bowed, placing his head into his hands.

Cremy, Darvin, Twilly and Gully with the two Patamodian couples emerged from the club looking for Pell and Grista. "I saw them leave," Cremy said, looking up and down the main street.

"I think they went towards the harbor," offered Gully.

They made their way to the dock where they saw the small boat carrying Grista and Forste in the distance, slowly making its way to the Isle of Delights. As Cremy began to rush towards the dock, Gully grabbed her arm and shook his head. "Let go!" she shouted.

Darvin grew alarmed and asked, "What's going on, mate?"

"We can't follow them," Gully said sternly. Cremy broke away from Gully's grip and rushed towards the dock. She was met by two large orange-gold attendants, who blocked her way without saying a word. Darvin came up behind Cremona and gently led her away. He walked her up to the group and apologized to Gully for his anger towards him.

• • • • • • •

The Kungerods were all having their evening repast, laughing and enjoying themselves. It was unusual to see such jocularity and good humor amongst Kungerods, who had a tendency to be dower. They were discussing the past events concerning Pell and Grista and their friends, looking forward to meeting all of them.

• • • • • • •

The small, pearl-colored boat containing Pell and Corindel landed on the shore of the afore spoken of isle. The stones around the beach area shown in the moon's blue light, oval-shaped, pink and pearl white, translucent stones. As they made their way to the beach hand in hand, there before them stood a very tall and wide wall of thick, green, impenetrable leaves in perfect uniformity to one another. Corindel looked up at Pell, smiled, then gently touched one of the leaves. The leaf responded as if it knew Corindel's touch and opened, flattening itself before them. They made their way onto the leaves into, as it were another world. The translucent blue stone path seemed to come alive beneath their feet, as they made their way to the center part of the leafy citadel, which was glowing with warmth beneath them, inviting them. As they continued to walk, the great crystalline Cartalasae trees came alive with light and color, shimmering as the crystal filled with liquid, brightening the whole island with majestic light. Bright blue, silver-pink, indescribable clear light flashed off of the bodies of the two visitors.

The entrance was guarded by two massive blue glass pillars perfect in symmetry. The pillars silently separated as the two entered. Six small figures approached the two. Pell wasn't sure what they were. They appeared to be children, but were composed of clear supple, soft glass. They knew Corindel and smiled as they approached. Corindel bent down to greet a little female figure. The little girl was lovely, her glass hair soft and combed back in a pony tail. She introduced Pell to the children, as Pell knelt to meet them. They loved to touch his thick mane, smiling to each other as they fingered lightly his features. The leader of this group whispered in Corindel's ear. "He's beautiful, isn't he?" she asked.

"Oh my, yes," Corindel said, looking admiringly at Pell. "He's a great king," she whispered softly. "Pell," said Corindel, "this is Perselana and her friends." Pell bowed courteously to the little girl and her friends. Then they took the couple by the hand and led them to the center of the isle. Forste and Grista were slowly catching up to Pell and Corindel.

After they reached the center, the children left them to meet Forste and Grista. The center of the isle was bathed in velvety-violet and dark turquoise light. Off in the distance, they could see two tables set, one to the right and the other to the left. Corindel and Pell made their way to the table on the right, walking over light blue sand, which was sprinkled with gold. The table was set on a platform of pearl with ivory-like steps. The table was of a thick blue, marvelously shaped glass, with a gold-glass goblet in the center, holding a silver spiral-shaped flame. The platform was about eight feet in length with a turquoise wall to the right side. To the right of the platform, was a small corridor of colored glass, which led to a small bedroom, dark with blue and purple glass and a background of stars. Off to the side was a bed, the base of which was made of a glowing white crystal as was the headboard. The mattress and pillows, if you could call them that, were made of soft, wonderful glass, royal blue in color. It was the bed of crowns.

Pell and Corindel made their way up the platform. Pell then pulled back a seat for Corindel. The seat was of wrought silver with a soft white glass cushion. After seating, the two stared into each other's eyes. He was enchanted by the woman's silver and violet eyes, her beautiful silver hair, full and rich magenta lips, her skin shimmering as only Grista's could. She is an overwhelming beauty, Pell thought. They stared at each other silently, penetrating and discovering hidden treasures in one another.

A glass figure approached the preoccupied couple and courteously bowed. Like the children, he was composed of glass, but his color was dark blue. In spite of this, they could see every detail of his handsome face. He was wearing a turquoise glass tunic, wrapped in the center with a thin belt of golden glass with sandals of the same composition. His voice was rich and melodic.

Just then Forste and Grista were walking across the light blue sand, smiling at them. Perselana and her friends were at the entrance, watching and giggling. Forste and Grista seated themselves across the sand on the left side. The glass attendant spoke to Pell and Corindel. "I'll be attending to all of your highnesses needs this evening. I am called Diamine," he offered courteously. "I will return with your Hormeciles."

Pell was at a loss as to what this was. Corindel, noticing his questioning eyes, began to explain to him what a Hormecile was. She looked at him reassuringly. "The Hormecile," she said, "is a brew for potentates beloved. It is an exotic beverage of herbs for regals," she added. "It will dislodge memories, sensations, fears and indescribable erotic propensities." Diamine returned with the Hormeciles in deep red, glass chalices, trimmed with gold rims with golden emblems embossed on the sides.

They both lifted their goblets and sipped slowly. The drink was bitter, heady and mind numbing. His head began spinning, everything swirling around him. Corindel leaned over to assure and comfort him. He began thinking of Drue and the way he was drugged by her, wondering if this was to be his fate again. Then he remembered that Grista was close by. He was safe. Corindel stood up and grabbed Pell's hand and led him to the dark, velvety bedroom. She steadied him as she pulled back the liquid-glass blanket. She helped him to lie down, then laid next to him, holding him close to her as he began his descent into his mind.

Memories and visions began rushing through his mind. Corindel continued to hold him tightly, sensing his apprehension, her strong arms comforting him, as he kept descending to worlds upon worlds, thousands of cycles past. Images of unimaginable destruction, decay, Thermedytes, the Earth and hosts of other worlds. But Grista, always Grista, there on every world. He saw himself crowned with majesty and power, with Grista his queen by his side. When he saw Forste and Corindel, he began to understand. Corindel continued to hold him tightly, as he passed through the eons of his life. Then he saw Agrimore and Algenmere and he understood, home. A feeling of warmth and comfort replaced the apprehension he felt. His body relaxed and went limp. Corindel, sensing this, loosened her grip. He opened his eyes and looked at the ravishing figure next to him. He smiled at her, understanding what she had done for him and who she was. He lifted himself, resting on one arm, and said softly, "How can I ever thank you?"

She touched his lips with her finger. "Sssh. We will speak later, when Forste and Grista are finished." He understood what she had done, that she was Grista's sister and that Grista could not have performed this because she, too, had to remember. Also, she had been with him. Part of Pell was in Corindel, as with Forste and Grista. They were a royal family, apart for eons upon eons.

Pell kissed Corindel gently on her lips and said, "You are worthy, forever worthy." She became filled with honor, resplendent in her glory.

The two couples emerged from their rooms. Grista's eyes filled with tears as she rushed towards Corindel, her sister, holding her and not wishing to let go, filling her lovely face with kisses. Pell looked at Forste, his brother. Slowly, both mighty men drew closer to each other, studying each other, then flung themselves at each other. Forste held his dear lost brother in his massive arms tightly, a tear inching its way down his cheek. He kissed Pell's forehead. He had found his brother and would never, never again lose him. Grista and Corindel, still holding each other, turned cheek to cheek to look over at their kings and smiled at the two clutched men. Forste held his brother, his younger brother, protectively, securely, not wanting to let him go.

• • • • • • •

The Kungerods arose and followed the smell of the hot caone. They entered the kitchen area with all of the staff rushing about preparing for the days events. The Kungerods were still sleepy and shuffling about the kitchen picking on this and that, getting in the way of the chefs and being slightly disruptive. They had not slept most of the night, as they had been engrossed in jovial conversation. They wobbled their way to the kitchen anteroom and sat down, silently sipping their hot caone. The Vernacian was busy sipping his beverage as he looked up at the Athelonian. "Did any of us sleep last night?" The Athelonian looked around at the other sleepy Kungerods and yawned.

• • • • • • •

Darvin, Cremy, Gully, Twilly and the two Patamodian couples grew tired dancing and partying all night and dawn was approaching. They made their way back to Forste and Corindel's home, with the two Patamodian couples taking their leave. They entered the house and realized that Pell, Grista, Forste and Corindel had not returned. They looked in the bedroom to find the child sleeping with a Patamodian housekeeper.

• • • • • • •

The Kungerods were sitting quietly, drinking caone and eating pastries they had pillaged from the kitchen. The Athelonian noticed that the Vernacian was missing from amongst the group. He quietly rose in search of him. He made his way to the conference building and entered the Pollidecreum to find the Vernacian staring at an emblem on the activated globe. The Athelonain approached the globe. He looked up to see what the Vernacian was observing and saw a small, unusual emblem, which they had apparently overlooked. The Vernacian looked at his colleague and said, "You see it, don't you?"

"Yes, yes. How did we overlook this?" he asked.

"Well," answered the Vernacian, "we were all concentrating on the major emblems, that we had overlooked this little one."

"Fascinating!" exclaimed the Athelonian, still gazing at the emblem upon the globe.

• • • • • • •

Cremona sat next to Darvin, looking over at Gully and Twilly. Cremy yawned and droned, "When are they coming home?"

Darvin laid his head back, shut his eyes and groaned, "What a night. I don't think I've danced so much in my life."

Gully smiled and put his arm around Twilly. "What about you?" he asked.

"Me?" she asked. She stretched her arms in front of her and smiled at him. "I had a wonderful time," she swooned, placing her head on Gully's shoulder. "You," she added, "were wonderful."

He looked at her lovingly, "Oh, yeah?" he asked, wanting more.

"Mmm," she moaned, cuddling closer to him. She looked at him and whispered in his ear. "You move so well on the dance floor. For someone so big, you're so sensual in your moves," she said, nuzzling her head on his chest. Gully kissed her on her little boyish head and held her close.

Cremona looked at them visibly annoyed. Gully looked over at her, noticing her wrinkled brow, and sighed, "What is it Creme?" he asked.

She looked at him sternly. "I can't believe that everyone is all right with what happened last night."

"You mean about Pell and Corindel, don't you?" he asked rhetorically.

"Yes!" she shot back. "Why is it I'm the only one that has a problem with this?!"

"Yes, why?" asked Gully, sitting up and looking at Cremy. "Why do you have such a problem with it? You didn't take your eyes off of them until they left. Plus, you practically ignored poor Darvin over there," he said, reprimanding her.

Darvin awakened and raised his head, trying to shake off the dreariness. "What's going on, Creme?" he asked, staring at her. She put her head down and stared at the floor.

"Creme?" asked Gully softly.

"Yes, what's the trouble sweetie?" inquired Twilly.

"I don't know," she said softly, everyone straining to hear her.

Darvin put his arm around her and rubbed her back softly. "What is it, baby?" he asked concernedly.

"All right. All right. I'm jealous!" she shouted, sobbing. Everyone looked at each other. "Pell used to belong to us," she went on. "First it was Pell, Darvin and me. I felt so special back then. Then Grista came with Gully and Twilly. Oh please, don't misunderstand. I love you all and it felt cozy again with all of us. But now, Corindel?" her eyes widened. "I feel as if we're losing him."

Gully came over to sit on the other side of her and spoke gently, "Don't you understand? The type of person he is, we could never lose him. He loves us. I don't pretend to understand what's happening, but I know that this is part of the Pell Provance legend or saga. He's different from us, lovey, but I do know we will never lose him. We'll be together forever. I know," he continued, "that this encounter with Corindel is necessary and vital to him," Gully concluded.

Just then the door opened, with Corindel and Forste entering, followed by Pell and Grista. Cremy looked up at Pell. There was something different about him. Something had been added to him, transforming and enhancing his manliness. He was a more complete Pell Provance – stronger, mightier, kingly, overpoweringly attractive. Grista was beholding him, entranced by him. She was also transformed into, if possible, a more glorious queen, full of grace and beauty, yet more sensual and womanly.

Pell stood in the room, unable to take his eyes off of her, completely enthralled by her. She was a drink he could not put down. Corindel and Forste knew that the others were tired and showed them to their rooms. When the couple returned, they found Pell and Grista still staring at each other, silently paying homage to each other's greatness. Corindel smiled up at Forste, enjoying the spectacle. Forste quietly interrupted the solemnity of the moment. "Let us show you to your room," he asked softly. Grista took Pell's hand and swung it, as they climbed the stairs to the bedroom at the end of the hall. They both entered the darkened room, with Corindel and Forste quietly closing the door behind them.

They were alone in the dark. The scent of Grista overwhelmed Pell. His great strength began to leave him. He trembled, as he drew the unseen Grista to him, engulfed in darkness, her beauty pulsating and glowing through the darkness. He held her tightly and fell to his knees before her, offering fealty to his queen. Then he kissed her magnificent left leg, from her hip to her knee, composing every kiss, adorning her in the darkness. She, being overcome by him, bent over and kissed his beautiful aromatic mane, then crouched down in front of him. She grabbed his mane, being filled with ecstasy, and in controlled violence pulled him towards her, searching in the darkness for his lips with insatiable hunger taking possession of them. When she found them, their embrace was legendary. She was strong, trying to overpower him, but he was mightier, lifting her, their lips still sealed. Her heart pounded within her. As this mighty one carried her towards the bed, she was helpless in his grip, struggling to no avail, her wondrous eyes filled with tears, as her love carried her away to unknown worlds.

He found the bed and sat her down, holding her writhing body firmly with his might, but not saying a word. There was no speech allowed in this sacred grotto of delight. He encompassed her. Her limbs titillated with desire. She was his domain, his realm and she became subject to him, wonderfully surrounded, captivated and conquered by her king. Then he whispered to her, "After our coronation, my beloved."

She understood that the consummation of their love would have to be reserved until then. She moaned in acknowledgement, completely spent by her lover's mastery over her. "Mmm," she smiled. She adored him, but she thought to herself, I will bide my time, but I will yet overcome him and then slept sweetly in his arms.

Chapter 31

AN HOUR OF DESPAIR

The Athelonian gathered the other Kungerods to show them the emblem that had been overlooked. They entered the Pollidecreum. The Athelonian, leading them, pointed to the overlooked emblem. They all stared amazed that they had overlooked such an important feature. "Well, well! Now this is astounding!" exclaimed the Can-Chimeran. The female scanned the emblem with marked fascination. She turned and faced her colleagues.

"You look delighted, my dear," offered the Patamodian.

"This is exquisite," she remarked.

"So you see it?" asked the Atelonian.

She smiled. "Oh yes, my friends, oh yes. He not only focused the evil in the Earth dwellers, but," she glowed as she widened her eyes, "he increased every major factor in the royal seed." She continued, "Everything that was excellent, came to the forefront until they were filled with majesty. The inferior Earth dwellers were envious of them. At one time the commoners exalted themselves above them, but not now. Pell Provance increased them richly. Before that, the wretches were treating them with much contempt, glorying over them, mocking their royal lineage, spitting on them and even killing them. But, in steps our lord Pell and changes the game."

"Yes, quite marvelous," added the Can-Chimeran.

· · · · · · ·

The home of Forste and Corindel was alive with activity. Hot caone was being brewed. Corindel, with Forste assisting her, was preparing the morning repast. Forste wasn't much help. He just wanted to be close to his bride, nibbling and frolicking with her, as she tried to prepare for the day.

Grista was awake, studying her heart's desire. He was still asleep. She began playing with his nose and touching his lips, running stringy things across his face and blowing in his nose. She was filled with mischief as she imagined things to do with him while he was asleep. She climbed on him and straddled him, holding his arms firmly by his sides with her knees. Then she began tickling him ferociously. He awakened laughing hysterically, trying to dislodge her. "Grista, stop!" he shouted. He was lunging wildly with Grista riding him.

Corindel and Forste heard the wild goings on upstairs and laughed, as they heard the mighty Pell pleading for Grista to stop. Darvin and Gully awakened to all the noisy frolicking. Gully lifted himself against the backboard, with his hands clasped behind his head. He smiled at Darvin as they listened to the noisy gamboling and yelling from Pell and Grista's room. "She's the only one that could make Pell plead for mercy," laughed Gully.

Then they heard a door slam and someone running. It was Pell trying to get away from Grista. His hair was hanging down in front of his head, he was running and trying to tie his bathrobe. Corindel and Forste were holding their sides with laughter at the sight of Pell with the wild Grista chasing him. She caught him around the waist and kissed him, laughing intermittently as their lips met. "Grista, what are you doing to this poor child?" asked Corindel, laughing and trying to comb Pell's hair.

Forste put his arm around both of them, laughing. "Little babies having fun?" he asked.

Grista was looking up at Pell, giggling and saying in baby talk, "The bad, bad Grista, too tough for little Pell, hmmm? Comes downstairs so Forste and Corindel can protect you fwom me. Hmmm, my baby?" Pell was a mess. No female in creation could have made him look so unlike Pell Provance. Grista was capable of making him feel like a toddler. She was full of grace, beauty, and majesty. At the same time, she was playfully naughty, full of mischief. She would give him an eternity of delight and he loved it. Grista looked up at him, combing his hair with her hand and said, "Come on, my king, can't have everyone see you so scared of a little woman." She took his hand and led him back upstairs, smiling girlishly, her eyes twinkling.

Cremy and Twilly had their heads stuck out of the bedroom door and watched Grista leading Pell by the hand back to the bedroom, Pell looking apprehensive about what she would do next. Twilly laughed. "It's Grista. She's sooo bad," she said. "Poor Pell, he's in for a world of wild surprises."

• • • • • • •

Back on Pathenune, they were all busy preparing for the arrival of their king and queen. Everyone was rushing about: young men and women placing garlands over newly constructed archways; children with baskets full of flowers, placing them in designated areas; men carrying crystalline light poles, planting them along the paths where Pell and Grista would walk. In the huge kitchen, they were preparing delights of all five continents. The Kungerods were rehearsing their roles and speeches in anticipation for the arrival of the royal couple. It was the busiest day in the history of Pathenune.

• • • • • • •

Corindel and Grista were occupied dressing each other. Corindel opened a special chest of royal garments prepared for such a day, prepared for Grista. Forste took Pell into his room and brought out a large jeweled chest from the closet. "These are yours, my brother," he said, looking at Pell intently, handing him the chest. "This chest contains your royal armor to be worn at Pathenune."

Corindel was combing Grista's golden, curly hair. Corindel loved fussing over her sister. She was so proud of her sister, who was resplendent in beauty and she would never lose her again. Grista loved it when Corindel touched her. It made her feel warm, loved and cherished. She admired Corindel's great beauty. This is my sister, she thought. My flesh, spirit, and soul. Grista grabbed Corindel and held her tightly and whispered, "I'm so glad I've found you. I cannot imagine a moment not having you near me."

Corindel held Grista's beautiful head and kissed her tenderly on the forehead and said, "Until the ages of ages, I'll be close to you, my sister."

The group left together with Forste and Corindel for Crofty Bellar's. A philbee pulled up beside them, the occupant, a crew member of Purnis's terraspan. He opened the canopy and said, "Mr. Provance, your wardrobe has been delivered to Crofty Bellar's. Is there anything else, sir?"

Pell walked over to the philbee. "There are two chests at the home of Forste and Corindel," he said, pointing at the couple. "Would you be so kind and store them on your terraspan?"

"My pleasure, sir," the attendant answered and ran up the stairs of the house.

Forste looked handsome in his attire. He had Pell's taste, wearing a crème-colored blazer that was double-breasted with an exquisite black shirt, with two small gold lions subtly sewn into each collar, black pants, as sharply creased as a Toledo blade, and black boots of tacla plant leather, soft, shiny and supple. Corindel was clad in crème-colored, sweater-like blouse, open at the shoulders and arms, with two ringlets of the same material, as the blouse adorning her upper arms. She was also wearing black, soft slacks, with a silver belt around the waist. Her feet were clad in open-toe soft red shoes. Their daughter, Fanelle, came running down the stairs all dressed in red, with the Patamodian housekeeper putting some last touches on the child's dress. All four couples and Fanelle made their way up to Crofty Bellar's.

The Agrimorian sun was blazing with golden warmth, as they made their way closer to Crofty Bellar's. The smell of Patamodia's Carolunde Ocean filled the air as they walked. When they arrived at Crofty's home, they unlatched the wooden gate and walked up the stone path, past the thick blue-green lawn, with the stone seats. They approached the Chatham blue door and knocked. Someone came rushing to the door and opened it. It was Faengle. He had a broad smile on his face. "Well, well, well, come in," he said cheerfully. "The lady will be down presently," he offered, as they all took their seats in the large parlor. Pell paced the room, anxious to change his clothing, with Grista's eyes following his every move.

Faengle opened a box of puigos and set it on the glass table before them. All the men partook and so did Grista, with Twilly smiling at her, as she lit the puigo and bit it, trying to look like some sea farer or female pirate. The smell of hot-brewed caone filled the house. "Be right with you," came a shout from the second floor. Crofty Bellar descended the spiral stairwell. She was dressed in a smart, business-like suit, dark blue and pulled together in the center, with a thick, red, leather belt. She wore soft leather high heels. Her blonde hair hung naturally over her right shoulder, parted on the right side. They all smiled and rose to greet the woman. "Well, little ones, did you have an eventful night?" she asked in a booming voice. They all nodded in acknowledgement. Faengle entered the room, pushing a cart of hot caone. They all partook and sipped silently.

Crofty broke the silence, "I've arranged for two terraspans to carry us to Pathenune. Oh, by the way, your luggage was delivered, so I had them put in the second floor bedroom, so you can all change at your leisure," she said, smiling broadly. She looked up at Faengle, who was busy serving more hot caone. "You'll be joining us, Faengle," she said.

Faengle put down the pitcher slowly, not sure if he heard her correctly. "Me, my lady?" he asked astonishingly.

"Yes, my dear," she said gently. "I've cleared it with the Kungerods. I told them of your faithful service and loyalty and they agreed." Faengle was quite overwhelmed, for this was no small honor. "There's a complete change of clothing in your bedroom," she added.

Then she turned her attention to Forste and Corindel and said, "You both honor me by visiting my humble home."

Forste smiled and said, "Well, Crofty, I couldn't leave you alone with those two running amok in your home," pointing to Pell and Grista. Corindel laughed, watching Grista puffing mischievously on a puigo, watching Pell's every move. They all looked at Grista and laughed, but she just stared at Pell, planning something devious.

Gully smiled and whispered to Darvin, "Look at her. She's got something really bad in mind for Pell."

Darvin laughed and whispered to Gully, "Can you imagine such a woman? Look at her, like a huntress. A woman like that would kill either of us, but she's perfect for Pell."

Gully concurred. "She keeps him on his toes."

Pell, Darvin and Gully left for the second floor together, leaving the three girls with Corindel and Forste in the parlor. They entered the large bedroom to unpack their luggage. They were amazed how neatly folded everything was. So much care was taken. Gully and Darvin were looking at Pell, laughing.

"What's with you two?" he asked.

"Grista's going to get you," laughed Gully.

"Bugger," muttered Pell. "Don't worry. I've got my plans for that playful sprite."

Cremy, Twilly and Grista walked up the stairs towards their bedroom. Grista tiptoed towards the men's bedroom and listened in at the door. Cremy looked at Grista. "Grista, what are you doing?" she whispered.

"Sssh," said Grista.

Twilly tiptoed over to the door excitedly. "What's up?"

"Sssh!" said Grista. Pell noticed shadows under the door and flung the door open, and the three girls tumbled into the room.

Darvin stood there looking at the three sitting on the floor. "Bloody hell!" he shouted. "Are all of you becoming like Grista?!"

Grista laughed and looked at the other girls, "Well, are you?" she asked.

Cremy smiled and said, "Sure, why should you have all the fun? We're all going to get you three little cuties."

Darvin looked at Pell, perplexed. "What are we going to do with these playful little harpies?"

Pell walked over to where the girls were, hands on his hips and looked down sternly. "We're going to fix these little vixens, that's what. We'll have to teach them a lesson," he said quietly, but forebodingly. They helped the girls up, then Pell went up to Grista, with her smiling at him girlishly, turned her and escorted her out of the bedroom, slapping her derrière on the way out. They closed the door after the girls had left then laughed.

"That'll give them something to think about," said Gully.

Pell donned a pair of slacks from his luggage, soft and white as the tips of Everest, tightened with a fine thin gold belt. Then he put on an exquisitely tailored white shirt, threaded with fine gold. After that he picked a thin maroon tie from the luggage rack and tied it. He picked a soft black blazer with pure gold lion headed buttons. The blazer was as black as the mines of Coredon, deep and dark. Finally, he was shod with dark, rich, soft brown ankle boots. He would be the envy of all of the Earth's royal families, which to him were neither families nor royal. Darvin looked smart and menacing in his black leather suit and tie. Gully had on a finely tailored, dark green, double-breasted suit with a gold tie and brown shoes.

The girls entered their bedroom giggling. "I think we're in trouble," said Twilly.

"Yes," giggled Grista, "did you see the look in his eyes?"

Cremy was undressing and looked up at the two girls. "Grista, you're getting us into so much trouble," she said soberly. Then they all broke out with raucous laughter.

Soon afterward, the beautiful Corindel entered the room and greeted the girls, but came in to dress her sister. She helped Grista off with her clothing slowly and carefully. She began by tying and tightening a soft, brownish-red leather vest around Grista's bosom and waist, enhancing every nuance of her upper body. Then she helped her with a soft, crème-colored, pleated skirt sewn with a gold thread. It hung about six inches above the knees. After that, she tightened a thin black velvet belt with a gold buckle around her waist. Corindel looked at her sister, kissed her cheek and said, "I'll be right back," and left the room.

Cremy was lying on the bed and propped up against the backboard and asked, "You really love that don't you?"

"What?" said Grista.

"You know, Corindel dressing you and fussing over you," she said with a slight sneer.

Twilly shot a fierce look at her and walked over to the bed slowly. "How dare you!" she erupted. "How could you make such an insinuation, Cremy?!" she continued, enraged. "Corindel has not seen her sister in ages and I for one love to see her sister give her so much attention!" Then she walked over to Grista who was visibly shaken and moved. She groaned within herself, her eyes filling with tears. Twilly took Grista's head and held her to her bosom, comforting her, rocking her and speaking softly to her. Cremy grew ashamed at what she had done and rushed out of the room.

Corindel entered the room with some rich finery for her sister. She looked over at Grista with Twilly holding her, noticing her sister's tears and pain. She rushed over to her sister, her eyes widening with rage and shouted, her voice resonating, echoing and repeating through the manor, "Who dared to hurt my sister! Who had the audacity to sadden this beautiful face?!" Grista grabbed Corindel and Twilly.

"No," she sobbed, "please, please," she pleaded, trying to allay her sister's fierce anger. Fearing for Cremy, she continued, "Please, Corindel, no, please. Twilly defended me ably and shamed her. I'm afraid for Cremy, please."

Her sister calmed herself and looked at Twilly. "Thank you for coming to my sister's defense, Twilly," she said gently and kissed her forehead. "I've something special for you. I hope you'll accept it."

Grista recovered herself. Growing more worried about Cremy, she said urgently, "We must find her. I'm afraid for her."

Cremy was running and sobbing, saying to herself, "What have I done?" She ran outside of the house, across the lawn towards the grotto. When she reached it, she wept bitterly, her regrets overwhelming her. Her heart was breaking within her. The girls rushed out looking for Cremy. Pell, Darvin and Gully had gotten wind of what happened and grew concerned. They left to join in the search. The girls searched the manor with Crofty and the men searching the grounds.

Then Darvin espied a figure on the ground in the grotto. It was Cremona weeping. He rushed to her, his heart groaning and feeling her sorrow and took her in his arms. She was like a little child, with her eyes red and her nose running. He held her tightly and whispered, "Oh my little Creme, beloved."

She was sobbing and said, "Oh, Darvin, what have I done? I'm so sorry for what I said to Grista." Darvin just held her and rocked her in his arms, with Pell and Gully watching. The three girls had just arrived on the scene with Crofty, Forste and Faengle following after.

Grista came up to Cremona and knelt beside her, Darvin still holding her. She stroked her hair and wiped her tears. Cremy's sorrow so moved her. She took Cremy from Darvin and held her tightly. "Sssh," she said, stroking her.

"Grista," sobbed Cremy, "Can you forgive me?"

"Of course, little sweetie, of course I forgive you."

Cremy continued looking at her with teary eyes. "Grista, I was so envious of you with all the attention you were receiving from Pell, Corindel and everyone."

Grista smiled and rocked her gently. "Hey, I've an idea," said Grista, looking at Cremy lovingly. "Why don't you and I go back to the manor and you let me fuss over you. I've a chest with the most wonderful finery and I'd love to adorn your beautiful body with them."

Cremona looked at Grista, this time differently. She saw what Pell saw, the astonishing beauty of her spirit. She is truly a queen, she thought.

"Oh, don't you forget your prince over there," Grista added. "He was the first one to find you. Look at him," she said. "He's your lovely prince and his heart is so broken for you."

Cremy slowly rose and walked up to Darvin, looking into his teary eyes. She pulled him violently towards her and kissed him. She held him around the neck and would not let go. Pell knelt down next to his queen and paid homage to her, bedazzled by her wondrous spirit. Forste held Corindel, happy for Cremy and Darvin. Twilly put her arms around Gully's massive physique and looked up at him smiling. Faengle even gave Crofty a pie-eyed look. She turned and shot back at him, "Don't even think of it!" They all laughed at the silly sight of Faengle walking away muttering to himself. But Cremy and Darvin were oblivious to anything but each other in an endless embrace. Grista walked over to the lovers and cleared her throat, carefully trying to be as subtle as possible. Cremy looked over at Grista, kissed Darvin on the forehead then took Grista's hand. The two girls then left for the manor together.

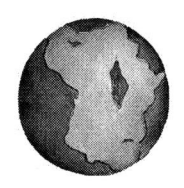

Chapter 32

ONWARD TO PATHENUNE

The preparations for the king and queen continued on Pathenune. The island was full of joy and merriment. Flowers were strewn over all of the walkways. Ribbons of wondrous colors with banners, were hanging from the archways. Songs were in the air, as the orchestras fine-tuned their instruments. The chorales were busy rehearsing. The joy was so contagious that even the forest creatures were curious, peeking through the trees at the festivities.

The Athelonian went to his quarters and opened a thin wooden box, which contained a flute-like instrument, but like no flute ever created on Earth in that it was pinkish-gold and glass, with a movable ring around the upper body. The Athelonian took the box and walked to an area of the forest which was very quiet. He played the flute, which resonated through the forest with a sound that made even the leaves to vibrate. The tune echoed and carried through Pathenune, a sound and tune which would have stunned any on Earth that heard it. This was the summoning of the Regunelus. (The wings of the kings.) Regunelus were the sacred birds of Agrimore about ten times the size of an eagle. Their heads and feathers were of pure, soft gold and bodies as white as pearl. Their eyes were the eyes of the morning, filled with flame and glory. Their heads were like unto eagles' and their bodies resembled swans'. They flew toward the highway of Potentates and perched themselves around the circle of monarchs, the place reserved for Pell, Grista, Forste and Corindel.

Grista took Cremy into her bedroom and slowly undressed her, admiring her beauty. Grista took her brush and brushed Cremy's beautiful auburn hair, until it hung over her naked porcelain body. She looked into Cremy's eyes and said, "You are magnificent."

Cremy closed her eyes and swooned, loving Grista's attention. Her touch made Cremy feel warm, comfortable and loved. She could have slept in Grista's arms. Grista took Apicella leaves given to her by Corindel and gently applied them to Cremy's body, covering every inch until Cremy's body began to glow orange-tan in Patamodian fashion. Cremy looked down at Grista, who was on her knees before her, applying the leaves to her legs, the queen serving her subject. She fingered Grista's lovely golden hair as Grista smiled up at her.

Cremy understood how important this was to Grista and it made them inseparable. She was connected to Grista eternally. Grista then took the blue bulb Corindel had given her and applied the fragrance to Cremy. Cremy could not take her eyes off of Grista. All she knew was that she wanted all of them to be together eternally. Grista, she thought, a superlative beauty – sensual, playful, yet holy, so holy. Grista pulled out an exquisite, white, pleated blouse from her luggage, subtly sewn with turquoise thread, befitting the classical Cremy. She then took a light marvelous blue-green dress wonderfully embroidered with blue-green roses. The dress hung just above her ankles. It was light with many folds. After that, she picked up a gorgeous belt. It was wavy and curved, so that the large part was in the front and bucked in the rear. It was made of pearls and silver, fine spun.

Cremy glowed with the care and attention Grista was giving her. Grista then took the second part of the dress, which covered the blouse. A blue-green flowered armlet connected on either arm by a beautiful blue-green robe like train, which slightly touched the ground. Grista was proud of her. She kissed her cheek and told her how lovely she was. "I'm not done," she whispered in her ear, then pulled out a small gilded chest which contained a tiara thin of spun silver and fine tubular shaped turquoise stones integrated into the fine silver. She gently and adoringly placed it on Cremy's head, then stood back to admire her. A fusion of beauty and grace stood there before her.

There was a knock at the door. It was Twilly and Corindel. Twilly came running up to Cremy. "Oh, Creme, you look luscious."

Cremy looked at Grista and walked over to her and whispered, "I understand what this means. Thank you for sharing this with me."

Grista kissed her forehead and said, "Now go and get your dear prince and ravish his heart." Grista walked over to the lovely little Twilly and said, "We've already performed this act together, my sweet. You remember, back at Faxburn?"

"Uh huh," Twilly said nodding. Grista said this to reassure her.

Pell, Darvin and Gully were walking towards the manor. Pell put his arm around Darvin and asked, "Hurts, doesn't it?"

"What?" asked Darvin.

"You know," Pell continued.

Gully stretched his neck over Darvin's shoulder with a broad smile and said, "He means looove, loooove." Pell laughed at Gully's antics. Darvin moved away, trying to dislodge Gully's large head from his shoulder. Gully chased Darvin around the grotto saying, "Looove, loooove." They were all laughing at Gully's silly expressions. Pell sat on the ground laughing and thinking of how rich he was to have such good friends. He loved them and was even more determined that no evil would ever come near them.

Three philbees pulled up to the manor to take them to the terraport. Pell grew apprehensive of what he had yet to face. Gully and Darvin noticed the change in his countenance and moved close to him, flanking him on either side. They grew serious, not sure of what Pell had to face, but they would never abandon him no matter what the future held.

• • • • • • •

On Pathenune, last minute preparations were being made. Everyone on Pathenune, from the children to their parents, was to be present and clad in the finest attire. The four orchestras placed themselves on either side of the highway of Potentates. The chefs, with their assistants, were wheeling tables and carts with flame pits in the center, to the circle of monarchs, careful not to step in the center, which had four circles of crystalline glass reserved for Pell, Grista, Forste and Corindel. The isle grew with excitement and anticipation, as the hour of arrival approached.

The beautiful Grista quietly waited with Cremy and Twilly for the men to return from the grotto. She saw Pell and felt his apprehension and the heaviness of his heart. She groaned within herself to see her beloved troubled. She walked slowly over to him, looking into his eyes. Her heart pained for him. There was nothing she would not do for him, even to take his place and face whatever was causing him so much dread. Everyone was quiet as they saw Pell's face. They had never seen such a look on his face and were all troubled in their spirits.

Forste and Corindel emerged from the manor. They saw Pell's face and their hearts were almost rent within them. Forste ran over to his brother, pulled him to himself and held him in his powerful embrace. He whispered, "My poor brother. Don't be so troubled. I'll be with you every inch of the way. We'll face this thing together, my dear brother." He pulled himself away and held Pell firmly by his arms and looked straight into his eyes and shouted, "king to king! You will never be alone! Do you understand, my brother? Never!" Pell drew strength from his brother and smiled gratefully.

Corindel held Grista tightly, comforting her. Grista was grateful for Corindel and Forste. My love has a powerful ally, she thought. A mighty man of war and greatness as mighty as his brother Pell. These thoughts comforted her. Crofty and Faengle witnessed all of this with great concern.

They all entered the philbees and made their way to the terraport. They rode through the exotically beautiful Applendice, past the Pandora clubs and the streets filled with inhabitants. The shops and cafes were alive and busy, as they continued past the pastel colored homes. The air was fragrant and vibrant. They approached the outskirts of the city with the terraport in the distance. As they approached the terraport, they could see the crews standing at attention beside their terraspans. The philbees came to a halt on the tarmac. Pell could see Purnis's terraspan glistening in the sun on the elevator, with Denara and Brighel standing with their crews awaiting their arrival.

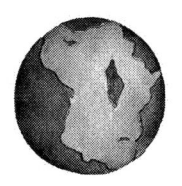

Chapter 33

THE ARRIVAL OF THE KINGS

Pell exited the philbee with Grista hanging on his arm. He walked over to the smartly dressed couple. There was something different about them. He excused himself from Grista and approached the two. He smiled at them. "No, you didn't!" he shouted with joy.

"Yep, sure did," said Brighel, grabbing Denara around the waist and holding her tightly. "Didn't we, my sweet?" he asked. Pell was overjoyed for the couple and hugged both of them.

Denara kissed Pell on the cheek and said, "You're a sweet prince for what you did for us. But," she said mischievously, "I could always ditch him and give you some special attention." Pell laughed as Brighel slapped Denara's backside. It lightened his heart to see the married couple.

"Remind me to give you something when we arrive," he said to them.

Pell, Grista together with Forste and Corindel entered Purnis's terraspan. As they entered, Denara presented Pell with a sealed parchment tied with a blue and red ribbon.

"The terraspan is officially yours now Pell," she said, "a gift from Purnis. Plus, all expenses have been taken care of indefinitely," she added.

Two cabins had been prepared for the couples, luxurious and well stocked. Grista followed Pell into the cabin and closed the door behind them. She gently helped him off with his jacket, then took him by the hand and led him to the couch. He laid back with Grista, laying her head on is chest. "My heart was so troubled when I saw you at the grotto," she whispered. Then, looking up into his eyes with tears streaking down her cheek, she said, "I've never known such pain." She moved herself over him looking down at him. "I can't endure anything that causes you pain," she said and gently kissed his eyes.

He looked up at her wondering to himself, How can a man be so loved? How could I have lived so long without her? He quietly studied her and kissed her tears. The universe is not large enough to contain the love I have for her. Then he gently laid her below him and kissed her fervently knowing that she, Grista, his queen, was his life, his soul, his breath. He had seen thousands of worlds, stars with their systems of glory, kings with glorious armies arrayed in the finest robes of victory with their bejeweled queens. But they were all dusty memories, dross images of folly, compared to her, this one named Grista, the zenith of majesty, comprehensively beautiful.

Forste and Corindel entered the cabin. "What is it, my love?" asked Corindel.

"It's my brother," answered Forste.

She moved close to him and stroked his hair, looking into his eyes. "You love him so much, don't you?" she asked.

He looked down at his love. "Our souls are one. I can't lose him, even at the cost of my life," he answered.

She grew frightened. "No, no, neither of you must die. This thing cannot happen, for it would mean the destruction of everything we love, our realms, our worlds, our hopes and dreams. No beloved, you must both return full of victory and glory."

Grista looked at Pell, "I love and admire your brother. Truly he is worthy of you. It gave me strength when he held you and spoke to you firmly," she said.

He looked down at her, then rose up from the couch and walked to the portal. He could see the crew making last minute preparations for their departure. He stared out of the portal and said, "Yes, it's true that my brother is strong, but I would wish he was not going with me. I don't want to lose him. Besides," he went on, "if anything were to happen to me, our realms would still be intact, but if both of us should be lost..."

Grista jumped off of the couch and ran up to him. "No!" she shouted. "You will not go there by yourself. You will take your brother!" she commanded. She grabbed his mane gently with both hands and looked into his eyes, her heart heavy within her. "Do you have any idea what existence would be without you? No Pell Provance!" she shouted, walking away from him and trying to compose herself. "A world without Pell Provance would be an empty dismal place. I would scorn the sun and mock the birds with their songs. I would defile the beautiful world of floral creations and despise the lovers of Patamodia. I would not cease, until I saw this world sink into the despair of that dark veil called Earth." She turned to him and pulled him towards her. "My love for you is beyond the limits of existence, deeper then the dark abyss of the uncreated." She turned and drew him to herself with great strength. She held him close and looked into his eyes and said, "I cherish every breath you take. Do you understand?" She was holding him so tightly that he could barely speak.

"My love," he said, struggling, "you're holding me too tightly."

"No!" she shouted. "I won't let you go alone! Even if I have to physically prevent you from going!" she said assertively. "You will take Forste, your mighty brother, or I will go with you, or you will not go at all!"

He finally relented and said, "I'll take Forste. Now, please let go, you're crushing me."

"I'm sorry, my sweet," she said apologetically. Then she gently kissed his hands.

Corindel and Forste knocked and entered the cabin, concerned about the shouting of Grista. They walked over to the couple. "Is everything in order?" Forste asked, looking intently at the couple.

Grista walked away from Pell, then turned and looked at him and said, "Do you know what he was about to do?" she asked sternly. "He was going to go and face the evil alone!" she said, her voice rising.

Forste and Corindel looked intently at Pell, their anger rising. "Is this true, my brother?!" he asked fiercely.

Pell put his head down and answered, "The realm must be preserved if anything should happen to both of us."

"Enough!" shouted Forste. "The realm preserved without its king!" he continued, enraged.

Corindel moved up to him and stared at him with her marvelous eyes, anger and sorrow mounting in her heart-heaving breast. "Pell," she said, the words sticking in her throat as she tried to hold back her tears, "don't you realize who you are? Pell," she asked, searching his eyes, "what is a realm, but empty memories of its king? Without you, it's worthless. "Another thing," she continued, her eyes widening with anger, "how could you ever consider putting yourself at such risk? Do you know what would happen to my sister if she were to lose you? Forste your brother would be grieving for all eternity. How dare you even think of such a thing!" Then she caressed his head. "No more Pell Provance, no more dashing looks, that beautiful face would be seen no more, your wonderful kingly gait, no more. A world deprived of Pell Provance is a world of shadows, an unhappy place, a place of the dead," she concluded.

Pell realized how wrong he was to think of such a thing and recovered himself. "Forgive me all of you, especially you, my queen," he said and he took Grista into his arms.

All three terraspans lifted simultaneously. Slowly, the three gleaming crafts made their way towards the magnetic corridor, gently climbing and searching for the cushiony field. Higher and higher they climbed, feeling for the magnetic waves that would scurry them to Pathenune.

Darvin and Gully were in the cabin of the second terraspan. Gully exited the galley with two perlees and handed one to Darvin, who was reclining in his seat and staring at the wall. "Troubled, my friend?" asked Gully.

Darvin looked at Gully and said, "All of these preparations, all of this activity, the whole world waiting quietly standing at attention for Pell Provance. I've a terrible foreboding, an uneasiness about all of this. He's going to face something terrible. I know it," he continued, "and we can't be there to cover his back." He then took a swig from the perlee bottle.

Gully sat down and stared at the carpeted deck of the terraspan. "I know, Darvin," he said gravely. "I've been so frightened ever since we arrived at Crofty's manor the second time. There were times I went alone to my room and began to shake. That's never happened to me before."

Darvin studied Gully. His smile, which brightened a room was gone, his countenance was dark and sad. Darvin nudged him on the shoulder. "Come on, Gulls," he said, trying to cheer him. "He's got his brother Forste with him. Did you take a good look at him?" he asked. "I've never seen anyone like him, except Pell of course, and he's going with him, two mighty men going into battle together." He looked at Gully and assured him. "He's not going to be alone, Gully. He's got his brother with him. They'll face whatever together and both will emerge victorious, mate," he concluded. Gully smiled slightly and downed his perlee.

The terraspan shuddered slightly, as it caught the field then smoothly whisked it's way towards Pathenune.

• • • • • • •

At Pathenune, the preparations were complete. Everyone waited silently for the arrival of the terraspans carrying the kings and queens. There was hardly a whisper as the Kungerods and the inhabitants searched the skies in anticipation. Some last minute preparations were being made.

In the living quarters the attendants were pulling out and preparing the Kungerods' finest attire for the night's festivities. Gorgeously designed robes representing each continent, were carefully being laid on the beds.

The air was still, as the Kungerods gathered near the terraport. The Athelonian walked over to his colleagues. They were all staring at the sky in anticipation. Noticing their uneasiness, he said, "Dear friends, what is troubling your hearts?"

The Vernacian looked down sadly. "I," he hesitated, "I wondered what Agrimore would be like without a king and queen. What would happen if we lost him?" They were all tormented by the same thoughts. The Athelonian fought back the same apprehensions.

He looked at his friends confidently and said, "My dear, dear colleagues, It's true we have never faced such an hour as this, but remember, this is Pell Provance, our king, skilled in warfare, never lacking in courage, the experience of thousands of ages within him, filled with wisdom immeasurable. Also, there's something I wish to show all of you after the arrival of our guests, if you'll permit me."

• • • • • • •

Grista was sitting on the couch with her arms around Pell's neck, holding his cheek close to her own. "My love is going to be splendid in battle," she said softly. "I'm so proud to be your queen. You'll put on your mighty armor and gird your sword to your side, my mighty one, terrible in battle, with your great brother at your side. Your deeds will be fearful," she went on, "unleashing your glittering blade against the enemies of the people you love. My heart is so ravished for my mighty king, so go forth my king and let thy sword perform wondrous deeds for thee." Then she bowed herself before him on one knee.

Corindel looked at Forste and said, "I know my beloved of your great strength and am confident in your abilities and exploits, but be on guard concerning your brother. Do not to let him take useless risks, or throw away his precious life in a battle he cannot win. Cover him my love and stay close, do not let him wander off alone," she said with great concern.

"Do not fear, my queen. I will be his shield. My brother is great in battle, but we will both face an evil that hithertofore we have not faced, something so hideous, as to do violence to the mind, in total opposition to the streaks of creation, the framing of filth incarnate, anti-light, anti-life, whose shadow scrapes the floors of all creation, a maddening darkness and blackness that rages at the formulation of unity, composition, symmetry. It cannot even abide chaos, Toto Belurum, the shrieking darkness," he quietly concluded, then put his head down into his hands, as Corindel comforted him.

• • • • • • •

On the isle of Pathenune, the sea breezes were gently fingering the banners and streamers, folding and refolding them, as the isle waited in complete silence for the arrival of the monarchs. Everyone's heart was heavy with a terrible foreboding in the air around them. All at once, the sun, which seemed to be poised and waiting, caught a glint of gleaming metal, as one terraspan emerged from the magnetic corridor, then another, finally the last terraspan emerged. Slowly, gracefully, gently, the three gleaming vehicles descended. Their descent was like three silver leaves falling from an oak tree in autumn, slowly, gently, quietly, solemnly. All the eyes of Pathenune were on the descending terraspans, as they carefully alit upon the waiting elevators.

The Kungerods made a semi-circle around the passenger elevators in anticipation of the appearance of their monarchs. The first terraspan's hatch opened with the crew at attention, as Crofty and Faengle quietly traversed the gangplank. The second terraspan opened it's hatch with Darvin, Cremona, Gully and Twilly advancing down the gangplank and waiting near the passenger elevator for the occupants of the third terraspan. No one said a word, as if a holy quietness overcame the entire isle. Twilly held Gully's hand tightly, sensing the foreboding atmosphere.

Finally, the third terraspan slowly and quietly opened its hatch, with the crew standing superbly at attention. Brighel and Denara stood at the head of them, waiting for the royal couples to appear. Forste and Corindel stood at the entrance, waiting for Pell and Grista. Pell and Grista arrived at the hatchway. Then Forste and Corindel lead the way. Slowly, regally, they began to negotiate the gang plank, with Pell and Grista following. Pell looked up and sensed the stillness and the enveloping fear. His spirit was troubled within him. The passenger elevator descended slowly, carrying Crofty and Faengle. The Kungerods bowed slightly at the two, who immediately walked over to the left side of the Kungerods. Once again, the elevator descended, bearing Darvin, Cremy, Gully and Twilly. The Kungerods bowed courteously at them. They then walked over to stand beside Crofty and Faengle. Then the elevator descended and stopped at ground level. Forste and Corindel walked over to the semi-circle of the Kungerods, with Pell and Grista following.

The Kungerods bowed on one knee before Forste and Corindel. "Your highnesses," they said quietly. Then the couple stood to the side to make way for Pell and Grista, who walked to the forefront. The Kungerods fell on their faces before them and shouted, "Your majesties!"

Pell and Grista were quite overwhelmed by the honor paid to them, but Pell slowly began to understand who these faithful subjects were and how important they were to Agrimore. He walked over to them and said, "Please, my dear friends, rise up so I can look upon you." They all rose up on their feet.

Chapter 34

THE SILVER GOBLET OF FORGIVENESS

Pell understood more and more about these wonderful people. He made his way over to the Can-Chimeran, who was standing on the left of the semi-circle. He stood face to face with the Can-Chimeran, then hugged him and said, "Thank you, my friend. Your might and power kept Agrimore safe, protected and secure."

The Can-Chimeran came to attention, overcome with honor, bowed his head and whispered, "Thank you, sire."

Pell then faced the handsome Patamodian. "Wisdom and understanding are your constant companions and you've shared them with Agrimore," Pell declared and hugged him.

The Patamodian responded, "It was my pleasure, sire," and bowed his head.

Pell then faced the Ilgestanian and smiled at her. She was slightly nervous for her impetuous proposal earlier. Pell looked at her tenderly, sensing her uneasiness and held her hands. "Grace and beauty have adorned Agrimore because of thee and abide with thee, fair one." Then he whispered to her, "Stop troubling your heart, dear one. You've beautified this world with your presence." Then he kissed her forehead. Her beautiful eyes filled with water as she bowed to him. Then he walked over to the Vernacian, smiling at him, looking into his gentle eyes. He held the little Kungerod by the arms and said, "Your warmth, kindness and tender love, with sweet humor, tempered all the Kungerods wonderfully. I am in your debt, dear friend." He hugged him tenderly.

Then Pell finally made his way to the Athelonian and gave him that silly smile that the Kungerod spoke of. He stood in front of him and exclaimed, "Your great leadership and masterful piloting kept this great ship of Kungerods on course! You are the rudder of this vessel, without which, it would have run aground. Your authority is well deserved and I, for one, am so honored by your steadfastness. Your indomitable spirit was the lighthouse in a troubled sea."

Then Pell bowed to all of them. The spectacle of the king bowing to his subjects was marvelous to them and made them love him. Pell's actions broke the stillness and completely dissipated the apprehension and heaviness of heart. They all walked back together with joy to the living quarters, laughing and recounting the past events. They all became close friends with their king and queen.

As they walked, Pell asked about the city of Candorey and mentioned that he would like to visit it with Grista. Forste interjected, "I've heard it's a fascinating place with inhabitants from all five continents."

"That must mean that there are districts representing each culture," added Gully.

"Yes, yes!" offered the Vernacian excitedly. "We must all go together." The Kungerods all concurred, feeling relieved that their king was with them and was easy to be with. Everyone hurried to the living quarters to get ready to visit the city of Candorey.

The Kungerods were all abuzz with the appearance of their king. His demeanor so impressed them. "Now remember," said the Athelonian to his colleagues, "no dower attire for tonight. We're going to enjoy this night with our king."

The Vernacian looked up at the Athelonian puzzled. "You mean we're going to patronize the cafes, bistros and clubs?" he asked. The Athelonian smiled warmly at him. "Yes, my dear friend. Tonight we'll enjoy ourselves." The Vernacian walked away smiling to himself.

The Can-Chimeran looked over at the others and said, "Our king honored us greatly. He bowed to his subjects."

The Patamodian inserted, "That's why he's a king."

The Athelonian looked at the female Kungerod and asked, "And how is it with you, my dear?"

"Wonderful!" she beamed. "I'm going to don my most exotic attire and I'll look hot, not as Kungerod, but a hot sizzling female." They all stared at her with question marks written on their faces, at which she burst out with laughter at their expressions, then she left for her quarters to change. The Athelonian had finished dressing. He looked quite dapper in a black suit, with all three buttons fastened, a perfectly-tailored white shirt, a pearl-white shimmering scarf and a hat that looked like a bowler. Finally, his feet were shod with dark brown boots. The handsome Patamodian put on a gray tweed with an ascot, blue in color. The Vernacian looked smart in a dark blue, double-breasted suit with an open-collar and a black-striped white shirt. The Can-Chimeran looked excellent in a blue sport shirt, black pants and a three-quarter-length leather jacket, black in color.

Now the Ilgestanian was anxious to dress provocatively. She had dreamt of the opportunity to break out her sultry attire. The tall, black-haired woman took a white blouse and put it on, revealing her extravagant breasts. Then she slipped into a chocolate-brown leather skirt, bound loosely with a fine-spun thin gold belt. She was smiling, as she put on the matching dark chocolate-colored leather vest. Then finally, she donned soft, dark chocolate colored velvet boots. Slowly, she negotiated the boots, until they reached above her knees, caressing them with both hands, for they felt "soooo gooood." Finally, she put a black velvet mask that covered the eye area in her purse, to be worn at one of the clubs.

Grista looked at Pell and whispered in his ear, "I want to dance with you." She pushed her thigh into him, knocking him off balance. Then she knelt and gently bit and nibbled the back of his upper calf, looked up at him cattily, full of playfulness and began crawling around him.

"Grista!" shouted Pell. "Not now!" But she was unmoved, still crawling around him. He moved away from her, but she followed him, still crawling. Then he lunged toward the door, but she sprang up and blocked it, spreading her arms and legs across the door. He then ran around the bed and she jumped on the bed to corner him. "Grista," he said pleadingly. "Not now, please."

Gully and Darin were outside of the door, listening to the goings on inside. Gully smiled and said, "They're at it again."

Grista tried to lunge at him. He avoided her, grabbed the spread and wrapped her in it, then ran from the room, shaking his head with Darvin and Gully looking on. Corindel entered the room, with Grista trying to extricate herself from under the spread. Corindel sat on the bed, helping her sister uncover herself. "Grista," she said scoldingly, "are you up to mischief again?"

"Uh, huh," said Grista in a child's voice.

"Poor Pell, you chased him out of the room," said Corindel. "Well, are you ready for tonight's festivities my sister?" asked Corindel.

"Yes!" she answered robustly. The Kungerods, clad in sharp, tasteful, night-on-the-town attire, waited in the lounge for the group.

Pell dressed himself in Darvin and Gully's quarters. He donned a pair of midnight blue slacks, elegant and well creased, then he took a crème-colored sport shirt wonderfully tailored and sewn with pure silver thread. It fit snuggly, accentuating the contours of his superb frame. He then fastened a decorative gold spun bracelet around his left wrist. Finally, he took soft, suede, loafer-like shoes and put them on.

Grista put on a sultry pure gold skirt that hung above her knees. Then she put on a matching top, which left a space, exposing her wonderful midsection. She then took two crimson velvet belts and crisscrossed them around her hips. She then put a gold and crimson choker around her neck and a thick gold cuff on her left wrist. Finally, she shod her feet with gold sandals and gold anklets.

The group met the Kungerods in the lounge. Pell looked at the Kungerods and addressed them, "It is my command to all of you that you go out with us tonight and have the time of your lives. No Kungerod activities, no dower conversations. I want you all to completely enjoy yourselves with song, merriment and good food. This is my command." He charged them all with a smile. He then walked over to the female Ilgestanian, smiled and whispered in her ear, "Hot, very hot." She smiled bashfully at him.

Crofty and Faengle were now a couple and stood arm in arm, as they waited for the five philbees that would carry them to Candorey.

They all gleefully piled into the waiting philbees. Kungerods, kings, queens and friends were all equal now, all in a festive mood.

· · · · · · · ·

Back at Firwith, Purnis was walking with Drue. Drue was glum and downcast. "Little sweetie, why so glum?" asked Purnis. The girl did not answer. "Is it Pell?" she asked, staring at Drue with concern.

Drue turned to look at her aunt, her beautiful silver hair glistening in the sun. The breezes of Firwith gently blew the ribbons in her hair. Her eyes filled with water, as she asked, "How? How auntie? How do you heal a broken heart?" She rested her head on the woman's chest. "I was so happy to be with him," she continued. "How can I settle for anyone else after being with someone like him? Handsome, beautiful, gracious, manly, sexy and compassionate all in one man. Oh, auntie, I don't know if I'll survive without him," she went on. "I think about him every moment of every day," she said sadly. "I actually go back to the room he stayed in and I fantasize that he's still there. I try to smell his scent. Yes, auntie. I actually snuck away a few times and went back to the manor to relive the memories of Pell."

Her aunt was moved by her niece's sorrow, "Well," said Purnis, "I've some news for you." Drue's ears perked up. "I wasn't going to show you this because I wanted you to recover and forget about Pell, but it may help you."

"What is it?!" Drue asked excitedly. Purnis looked into the girl's eyes hesitantly, "What is it, auntie?" she asked, her eyes widening with emotion. Purnis slowly pulled an elegantly sealed parchment from her purse and handed it to Drue. "What, what is this?" she asked, anxiously undoing the seal. Her eyes brightened, as she read the official invitation to Pathenune. "I don't believe it!" she exclaimed, wiping her eyes. "It's an invitation to Pathenune for the both of us to join in tomorrow night's festivities!" She danced in a circle, smiling, holding the parchment in the air. "And it's officially signed by Pell!" she shouted with joy. "Auntie!" she searched her aunt's face. "He must be someone of very great importance. I mean, no one goes to Pathenune, except Kungerods!" The young girl was elated. She was so happy that Pell personally invited them.

Her aunt looked at her sternly. "You'd better behave yourself, you understand?" she said sharply. "Don't try to pull any of your shenanigans at Pathenune."

"Oh, auntie, of course not. Anyway, he'll have his guard up with me around," she said, smiling mischievously. "Mmm, what I'd like to do to him, though." Then she said, looking at her aunt, "Just kidding, Auntie." Her aunt looked up into the sky and shook her head.

• • • • • • •

The five philbees made their way to the countryside of Pathenune, past the red forests with violet shrubbery, past the towering Poncille trees. These trees were enormous in size, light green and translucent, three, four, even five hundred feet high. The city of Candorey appeared in the distance down in a valley. The grassland of the valley was lush, with ice blue, glowing grass that gave off glowing seeds, which would light up the dusky sky. The city of Candorey was filled with thousands of inhabitants from every continent of Agrimore, each culture represented by its own architecture. The sultry pastels of Patamodia were clearly seen, the monolithic towers of Athelone, the streamlined domes and curves of Ilgestania were in the distance, the classical subtleties of Vernace, finally, the Spartan, garrison, practical architecture of Can-Chimera, pock marked the right side of the city.

The five philbees entered Candorey, past the gate house and towards the Patamodian district. They parked the philbees and began to stroll past the pastel-colored buildings, homes, shops and cafes. The streets and sidewalks were full of strollers, golden-orange-skinned lovers walking arm in arm. Two young Patamodian females were leaving a café when they saw the group. They were intrigued with the Can-Chimeran and the cute Vernacian.

One girl was tall with golden, braided hair swept back. She wore a crème-colored top that sat slightly below her shoulders, revealing a well-developed upper body. Her eyes were violet and silver, her brows and lashes were full and golden. Her face was wonderfully chiseled and her lips were full and orange, offset by her golden complexion. Her top hung just short, above her waist, revealing a most marvelous midsection. She was wearing form-fitting, black velvet slacks that caressed her long, well-developed legs. Her feet were shod with golden sandals. She boldly walked up to the mighty Can-Chimeran and stood in front of him, looking straight into his eyes. The Can-Chimeran stopped and became uneasy, not knowing what to do.

Pell and Grista were giggling with delight at the encounter. The girl touched the strong face of the Kungerod, admiring his strength and character. "I'm speechless," she said, looking and feeling the lines of his face. Then she looked into the Can-Chimeran's eyes. "Beauty and strength abide in you. Will you enjoy this evening with me?" she asked. The Can-Chimeran was at a loss and looked around at his colleagues for help.

The Athelonian gave him a nudge towards her and smiled. "Go, my friend. We'll meet later." The Can-Chimeran took the girl's hand and left with her.

The girl that she was with, was a little shorter, a silver-haired beauty. Her silver hair was cut short, with silver brows, lashes and a round, pixie-like face, with golden-brown eyes. She had a long, lovely neck with a black velvet choker. She wore a dark, shimmering brown top, exquisitely tailored, and a brilliant silver-blue skirt with dark brown boots. She walked over to the Vernacian, smiling and touched his curly hair, "You're adorable!" she exclaimed. The Vernacian responded happily to the attention. He looked over at the Athelonian, who smiled, beckoning him to leave with the girl. The rest of the group continued down the festive boulevard.

The female Kungerod of Ilgestana crossed the boulevard towards a Pondora club, the group following after her. She pushed open the doors, as if she were looking for someone. She walked down the center isle, with all eyes on the beauty. She felt the eyes of the male patrons and liked it. She knew she was flaming, burning, sizzling hot.

She looked around the club and saw a handsome Patamodian with long brown hair standing alone. He looked rather shy and this made her even hotter. She strolled over to where he was and looked at him. She was intimidating to the young man, but extremely alluring. She stared at him, scanning his entire body and thought to herself; Mmm, yes him, he is what I want tonight. I'm going to take him with me. The young man grew weak next to the powerful female Kungerod.

She took her black mask that fit around her eyes and part of her nose and fastened it. Then she approached him closer and closer, threatening and menacing. The air around them was thick with sensuality, quite like the eye of a hurricane. She was only inches away from him staring into his eyes behind the mask. The young man's heart was beginning to melt within him, his entire body tingled in the presence of the beautifully aggressive woman. Their breaths were touching, tropical and exotic. She looked at him, her eyes slightly closed, then she grabbed his thick brown hair, bent him backwards and kissed him forcefully on his lips. The young man was completely overcome. He knew he belonged to her. She looked him over, kissed his cheek, then took him by the wrist and led him away. He would never be the same, nor would he ever forget this night. He had no idea that he was being led away by a Kungerod.

Grista put her hands to her mouth. "Oh my!" she exclaimed. "I hope she'll be gentle with the young boy." Then she smiled at Pell with amazement. Pell looked with fascination as the two left the club. The Athelonian looked at the Patamodian with his brows raised.

"You think the boy will survive the night?" asked the Patamodian smiling.

"Oh, she'll be gentle. I'm sure," he responded. The Athelonian then burst out with laughter. Pell, Forste, Corindel and Grista relished the fact that the Kungerods were having a good time.

The Athelonian and Patamodian took their leave and excused themselves, deciding to go off on their own. Crofty and Faengle had left to dine at one of the splendid restaurants of the Athelonian district, leaving Pell, Forste, Corindel and Grista by themselves. Grista looked at Pell, the light of the club flashing off of her beautiful hair and eyes, her eyes growing in brilliance and golden flame, as she looked into Pell's eyes. She whispered in his ear. "I want to dance with you, my love," her voice, like a claxon awakening his senses, titillating him.

His heart began burning for her and she sensed it. She slowly began removing the magenta sarong she was wearing, revealing a short skirt of pure gold. The gold looked molten from Grista's fiery body. Her eyes were now filled with flame and light, as if lit from within. Her fragrant wondrous mouth was beckoning him. Her deep aroma from her breath was heady, dizzying, fragrant. Her matching midriff was also molten gold revealing and sensual. Her beautiful shoulders exposed a symphony of symmetry of muscle and bone with shimmering sweat. Her lovely neck was adorned with a gold and velvet choker crimson in color. Her powerful legs of muscle and grace were cuffed with golden anklets, alighting upon gold and crimson sandals. Grista moved gracefully around Pell, stalking him and caressing his frame with her hand, then with a sudden leap she jumped on his back and clamped her legs around his waist. Then Pell bent over slightly as Grista climbed higher on him and sat on his strong shoulders. He grabbed her hands and lifted her high into the air, with her toes straight up into the lights and her face even with his, he kissed her.

The music changed to accommodate the erotic dance, drum beats and flutes rhythmically erotic. He then swung her around his body, she wrapping herself tightly around his ribs. She was coiled tightly around him, then he grabbed her around the waist and lifted her over his shoulders, the back of her legs clamping tightly around his shoulders, with her backside against his chest, her head hanging towards the floor.

Forste and Corindel were watching with wide-eyed astonishment as the lovers performed the great exploits of dance. He then grabbed her hands that were clutched around his waist and held her up straight with his hands. With little effort, she flipped twice in the air and landed on her feet. The club patrons were amazed by these maneuvers. Then Grista rushed at Pell negotiating two cartwheels, as she approached him, the music beating and rising to a crescendo. She leapt upon his shoulders, then twisted her body around, until she reversed her position. He grabbed her calves and held her in front of him, as she ferociously ripped his jacket and shirt off of him, leaving his upper body naked. Grista could see the blood running through her beloved, through his arms and muscular neck. They were both soaked with sweat, as he twisted her body in front of him like a pinwheel and then stopped.

The music revealing its cue, everything was silent as they stared into each other's eyes. They were now engulfed with passion, their bodies throbbing, pulsating for each other. She breathed her breath into his mouth and then pulled it back until he had no breath left in him. His heart was beating rapidly within him, as he looked into the eyes of his queen and thought to himself, An epoch of ecstasy would not suffice. Eons would be a passing moment; the torrent of passion within me would be a sea without boundaries without shores. The flood within me would continue to the limits of eternity itself and would still hunger for more, for Grista, forever my queen. Then he took her into his arms and kissed her deeply downward. They proceeded into each other's souls. No one else danced that night, not in the light of that spectacle. The club became a holy shrine for that night.

The Patamodian and Athelonian Kungerods walked into an elegant restaurant together. They were seated at a table on a balcony, with a glass dome. They could view all of Candorey from there. Across from them, an attendant was preparing a table for another patron. After he had finished, the maitre d' escorted an imposingly attractive female to the table. The two Kungerods watched the female, noting that she was a Can-Chimeran. She had long black full hair parted to the side. Her skin had a dark tone, as with Can-Chimerans. Her brows and lashes were full and black outlining flashing turquoise eyes that were full of life and dangerous looking. Her nose was scaline and perfect, which sat just above a full, rich, marvelous mouth, red and heated. She wore a lovely soft white dress, covering a body that would take time and many pages to explain. Her dress hung just over her ankles, bordering the hem which was adorned with golden vines. The Athelonian motioned for the attendant who briskly walked over to the table. The attendant bent over while the Kungerod whispered in his ear. "Please send a Paximunte over to the lady's table." The attendant left for the kitchen. The Can-Chimeran female was scanning the menu and occasionally looking over the top at the Athelonian.

She put down her menu and tried to occupy herself with the rooftop sights of Candorey, occasionally catching the eye of the Athelonian. She was fascinated with him. His severe, but strong features attracted her. She liked the way he would occasionally look at her, but tried not to show it. The Patamodian noticed the interplay between the two and finished his drink, excusing himself. "Where are you going, my friend?" asked the Athelonian.

The handsome Patamodian bent over and whispered in his ear, looking at the female. "She's all yours, my friend. A Can-Chimeran female is a lot to handle."

The female noticed his gracious gesture and smiled at him respectfully. The attendant arrived with the enchanting Paximunte. The female smiled at the Athelonian, then stretched out a muscular leg from under the dress and shoved a chair away from the table, welcoming him. He walked over to the table and joined her.

The handsome Patamodian walked down the Athelonian district of Candorey by himself. He made his way to the Vernacian district. This section was different from the rest, in that many of the houses and shops had orange-colored glass with vines hanging down the stone facades of the buildings. The streets in the Vernacian district were quaint and winding. The inhabitants were colorfully dressed and reserved. He walked into a bistro filled with Tendrats, Hogomeans, and officials. The Kungerod made his way to the front with serving girls rushing to and fro in his path. All of a sudden there was a commotion between the Tendrats and the Hogomeans. One of the Hogomeans shoved a female Tendrat into the Patamodian, who was astonished that a woman was so treated on Agrimore, then thought to himself about the latent and sleeping evil slowly taking over Agrimore. The Patamodian walked slowly over to the group of Hogomeans, which were about seven in number. He looked at the one standing, which had shoved the young woman, who was standing behind the Kungerod.

He stood face to face with the young man. His companions arose from their seats, in support of their comrade. The Kungerod was unmoved by their numbers. His face was now just inches away from the young man. The Kungerod raised his eyebrows and stared intently at the antagonist and spoke softly, but sternly, "You dare touch a woman in the world of Agrimore," his voice rising. The young man stood there defiantly, sticking out his chest at the Kungerod.

The Kungerod noticed that he was not getting through to the Hogomean, so with lightning speed grabbed the young man by the shirt and threw him sprawling across the floor. Then he quickly turned to face the Hogomean's friends. Cowardice is not a stranger, even on Agrimore. The Hogomean's friends backed off at the sight of the fierce Kungerod, seeing their strongest friend sprawled on the floor. The Kungerod turned to the young woman and asked, "Are you unharmed?"

"Yes, thank you," she said. He then escorted her to her table of two other female Tendrats. They thanked him for his chivalry and asked him to join them.

The girl he had championed was named Porinora. She was dressed in traditional Tendrat garb of brown leather. She was a slight girl with dark brown hair with bangs. She wore a yellow blouse with a silver chain hanging over her neck, containing a fiery blue jewel. Her blouse was covered with a leather vest and she wore a brown leather skirt. Little did they know that they were sitting with a Kungerod. She introduced her friends to her champion. The first girl to her left was named Fodince. She was a red head with a short bob cut. The second girl was called Kartharnay, she had very long golden hair. Then the girl who was championed spoke. "My name is Porinora. I am very impressed with the way you stood up for me," she added.

"You are very powerful and handsome. Who are you?" asked Fodince.

"Just a man traveling about Candorey," answered the Kungerod.

"Listen," said Kartharnay, "how would you like to come home with us?" she asked.

The Patamodian was slightly taken aback with the invitation. But he thought to himself, Our king did order us to enjoy ourselves. So he rose, paid the tab and left with all three female Tendrats. The Athelonian sat in the chair that the Can-Chimeran had thrust with her foot. He looked over at the imposing female, she smiled as she silently scanned his features. Then she spread her powerful legs and leaned towards him across the table.

"You" she noted, "are one powerful looking man!" The Kungerod stared at the female, not knowing what to answer. She moved her chair closer to him and just stared at him, waiting for a response.

Why do I feel so intimidated? he thought to himself. After all, I am a Kungerod.

That didn't seem to matter to the Can-Chimeran. Even if she knew what he was, it wouldn't have made a difference. She looked at him, holding her head with her hand, her elbow on the table. "Aren't you going to say anything to me?" she asked boldly.

"Well, what more is there to say?" he responded. With that, they both rose and left together.

Chapter 35

THE SPECTRE OF DARKNESS

After their dance Pell and Grista left the Pandora club, her eyes never leaving her king. She loved the attention he received from the females of Candorey. She continued to look at him, his flashing eyes, his wonderful dimples, his roguish smile, the way his clothing seemed to respectfully adorn his mighty body. She was completely captivated and entranced by him. She smiled mischievously. Then she grabbed the tie around his neck and pulled him towards her and kissed him forcefully in front of all onlookers who began giggling at the couple.

Forste and Corindel left the club to follow after Grista and Pell, not wanting to dance after Pell and Grista's performance. Pell and Grista decided to dine, so they walked towards the Ilgestanian section. The architecture of this section was marvelous indeed. The buildings and homes, as in Ilgestana, were made of shaped colorful translucent crystal, beautiful green, blue, and magenta glass, reflecting the Agrimorian moonlight. The walkways paved with stone and crystal. The Ilgestanians were a quiet and serene race. They were careful of whom they befriended, but were loyal lifelong friends, once you were accepted by them. Pell and Grista continued walking along the main street, with Forste and Corindel following at a distance behind them. There were many shops and cafes on the strip, but there was one shop in particular that caught their eye. It was different from the other shops on the strip, darker perhaps. The couple walked over to the shop with the black and gold awning. The name on the awning was Rexibonte. The curious thing about this shop, was that it contained the most mundane items of little value. They entered the shop, which displayed crystal goblets and other ordinary items.

Forste and Corindel stood outside, as the couple entered the shop. The store keeper was busy opening boxed items of stock. It was as if this store had recently opened. The look of the storekeeper was curious. His motions were fast and jerky. Pell watched the man curiously from behind the counter. The shopkeeper seemed to be oblivious to the couple, but there was something about him that disturbed Pell.

Pell moved towards the man, who was crouched over the boxes. He stood in front of the man with only his shoes in view. The man looked up at him slowly and met Pell's eyes. The man immediately rose to his feet and backed away from Pell. The man's face was uninteresting and ordinary, but not that of an Ilgestanian. The man's eyes were murky brown and dead. Pell moved closer to the man, who backed off knocking things over in the process. Pell moved closer, with the man constantly moving away from him.

Just then the front door flung open, with Forste and Corindel entering. "What is he?!" shouted Forste blocking the front entrance. Pell cornered the man. He grabbed him by the lapel and pulled him close, staring at him. "What in the tigriste domains are you?!" he shouted, holding the petrified creature. Forste came over to his brother and said, "This thing is not of Agrimore."

The girls stood there staring at the scene. Pell, firmly gripping the man asked, "What do we do with it?"

"Well, we can't slay the thing here," answered Forste. "Nor can we turn it over to the authorities. They wouldn't understand." The man stood cringing before Pell and Forste. Pell couldn't bring himself to slay the pathetic creature. He released his hold and determined to inform the Kungerods of it's presence. They all departed, troubled by the presence of the man in the shop. Pell walked with his brother, silently contemplating the presence of the creature and if there were others on Agrimore.

Crofty and Faengle walked into an exquisite Athelonian restaurant. The décor was distinctly Athelonian, with a green marble floor with fluted brass, floral designs and imposing marble pillars. They were seated at the end of the restaurant, which had glass tables with brass posts. Faengle sat across from Crofty admiring her opulent bust. Crofty asked, "What are you staring at, Fengy?"

Faengle immediately caught himself. "Oh, nothing," he said ashamedly.

"Were you staring at my breasts?!" she asked in a scolding manner.

"No, no, not at all," he answered defensively. "Why not?!" she shot back.

"Well err um," Faengle tried to get words out.

"Oh, it's all right, Fengy. I'll show you more after we finish our meal," she purred.

The female Kungerod took the young man from the Pondora club to an inn. She took the young man by the wrist and ordered a suite. Then she led him to the suite, unlocked the door and pulled him in. She stood there clad in a dark brown leather, wearing a black velvet mask, staring at her captive. She took off her mask, smiling at the young man, who was beginning to flame up with passion. "What is your name?" she asked quietly.

"Amborine," he answered. She gently undressed him, kissing his neck and caressing his frame. He then grabbed her ferociously and threw her onto the bed. He stared down at the beautiful Kungerod, as sweat trickled down his forehead, his thick brown hair hanging over his eyes, droplets of sweat finding their way down his nose onto the female's face, as he held her wrists tightly and searched for the mighty woman's lips. She closed her eyes and kissed him, her desire deepening.

Pell and Forste left the shop, with Grista and Corindel following after them. Pell turned to his brother and said, "We'll inform the Kungerods in the morning. Let them enjoy this night." Forste agreed with him, adding that they deserved this night to themselves without being disturbed.

• • • • • • •

Pell and his brother continued walking along the Ilgestanian section, with Grista and Corindel following after them. They continued walking past the shaped glass buildings, looking for an eating spot. They espied a restaurant a few meters away. The name on the front of the light green translucent glass building was the Palidor, written in large brass-like letters across the front. An Ilgestanian doorman opened the thick-glass doors for them. The restaurant was breath taking, with green-glass pillars and a fountain set between the pillars. There were four glass pillars on each side, with three fountains on each side between the pillars. The floor was of shimmering thick mica, dark orange in color. There were also Folocache trees, which were indigenous to Ilgestana, behind the fountains. The Ilgestanian maitre d' bowed courteously and led them to a table. The female servers approached the table as the other patrons stared over at the foursome. Pell and Forste drew the attention of all the female patrons. "Four Paximuntes," said Pell to the servers.

Pell looked over to the table next to theirs, as they were being served a most fascinating entrée. It was a piece of meat engulfed in orange flame, set in a silver bowl with thin a skewer or rod positioned in the middle of the bowl, with the flaming meat at the end of the skewer. Pell asked the serving girls who returned with their cordials what the entrée was that the four girls at the next table were having. "Oh, you mean Cocaba," answered one of the servers.

"Cocaba is an Ilgestanian delight," answered the other girl. The four Ilgestanian girls at the next table were flirting and smiling at Pell and Forste, who ignored them.

Grista and Corindel were becoming annoyed, as the girls at the next table grew more provocative and louder as they tried to catch the attention of Pell and Forste. The four girls moved their table closer to Pell's and Forste's, completely ignoring Grista and Corindel.

The maitre d' became concerned, as he looked at the faces of Grista and Corindel filling with rage towards the disruptive girls. He tried to speak to them, but to no avail. They began raising their voices, trying to get the attention of Pell and Forste. Grista looked at her sister. "Shall we handle this lot?" she asked.

"Uh, huh," she nodded. The two girls slowly rose from the table and walked over to the four Ilgestanian females. Pell and Forste watched Grista and Corindel carefully, knowing what they were capable of. The four girls rose to meet them with one girl who was especially large. They were moving closer to meet Grista and Corindel. Grista moved to the left to flank the girls, as Corindel moved to the right, with Pell and Forste watching everything carefully. The other patrons moved away from their tables to the rear of the restaurant. Grista closed in on the two girls at the left of the group, while Corindel slowly and carefully approached the two on the right containing the large girl. Grista closed fearlessly, but the two girls did not flinch and stood their ground. Corindel came within a few feet of the others.

Grista, standing a few feet from the girls said, "I'll give you both a chance to retreat with honor. You don't have to do this."

"Retreat?!" shouted one of the girls. "And why should we do that?!"

"Because," said Grista in an even and slow voice, "my sister and I are very skilled in arts of combat and could inflict much damage, if you should choose to engage us." The two girls looked at each other, while the other two stared at Corindel, without saying a word.

Corindel closed swiftly on the two and slid beneath them, turning, then kicking the large one on her backside with such force that the girl flew sprawling across the restaurant floor. The other girl backed off, seeing her companion moaning on the floor of the restaurant. The other two approached Grista and lunged at her. Grista easily bent low beneath their grasp and placed both of her fists in the solar plexuses of the two females. Both bent over in pain, as Grista shoved both of them with her feet to their backsides and sent them sprawling to join the larger girl still on the floor. Corindel approached the last girl, who immediately apologized nervously. Corindel continued to approach her, as Grista mediated for the penitent girl. "No, my sister," said Grista softly. "It is done. She's finished."

Corindel broke out of her combative stance and looked at her sister smiling. "Of course dear one," she relented.

Just then, three Ilgestanian officials entered the restaurant. The maitre d' immediately approached them and informed them of what had happened. The officials then took the four girls into custody. The maitre d' approached Pell's table and apologized profusely and would not let them use their mica as payment. Pell decided it was time to leave and make their way back to the conference center in the light of the individual they had encountered at the shop. So they walked back to the Patamodian district to where the philbees were parked. "Shall we find the Kungerods?" asked Forste.

"No," answered Pell, "let them enjoy this night."

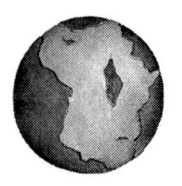

Chapter 36

CORODORBUS

They drove back to the conference center quietly. No one said a word, realizing in a short time that Pell and Forste would have to face an unspeakable evil. The philbee approached the conference center, which was quiet and stark with the blue Agrimorian moons shining their blue light on the quiet isle. They quietly made their way to their quarters, with Corindel and Forste walking together. Pell and Grista entered the darkened room of the living quarters.

She began undressing Pell, kissing his back as she removed his shirt, thinking to herself that this was their last night together before he and Forste would leave to deal with the darkness that was slowly enveloping Agrimore. Maybe the last night we'll ever be together, she thought as she looked into Pell's eyes.

Tears began streaming down her cheeks, as Pell kissed her tears and asked softly, "What? What is it?"

She looked at him, her eyes and cheeks wet with tears and held his face in her hands and said, "I'm afraid. Actually, I'm terrified for you and your brother. What if something should happen to either of you, or to both of you? How would my sister and I survive? These beautiful worlds would come to their end."

He was so moved by her tears and fears. He held her close and kissed her forehead. "What is all this?" he asked. He lifted her head and looked into her wet eyes, the Agrimorian moonlight reflecting off of both of them. "Grista," he said quietly, "you must have courage and understand that Forste and I are not ordinary men, but kings and quite adept in warfare. We not only are well equipped, but we are the only ones that are capable of defeating whatever it is that's spreading the darkness. Not only that, we will be well armed, with might, courage, determination and destiny. Also, we will have a terrible weapon in our hands. So be not fearful my love, for I promise you that both of us will return." He looked at her intently and held her head firmly in his hands. "I promise you, we will both return," he said firmly and forcefully.

Corindel and Forste quietly disrobed, not saying a word. Forste sat on the bed, with Corindel sitting beside him. She stroked his thick silver hair. "What is it, my love?" he asked tenderly. She held him tightly and looked out the window, at the blue nighttime scenery.

"I'm troubled about your confrontation," she said quietly.

He turned to her and held her tightly. "Do not be troubled, beloved. Pell is strong and not easily defeated; we will emerge victorious. This I promise you!"

The Kungerods were making their way back from Candorey after a night to remember. They left the city before dawn because of the festivities that were being prepared. Pell and Grista were asleep in each other's arms, as were Forste and Corindel. The Kungerods arrived and made their way quietly to the living quarters, trying not to disturb the sleeping couples, knowing that this would be their last day they would spend together before facing their ordeal.

The Agrimorian sun began to shine brightly, brightening and beautifying the isle of Pathenune, awakening all of the inhabitants. The specially invited quests began arriving, silently terraspans began emerging from the magnetic corridors. Leaders of all five continents were invited dressed in their finest official attire. There were also other guests from some of the most prominent families of Agrimore, including Purnis Huelett and her niece Drue.

Pell awakened and looked over at the beautiful Grista, who was fast asleep. He began playing with her golden curly hair. He thought back to the time they had first met on Athelonia. She was sweaty, soiled and fragrant from the fens. He loved her courage and honor, how she tried many times to defend him, not that he needed defending, but he loved her attempts. Corindel awakened Forste with kisses to his eyes, "It's time to arise my love," she said.

Forste opened his eyes and saw Corindel straddled across his waist smiling at him. "My lady is playful today?" he asked. She smiled, moving her waist rhythmically. He reached up and pulled her off of him and kissed her. "We have to get ready for the festivities," he announced.

"I know," she answered, "I just wanted to spend some quiet moments with you until we leave."

Grista opened her eyes and looked at Pell, who was staring at the ceiling, "What is it my darling?" she whispered.

He turned to look at her and said, "You must trust my brother and I!" he said sternly. "Forste and I are quite capable of dealing with this, so you must trust us. We will return victorious. This I promise you. Do you understand my sweet?"

"Yes, I do and I trust both of you," she answered. After that he kissed her and rose to dress.

The Kungerods made their way to the kitchen anteroom, waiting for their hot-brewed caone. They were all tired form the activities of the past evening. They all sat quietly as the attendants brought their hot beverages. They quietly sipped their hot caone, thinking to themselves of the events of the past evening. "Well, my friends, did you enjoy yourselves?" asked the Athelonian. The Ilgestanian smiled.

"Were you gentle with that poor lad?" asked the Patamodian

"Poor lad," she laughed. "It was just an act. You should have seen him. He was a bloody Gerathen."

They all laughed as the Vernacian asked, "You're going to see him again, aren't you?"

"Mmm, I'm not telling," she said, smiling.

"What about the Can-Chimeran that you met last night?" asked the Patamodian of the Athelonain.

"She'll be at the festival tonight," responded the Athelonian. "She's from one of the noblest families of Can-Chimera," he concluded. The Vernacian laughed to himself, thinking about his night out. Yes, they all needed this respite.

After finishing their morning brew, the Kungerods made their way towards the conference center. The isle was filling with visitors, continental leaders with their entourages, noble families, personal invitees and retired rulers. Everyone who resided on Pathenune was also invited, so that everyone was busy in preparation for the night's festivities.

The Kungerods rose and made their way towards the conference center. All were silent, tired from the past evening's events.

Pell arose from bed to dress with Grista still asleep. He was anxious to meet with Forste and looking forward to some hot-brewed caone. Grista turned on her side and opened her eyes to watch Pell readying himself. She pulled down the cover with all of her beauty in full view. "Hey you!" she yelled. "Who gave you permission to leave?" she asked playfully. He smiled at her and blew her a kiss. She crawled over to the edge of the bed where he was dressing. "You think you could just blow me off with an imaginary kiss? Hmm," she purred. He smiled and continued dressing. She got up on her knees still on the edge of the bed and began blowing in his ear, then messing up his hair, which he would immediately comb back, which she would immediately mess up again.

"Come on baby," he reacted. "I want to meet up with Forste and have a morning brew."

She threw her arms around his neck from behind and whispered, "Oh yeah, well suppose I don't want you to leave? Hmm? Suppose I decide to keep you here all morning, hmm?"

"Come on Grista," he pleaded. "Not now, please."

"Uh huh, now," she said smiling.

"Grista!" he yelled, but she would have none of it. She kept messing up his hair and undoing the buttons on his shirt, while he tried in vain to dress himself.

All of a sudden there was a knock on the door. Saved, he thought to himself. He went to the door where Forste was there to greet him. As he began to speak, Grista slammed the door shut. Pell opened it and looked at the surprised Forste. "I'll be with you shortly," he said.

"Oh, no he won't!" Grista shouted and slammed the door. Forste continued to knock, with Pell trying to open the door, as Grista was trying to drag him back to the bed. He finally opened the door to find Forste with a frustrated look on his face.

"The baby's very playful this morning," said Pell. Grista smiled at Forste and Corindel, who had just joined him outside of the door. Then she slammed the door again, grabbed Pell's hair and dragged him back to the bed.

Forste and Corindel laughed at the scene, then Corindel began walking away. She turned to Forste and said, "Forget it. Your brother is not getting out of that room for a while." Forste was disappointed, wanting to talk to his brother.

The Kungerods finally made it to the conference center and to the Pollidecreum. They all took their positions around the globe and placed their tundrils into the slots. The inner globe came to life. The Athelonian moved around the globe and said, "Now we shall seek to discover what the evil is that plagues our two worlds and its location." The Athelonian went back to his position and in unison they all turned their tundrils. All at once, the globe brightened and darkened, as if it shut itself down completely. They were all at a loss circling the dead globe, bewildered as to what had happened. The Athelonian spoke to them, "My dear friends, it's obvious that we are not authorized to access this information. This is for Pell alone to access. Not even his brother is able to derive the information needed," he added. "Only him, our king, is able to suss this out," he concluded. With that they withdrew their tundrils and continued to make preparations for the evening's events.

Darvin and Gully were in the kitchen ante-room enjoying caone and hot hethesh, which is a hot Pathenune cereal. They were waiting for Cremona and Twilly. Darvin looked over at Gully and asked, "What do you think, mate?"

"About what?" Gully inquired.

"About what Pell and Forste are going to face," responded Darvin.

"Well, it's something they're going to have to face, what's to think about?" added Gully.

"Well, I've been thinking, mate. What if we went along as backup?" asked Darvin.

"Are you out of your bloody mind?!" shot Gully. "We don't even know what they're up against. Furthermore, our being there might jeopardize this mission." He moved closer to him and looked at him intently. "Look, Darvin, I know how much you care for Pell and I don't doubt your courage, but you've got to get this out of your head, you got that? Not only that, you might put us at risk, including these worlds, we are not prepared," continued Gully, "or sanctioned for this type of combat. It's only for kings, you got that?" He stared at him, waiting for an answer.

"Yes, I guess you're right," answered Darvin.

Pell went to where his luggage was stored and pulled out a gilded box. In the box were two splendidly crafted chalices of the richest gold and silver, with a ruby like jewel in the stems. "Oh my!" exclaimed Grista. "Who are these for?" she asked.

"I have to give them to Brighel and Denara as a wedding gift from both of us," he answered. They both dressed and left the living quarters in search of the couple.

The Kungerods continued to make preparations for the evening's festivities. They had prelacian plants placed along the highway of the Potentates. These would open at night and fill their air and sky with wonderful pastel colors. The seeds they would eject, were luminescent and would fill the sky with colored light. The Regunelus were all in place around the circle of monarchs. All of the streamers and banners were in place.

The orchestras and choruses were beginning to fine-tune their royal arrangements. The Kungerods arrived at the living quarters and prepared to dress in the robes of authority, representing each continent they were in charge of.

Pell and Grista made their way to the terraspan, which was a gift from Purnis. They entered and made their way to the crew quarters. They heard the crew talking and laughing from behind the door. They knocked and a female crew member opened the door. She smiled delightfully when she noticed who it was. "Oh, sir, and Miss Grista," she said joyfully. "Please come in." They all stood on their feet. Pell motioned for them to recline as they were. Another crewmember brought two seats over for them, then asked what they would like to drink.

"I'll have what everyone else is drinking," answered Pell.

"Same here," said Grista. The crewman returned with two perlees.

After they had sat and enjoyed their perlees, Brighel asked about the unexpected pleasure of their visit. "Well, remember I said I have a wedding gift for you? Well here it is." Then he handed the gilded box to both of them.

They opened it and were astonished at the beautiful craftsmanship of the two chalices. "Sir, we cannot accept something like this," said Brighel. "Why, we've never seen anything like it before. It's much too valuable," he added.

"No," said Pell, "it's for both of you and you would offend us if you did not accept it."

"Well, in that case we accept gratefully."

"It's from another world," Pell added. "There's nothing like it on Agrimore." Brighel and Denara stared at the beautiful chalices speechless with the magnanimity of Pell and Grista. "One more thing," said Pell, as he was leaving. "It's Pell, not sir, got that?!" They hugged each other and left.

Pell walked slowly back to the living quarters with Grista by his side. Grista noticed that he was quiet and troubled. She moved closer to him and linked her arm into his tightly. She looked at him and asked, "What troubles you my love?"

"Last night I dreamt the most terrible dream of my life," he said quietly.

"What was it?" she asked.

"So terrible that I cannot speak of it." She held him closer. "I know what it is, though," he added and looked at her. "It's him, Corodorbus. He's trying to weaken me as the time of battle is drawing closer. He's awake and active awaiting the battle," he said, staring straight ahead as they walked. "I must meet with Forste to gain strength," he concluded.

"Is the thing that strong?" asked Grista.

He turned and looked at her sternly. "He's the most fearsome adversary to ever engage anyone in battle. One of his strongest powers is to work on your mind, to make you doubt yourself. Fear is a mighty weapon of his, then doubt, that being accomplished half the battle is already won. Another weapon is when he tries to converse. He can lull an enemy to sleep with conversation, then he strikes out with terrible power. So we must be most vigilant and alert every second." With that they entered the living quarters.

Forste was walking towards his room, when he noticed his brother. He looked at him grimly and asked, "What is it, Pell?"

"He's awakened and active," answered Pell.

"Are you all right?" asked Forste gently.

"He tried to reach into my mind last night," said Pell.

"What?!" asked his brother astonished.

Grista excused herself and left to meet with Corindel. "What did he do?" asked Forste.

"He gave me the most terrible images that I awakened in a cold sweat. So terrible," he continued, "that I cannot even speak of it," he stated.

"Don't worry," said Forste. "We'll put an end to the filth and darkness of Corodorbus."

"Beware!" said Pell, grabbing his brother by both arms and shaking him. "Don't become overconfident!" he warned sternly. "We have never faced anything like this before. This thing has a myriad of weapons and strategies at his disposal and has vanquished many enemies he's faced. Mighty ones have lost their lives and souls facing this monstrosity. Do you understand?!" Pell shouted. Forste, visibly shaken with his brother's intensity, nodded in acquiescence. Pell walked quietly with his brother to where the festivities were being held to find the Kungerods.

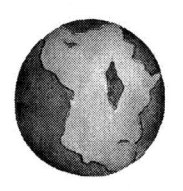

Chapter 37

A DARK APPEAL

They found the Athelonian busy at the circle of monarchs. Pell walked over to the Kungerod. "We need all of you!" he commanded. The Athelonian noticed the dower countenance of Pell and rushed to gather his colleagues. Pell and Forste silently made their way back to the conference center, with the Kungerods following. They entered the Pollidecreum with Pell at the forefront.

The Kungerods took their places around the globe and waited as Pell walked over to the part of the globe, which could not be accessed by them. Again, the Kungerods turned their tundrils as the globe came to life. Emblems, symbols and legends lit up with the golden blood streaming through the globe. Pell stared at the darkened spot on the globe, which seemed to have grown darker overnight. The darkened spot was growing, which meant Corodorbus was getting larger. It was feeding!

Pell looked at his brother and the Kungerods gravely and said, "The festivities are going to have to wait until we return." The Kungerods looked at each other in astonished disappointment. "I know," continued Pell, "that you were all looking forward to this evening, but we have no time my friends. That thing attacked me in my sleep last night."

Fear grew on the faces of the Kungerods and they left their places and circled him their faces full of concern. "Are you all right your majesty?" they asked.

"Yes, I'm fine. Shaken, but fine," he answered. "The thing is growing even as we speak and feeding," said Pell gravely. "We will celebrate after we have dispatched the abomination. Now my friends, back to your places. The time is short and our worlds and lives are at great risk." The

Kungerods quickly moved back to their places around the globe. Each face filled with fear wondering if it was too late. Pell moved closer to the darkened spot on the globe and placed his hand firmly against it. At that moment there was a loud screech and roar that resonated throughout the entire world of Agrimore. All who heard turned white with fear.

Pell continued the process of keeping his hand on the spot, until a small part of the globe emerged from the small orb. They all stared at the part of the inner globe that rose from the orb. It was the location of Corodorbus. The Kungerods circled around the disconnected piece of the globe. "What is this?" asked Pell.

The Athelonain strained to look. "Why, this is the isle of Assilene!" he exclaimed.

"Then that's where we will go," said Pell, firmly turning to Forste. Pell and Forste left for the living quarters, both feeling grieved in their spirits.

Pell entered the room with Grista still in bed. His spirit inside of him was in torment. He laid down beside her and held her. She opened her eyes and stared at the ceiling. "Why?" she asked.

Pell looked at her questioningly. "Why my love?" he asked.

"Why do you have to fight Corodorbus?"

Pell was astonished at this question. "What are you saying Grista?"

Grista grew visibly annoyed. "Maybe this is the purpose of the creature. It's been doing this for cycles or even eons. Why do you think you have the right to stop it?"

"What is this?' he asked sternly. She turned and shot an angry look at him and turned away. He began to realize that Corodorbus was affecting even Grista. He knew that if he did not deal with it immediately, that all would soon be affected. He left the bedroom for Forste's quarters and rapped on the door. There was a voice from within. It was Corindel.

"It's your boring brother. I guess this means you're going to go with him on this useless quest." Forste emerged from the room quite shaken.

Pell grabbed hold of him. "Are you all right?" he asked sternly.

Forste's hands were shaking as he spoke. "She, Corindel, she's become so different, mocking and insulting," he said, his voice shaking.

Pell looked at him intensely. "Listen to me! It's not Corindel. Grista acted the same way. It's Corodorbus. He's affecting all of us. Now get control of yourself!"

Forste calmed himself at his brother's upbraiding. "Yes, you're right. We must hurry!" he said urgently.

Both men left to find the Athelonian at the other end of the living quarters. When they found him, he hurried them into his quarters. He looked at both men sternly and said, "You've felt it, haven't you? The affect of Corodorbus?!" he asked sharply.

"Yes, it's affecting everyone, even our women," answered Pell.

"Well, it's going to get much worse," the Athelonian went on. "You must find the thing and dispatch it immediately. Come with me," ordered the Athelonian, rushing towards the conference room ahead of them.

• • • • • • •

They entered the conference center following the Athelonian, who rushed to a room past the Pollidecreum. The room was stark with walls of stone and wood. There was a large window at the end of the room. In the middle of the room were two stone benches and something that resembled an altar in the center. The Athelonian walked over to the altar-like platform and moved the top slab to the right. All of a sudden a draw opened at the bottom of the altar. The Athelonian stooped down and removed a gilded box from the draw. The box he opened held a strange looking device. It was of a gleaming light blue metal. It was shaped like a malformed trident. The center was long like a sword. Half way up on each side of the sword-like piece was another piece, forming a "T." The "T" was formed by two sharp dagger-like shapes on each end. Up above the "T" shape was an oval dark gem that covered the circumference of the upper stem near the handle. The handle was like black onyx, slightly inverted on each side with a golden knob at the end. The instrument had been wrapped in a cloth of scarlet and gold material.

The Athelonian wrapped the instrument in the cloth, walked over to Pell and handed it to him. He looked up at him and said, "This weapon is called an Asclodent. For eons it has waited to be used by only one person, the only one that can wield it is you Pell, the king of our worlds." With that he handed the weapon to Pell. Pell unwrapped it from the cloth and held it tightly staring at it. As he continued to hold it, the gem below the hilt began to glow, giving off purple and magenta colors. "With this Asclodent you'll be able to kill Corodorbus by placing it deep within its body up to the gem and then removing it," said the Athelonian. The Athelonian then returned to the altar, stooping down and then pulling another box from the draw. He opened the box and removed a large object covered with a blue and silver cloth covering. He walked over to Forste and unwrapped the object, which was silver in color, extremely brilliant, like platinum. The object had two prongs, much like an oversized tuning fork, as well as a gem, blue in color, which occupied the circumference of the upper stem. The handle was of blue sapphire-like stone with a silver top.

The Athelonian handed the object to Forste and said, "Forste take this Ascolande and support your brother in battle."

Forste took the instrument from the Athelonian and raised it into the air, the sun shimmering off of the gleaming metal, then turned to the Athelonian and said, "I will support and protect him with my life," looking over at Pell as he spoke.

The Athelonain took the weapon from Forste's hand and said, "This weapon will disrupt any sound coming from the creature, all you have to do is aim in the direction of the creature and it will disrupt its speech, as well as cause the creature great torment." Then the Athelonian faced both men, looking severe and spoke, "Your majesties," he said firmly, "you must under no circumstances engage the creature in conversation," he continued. "To engage the creature in conversation means death for both of you. Remember to use it whenever the creature begins to speak. Speech is its greatest weapon," he concluded. Then he handed the Ascolande back to Forste and bowed to both men. "Now, sires," said the Athelonian, "your armor awaits you. Please follow me."

He led them to another small room on the other side of the Pollidecreum. The room was stark, with only a small round stained glass rosette window. He walked up to a raised section of the room, just under the window, with Pell and Forste following behind. Under the window were two very old chests covered with blue and gold linen. He pulled back the covering revealing the old chests. He slowly unlocked the first chest and opened it, the top creaking as it opened. The Athelonian reached in and pulled out a breastplate, which seemed to come alive with flame as the light caught it. The breastplate seemed to have the flame contained within it.

The Kungerod looked at Pell intensely and said, "This armor is made of Thuladite, which will allow you to come close to the creature without harm to yourself. Remember," said the Kungerod sternly, "the greatest weapon against you is your mind. It cannot harm you physically, but could destroy your mind if you converse with it. Do you understand?!" asked the Kungerod fiercely.

Then the Kungerod moved over to Forste, stared at him then stooped down and pulled a different breastplate from the other chest. This breastplate was different from Pell's. It was filled with bright blue light coursing its way through the contours of the breastplate, as if it were filled with electrical activity. He moved over to Forste and said, "This armor, Forste, will make you invulnerable to the creature's attacks, but only at a distance. You must not approach the thing, or try to take any offensive action. It will kill you easily if you approach it. Just support your brother's mind with the Ascolande. At a distance it cannot harm you. Approach it and you're dead. Do you understand, Forste?" Forste nodded with concurrence.

The Athelonian turned and faced both men and said, "You are now completely equipped and prepared your majesties. There is no more I can do. I instructed you with all I know concerning your coming conflict." Both men moved closer to the Kungerod and thanked him, then departed to the living quarters.

Pell entered the bedroom carrying the chest with the armor and the Asclodent. Grista was dressing when he entered. "What is that?" she asked curtly. "Oh, don't tell. Let me guess," she went on. "It's for that stupid battle you're going to fight, isn't it?" Pell completely ignored her and readied himself for the battle. Forste walked into the room to help his brother with his armor. Grista looked at Forste and said, "You both look like two dopes on a rope, ridiculous," she sneered. Both men continued to ignore her as Forste helped his brother on with his armor.

Just then Corindel walked in and stood beside her sister. "Can you believe these two?" she asked Grista, sneering.

"Oh," answered Grista, "have you not heard? The two little boys are going off to fight the big bad beastie." With that they both laughed the men to scorn. Pell and Forste did not say a word, but continued to don the armor. Pell went with Forste to his room to help his brother with his armor, with the women continuing to mock them.

When both men were finished, they took their weapons and left without saying a word to Grista or Corindel. They entered a philbee and quietly drove to the terraport without saying a word. They parked the philbee and walked over to the terraspan given to Pell by Purnis. They entered the terraspan and walked to the crew quarters where they found Brighel and Denara. Pell looked at Denara and commanded, "We're leaving for the isle of Assilene." Denara and Brighel looked at both men with disdain and grudgingly made preparations to leave.

• • • • • • •

Forste followed Pell to his quarters and sat quietly. Pell went to the galley and took two perlees from the fridge and sat across from his brother, and offered him one of the perlees. They both drank quietly as the terraspan's turbines began their warm up mode. "I've never felt such anguish," said Forste.

Pell turned to look at him and asked, "You mean Grista and Corindel?" Forste nodded. "I too, my brother," answered Pell. The terraspan lifted higher and higher until it reached the magnetic corridor. With a jerk and a lunge, it had found the magnetic field, then began its trip to the isle of Assilene.

"Did you notice the atmosphere?" asked Forste.

"Of course I did," answered Pell. "Grim, black and hopeless, as it was on Earth when I was there," he concluded. Then he turned to Forste and stared at him intently. "Remember, Forste, do not under any circumstances approach the thing, no matter what you see. Do you understand?!" asked Pell intensely. Forste nodded quietly. "Just keep the Ascolande pointed at the thing. I cannot be harmed by the creature, but he can destroy my mind, so be vigilant," said Pell gravely. Then he added, "If anything happens to either one of us, the battle is over and the creature has won, so aim your Ascolande well and keep back," he concluded.

Denara and Brighel were at the controls, when Brighel looked at Denara and said, "Why do we have to do the bidding of those two?"

Denara stared at him, with anger growing within her. "You're right!" she shot back. "Why do we have to do their bidding? We're not lackeys!" She then angrily grabbed a lever and pulled it back with violence. The machine lurched forward and came to a full stop, suspended, motionless in the corridor. Pell and Forste were lifting themselves off of the floor, being thrown by the sudden stop.

Everything was strewn over the deck of the stateroom, spilt perlees, puigos and their weapons. After lifting themselves off the deck, they made their way swiftly to the control room. They opened the door to see the crew staring at them. "What's the problem?!" shouted Pell. Denara and Brighel ignored both men as the rest of the crew carefully reclined in their seats smiling at them. Pell walked over to the couple enraged and said, "This is my terraspan and you work for me, you got that?!" They both turned their backs to him. Pell turned them around to face him and leaned over with his face only inches from theirs and said quietly, but menacingly, "I will ask you both just once to start those turbines. After that I will not speak, but the result will be great pain to Brighel, you got that?!" his voice rising in anger. The couple quietly swiveled their seats around and Denara, with her hands shaking, pushed forward the lever. The turbines came to life as the machine lunged and continued on its way. Pell and Forste went back to Pell's stateroom, tidied up and sat back wearily.

"It's going to get worse, isn't it?" asked Forste.

Pell nodded and said, "Much worse."

• • • • • • •

The Athelonian walked back to the living quarters to meet with his colleagues. They were all in the lounge area of the living quarters. Their faces were all ashen and stony. He walked over to where they were and seated himself next to the Can-Chimeran, "You've all felt it, haven't you?" he asked. They looked up at him without saying a word. "I've sent them both on their way fully equipped to dispatch the darkness."

"You did that without us?" asked the Ilgestanian.

"Yes," he answered, "there was no time for festivities, or to try to find all of you. They had to leave immediately and they have left. So take courage my friends. These two great ones will accomplish their task and our two worlds will be free of this abomination."

The terraspan slowed as it emerged from the corridor and gently descended slowly towards the isle of Assilene. Finally, the craft gently alit on the surface of the isle. The isle, which had at one time been beautiful, was now stark and almost barren. The trees were black and lifeless and the lovely fauna was withered. Even the grass was hard and lifeless. Pell and Forste, completely clad in armor and well armed, exited the terraspan.

Chapter 38

THE DARKNESS AND BLACKNESS OF CORODORBUS

"How do you know which way to go?" asked Forste.

"Look at the desolation. Wherever it is, the desolation will be greater. All we do is to follow where the desolation is greater. Also, do you smell that?" Pell went on. "That scent is the filth of the creature."

"Yes," said Forste, "I do smell it. It's abominable."

"Well, it'll get worse as we get closer to where it is." They continued to walk past rotted and dead trees, until there was nothing. The odor was becoming stronger and overwhelming.

"The stench!" exclaimed Forste. "How can we abide with the stench?!"

"Keep your faculties about you!" shouted Pell. "And get control of yourself!" The stench was almost vomitous. At this time both men were fighting just to compose themselves. They kept walking until they came to a clearing, the ground was black and slimy. They fought to keep themselves from slipping into the muck and mire left by the creature. As they both walked together into the clearing, they noticed a huge chasm where Corodorbus had eaten its way into the planet.

"That's where we must go!" exclaimed Pell. They both walked up to the chasm and gradually descended into it. Forste's breastplate grew brighter as they descended, lighting the way. Then the gemstones on the stem of their weapons began throbbing with light. They continued to descend as Pell turned to Forste and shouted, "Be alert brother and keep your Ascolande prepared!"

All at once there was a soft calm voice out of the darkness. "Ah, Pell and Forste, I've been waiting for you. Yes, I've been-"

Pell interrupted the voice and shouted at Forste, "Aim your Ascolande!" Forste raised the gleaming instrument in the direction of the voice. The stone on the stem was now pulsating rapidly as the Ascolande grew in brilliance. All of a sudden there was a deafening scream from the direction of the voice and then there was silence.

"That will be something that the fiend will remember if it ever tries to engage in conversation again," said Forste.

Both men continued to descend the chasm towards the direction of the voice. Deeper and deeper they descended into the chasm, slipping occasionally on the slimy paths. Then the voice boomed, "Do you think you can face me?! Do you know what I've...?" Forste raised the Ascolande in the direction of the voice and once again, there was a bone-chilling scream that resonated throughout the world of Agrimore.

They continued to make their way downward towards the voice slipping and sliding occasionally. Forste rested against a stone slab, trying to cover his face from the overwhelming stench. Pell approached his brother. "Are you all right?" he asked.

"All right!" retorted Forste. "All right?! Is that what you are asking me, brother?! Don't you smell the stench of that denizen?! How can you ask if I'm all right?!"

Pell put down his Asclodent and grabbed his brother firmly by the shoulders and stared into his eyes and said quietly, but firmly, "Listen, Forste I need you to get control of yourself. I cannot do this without you, you are my shield!" he shouted. "If you lose control, then all is lost. Do you understand?!"

His brother looked up at Pell and sighed. "It's all on our shoulders, isn't it brother? Two worlds resting on our shoulders."

He then composed himself, rose up as they continued their trek downward to where the adversary was. "Why? Why do you approach?" came a sweet feminine voice. "I'm not your enemy. Why, Pell? I've known you for so long. We've me-"

"Your Ascolande!" shouted Pell. "Forste!" he bellowed. Forste came out of his trance and raised the weapon, the gem on the stem now glowing wildly as he aimed the instrument. All at once, there was a blood-curdling scream.

Forste looked at Pell. "His attacks are becoming stronger," he said, shaking.

Pell concurred and said, "We must be getting closer." Then the two men continued their descent. They finally came to a wide cavern glowing with stinking light. Both men were gagging from the stench. They slowly made their way into the cavern and towards the hideous light. Indescribable things were scurrying away from them, black, wormy and slimy. They could see a shadowy mass in the distance. "We've arrived," said Pell. Forste's eyes grew as he tried to focus on the incomprehensible form. Both men walked slowly and carefully towards the mass.

"Welcome, dear friends," said a voice coming from the distant mass. "I've been expecting you."

"Forste!" shouted Pell. Forste raised the Ascolande and aimed towards the mass. The cavern echoed with fearful screams as the mass lunged away from them.

They proceeded slowly, inching closer to the distant mass. All over the cavern, were translucent capsule shaped things, thousands of them, maybe millions strewn everywhere. Pell looked down closely at one of the capsule shapes. There was movement inside, a black, reddish and slimy substance was moving within the capsule. Pell stood upright and stared at Forste. "Offspring!" he said. "The abomination is giving birth." Both men, their faces white like ash, proceeded forward towards the mass. The mass had moved to the far end of the cavern. Pell's breastplate began to glow like flame. "Danger," announced Pell. "We're in danger. Keep alert, brother!" They continued to move closer to where the mass was.

They began to notice something in the distance. To the left of them, it looked like blood trying to take form. Both men stopped, staring in horror, as the blood tried to shape itself. It started to take an indescribable form and they could hear the sound of the sucking liquid. Finally it took a shape, which could only be described by a madman. Its skin was so tight that you could hear it stretch. Blackish, red and monstrous, like a bat wing with feet is the only way to describe what they were looking at. While they were concentrating on the form to the left of them, the voice of the mass at the end of the cavern began to speak, "How do you like my creation? Lovely, isn't it?" Forste at once knew what to do and aimed the Ascolande towards the distant mass. Once again, there was a heart-rending scream.

Then the unknown to the left of them began to close in on them. Pell stood to the forefront to intercept the unknown monstrosity. Pell raised his Asclodent as the form came closer, stretching itself to envelope him. Silently, the hideous form moved closer to him, picking up speed as it closed in on its prey.

The clumsy thing lunged at Pell with Forste captivated by the horrible configuration. Pell threw himself out of its way and rolled on the ground as the thing pursued him. As he laid on his back, the monstrous shape sought to cover him. He then got up and lunged towards the shape with his Asclodent, as a charging lancer. He struck the impure violation of creation in the center of the bat-like wing formation. The thing immediately shriveled up. All there was left was a pile of something, which resembled dead brown leaves. Forste stood staring at the residue on the ground. Pell walked over to him and said, "You see what we're up against, don't you, Forste?"

Forste looked up at him slowly and stated, "How? How can we fight such things? Spectres, abominations, things not even seen in nightmares. How, Pell?" he pleaded. "How do we deal with such unimaginable horrors? How? Please tell me if you can." He then put his head in his hands.

Pell put his hands around his brother's head and lifted his head to look at him and gently said, "Forste, my dear brother, you are stronger than you realize and you are not alone. I am here with you. We're kings and not ordinary men. In fact, ordinary men are depending on us. We can do this, Forste. Only we can accomplish this," his brother concluded. Forste looked at his dear brother and took courage. Then both men continued towards the darkened mass at the end of the cavern.

"How dare you!" came a voice out at the end of the cavern. "You would dare to raise arms against me? No one has ever successfully defeated me." Forste aimed his Ascolande towards the mass. Immediately there was a scream and moan, then silence. They both made their way towards the mass.

Then Pell turned to Forste and said, "We're nearing the darkness." Then he turned and faced Forste. "Remember, brother, when we near Corodorbus you must cover me with your Ascolande, but you must stay behind. You must not venture close to the creature, no matter what you observe. Is that clear?" Forste nodded in approval. Pell and Forste ventured further into the vast cavern to where the mass was located. They edged their way slowly and carefully, closing in on the dark form at the end of the cavern.

"You've fed me for eons, Pell Provance," came a voice echoing through the cavern, "magnifying evil for me to feed on. Now you wish to end it all? What gives you the right?"

• • • • • • •

Pell turned around to his brother. Forste had a questioning expression on his face. "What?" he asked.

"Do you not hear that?" asked Pell.

"Hear what?" Pell was at a loss as to his brother's lack of hearing.

Unless, of course, the creature is speaking in my mind. The thought came to him like a report of a three inch deck gun. Pell walked up to Forste and gestured for him to stop. Pell looked at Forste and said, "The things gotten into my mind. Don't proceed any further than those rocks over there." Pell gestured with his Asclodent to a pile of large stones. "Now brother, you must aim the Ascolande at me. It will protect my mind as I close in on the obscenity," he concluded.

Forste situated himself between two large stones and aimed his Ascolande at Pell. Pell was thinking about what the creature had said to him. Have I been feeding that thing? he thought. For how long? He continued slowly towards the dark mass, now huddled against the far wall. This time, he was alone, without his brother by his side. But he knew that his brother would never take his eyes off of him. He continued to close in on the mass.

All of a sudden the huge black mass turned into a sheet, then into some sort of ugly black umbrella shape. Forste grew concerned, but remembered that he could not move from his spot, only to keep his Ascolande aimed at Pell. The monstrous mass kept changing its shape, trying to frighten Pell, but to no avail. Pell closed in on the filthy mass now only about ten feet away from it. He continued closer to the filthy creature, trying to understand what he was looking at.

All of a sudden the misformed mass grew before him higher and broader. It was beginning to fill the rear end of the cavern. It was brownish black and slimy. It was now maybe hundreds of feet high, with a hole of dark blue light. Within, it looked like a bottomless maul, deep and terrible. The aperture is where it consumes evil, Pell thought.

Forste attempted to take a step forward after having seen the mass enlarge itself, but remembered the directives of Pell, the Kungerod and the dire warning of taking offensive action and its consequences. He kept his ground and just kept aiming the Ascolande at Pell. Pell inched closer to the mass, studying it with doleful fascination. The mass was fully aware of Pell's presence and stood motionless, not having room to retreat. Pell raised his Asclodent and moved closer to the mass. He began thinking to himself, Do I have the right to end this creature's existence?

Pell hesitated, then the creature lunged at him, overwhelming him. He felt himself sinking into the maul, into blackness of darkness, into a bottomless pit. His mind became filled with images of horror, he was frozen with fear and could not move, as he became enveloped. Forste saw that his brother was in great danger. He could see his brother descending into the maul. He began frantically shouting, screaming in frenzy at his brother. Pell recovered himself and overcame his fear. He raised his Asclodent and drove it deep into the creature from the opening of the maul. The massive creature convulsed violently, twisting and screaming, filling the cavern with a cacophony of sounds indescribable to the human ear. Forste covered his ears protecting them from the din. The echoes continued filling the cavern like a cathedral with hundreds of out of tune pipe organs.

Pell remembered what the Athelonian had told him, to remove the Asclodent. He struggled to reach the hilt as the mass lunged from side to side violently. With much effort, he reached up and grabbed the hilt of the Asclodent and forcibly removed it. The creature grew still and began to shrink moaning in despair as it died. Finally, all that was left was a liquidy mass on the ground of the cavern. Corodorbus was dead! Forste walked slowly over to his brother, who was still staring at the residue on the ground of the cavern. Pell turned to Forste and embraced him tightly. Forste, with a tear making its way down his cheek said, "My dear brother, for a moment I thought I had lost you forever. I never wish to recall the anguish of that moment again." He kissed Pell on the side of the head and said, "Come dear brother, let's leave this miserable place."

Both men slowly made their way out of the cavern, past the capsules, which were now beginning to disintegrate. They were both weary and spent. They continued to scale the opening the creature had made, helping one another. These two, kings true, with honor and grace filling their faces, saviours of their worlds, potentates of courage made their way upward towards the Agrimorian sun, which waited patiently for their arrival, waiting to reward them with glory well deserved. Slowly, they continued to climb together, supporting one another, hope and joy filling their souls.

Chapter 39

THESE TWO, KINGS TRUE

The Kungerods knew that the two kings were victorious. Great joy filled their faces as they all embraced one another in exultation. Grista and Corindel emerged from the bedroom, their eyes full of tears and their hearts longing for the men they loved. The painful memories of how they had behaved earlier afflicted both of them. They were weeping bitterly in the hallway. Grista crouched down and sat on the floor of the hallway holding her head in uncontrollable weeping.

The Athelonian was making his way back to the living quarters to prepare for the greatest festival Agrimore had ever known. He entered the living quarters spritely, when he had heard sobbing coming from the left side hallway. He walked towards the sound of the sobbing and saw both Corindel and Grista sobbing uncontrollably. His heart dropped within him as he beheld their grief. He swallowed hard trying to contain his own spirit. He walked slowly over to both women, who were completely overcome.

He stooped down to where Grista was and looked up at Corindel, who was facing the wall sobbing. Then he put his arms around Grista and took Corindel's hand, pulling her over towards her sister and motioned for her to sit. He put his arm around both girls and spoke gently to them. "Grista, Corindel," he said, "what is the meaning of all of this weeping? Your hearts are so broken, but your kings have been victorious and are on their way back," he said smiling.

Grista looked up sobbing and said, "You don't know the things we said to them, the utter disrespect we showed to them, just when they needed us most," she concluded, still sobbing.

"Dear, dear children," he said, "It was not you, but Corodorbus, who is now dead, slain by your two great men. Now stop this weeping and prepare yourselves for the arrival of your beloveds who love you both dearly and are longing for you." With that, both women wiped their eyes and rose up. The Athelonian smiled at them and said, "Now, no more of this nonsense," then left to continue the preparations.

Pell and Forste continued their ascent out of the aperture with the waiting Agrimorian sun beginning to shine on them. Forward, they climbed together their faces now full of sunlight until they reached the clearing of blackened trees and fauna, which slowly seemed to be coming back to life, even the slime had disappeared. Both kings continued on their way with the desolation disappearing as they walked to the spot to where Purnis's terraspan was to meet them. Finally, they approached the original site where they had been deposited. There with the Agrimorian sun glistening off of its skin, was the terraspan. As they approached, they saw the entire crew at attention with Denara and Brighel at the center. Pell and Forste stumbled towards them, finally reaching the small entourage. They walked up to Denara and Brighel who bowed their heads and asked softly, "Can you both forgive us for our earlier actions?"

Pell looked at them, being quite spent, and said, "Please, no more of this; there is nothing to forgive, but if it makes you feel better, yes, we forgive you. Now can we get on board before we faint before you?" With that they all smiled and helped both men on board.

Pell and Forste entered their quarters with the help of some of the crew. Pell and Forste sat down as a crewmember asked if there was anything he could get for them. "Yes," said Forste, "two perlees please." The crewmember smiled and walked to the galley and came back with two perlees in hand. He excused himself and left. Pell and Forste raised the perlees and toasted each other, took swigs and reclined.

The entire isle of Pathenune was full of activity and abuzz with the exploits of Pell and Forste. The entire world of Agrimore was full of joy and celebration. Everyone was rushing about on Pathenune waiting for the arrival of Pell and Forste.

Grista and Corindel were in their bedrooms awaiting for the arrival of their kings. Corindel walked into Grista's bedroom and sat on the bed and yawned with exhaustion from the grief that both of them had suffered. Grista sat next to her sister and put her arm around her, holding her closely. "How are you feeling my sweet?" she asked.

Corindel looked at her sister affectionately. "So, so tired." Then she laid her head on Grista's shoulders.

The Kungerods were rushing to the terraport to greet the two victorious kings. They were all abuzz concerning their exploits.

Grista and Corindel were rushing around getting ready so they could meet their heart's desires at their arrival. They hurriedly dressed and ran to a parked philbee behind the conference center.

Pell and Forste had been sleeping when they were awakened by the sudden shift of the terraspan exiting the magnetic corridor. The terraspan gradually descended on the isle of Pathenune where Grista, Corindel and all of the Kungerods were waiting for them. Slowly, the terraspan descended, until it finally settled on the elevator. Pell and Forste made their way down the gangplank where the crew was waiting at attention. The two mighty men walked through the small gauntlet of honor formed by the crew still standing at attention.

Pell walked over to Denara and Brighel, thanked them and invited them to attend tonight's festivities, as well as the crew. They made their way to the passenger elevator where Grista, Corindel and the Kungerods were waiting for them. The elevator descended slowly and then settled on ground level. They stepped off of the elevator where the Kungerods had formed a semi-circle. All five Kungerods bowed down on one knee and shouted in unison, "Your majesties!"

· · · · · · ·

"Please rise to your feet," asked Pell. "Thank you all for what you've done for us," he said. Then Pell walked over to the Athelonian, grabbed and hugged him tightly. He loosened his embrace and looked at the Kungerod respectfully. "My dear, dear friend, how can we ever thank you for your invaluable assistance in this terrible battle? You armed us, equipped us and directed us without which, we might not be standing here at this time. Please kneel," he asked. Then he took the Asclodent, raised it until the blade was positioned in front of the face of the Kungerod, then said, "I confer upon you the honor of Ex-Cathelara with all of the authority that pertains to that title." Then he turned and shouted for all to hear, "I pronounce Ex-Cathelara upon the Kungerod of Athelone." All of the other Kungerods were astonished, for there was no higher honor for a Kungerod.

This honor had not been conferred for thousands of Agrimorian cycles. It gave the Athelonian absolute authority as a Kungerod. The Athelonian knelt there on one knee, completely speechless.

Then Pell and Forste turned and walked over to where Grista and Corindel were waiting for them. Grista stared at Pell as he approached her, as did Corindel at Forste. Both men were quite spent, soiled and disheveled. They both stumbled towards their queens with every step more burdensome than the previous one. Grista ran over to Pell and Corindel rushed to Forste. Both women helped their men to the living quarters.

The Kungerods were busy with the preparations. The Athelonian went to the Pollidecreum and walked past the globes to the far side of the room, to a wooden panel. The panel had a small square metallic symbol. He pressed hard on the symbol with his thumb. The panel receded into the wall, revealing a small staircase. He proceeded down the staircase to a small dimly lit room. In the center of the room, was a stand supporting a box of blue glass with gold edges. Inside of the box was a marvelously crafted crown. He carefully lifted the white satin like pillow, which held the crown and whispered to himself, "The crown of Auduxiare," and left the small room taking the crown with him.

Grista helped Pell into the bedroom and began removing his armor and tunic. He laid on the bed while she went to prepare a bath for him.

Meanwhile, the Kungerods were engrossed in their preparations for the night's festivities. The highway of potentates was now strewn with ribbons, banners and flowers. Children were everywhere laughing, placing flowers over the highway and tying ribbons to the small poles along the roadway. The chefs were rolling their tables into position; there were also great chefs from Faxburn, Lathernae, Firwith, Applendice and Selverna. Artistic fire shapers were also present. The terraport was also full of activity with continuous traffic of landing terraspans. Some exotic plant life had also been transported for the festival.

The Athelonian used the pink glass and gold pipe to summon the Regunelus back to the circle of monarchs. The magnificent creatures were a delight to behold as they gracefully maneuvered their way to the circle. Every eye was upon these aviators. The living quarters were becoming filled with visitors as special refreshments were being prepared for them. Dignitaries, officials and persons of importance filled the lounge area. All were fabulously attired.

Pell was sleeping soundly with Grista holding him. She had bathed him in spices and oils then rubbed down his entire body and put him to bed, as Corindel did the same with Forste.

• • • • • • •

Purnis and Drue were walking outside of the living quarters. Drue was wearing a sleeveless silver-blouse, with black slacks and tan boots. She also wore a thin gold belt around her waist. They continued to walk quietly together when Drue asked her aunt about the festivities. Purnis was not completely sure of the reason for the festivities, but added, "I think it's some sort of coronation for a person of some importance, but I'm not sure."

"Well, it's got to be someone really important and Pell seems to know whoever it is because he was allowed to invite us," said Drue.

Pell opened his eyes to find Grista asleep next to him. He kissed her cheek and gently woke her. "Time for us to get ready my love," he said softly. Grista moaned and asked if it was evening yet. "Not yet, but close," he answered. He rose up and walked to the closet and pulled out an old trunk. He opened it and took out a fabulous tunic and laid it on the bed. The tunic was sewn with pure gold. It was indigo blue with touches of red. It had a high collar with edges curved around the throat area. The collar was white, finely sewn with pure gold. The coat had six golden buttons shaped like lions' heads. The sleeves had two thin red stripes near the ends. Then he removed a pair of white slacks from the chest. These slacks were so blindingly white that they almost shimmered whiter than the snows of Everest. He then removed a pair of finely crafted black boots with a brilliant luster. He next removed a red sash, then a belt. The buckle was a gold lions' head. The belt itself was made of pure, soft, spun silver.

Grista opened her eyes and beheld the noble attire on the bed next to her. She sat up and gently ran her hand over the tunic. "How wonderfully lordly," she noted.

Corindel was awake and gently nudged Forste. "Hey, my silver-haired beauty, wake up."

"Ugh, hmm," moaned Forste.

"Come on baby, this is your brother's big night and my sister's," she said.

"How late is it?" he asked.

"It's close to sundown. Come on, up with you."

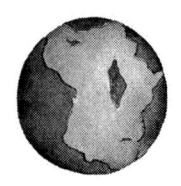

Chapter 40

THE RECOVERY OF TWO JEWELS

Purnis and Drue were walking back towards the living quarters when Drue asked her aunt, "Auntie, do you think we'll see Pell before the celebration?"

Her aunt looked at her sternly and asked, "Why do you wish to see him?"

"I don't know," she answered, "maybe, just to thank him for the honor he paid us, or maybe if he sees me another time, he'll see how beautiful I am and decide to be with me. I am beautiful, aren't I, auntie?"

Her aunt looked at her compassionately and held her lovely face in her hands and answered, "Of course you're beautiful, lovey. Why, most men would do anything for just a moment with you."

"But not Pell," said Drue. "Huh, auntie? Not him, right?" Her aunt looked away in distress.

Forste went to the closet and took a trunk out and dragged it near the bed. He opened it and removed an exquisite tunic from it. It was white, sewn with silver thread. The buttons were red gems shaped in the faces of lions. The collar was high and curved, opened around the throat area, indigo blue in color. On the sleeves, were two thin indigo blue stripes. He then removed an indigo blue sash from the trunk and a belt with a buckle of platinum lions head. The belt was of dark, rich, spun gold. Then he took a pair of rich, soft black slacks as black as the shadows of Ilgestana.

Purnis and Drue entered the lounge area where most of the guests were gathered. Drue noted with excitement, "Auntie!" she exclaimed. "Look at all of the dignitaries. Why, there are Ilgestanians, Can-Chimerans, Patamodians, Vernacians and Athelonians. This must be an event of great importance," she said excitedly. "Also, they're all so fabulously dressed," she concluded.

Her aunt looked around and remarked, "Hmm, in all of my years I've never seen such a gathering." Then she turned to Drue and said, "Honey, we'll never see anything like this again, why, everyone of significance in all of Agrimore are here, even the old noble families and they don't attend anything, but they're all here."

A large Vernacian male approached the two females and offered them refreshments. "Well, well," noted the corpulent Vernacian, "two lovelies without refreshment will not do. No, not at all," he said energetically. The man was bright eyed with curly white wooly hair and a wonderful smile. He handed the cordials to the two women and bowed respectfully. "The name is Pyderyn," he offered with enthusiasm.

"I'm Purnis, and this is my niece Drue."

"Well," said Pyderyn, "let me introduce you to some of the guests."

Purnis interjected and asked, "Tell me, Pyderyn, who is being so honored that all of Agrimore is poised for tonight's celebration? Who is this person to be crowned tonight?"

Pyderyn looked at both women with questions running through his face astonished that both women were oblivious to the happenings of the past few annots. "You mean you don't know?" he asked, staring with disbelief.

"No, we don't know, now would you please inform us?!" asked Purnis sharply.

The Vernacian composed himself and recounted the destruction of Corodorbus and the two kings that saved both worlds. "Who are the two kings?" asked Drue with excited anticipation.

He looked at them, smiling. "Why it's our lord Pell Provance and his great brother Forste," he answered proudly.

Drue put her hand to her mouth and looked at her aunt with astonishment and shame. "Did you say Pell Provance?" asked Purnis.

"Yes," said Pyderyn, "why, he's our king, long gone from us, the king of our two worlds and much, much more," he answered with joy.

Purnis looked at Drue with amazement and excused themselves. They rushed out of the lounge and walked down the path away from the living quarters. Purnis stopped and looked at Drue. "A king," she said, her voice shaking. "Our king."

Drue looked at her aunt with concern. "Are we going to be all right, auntie?" she asked in a frightened voice.

"I don't know, my sweet. I don't know," she answered, holding Drue tightly.

"We should leave, auntie, huh?"

"Yes, I think it may be for the best." They both headed towards the terraport.

• • • • • • •

Pell quickly dressed in normal attire and rushed to leave. "Where are you going?" asked Grista.

"I'll be right back," he said anxiously. "There's something I must take care of." He left the living quarters and headed towards the terraport.

• • • • • • •

Purnis and Drue quickly headed towards their awaiting terraspan when a philbee pulled up to them. The canopy opened and Pell exited the philbee. Purnis and her niece began to be filled with terror. Purnis grabbed her niece tightly as Pell approached them.

Pell noticed at once their fright and spoke softly to calm them. "Please," he said quietly, "why are you so afraid of me?" He moved a little closer to them, with a pleading and compassionate look on his face, pained that they were so afraid of him. "Purnis, Drue," he said addressing them, "Why, why do you treat me so? What have I done to deserve this? From two people I care for, why? Why treat me like a monster?"

Purnis spoke hesitantly, "Why did you not tell us you were a king, and not only that, but our king?"

"Because," he answered, "I myself did not know it. It was only revealed to me a short time ago by the Kungerods. Please, Drue, Purnis, I would not harm you. In fact, I protected both of you by not revealing anything to anyone. Did you think I would invite you here for ulterior motives? How could you think such a thing of me?"

Purnis and Drue now felt more at ease. "So you're not mad at me?" Drue asked.

"Mad at such a beauty as yourself? Mad at being loved? Even though you took some extreme measures to demonstrate your love, in a way it was really flattering. No, in fact, you've both become precious to me. Now stop this nonsense and come close to me." They walked over to him hesitantly. He then grabbed them both and hugged them.

Then he took Drue and held her head with his hands and kissed her forehead and said, "Now, you little beauty, I've something special for you. Now come, I've got to get prepared and I want you both to attend."

They walked back to the living quarters together when Drue asked, "What shall we call you Pell? Sire, your majesty or what?"

Pell smiled at Drue and gently pinched her cheek and answered, "Well, why don't you call me Pell, except when I'm sitting crowned, then you can use titles, but when we're together we're friends, got that?"

"Uh, huh," said Drue sweetly, then said, "I still think you're hot, the hottest man I've ever seen."

Pell looked at Purnis and said, "It's hopeless, isn't it?"

"I'm afraid so," she said as they both laughed.

Chapter 41

DOWN THE HIGHWAY OF POTENTATES

The preparations on Pathenune continued at a rapid pace seeing that evening was almost upon them.

Along the highway of Potentates on either side, were fire shapers twisting and shaping swirls of flame into the dusky sky. The chefs from five continents were rushing about followed by attendants. Workers were placing the wondrous Cartalasae trees in place like glowing crystal sentinels lighting both sides of the highway of Potentates. Others were getting the beautiful Retazuna plants ready for flight. Hundreds of workers, attendants, chefs, fire shapers and fenfitters were hard at work for the evening's festivities.

The Athelonian carried the Auduxaire back to his quarters. Then he left the living quarters and headed for the conference center.

Darvin and Gully were lying back on their beds. Gully turned to Darvin smiling and asked, "Well, my good mate, what do you think?"

Darvin looked over at Gully. "What are you going on about?"

Gully tossed his pillow at Darvin and said, "You know," then said, "think of it, mate, we're good friends with a king. I mean a king of two worlds and so much more. You know Pell, we'll be friends forever," he continued. "Did you ever think that that handsome heart breaker, perlee drinker, party goer and all around weirdest rascal we've ever met would be anything like this?"

Darvin looked at Gully and said, "You know, Gulls, I've always thought that there was something strange about Pell, so I'm not that surprised."

Gully laid back and smiled at the ceiling. "Yeah, I wonder what's going to happen next, you know our next adventure." Darvin looked at him, then looked away shaking his head.

Grista was outside of Cremy and Twilly's bedroom when she heard Twilly screaming and pleading for mercy. She opened the door to find Cremy on top of Twilly, pinning her to the floor and ticking her. Grista laughed and asked, "What's going on you two?"

Twilly pleaded, "Grista make her let me up, please!" she pleaded, laughing.

Cremy held her down, "Oh no you don't," she said. "You tell her what you did to me." Cremy turned to Grista and said, "This little sprite filled my bath with so much bath soap that the whole bathroom's filled with suds, while I was in the bath!" she yelled. "You can't even open the door to the bathroom because of all of the bubbles!"

Grista walked over to the bathroom and sure enough there was a wall of bubbles, you could not see anything in the bathroom. Grista looked down at Twilly still being held by Cremy. "You deserve whatever Cremy does to you," she said laughing, then said to Cremy, "Don't let her up until she's learned her lesson." Then she turned and left, laughing, with Twilly still pleading for help.

The Athelonian entered the conference center and walked into the Pollidecreum. He walked past the globe to the end of the room. Then he took his tundril and placed it in a slot in the floor and turned it, a stone slab slid back, revealing a parchment of pure gold paper sealed with a platinum seal. The Athelonian removed it and carried it back to the living quarters.

• • • • • • •

Pell led Purnis and Drue to the lounge. He introduced them to Diamine and Persalana. They were fascinated with the glass beings. He also asked the Vernacian Kungerod if he would make them feel at home. Drue began enjoying herself and caught the eye of most of the young available males. Pell then excused himself and went to look for Grista.

The preparations were continuing at a feverish pace. The chefs had their tables placed on either side of the highway of Potentates and began preparing their sumptuous fare of Plaporis Carib with fig nuts, Tandelon with gretheline sauce, Athelonian silk strips, Folineese Foderich and Mutrish. The great desserts of Agrimore were also readied, Merokosian Canae, Aspicone, Paximunte and the great Aquidale the king of desserts. Appitizers were also made available, Quanta berries, Todo Pon breadrolls, Poscen breadrolls and malen chips.

Pell walked down the hallway of the living quarters towards his bedroom. He entered the bedroom to find Grista dressing. Just then there was a knock on the door, he opened it and Corindel entered. "No, no, sweetie," said Corindel to Grista. "That won't do. You have to change and put on your royal gown." Corindel walked over to the closet and pulled out Grista's trunk. Pell kissed Grista on the cheek and excused himself, realizing that Corindel was there to help his queen get ready for the coronation.

Pell entered the lounge area and espied a black-haired beauty in the far end of the lounge standing by herself. He approached the solitary female. "Extella?!" he exclaimed.

Extella turned and looked at him. "Sire?"

"No Extella, not sire, unless I'm on my throne. I prefer Pell when socializing."

"Oh, sorry, Pell," she said apologetically.

"So, I'm glad you're here to attend my coronation, but you're a Thermedyte and I didn't think you would partake in such matters," said Pell.

"Normally you'd be right," she answered, "but I'm not a Thermedyte any longer." Pell had a surprised expression on his face. "Why are you so surprised?" she asked. "It was you that made this possible, so I've decided to keep this form and live here on Agrimore. After all, the purpose of a Thermedyte was ended with the destruction of Corodorbus. So we owe you a great debt." Then she kissed him on the cheek and said, "Thank you, great prince," and left.

Evening had finally fallen on Agrimore and the two blue moons were poised for the evening's events. Scores of Agrimorians were making their way down the highway of Potentates trying to find an area with a good view.

Pell returned to his bedroom to change into his kingly garb. The women had left to dress in Corindel's bedroom. Pell donned his tunic, slacks and boots. Soon afterwards there was a knock at the door. He opened it to three women of Pathenune. "Sire," a tall red-haired beauty said, "We are here to prepare you for this evening." They then removed his tunic, then brushed, combed and trimmed his hair.

Corindel took a magnificent white gown out of Grista's trunk. It was a shimmering white, satin-like material. Then she took a pair of platinum open-toe shoes out of the trunk. She then removed a glass box which contained a tiara of platinum with diamonds, sapphires and small rubies in the shape of roses. Three Pathenunian women entered Corindel's bedroom to help her prepare Grista for the coronation.

The Athelonian made his way to the circle of monarchs, followed by some attendants. He directed them to place a rostrum of blue glass in the center of the circle. He then directed them to place two golden stands on either side of the rostrum. Then he placed the Auduxiare on the stand to the right.

The Regunelus were perched in their places around the circle of monarchs. The orchestras and choruses were also in place poised for the appearance of the king and queen.

The three women were putting the finishing touches on Pell's attire. He was now kingly, royal and majestic. He was asked to wait until Grista was ready.

Corindel and the three women were preparing Grista. They first had bathed her in the finest oils of Pathenune. Then they brushed her golden curly tresses, which had grown longer after time. Corindel took the Apicella leaves, which she had used earlier on Grista and rubbed them all over her marvelous body. Then Corindel took the Phalmus bulb she had used on Grista at her home and spread the light blue fragrant liquid on her. After that, the women took the gown, white and brilliant. It was adorned with rubies shaped like roses in a diagonal pattern. The jewels were tiny, about a foot apart and ended in a circular pattern around the waist. The top of the gown came to a "V" at the breast area with the "V" covered with beautiful white lace, set with tiny sapphires. The sleeves of the gown were the finest embroidered lace that ended at the forearms, with tiny rose shaped rubies at the ends. They dressed her in the magnificent gown, then shod her feet with platinum shoes. They took a headdress with a veil and a long train studded with tiny diamonds and now the queen Grista was ready. Then Corindel went to her dresser and pulled out a beautiful box. Inside was a necklace of fine, spun, dark gold, with an indescribable jewel in the center and placed it around Grista's neck.

Forste now dressed in his kingly attire with a gold crown on his head, went to fetch his brother.

Corindel put on an ice blue gown sewn with silver thread. Around her waist, she wore a platinum fine-spun belt bespeckled with jewels. Her feet were shod with shoes of soft gold and on her head was a marvelous golden tiara. They were all ready for the procession.

Forste went to Pell's bedroom and entered to find the three women putting the finishing touches on him. He walked over to his brother holding an embossed blue box in his hand. He stared at his brother and said, "I'm so proud of you, my brother, you're the noblest person, full of honor, courage and a true king." Then he opened the box and removed a chain or Lavaliere, wonderfully designed with golden squares of lion's heads set a half inch apart. At the end of the chain was a indescribable blue gem. He fastened it around his brother's neck then said, "Come, my brother, your queen is awaiting you and they left.

The Kungerods were all gathered at the circle of monarchs, with the Athelonian standing by the Rostrum. All of the guests were now present on each side of the highway of Potentates. Streamers and banners were flowing in the gentle breeze, the Cartalasae trees giving off their wonderful light illuminating everything and everyone. All were silent as they awaited the royal couple. Many people were still making their way to the highway of Potentates. The Athelonian unsealed the parchment and held it in his hand until the royal couple appeared.

Pell, Forste, Darvin and Gully were waiting by the entrance to the highway of Potentates for Grista, Corindel, Cremona and Twilly to appear. Pell and Forste stood side by side with Darvin and Gully behind them.

Then Grista and Corindel appeared making their way to the entrance of the highway of Potentates, followed by Cremona and Twilly. All eyes were fastened on the approaching entourage, Grista in white resplendent glory. Slowly they approached the men at the entrance. Pell could see Grista's glistening eyes looking at him through the diamond-studded veil. As Pell looked at his queen, he tried to understand what he was looking at. His mind labored to put words to the scene. Words, he thought, would be profane descriptions, paltry, abysmal, futile, nugatory, vain and ineffectual in trying to describe Grista. He stared into the eyes behind the veil of the approaching Grista. The majesty of her movements overwhelmed him. The eyes behind the veil were as stars that had just been born, thousands of star clusters in those eyes that were staring at him. Pell felt his brother's strong arm steadying him as he lost his balance as his queen slowly approached in jeweled splendor. Finally, they were side by side and ready to slowly promenade up the highway of Potentates, with Forste and Corindel behind them, Corindel carrying Grista's tiara. Behind them were Darvin and Cremona, then Gully and Twilly. The orchestras played a magnificent march as they all made their way slowly up the highway of Potentates with Pell and Grista leading the way.

Chapter 42

THE ARRIVAL OF THE TEN KINGS

The Athelonian seeing that the royal couple had begun the march up the highway of Potentates unrolled the parchment, stood before the Rostrum, lifted his head to the heavens and declared, "I Kungerod Ex-Cathalara, authorized by the King of our realm beckon the most high King, Lord Bellemore at our King's request, that you join this most holy celebration." Everyone was quiet, as they looked heavenward. All of a sudden, there was a blue flash a great distance away in the heavens. Then, like a star that had just landed, was a blue crossed flash depositing the King Bellemore. Bellemore, dressed in royal blue robes, walked over beside the Athelonian. He was tall, handsome, with red hair and beard. The Athelonian once again spoke, "I, Kungerod Ex-Cathalara, summon at our King's request the high King Maridina." Again there was a flash in the heavens, this time magenta. Then a magenta flash-like exploding cross, which lit up the entire circle and everyone's face, deposited King Maridina. He was clad in gold armor, with a magenta robe. His face was young and finely chiseled with long black hair. He walked up and stood next to King Bellemore. Once again the Athelonian declared his rank and summoned King Dalamaxe. Again there was an orange flash in the heavens, then another starry cross on the ground, depositing King Dalamaxe. Dalamaxe was quite imposing looking wearing orange robes with silver trim. He was very large, with a black beard and short black hair. Again the Athelonian beckoned and again the heavens lit up, this time with bright green light. Then another crossed flash appeared in the circle. It was King Loenmere, dressed in green and gold flowing robes. Loenmere was very handsome, with long golden tresses and a short golden beard. He walked over regally to the side of Dalamaxe.

The royal couple slowly made their way up the highway of Potentates as the Kings arrived. They were about a quarter of the way there.

Again the Athelonian read from the parchment. This time there was an icy blue flash, which deposited King Moervil. King Moervil was dressed in icy blue armor with a silver robe. He was very handsome, with thick brown hair parted on the side and was clean-shaven. He walked over and stood beside King Loenmere.

Then the Athelonian read from the parchment again and invoked the name of King Alberaine. This time there was a golden flash in the heavens and a flashing golden cross on the ground depositing King Alberaine. Alberaine was clad in gold armor with a crimson robe. He was quite attractive with golden hair combed straight back. He walked over to the left side of the Rostrum facing the other kings. The Athelonian again summoned another King with a bright red flash depositing King Techance. Techance had a red breastplate of leather-like material, somewhat like a Roman Lorica and wore a bright white robe. Techance was clean-shaven with curly black hair. He walked over and stood beside King Alberaine, on the left side of the Rostrum.

The royal couple continued their march slowly up the highway of Potentates with every eye on them. They were about three quarters of the way up the highway, as the Athelonian again performed the ritual. The heavens flashed with purple light and on the ground another starry cross flashed across the landscape bathing all onlookers in purple light depositing King Auderom. Auderom was attired in purple and silver robes, light brown hair and a neatly cropped beard. He walked over and stood next to King Techance.

The Athelonian continued his exercise and called King Bathenelle. Again there was a flash, this time aqua in color and deposited King Bathenelle. Bathenelle was a striking figure of a man, though a little older than the rest with a salt and pepper hair and beard. His kingly attire was aqua.

Finally the Athelonian read the last name on the list and summoned King Danathera. There was a silver flash in the heavens, then a silver crossed flash appeared in the circle. Danathera was stunning, with Platinum hair, thick and wavy, with beautiful platinum brows. His armor was silver and gold.

Now, all of the Kings were present, clad in their resplendent attire. The royal couple with their entourage had finally arrived at the circle of monarchs. Pell and Grista stood before the Rostrum facing the Athelonian

Kungerod in the presence of the ten Kings. Corindel placed Grista's tiara on the platform to the left of the Rostrum. The Athelonian stepped from the Rostrum, clad in his official robes of blue and gold with a pendent around his neck declaring his rank of Ex-Cathalara. He stood there facing Pell and Grista and said, raising his voice:

"I, Kungerod Ex-Cathalara, present to you Pell Provance and Grista Menuelve, as your duly crowned monarchs. In this crowning." He went on, "they will also become one as bride and groom, husband and wife, King and Queen." He continued, "Therefore, let all here surrender to them the honor, respect, obedience and love due to their rank and their persons." Then he added, "If there be any here who would object to this conferring of authority, coronation or marriage, let him or her come forth now, for once the ceremony begins all caviling shall cease as will disobedience, dishonor, treason, or corruption of crown under the most severe penalty of Agrimore and Algenmere." The Kungerod stood and waited, looking over the crowds until he was satisfied. Then he took his tundril, raised it into the air for all to behold, then slammed it forcefully on the stone floor and declared in a loud voice, "Sunad En Barde Coronat!" meaning, "the coronation has begun."

Then he faced the couple and charged them both by saying, "I, Kungerod Ex-Cathalara, charge you both in the presence of all here gathered that you will rule with strength, courage, wisdom, and most of all love. Do you swear, Pell Provance?" asked the Kungerod, staring intently at him.

Pell looked at all present, then stared at the Kungerod and shouted, "Hie!" which was affirmative.

Then the Kungerod stared at Grista and asked, "And you, Grista Menuelve?"

"Hie!" she shouted.

He then turned and took the tiara from the platform and placed it on the head of Grista after Corindel had removed her veil and headdress. All bowed on one knee to the beautiful Queen filled with Excellency. He then turned to Pell looking sternly at him, then turned and took the Auduxaire and placed it on Pell's head as all bowed their heads and knelt on one knee. Finally, the Kungerod lifted with both hands, a long belt of purple and gold with a golden lion's head for a buckle and wrapped it around the couple binding them together. After buckling it, he shouted with joy, "All hail Pell and Grista our King and Queen for now and evermore beyond times eternal and may the great King, whose Name is unknown, be their glory forever!"

Pell looked into the eyes of his Queen his soul filled with inexpressible glory as he took her into his arms and kissed her. The entire circle of monarchs erupted into a thunderous deafening shout. Kungerods, Kings, Forste and Corinel, as well as Darvin, Cremy, Gully and Twilly and all present shouted for joy at the embrace of the lovers. The Regunelus also circled the couple and extended their great wings to honor the lovers in a canopy of white and gold feathers. Grista kissed her beloved searching his soul. Door after door opened to her until she found the place she would rest, bright and warm. Then she settled herself within him deep and endless, probing his being as he did with her. The seed of the uncreated rested within him not made with hands. Now, she thought, now we are one forever. They continued tightly in their embrace, then Pell looked into Grista's eyes for he knew what she did and it pleased him.

Pell turned holding Grista around the waist and declared, "This is a night of joy and merriment! My command is to feast, sing and fill this night with joy!" Everyone cheered loudly and gathered at the tables to eat and drink. The Retazuna plants were released filling the night sky. Multicolored balloon-like plants with electrical sparks within floated upward, lighting the sky with color. The fire shapers were honing their craft, twisting silver, gold and blue flame skyward.

Pell and Grista made their way through the throng with so many well wishers greeting them. Choruses filled the air with music as the gaiety was becoming contagious. Pell saw Forste and Corindel speaking to two of the Kings. It was Alberaine and Bathenelle. Pell and Grista walked over to greet the two Kings. Alberaine and Bathenelle bowed their heads when they saw Pell and Grista. Pell and Grista returned the courtesy. Forste who was with them, put one arm around his brother's neck and said, "Finally, we can rid ourselves of you two." He then turned to the Kings and said, "You should have seen these two, the goings on were enough to make a man blush." With that Forste, Pell, the Kings, Grista and Corindel burst out laughing. Alberaine whispered in Pell's ear that he left his wedding present with the Athelonian as did Bathenelle.

Pell saw Danathera by himself and excused Grista and himself. Pell and Grista walked up to the splendid Danathera. "King Danathera," said Pell, trying to get his attention.

The handsome Danathera turned, bowed and said, "My Lord and my Lady." Grista smiled broadly. She liked Danathera at once. Pell returned the courtesy as Danathera reached out and kissed Grista's hand and said, "Thy beauty, oh lovely one is like an arrow a King receives in battle which cannot be removed because of its depth." Then he said bowing to her, "My Lady, you are the glory of this realm." Grista blushed and smiled at Danathera. Then Pell asked Danathera if he'd found a Queen yet.

Danathera lifted his head and rolled his eyes, saying, "Alas, my friend, finding a Queen is harder than finding Meathurn the wanderer," he answered. Meathurn was a legendary planet in search of its mate, a twin star.

Pell was relieved and said, "There is someone I wish you to meet."

Danathera stopped Pell and said, "My dear friend, do you know how many times my fellow Kings have tried to find me a Queen and to no avail unless, of course, Queen Grista has a twin?" he said, smiling at her in admiration. Grista blushed. She could not remember blushing so many times before. Grista liked King Danathera because he reminded her of Pell not in looks, but in disposition. He was witty, handsome, roguish and playful in the same way that Pell was, but was also noble, loyal and courageous as was her beloved.

Pell asked leave of his Queen for a moment and led Danathera to where Drue was standing with her aunt. Drue was wide eyed and excited at all of the evening's goings on. She grew with excited anticipation as she saw Pell approaching. Pell walked up to Drue and her aunt who bowed to him in respect and he returned the courtesy. Then he grabbed Danathera, who began wandering off and said, "Drue, Purnis, I'd like you to meet King Danathera."

Danathera bowed to Purnis, then looked at Drue and said, "Well, well, now here's someone that just might keep my star in orbit." Drue blushed at Danathera's boldness. Then Danathera turned to Pell and whispered, "I'll say this for you Pell, you do have exquisite taste. Yes, indeed," he said, turning to Drue looking her over. Drue smiled with admiration. Then Danathera put his arm around Drue and walked away with her, saying, "Have you ever been told you are the most exquisite creature in the world? How would you like to become a Queen?" Drue was giggling as they walked away.

Chapter 43

GUESTS, BANTER AND MORE GUESTS

Grista came up to Pell and asked, "Who is that girl?" staring at Drue as she walked away with Danathera.

"Oh, just a friend," he answered, watching the couple.

"She's magnificent!" exclaimed Grista, and then she looked at Pell suspiciously.

The Athelonian came into the lounge followed by attendants carrying Pell and Grista's wedding gifts. There were ten treasure chests from the ten Kings, plus gifts from noble families, officials and old rulers of Agrimore. There were gifts also from Forste and Corindel, Darvin and Cremona, Gully and Twilly. The Athelonian directed the attendants to place the gifts in an unoccupied room. Then he directed them to clear out the lounge area for the coronation ball. He also had ordered a large Aquidale from Athelone, which he had the attendants place in the center of the lounge which was being transformed into a ballroom because of its size and high ceiling. Everything was removed except the giant Aquidale, which was being prepared.

Meanwhile, Pell and Grista went looking for Drue and Danathera. The Athelonian left the ballroom and made his way back to the outside festivities. He was looking for someone he had invited to the festival. He was looking for the Can-Chimeran female he had met at Candorey. Then he saw the tall imposing female. "Asydina!" he shouted over the throng of wedding guests. She turned and tried to lift herself above the crowds, in the direction of the voice. "Asydina over here!" shouted the Athelonian. She noticed him and waved over the heads of the wedding guests. The Athelonian slowly made his way towards her. "Asydina!" he said, when he had finally reached her. She was delighted to see him. He led her to a spot where they could converse alone. "Well," said the Athelonian, "I'm so glad you made it to the festival."

"How could I refuse such an offer?" she said smiling. "I mean, Pathenune?" She then continued, "Look around at the guests and festivities and all of those magnificent Kings. It's all so breathtaking," she said with enthusiasm. "Thank you so much for inviting me," she offered gratefully.

"Oh, it was my pleasure my dear," said the Athelonian. "Anyhow," he added, "I wanted to see you again after our night in Candorey."

"Oh, so you enjoyed that night, did you?" she asked candidly.

"Best night I've ever had," he answered.

"Tell me something," she asked. "Were you ever going to tell me that you were a Kungerod?"

"Eventually my sweet," he answered.

Pell and Grista found Drue and Danathera outside of the ballroom. He could see that Danathera had Drue enchanted by all of his stories. "Don't believe a word he tells you," said Pell smiling. "Has he been filling your pretty head of his travels to distant worlds, the rescuing of fair maidens and all the dangers he's faced?" asked Pell of Drue.

"Look whose talking," laughed Danathera, "the cosmic heartbreaker himself."

Then Pell turning to Drue, asked, "Drue, do you remember anything of your childhood or your parents?"

"Umm, no, not much," she answered thoughtfully.

Then Pell looked over at Danathera and declared, "I would like to introduce you to Princess Dunemare." Drue's eyes widened and stared at Pell as if he were beside himself.

Danathera looked at Drue quizzically, then turned to Pell. "You mean this walking piece of rare jewels is royalty?"

"Precisely," answered Pell. "She's from an old royal family from the far flung ends of the stellar regions. She's been lost and I arranged her relationship with Purnis long ago." Drue just stared at Pell with her mouth open in disbelief.

"Are you telling me she's immortal?" asked Danathera.

"Yes," answered Pell, "and she's a slow cycler, that's why she's taken so long to reach sixteen," he added. Then he turned to Drue and said, "Your family misses you and are waiting for you." Finally, he turned to Purnis and said, "Thank you for all of your help over these cycles in raising Drue and for keeping everything to yourself until the proper time."

Purnis bowed her head and said quietly, "It was an honor, my Lord." She then turned and walked away broken hearted, for she loved Drue.

Drue watched her slowly walk away through the throng, her eyes filling with tears, as she saw Purnis leaving and shouted, "Auntie!" Purnis turned as Drue ran up to her and hugged her crying, "No, Auntie, you can't leave me! You've been my family for so long and I couldn't bear not being with you. Please, Auntie, don't leave me!" she cried.

Purnis overcome with emotion hugged and kissed Drue and wept saying, "Oh, my dear lovely child."

Drue composed herself, looked at Purnis and said, "I will go to see my family with Danathera, then I'll be back to Agrimore and to you, auntie. Royalty or no royalty you are part of my family forever. So please don't leave without me," she pleaded.

Purnis looked at Pell who said, "I think it's a good arrangement. I'll speak to her family and make all of the arrangements."

Danathera looked at Drue. "Cool, isn't he?" he said, referring to Pell.

"The coolest of all," answered Drue, smiling at Pell. She then jumped up and grabbed Pell around the neck, kissed him hard on the cheek and whispered, "You are the most excellent, coolest man ever and the hottest." Then Drue left with Purnis and Danathera.

Grista looking down at the ground said, "I don't know the history between you two, but I know this: you are always honorable in everything you do. And she's right, you are the hottest." Then she kissed his cheek.

Asydina looked at the Athelonian searching his face and asked, "Do Kungerods have a name? I mean how do I address you?"

The Athelonian looked down not knowing how to answer her or if he should answer the question. Then he looked at her and stared into her eyes. "Well, maybe its time, I mean now we have our King. I'm not sure what our roles are, if we indeed are Kungerods any longer." At that point Pell and Grista came over to the Athelonian. "My dear, I'd like you to meet our King Pell and Queen Grista," said the Athelonian turning to face them.

"Your Majesties," said Asydina.

"Please," interjected Pell, "just Pell and Grista for now." Then Pell whispered to the Athelonian, "It's all right to tell her." He turned to Asydina and said, "It was our pleasure to meet you." So they took their leave of them. Pell turned as he was walking away and said, "By the way, you're still on the job, all of you." Then he and Grista left for the ballroom.

Asydina noted, "He is gracious, isn't he? And most handsome, as for Grista his Queen!" she exclaimed. "I've never seen such a beauty!"

The Athelonian concurred. "Yes, our worlds are most blessed to have such monarchs," looking at the royal couple with admiration as they left.

"So?" asked Asydina. "What is your name?"

"Athelone," he offered. "You see, the continents were named after us."

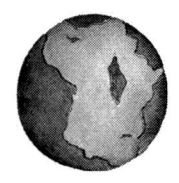

Chapter 44

THE WALTZ OF ETERNAL CYCLES

Pell and Grista entered the ballroom where everything was prepared for the waltz. In the center of the ballroom was the great dessert, which they had enjoyed at Firwith while awaiting the freightliner. It was a giant Aquidale which reached almost to the ceiling, with a large goblet wide at the bottom and tapered up to the stem. Inside, was a liquid crystal fruit, which was being heated with a blue flame around the base, boiling the fruit and causing the foam to rise.

The orchestras were seated and waited for the cue to begin the waltz. The Athelonian made his way to the circle of monarchs to announce from the Rostrum that the royal waltz was about to commence.

The guests began filling into the ballroom for the commencement of the waltz. Drue and Danathera were there as well as the Kings, whose Queen's had just arrived. Asydina was waiting for Athelone to return from the circle of monarchs. Ilgestana was also present with Amborine at her side. Faengle and Crofty Bellar were also there, as was Can-Chimera coupled with the golden-haired beauty he had met in Patamodia named Sprinda. Vernacia had also joined them with Hyperdia, whom he had also met at Patamodia. Lastly, Patamodia was there with the Tendrat girl he had championed in the Vernacian district of Candorey. She was named Porinora. Everything was in place for the waltz to start.

The music in the ballroom began slowly, a sweeping majestic waltz. Pell looked into Grista's eyes knowing that this was their waltz and only theirs. He took the hand of his Queen then bowed to her as she accepted him, then began a speedy fox trot, round and round they went with every eye upon them. Pell looked into the eyes of his Queen turning and spinning to the music. All of a sudden there was a flash of light, not as when the Kings arrived, but much much brighter, brighter than the sun, so bright and dazzling that everything disappeared that was touched by the light. Pell and Grista were astonished by the light and stopped waltzing as the orchestra ceased. Everyone stared in the direction of the effulgence.

Pell and Grista left the ballroom in the direction of the light, with Forste and the Athelonian following them. Corindel, Cremona and Twilly also slowly made their way out of the ballroom. Soon the entire ballroom was empty with everyone walking towards the light.

Pell and Grista continued to walk towards the resplendence, which seemed to originate around the circle of monarchs. Pell and Grista continued slowly towards the light with everyone slowly following after them. They continued until they neared the circle of monarchs. The royal couple strained to see through the blinding light. As they neared, they saw a figure, then another figure. The first figure was even brighter than the emitted light as was the second. They walked closer shielding their eyes when they saw the blazing figures. Pell immediately dropped to the ground, lying flat on his face with Grista following his lead. The Athelonian turned to Forste and whispered with astonished fervor, "Down, down Forste on your face!" then turned and looked over his shoulder and whispered, "Down! Quickly all of you on your faces!"

Forste, lying flat on the ground, asked, "What? Who is it?"

The Athelonian turned and looked at him from his prone position and said, solemnly whispering, "It's the King whose Name is unknown and His Son." Forste upon hearing this put his head down and faced the ground. Slowly the two figures of light approached Pell and Grista, who were still lying flat, not even looking up.

The first figure touched Pell on the shoulder and spoke, "Rise, Pell and Grista, on your feet before me and face me." The voice was unlike anything ever heard before, thunderous, reverberating, which penetrated everything and would even cause the stones to rise, had he not personalized the command. Pell and Grista rose slowly and fearfully because of all the consuming glory and power of the One which spoke, a voice so mighty, yet so comforting and gentle as the music of creation itself. They both rose to face the One which had commanded them. Through the binding light they could make out the most astonishing features of both King's unspeakable beauty, which diminished the glory of Agrimore. Eyes so gentle yet so noble, mighty and penetrating, His Son, resplendent in his diadem beyond description. The King and His Son walked with Pell and Grista beyond the circle of monarchs.

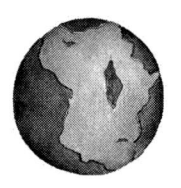

Chapter 45

A SAD FAREWELL?

The four of them stopped at the clearing. Pell and Grista noticed four tall mighty beings standing guard in the distance. They appeared to be made of diamonds whose facets gleamed and flashed with light erupting and playing off of the surface of their faces and their gleaming armor. They were silent and vigilant.

The King whose Name was unknown turned to them and said, "Do not fear my beloveds; you've both discharged your duties with great honor, alacrity and valor. My Son and I are Proud of both of you and all of your accomplishments. In all of your lives and travels to countless worlds you've both acquitted yourselves as the true sovereigns and dear children that you are! For that receive both of you, the diadem of life." Then the Great Son walked over to them and removed the tiara from Grista's head and replaced it with another tiara blue, white and brilliant encrusted with stones and jewels that could never be identified in this plane of existence. Then He the Son moved over to Pell. Pell noticed through the light of his glory the unspeakable beauty of the Son's face and tried to define or describe Him to his own mind, His hair gold of the purest spun gold, His eyes eternal flame, His features delicate and marvelous. His age was ageless – young, but ageless. He took the Auduxaire from Pell's head and replaced it with an unspeakable diadem with an eternal lustrous gold, brighter than the sun and jewels so enchantingly beautiful, that it would take much effort to remove one's eyes from. Then the King whose Name is unknown kissed them both on the forehead, then with a blinding flash both Kings were gone.

After the light had subsided the Athelonian raised his head and lifted himself off of the ground with all present following suit. Athelone stared at where the two figures had been to see Pell and Grista emerge from the circle of monarchs. They were both changed and different somewhat. He noticed the diadems upon their heads and stood astonished. Athelone knew that the radiant diadems upon their heads meant their powers were increased a hundred fold as was their authority and sovereignty. They were shimmering with light and power.

Athelone slowly approached them with Forste and Corindel by his side to behold Pell and Grista. Pell looked at them and quietly spoke, "I'm not sure of how to explain to all of you of what just happened. I don't know what speech to use." Pell and Grista had changed. Their beauty increased as well as their dignity and nobility. "One thing I can tell you is that our realm will never end as well as Agrimore and Algenmere." Pell then turned to the Kungerods and said, "With the increase of our realm, so we increase your authority." The Kungerods bowed in obeisance and took their leave as Pell and Grista turned to Darvin, Cremona, Gully and Twilly and smiled at them.

Pell stepped forward and looked at Darvin and Cremona and said, "Both of you, my dear friends, have been with me for so long. All of those parties, trips, perlee halls and concerts, faithful unto death both of you." He then whispered to Darvin, "I know of your plan to help and support Forste and myself in our battle with darkness and how Gully dissuaded you. I admire your courage and devotion even though your attempt would have put us all at risk. Nonetheless, your great loyalty is admirable." Then he motioned for Cremy to stand next to Darvin and looked at her lovingly, "Sweet and lovely Cremona, always queenly in your disposition and actions. We had fun, didn't we sweetie?" he asked smiling.

She blushed, looked at Pell with admiration and answered, "The best fun of my life is when I first met you," she said, staring up at him. "You were so intriguing, mysterious, dashing and handsome." She went on, "I used to think to myself how would any female hope to land that gorgeous whirlwind of a man. I used to daydream about you, but knew in my heart that you had another destiny to follow," she said teary eyed.

"What is this, Creme?" he asked softly. "Did you think I was just going to let you depart from our lives taking all of those marvelous qualities with you and never enjoy them anymore? Be it far from me to let you leave a vacancy in our lives," Pell assured her.

He then walked over to Gully and Twilly. "Gully," he said heartily, looking into his eyes shaking his head. "Where?" he asked. "Where would we be without you Gully?" Pell asked. "You gave up everything to come on this journey not knowing where it would take you," Pell said smiling.

"Without you the journey would have been grim. Your laughter," he continued, "and smile took the edge off of the most dire circumstances, always faithful and understanding," he affirmed.

Then he looked down at Twilly and said, "You, sweet little tender Twilly, life-long friend of my Queen. Your friendship to Grista is praiseworthy as you are dear one." He then turned and headed back to the ballroom, leaving Grista alone with the group saying his sorrowful farewell.

Chapter 46

REXUS DELETHARUM

Pell entered the ballroom where everything was waiting for them. Then he asked for all of the Kungerods to assemble themselves. They came at once led by Athelone.

Pell asked concerning the procedures of additional coronations and conferring of authority. Athelone assured, "Your majesty, Totta Detorum." Athelone then added, "You, Sire, have absolute power of coronation procedures, but I thank your gracious majesty that you still seek the counsel of your servants," Athelone said bowing.

Pell looked at all of them and asked, "Servants? When have I treated you as servants? I was under the impression that we were friends."

Athelone came forward and said penitently, "I beg your pardon, Sire. Of course, we are your friends, forgive the inexcusable oversight my Liege." Pell smiled broadly at all of them. Grista came back to the ballroom followed by the group.

The orchestra began playing the waltz when Pell motioned them to stop. Then he asked the Kungerods to gather round. He motioned for the group to stand before him. He then asked Athelone if he might use his tundril to which Athelone complied happily. Pell then asked Darvin and Cremona to stand before him. After they had positioned themselves before him, Pell took the tundril and pronounced, "Darvin Scutter and Cremona Pinkerly. In light of your friendship, courage, loyalty and devotion, I, your true Sovereign confer upon both of you the Royal Order of Rexus Deletharum, King and Queen of part of my realm called Emorial. Together with the honor, authority and fealty due to both your rank." He then took the tundril and touched them both gently on the side of their left arms, then declared, "I also pronounce you bride and groom." Darvin and Cremona bowed their head's completely speechless and overwhelmed with joy. Pell then whispered to them, "Your crowns are now being designed, you also have star power as the ten visiting kings so we can see each other whenever you wish." Pell stepped back and lifted his hands, which cued a roar of cheers by all present.

Pell asked Gully and Twilly to stand before him, then addressing them said, "Gulland Tivaler and Tawnella Boste, as your true Sovereign, I confer upon you both, Rexus Deletharum, with the titles, authority and power due to the rank of King and Queen for your wisdom, discretion, loyalty and devotion. You will have rulership over the realm of Pargemet. May you both serve your people as you have served me." Then he smiled at them and said, "I also pronounce you bride and groom." Again there was an eruption of cheers throughout the ballroom.

Pell then took Grista his Queen into his arms and continued their waltz and motioned for all to dance, as Pell and Grista danced into eternity.

Agrimore had never in all of its eons of existence, known such joy and merriment as it had known this night. Ruled by a great King and Queen, with subjects never happier than these with an endless existence.

A Note to the Reader

Dear reader, I, like you, feel the same bereavement as this great saga ends and the participants fade away before our eyes into the pages of hoped-for fantasies.

Our world, different from Agrimore and Algenmere, is a world so far removed from those worlds. A world where the profane is glorified as noble, where mediocrity is heralded as genius and brutality is confused with strength and courage. We long for a Royal strain, as the base and the common are given fealty. Remember this: that Agrimore does exist somewhere in hearts with a noble spark. They may be few, but nonetheless, exist. They stand poised, watching the decay, waiting for their departure, as the Thermedytes approach closer and closer with each passing moment. The sentence has been passed, the destruction eminent. The Royal seed is prepared for departure to return to all of the Heavenly Realms from which they came.

TATE PUBLISHING & *Enterprises*

Tate Publishing is commited to excellence in the publishing industry. Our staff of highly trained professionals, including editors, graphic designers, and marketing personnel, work together to produce the very finest books available. The company reflects the philosophy established by the founders, based on Psalms 68:11,

"THE LORD GAVE THE WORD AND GREAT WAS THE COMPANY OF THOSE WHO PUBLISHED IT."

If you would like further information, please call
1.888.361.9473
or visit our website
www.tatepublishing.com

TATE PUBLISHING & *Enterprises*, LLC
127 E. Trade Center Terrace
Mustang, Oklahoma 73064 USA